Dear Readers,

Many years ago, when I was a kid, my father said to me, "Bill, it doesn't really matter what you do in life. What's important is to be the *best* William Johnstone you can be."

I've never forgotten those words. And now, many years and almost two hundred books later, I like to think that I am still trying to be the best William Johnstone I can be. Whether it's Ben Raines in the Ashes series, or Frank Morgan, the last gunfighter, or Smoke Jensen, our intrepid mountain man, or John Barrone and his hardworking crew keeping America safe from terrorist lowlifes in the Code Name series, I want to make each new book better than the last and deliver powerful storytelling.

Equally important, I try to create the kinds of believable characters that we can all identify with, real people who face tough challenges. When one of my creations blasts an enemy into the middle of next week, you can be damn sure he had a good reason.

As a storyteller, my job is to entertain you, my readers, and to make sure that you get plenty of enjoyment from my books for your hard-earned money. This is not a job I take lightly. And I greatly appreciate your feedback—you are my gold, and your opinions *do* count. So please keep the letters and e-mails coming.

Respectfully yours,

William W. Johnstone

BOOK YOUR PLACE ON OUR WEBSITE AND MAKE THE READING CONNECTION!

We've created a customized website just for our very special readers, where you can get the inside scoop on everything that's going on with Zebra, Pinnacle and Kensington books.

When you come online, you'll have the exciting opportunity to:

- View covers of upcoming books
- Read sample chapters
- Learn about our future publishing schedule (listed by publication month *and author*)
- Find out when your favorite authors will be visiting a city near you
- Search for and order backlist books from our online catalog
- Check out author bios and background information
- Send e-mail to your favorite authors
- Meet the Kensington staff online
- Join us in weekly chats with authors, readers and other guests
- Get writing guidelines
- AND MUCH MORE!

Visit our website at
http://www.kensingtonbooks.com

WILLIAM W.
JOHNSTONE

CRY

OF

EAGLES

PINNACLE BOOKS
Kensington Publishing Corp.
http://www.kensingtonbooks.com

PINNACLE BOOKS are published by

Kensington Publishing Corp.
850 Third Avenue
New York, NY 10022

All Kensington Titles, Imprints and Distributed Lines are available at special quantity discounts for bulk purchases for sales
promotions, premiums, fund-raising, and educational or insti-
tutional use. Special book excerpts or customized printings can
also be created to fit specific needs. For details, write or phone
the office of the Kensington special sales manager: Kensington Publishing Corp., 850 Third Avenue, New York, NY 10022,
attn. Special Sales Department, Phone: 1-800-221-2647.

Pinnacle and the P logo Reg. U.S. Pat. & TM Off.

First Printing: October 1999

10 9 8 7 6 5 4 3

Printed in the United States of America

Chapter 1

Falcon MacCallister walked his big black stud, Diablo, down dusty town streets until he came to the livery stable. "Give him a good rubdown and all the grain he wants. He's earned it," he said to the pimply-faced boy who appeared in the doorway of the barn. "And don't put him too close to any of the other horses. He's kind'a used to getting his own way."

When he left the livery, Falcon saw the Oriental Saloon just down the street. *A drink would be just the thing to wash the desert sand out of my throat,* he thought, walking toward the batwings.

He had just arrived in Tombstone after a long, hot ride across the desert. Though it was fall everywhere else, you couldn't tell it in Arizona. The air was hot and dry enough to suck the life right out of a man, and Falcon's face was wind and sunburned and raw from his trip.

He figured to have a couple of drinks, get a hot meal somewhere, and see if this godforsaken town had any bathtubs in it. He'd been on the road for a couple of weeks straight, and was getting mighty tired of his own cooking,

and his own smell. He was so ripe even Diablo shied away
when he approached him.

Falcon stepped through the batwings and hesitated for
a moment, letting his eyes adjust to the gloom of the room.
It was an old habit, one that had kept him alive more times
than he cared to remember.

The usual noises of a bar—clinking glasses, too-loud
talk, the plinking of piano keys over in the corner—died
down as patrons noticed him standing there. He often had
that effect on people. Standing slightly over six feet tall,
he had shoulders so wide and muscular and a waist so thin
that his suits had to be custom-made for him. His eyes
were a pale blue under wheat-colored hair, worn short and
neat. He favored black suits with crisp, ironed white shirts
and black string ties when he was working at his favorite
pastime, gambling. On the trail, he wore a dark, long-
sleeved shirt, denim jeans tucked into knee-high black
leather boots, and a gray vest with a black silk handkerchief
around his neck. On his hips were a brace of .44 Colts,
tied down low, and he carried an ace in the hole, a two-
shot derringer, in the top of his right boot.

Once his eyes were accustomed to the low light in the
saloon, he surveyed the crowd. Nothing much to worry
about, he thought—several tables of punchers and cowboys, in town to spend in one night what it took them a
week to earn, a couple of well-dressed Mexicans in for a
night of whoring away from the hacienda and their wives,
and a pair of star-packers of some sort.

From where he stood, Falcon couldn't read the badges
on the mens' chests. Probably town marshals or deputy
sheriffs; they looked too young and inexperienced to be
U.S. Marshals.

He straightened his hat and walked straight to the bar,
leaning on one elbow and standing sideways so as not to
put his back to the room.

"I'll take a whiskey, with a side of water," he said to the
barkeep.

"Yes, sir, right away," the man said, and pulled out a glass that had seen better days.

Before the barkeep could fill it, Falcon put his hand over the top of the glass. "How about washing that before you put my whiskey in it?"

The bartender frowned. "Wash it?"

"Yes, as in soap and water. You have heard of soap and water, haven't you?"

"No need to get ornery, mister. I just work here, I don't own the place."

Falcon took a long, thin cheroot from his vest pocket and lighted it by striking a lucifer on the hammer of his Colt. After getting a cleaner glass, he took a sip of his bourbon. It tasted great after three weeks of nothing but coffee and water on the trail. The bite of the alcohol on his tongue and the warmth as it spread out from his stomach were mighty good.

As he stood there smoking and taking an occasional sip of his drink, he reflected on what he was going to do next, where he was going to go after leaving Tombstone. Since his wife Marie had been killed by renegade Indians, Falcon had been on a continual jaunt around the country, trying to heal his heart by staying constantly on the move. Seeing new faces and different places every day kept his mind off what he'd lost when Marie was killed.

Occasionally, the cold sweats and the killing rages would still come, but the intervals between them were getting longer and longer as time passed.

Falcon snapped out of his reverie when he noticed the two star packers putting their heads together and whispering while looking in his direction He wasn't wanted for anything, as far as he knew. There had been some papers on him a couple of years back, but they'd been recalled when he convinced a judge he'd acted in self-defense.

It didn't matter; Falcon knew that look. The set face, the hard, suspicious eyes, the tensing of the neck muscles as a man makes a decision whether to put his life on the line and challenge another. He'd seen it all too many times before.

Finally, just as he'd feared, the two lawmen got to their feet, their hands hanging next to their pistols. "Hey you, there at the bar," the shorter one called. He was barely over five feet three inches, and heavy through the gut. A bad combination, Falcon thought, a short, fat man with a badge and a chip on his shoulder, needing to prove he's a big man.

Falcon slowly raised his eyes from his glass to stare at the pair. "Yes. What can I do for you?"

The taller man, who was reed thin and gawky and looked to be barely out of his teens, said, "What's yore name, mister?"

Falcon sighed. He knew what was coming. "Falcon Mac-Callister."

The two deputies looked at each other. "I done told you so, Jimmy. It's him, all right!" the short one said.

They squared their shoulders. "You'd better come with us, MacCallister. We got some Wanted posters on you over at the jail."

Falcon continued to smoke and drink, standing relaxed at the bar. "Gentlemen, if you'll look at the dates on those posters, you'll find they're over a year old. They've been recalled."

The younger, thin deputy frowned, a puzzled look crossing his face, but the short, fat one's lips tightened, and he stuck out his chin like a spoiled little boy. "I don't recollect no recall notice, MacCallister," he said, his fingers twitching next to the handle of his pistol. "I'm Deputy Stillwell, an' you better put them hands high."

Falcon shook his head. "Before you make the biggest mistake of your life, why don't you check with the sheriff or city marshal, deputy? I'm sure he'll remember the recall."

"Naw, cain't do that, fellah. Sheriff Behan's gone out on a posse. He left Jimmy and me here in charge 'til he gits back."

Falcon glanced over Deputy Stillwell's shoulder at the

other patrons of the saloon. Their confrontation had everyone's attention.

The table of cowboys, five of them, had stopped their jawing and were openly staring at the scene, grins on their faces as if they hoped for the excitement of a gunfight.

The two Mexicans were quiet and looking away, pretending not to watch.

Then Falcon saw someone he hadn't seen on entering. Over in a far corner, sitting by himself, a well-dressed man had a deck of cards spread out on the table in front of him in a game of solitaire. He had stopped playing and was smoking a cigar and staring at Falcon, an irreverent smirk on his face.

Falcon stubbed out his cigar and finished his whiskey in one quick swallow. "All right, boys. Let's go over to the sheriff's office and I can show you those recall notices."

"We ain't goin' nowheres 'til you put them hands up, mister," Deputy Stillwell said, and he and the other deputy grabbed for their pistols.

In the flash of an eye, Falcon filled his hands with iron, and had both guns drawn, cocked, and aimed before either of the two young men even cleared leather.

One of the cowboys at the table opened his mouth in awe, the cigarette stuck there falling to the floor as he whispered, "Gawd Awmighty! Did you see that?" to his tablemates.

The two deputies slowly raised their hands, Deputy Stillwell breaking out in a sweat in spite of the coolness of the room. "What . . . what're you gonna do with us, mister?" the thin one named Jimmy asked, naked fear in his eyes.

Falcon pursed his lips. "Damned if I know. I just came into town for a peaceful drink, good meal and a hot bath. I guess we can go on over to the jail, and I'll try and prove to you I'm not a wanted man."

Falcon's eyes shifted as the man in the dark suit got up from his corner table and approached them.

"Howdy, Mr. MacCallister. My name's John Henry Holliday, but everybody calls me Doc."

"Hello, Doc," Falcon said, a puzzled expression on his face. He'd heard of the infamous Doc Holliday, and wondered why he was taking a hand in this matter.

"Perhaps I may be of some assistance here." He pointed over his shoulder with his thumb at the pair of deputies standing with their hands in the air. "Those boys are both dumber'n cow flop, but they don't mean any harm."

Falcon nodded. "As slow as they are on the draw, perhaps they should find some other means of employment."

Doc chuckled. "I'm sure those thoughts are going through their minds even as we speak."

He turned and addressed Deputy Stillwell. "If I take Mr. MacCallister over to the city marshal's office and have Wyatt check him out, will that satisfy you boys?"

Both nodded their heads rapidly. "Yes, sir, Doc," Stillwell answered.

Doc looked back at Falcon. "That suit you, MacCallister?"

"Anything, Doc, just so I get something to eat before too long," Falcon said as he holstered his Colts.

Doc smiled, "Good. Then right after we go see Wyatt and get this straightened out, I recommend Campbell and Hatch's Saloon. They got the best food in town, an' their whiskey isn't half bad, either."

One of the cowboys at the other table stood up, his face beet-red, angry at the peaceful resolution of the argument. "Hey, Doc," he yelled, "why don't you keep your nose out of other people's business?" He was dressed all in black, from his hat to his boots, and he had the look of a gunfighter.

Falcon was a little puzzled to see none of the men in the saloon were heeled.

Doc's face went flat and expressionless, and his eyes turned cold as ice. "You planning on anteing up in this hand, Curly Bill?" he said, pulling the lapels of his coat back and tucking them into the back of his belt to reveal a pistol hanging on his waist.

"We might, Doc," he answered, as the man next to him stood up. "You just give us time to go git our guns from the marshal's office and we'll be glad to accommodate you."

Doc gave a lazy smile. "Curly Bill Brocius and Johnny Ringo, two of the most butt-ugly men God ever put on the face of the earth."

He squared his shoulders and spread his feet, his hand hanging next to his pistol.

"Well, go get your pistols and make your play, boys, and I'll put a tunnel in your skulls," Doc said, a grim smile curling his lips.

Falcon stepped to Doc's side. "I've heard of you, Brocius, and you too, Ringo," he said, staring at the two gunmen. "From what I've heard you men don't usually face someone. You usually come at them from behind."

Ringo and Brocius's faces showed uncertainty. Before they were two on one. Now the odds were even, and they'd seen how snake-quick Falcon was with his guns.

Doc addressed the other men at the table. "Ike, you and Billy want to join this dance?" he asked. "I've never seen the Clanton brothers miss a good fight."

The two men sitting shook their heads and got up from the table and walked toward the batwings. "Not right now, Holliday, but you'll be seein' us later."

The one called Billy Clanton motioned to Ringo and Brocius. "Come on, boys, now's not the time or place for this." He looked around the saloon. "There's too many people in here. We got plenty of time to deal with Holliday and Earp later."

Ringo and Brocius, with looks of relief, grabbed their hats off the table and walked out of the bar with the two Clanton brothers.

Falcon sighed and relaxed his shoulders. "Nice quiet town you got here, Doc."

"It has its moments," the dapper man said, fixing his coat smiling.

"How is it none of those men were armed?" Falcon asked.

"When he became town marshal, Virgil Earp posted the town off-limits to guns."

Falcon glanced at Doc's left hip, where he wore a pistol, butt first for a cross hand draw. "How about you?"

"Oh, I'm something of a special case. Now, let's go meet Wyatt Earp and see about those recall notices, so's you can get some grub."

Chapter 2

"What was that all about?" Falcon asked Doc as they walked toward the city marshal's office.

"The Clanton clan—Ike, Phin, Billy, and Newman, known as the Old Man—along with Frank and Tom McLaury, Curly Bill Brocius and Johnny Ringo, call themselves The Cowboys. Did you notice those red sashes they were wearing around their waists?"

Falcon nodded. "Yeah, now that you mention it."

"All the members of The Cowboys gang wear them. They're a bunch of local outlaws who've had a pretty easy time of it around here until Wyatt Earp and his brothers, Morgan and Virgil, showed up."

"What's that got to do with you? From what I've heard of you, you're not exactly a lawman."

Doc grinned. "I am a friend of Wyatt's, though. I met him over in Fort Griffin, Texas, a while back. We've kind'a been runnin' into each other off and on since then. The Clantons and McLaurys know where I stand, an' they've been tryin' to get me out of the picture so Wyatt will have one less gun backing his play."

"This certainly doesn't sound like a very healthy town," Falcon observed.

"That may be why they named it Tombstone," Doc said with a twinkle in his dark eyes. Then he grabbed a soiled handkerchief out of his pocket and placed it against his face as he bent double and gave several hacking, wet-sounding coughs. As he straightened up, Falcon could see streaks of crimson on the linen before Doc stuffed it in his pocket.

He gave a sideways smirk at Falcon. "In my case, the name of the town may be very apropos."

As they walked along the dirt streets Falcon could see the town was relatively young. It'd been founded only a few years before, on the basis of some rich silver strikes nearby. It was said the first settlers had to fight off Geronimo and his sons, Nachez and Victorio, in order to stake their claims, thus leading to the name Tombstone.

Most of the buildings were storefronts, with wooden façades in front and large canvas tents stretching out to form the main part of the building. Many of the lots between buildings had smaller tents staked out, with families living in some, and others serving as small stores, selling their goods out of the back of wagons.

They walked into the city marshal's office and found a tall man dressed in a black coat, white shirt with a string tie, and gray trousers loading a rifle in front of a gun rack on the wall.

"Wyatt," Doc called out, "I'd like you to meet Falcon MacCallister, the fastest man with a gun I've ever seen."

Wyatt raised his eyebrows. "That so?"

He stuck out his hand, and he and Falcon shook.

"Sheriff Behan's deputies, Stillwell and Jimmy, braced him over at the Oriental Saloon. Said they'd seen some paper out on him a while back."

Wyatt's smile faded. "Are you wanted, Mr. Mac-Callister?"

Falcon shook his head. "Not any more. A judge ruled my fight was self-defense and sent out recall notices about six months after the original posters were circulated."

Wyatt walked over to his desk and pulled a thick sheaf of papers out of the top drawer. After rummaging through them for a few minutes, he pulled one out of the stack. "You're right, Falcon. Here it is."

He passed the paper over to Falcon. "You'd better keep that while you're in town. Sheriff Behan's deputies aren't known for their intelligence."

Doc laughed. "Yeah, they'd probably have to get someone to read it to 'em if you pulled it out and stuck it in their faces."

"Well, if you're done with me, Marshal, I'm hungry and I'd like to go."

"By all means, Falcon," Wyatt said, sticking out his hand and taking Falcon's. "However, I'll have to ask you to leave your pistols here. There's a town ordinance against carrying weapons inside the city limits."

Falcon shrugged. "Okay, Marshal."

He unbuckled his gunbelt and handed the brace of Colts to Wyatt.

"Have a good stay in our town, Falcon," Wyatt said as he hung the belt over a peg on the wall. "And," he added with a wink, "if you're a gambling man, I deal the Faro table over at the Oriental Saloon starting at eight o'clock."

"Faro is a game for men who don't understand numbers," Falcon said. "I prefer poker, preferably stud."

Doc nodded. "A man after my own heart, Wyatt."

Falcon smiled and touched the brim of his hat nodding at Doc. "Thanks for taking a hand over there, and thanks for the advice on where to eat, Doc. I'll be seeing you."

As he walked down the boardwalk looking for the Campbell and Hatch Saloon, Falcon wondered if they had baths there or if he was going to have to check into a hotel to get clean.

Suddenly four men stepped out of an alleyway to block Falcon's path. It was the two Clantons and Ringo and Brocius, and they were spoiling for some trouble.

"Hey, mister. We don't appreciate no strangers comin' into our town and causin' trouble," Billy Clanton said.

He was a big man, about five feet ten inches tall, with a barrel chest and thick, muscular arms. Falcon thought he was probably a bully, starting fights with just about anyone who was smaller. He'd seen his type plenty of times before.

"Yeah," Johnny Ringo added, "so why don't you just get back up on your horse and hightail it on outta here?"

"I don't believe I want to do that," Falcon answered, a slight smile on his face.

"We ain't exactly askin'. We're tellin' you to leave," Billy said, flexing his muscles and sticking his chest out, as if that was going to scare Falcon off.

Falcon gave a lazy look at the four men. "Well, right offhand, I don't see anyone big or mean enough to make me leave," he said.

Clanton stepped out into the street and began to roll up his sleeves, revealing hairy, muscular forearms. "Oh, we'll see 'bout that, mister, we'll just see."

Falcon took his hat off and hung it on the end of a hitching rail and walked slowly toward Clanton. "You sure you want to do this, Billy?" he asked. "I don't particularly want to spread your nose all over your face. It's already ugly enough."

The big man growled and came running at Falcon, swinging his right hand in a roundhouse punch.

Falcon set his feet and didn't move, merely leaning his head slightly to the side so Clanton's blow whistled harmlessly by his face.

As Clanton twisted sideways from the force of his swing, Falcon threw a short left jab into his ribs, cracking one with a snap like a wooden stick breaking.

Clanton grabbed his side, bent over, and let out his breath with a giant groan.

While he stood there, Falcon swung from his heels with a right uppercut, catching Clanton flush on the bridge of his nose, flattening it and spreading it all over his face. Blood and teeth went flying as Clanton's head snapped back and he staggered upright.

He stood there in the middle of the street, swaying and shaking his head, trying to uncross his eyes, blood streaming from his ruined nose. He spat two more teeth from between split lips and howled in anger as he ran at Falcon once more, his arms spread wide as if to catch him in a bear hug.

Falcon bent under the arms and threw two quick jabs into Clanton's paunch, doubling him over. The big man stood there, leaning over with his hands on his knees, and began to vomit onto his boots.

Falcon doubled up his fist and slammed it in the back of Clanton's head, knocking him flat on his face in a pile of horse manure.

He took the toe of his boot and rolled Clanton over so he wouldn't suffocate, then turned to the three men remaining, his chest heaving from the exertion of the fight.

Ringo had a long Bowie knife out and began to walk toward Falcon, waving it back and forth, when Wyatt Earp and Doc Holliday stepped up behind him. Wyatt clubbed Ringo in the side of the head with the butt of a sawed-off express gun, knocking the gunman to his knees and making him drop his blade.

"All right, men, break it up," Wyatt said.

Curly Bill Brocius pointed at Falcon. "He started it, Marshal. Why don't you arrest him?"

"Arrest him? Hell, I ought to pay him for the pleasure of watching him beat the crap out of Billy Clanton."

Ringo shook his head and started to pick up his knife, until Wyatt eared back the hammers on the shotgun with a loud double click. "I wouldn't do that, Johnny," Wyatt said. "Not unless you want your brains scattered all over the street like Billy's teeth."

Ringo glared hate at Wyatt. "I'll be seein' you, Earp. This ain't over yet."

Doc grinned down at Ringo. "You look right nice on your knees, Johnny. Perhaps you should spend more time there."

Ringo jumped to his feet, his hand unconsciously going for his empty holster.

Doc let his hand caress the butt of his pistol under his coat. "You are twice lucky today, Johnny. First Wyatt hits you in the head, where he cannot possibly do you any harm, and then you face me with an empty holster."

"Damn the both of you!" Ringo said as he walked out into the street. He and Curly Bill Brocius lifted Clanton up by his arms and walked him off down the road.

Falcon retrieved his hat from the hitching post and dusted it off. "Like I said, Doc, a right unhealthy town you got here."

Doc laughed, "Don't be too critical, Falcon. After all, you haven't tried the local cuisine yet."

"Would you care to join me for supper, Doc? It's the least I can do," Falcon offered.

Doc shrugged. "Sure, why not? It'll certainly be a change for me, eating supper instead of drinking it."

After the meal at Campbell and Hatch's Saloon, Falcon got his saddlebags from the livery and checked into the Grand Hotel on Main Street. It was the newest and finest hotel in Tombstone, and Falcon was finally able to get his hot bath.

Afterward, dressed in his gambling duds, he walked out onto his balcony for a smoke. He stood there in the dark for a moment, breathing the crisp, autumn air and looking up at the night sky, marveling at the number and brightness of the stars as he often did while on the trail.

From the alleyway below his balcony, Falcon heard a familiar voice. He ducked back out of sight as Billy Clanton said in a hoarse whisper, "Hello, Frank. How's it going, Tom?"

Two voices answered in muted greetings. Billy continued to talk, pulling the men farther down the alley with him. "You boys all set for tomorrow night, Frank?"

"Yeah, you can count on the McLaurys, Billy. Is Ike ready?"

"More than ready. We're sick of those Earp brothers stickin' their noses in our business. So the plan's set?"

"We'll meet at the OK Corral and get our extra guns outta our saddlebags, and then we'll hunt those bastards down and shoot 'em like the dogs they are."

"It'll be easy, since they won't be expectin' us to be carryin'."

Then Falcon could no longer hear them talking. He leaned back against the wall and lighted his cigar, letting the tobacco calm his nerves. He'd never before heard the planned execution of three men discussed so openly. Now he had to figure out what to do. He usually made it a practice to mind his own business, but he liked and admired what the Earp brothers were trying to do in Tombstone. After a while he threw his cigar butt into the alley, where it landed in a shower of sparks. He decided it was time for him to play a few hands of Faro.

He walked down the street to the Oriental Saloon and entered the batwings. The place was full to the brim with cowboys, miners, merchants, bar girls, and gamblers. He threaded his way through the crowd to a corner table in the back, where he saw Doc Holliday playing poker with four other men. Doc didn't look good. His face had a fine sheen of sweat, and he was pale as a ghost. A large bottle of whiskey sat nearly empty on the table next to him, and a woman dressed in red satin sat on the arm of his chair, her arm around his shoulders.

Falcon stepped up and tipped his hat at Doc, who immediately waved him over. "My, Mr. MacCallister, but you certainly do clean up very nicely," Doc said in his soft Southern accent. There was no trace of a slur in his words, though it was evident he'd been drinking heavily all night.

"I would like you to meet my special lady friend, Kate Elder. Kate, this is Falcon MacCallister, from Colorado."

"Pleased to meet you, Miss Kate," Falcon said. The girl was pretty, in an overblown, western sort of way. Her features were less than delicate, and she had a thin face with a large nose that was her most prominent feature. Her eyes were gentle, and it was evident from the way she looked at Doc that she worshiped him.

Before Doc sat back down, Falcon leaned over and whispered, "We've got to talk. Meet me at the Faro table later."

Doc winked and nodded, then returned to his poker game. Falcon noticed that even with the drinking, the pile of money and chips in front of Doc was sizable. Evidently the man was a master card player. Falcon looked forward to playing with him.

Falcon slowly made his way to the Faro table, smiling at Wyatt Earp, who was dealing cards from a brightly painted and lacquered box with a bright yellow tiger emblazoned on it. Bucking the Tiger, as playing against the house was called, was a game of high rewards, if you could beat the tremendous odds against you. It was a game, as Falcon had said, played by men who either didn't know the odds, or were too drunk to care.

Wyatt grinned as he passed out cards to two drunken miners sitting before him. "You ready to give the tiger a go, Falcon?" he asked.

Falcon shook his head. "I'm going to get a table. How about you joining me when you take a break?"

Wyatt nodded, then said, "Queen. So house wins again, boys."

Falcon finally managed to find a small table against the wall that was unoccupied and settled in, sitting facing the crowd out of habit even though he, along with everyone else in the room, was unarmed.

After a while, Doc and Wyatt joined him at his table. Falcon leaned forward and put his face near theirs, so no one else could hear him. "Wyatt, I just heard something you need to know."

He told them of the conversation he'd overheard between Billy Clanton and Frank and Tom McLaury.

Wyatt sat there a moment, his face set and grim. Finally,

he smiled slightly. "Well, I guess I knew this was coming. It's time to put a stop to this feud, once and for all."

He stood up and shook Falcon's hand. "Thanks for the information, Falcon. I'm much obliged to you."

"What are you going to do, Wyatt?"

Wyatt took a deep breath. "Stick around until tomorrow afternoon and you'll see . . . the entire town will see."

Chapter 3

October 21 was a clear, chilly day without a cloud in the sky over Tombstone. Falcon was finishing lunch at Campbell and Hatch's Saloon when, through the window onto Main Street, he saw Wyatt, Virgil, Morgan, and Doc Holliday come out of the marshal's office. As the four men walked down the street, all dressed in long dusters over their suits, he noticed Doc put a shotgun under his coat, keeping it out of sight.

Falcon threw a couple of banknotes on the table, grabbed his hat, and strolled outside, staying well behind the Earps and Doc Holliday on the boardwalk. He was curious to see how they would handle the threat he'd overheard the night before.

They turned left on Fourth Street, toward the OK Corral, walking abreast in the middle of the street. Falcon stepped around the corner, and he could see Ike and Billy Clanton and Frank and Tom McLaury out in front of the corral at the corner of Third and Fremont Streets, standing next to their horses.

When Wyatt noticed the men were all wearing sidearms,

he called out, "You boys surrender your weapons, or you're under arrest."

Sheriff Behan hurried up to the Earps, saying, "It's all right. They promised me they weren't gonna stay armed."

Virgil elbowed the sheriff aside and continued walking toward the four cowboys wearing red sashes. "We don't want any trouble," he said. "Throw down your guns."

Billy Clanton and Frank McLaury drew their guns, and Doc shot Billy through the chest, the sharp report of a scattergun echoing up and down Fremont. Then he turned his shotgun on Tom and put a double load of buckshot into his chest, killing him instantly, dropping him in his tracks.

Ike screamed, "Don't shoot, don't shoot!" and began to run down the street. Wyatt allowed him to pass, but Doc fired twice at him, missing both times.

As Ike ran, his brother Billy tried to fire a last few shots before he died. Camillus Fry, the proprietor of a photo studio nearby, raced over and took his pistol away from him.

Frank shot at Doc, but the bullet hit Doc's holster and ricochetted into his hip, producing a minor wound. Doc whirled and fired his Colt, hitting Frank in the forehead as the Earps all opened fire.

In less than thirty seconds, Billy, Frank, and Tom lay dead. Virgil had a bullet through his leg, and Morgan was wounded in both shoulders. Wyatt was the only one unscathed by the fusillade of bullets flying up and down the street.

As Falcon watched the melee, he noticed movement out of the corner of his eye from the alley before him. Johnny Ringo was in the shadows, aiming a rifle at the Earps.

Falcon pulled his derringer from his boot and stepped up behind Ringo, placing the double-barrel against the back of his head. "I don't think I'd do that, if I were you," he said in a low voice.

Ringo dropped the gun and raised his hands.

Falcon hesitated, then said, "Get on your horse and get out of town. There's been enough killing here today."

Ringo glanced back, hatred in his eyes, then sprinted down the alley toward his horse and jumped into the saddle, spurring his mount into a gallop without looking back.

Falcon put his derringer back in his boot and went to help get the wounded Earps to a doctor.

Doc pulled out a silver flask, calmly took a deep swig, and announced that what medical care he needed Kate Elder could provide. He walked off toward his room over the photography shop, whistling a tune Falcon thought he recognized as "Dixie."

Chapter 4

Naiche, Chief of the Chiricahua Apaches, watched the tiny settler's cabin from mottled shade beneath a gnarled pinyon pine, resting his rifle atop the high withers of his starving sorrel pony. Behind him, below the rim of the ridge, ten warriors sat on their ponies, awaiting his signal.

Naiche was worried. He counted four white-eyes moving about the cabin and barns near the spring, and if they had repeating rifles an attack would be costly. Since leading their escape from Fort Thomas and the Indian agency he'd been careful to avoid army patrols and all other white men traveling in large numbers. Now the Dragoon Mountains, in what the white-eyes called Arizona Territory, was crawling with soldiers looking for Naiche's half-brother, sworn enemy of the white Star Chief. In the tongue of the People he was called Gokaleh. Now most Apaches called him by his white man's name . . . Geronimo . . . after the attack on a Mexican village on the day of the Feast of Saint Jerome—Santo Geronimo in Spanish—when Geronimo began his bloody war on all who settled traditional Apache lands in Mexico or the southwestern United States.

Chokole rode her pony quietly to a spot near the rump of Naiche's sorrel. She was a woman warrior, rare among the Apache bands, chosen for her bravery and marksmanship with a rifle. She had taken many white and Mexican scalps. "Why do we wait, Naiche?" she whispered, the sound of her voice lost on a breath of hot desert wind.

"There are four white-eyes men. If they have Winchester rifles, the price for taking their food and livestock will come high."

"Will we wait for the night?" Chokole asked, as her pinto stamped a hoof to rid its leg of a stinging horsefly.

"I will watch them a longer time, until the shadows come to hide our approach." Naiche often doubted his wisdom in the ways of war, for he was not like his brother, a master of illusion and disguise who always caught an enemy by surprise. Naiche's thirst for blood often made him reckless. He longed to hear the screams of the wounded and dying enemy, see the sight of blood, hear the sound of a scalp being torn from an enemy's skull. Waiting to enter a fight was hard.

"As you wish, Naiche," the hard-twisted Apache woman said, cradling her rusted Spencer carbine in the crook of a thin brown arm. Two Colt pistols were belted to her bony waist, and she bore battle scars all over her flesh from knife and bullet wounds. "I will tell the others."

She turned her pony with a plaited rawhide jaw rein and rode silently off the rocky ridge.

Naiche glanced at the sky. There would be no moon tonight, a sign from the Four Spirits that they approved of his attack on the cabin in darkness, hiding his warriors' approach. Thus he decided to wait, for it was unwise to ignore a sign from the Spirits, bad medicine that could cause their attack to fail, or cost them many lives.

With their ponies tethered in a rocky ravine, Chokole led them toward the cabin on foot, then later on her hands and knees through tangles of creosote brush, until finally she went down on her belly to crawl, slithering like a snake around clumps of cactus and creosote stalks, making no sound. Naiche crawled in her wake while the others were scattered, forming a deadly circle around a crude pinyon log cabin with windows alight. The scent of smoke came from its chimney. In pole corrals behind the cabin a half dozen horses nibbled at mounds of hay. Two mules were in a separate corral. In another pen several small calves settled down for the night beneath the shadow cast by a thatched roof of pine limbs and mud. He could almost taste the roasted mule meat on his tongue now at the feast they would have to celebrate the success of their raid.

Naiche heard Taza and two more warriors off to his left, a sound only a trained Apache ear could hear. The circle was almost complete around the settlers cabin. Very soon, the time for killing and scalping would begin.

A door into the cabin opened when a dog barked. Golden lamplight spilled out onto the hard-packed ground, framing the outline of a man with a rifle. It was too much for Naiche to resist, a perfect shot at an enemy even though the others were still inside.

Very softly, covering the cocking mechanism with his palm, he thumbed back the hammer on his Spencer and took careful aim. Chokole heard the faint sound and glanced over her shoulder, then she shook her head, asking him to wait until they were closer to the cabin under the cover of the creosote bushes.

Naiche ignored her, his blood coursing through him in rapid bursts, thinking about the scream of a dying man when his bullet passed through the white man's heart. Sighting carefully along the barrel until he was certain he could not miss, he feathered the trigger gently.

The bang of his Spencer crackled through the night silence blanketing barren mountains around the cabin. The man in the door frame let out a yelp and dropped his rifle, bending over to clutch his belly as his wail grew louder. He staggered forward a half-step when another rifle exploded from the brush, ripping open one side of his skull in a shower of blood, bone, and plugs of his hair.

Another figure dashed to the doorway with a rifle. Chokole was ready. Her gun roared while Naiche sent another cartridge rattling into the firing chamber of his rifle. In the same instant three more guns erupted from scattered positions near the front of the cabin.

The second white man screamed the cry of a young man as he sank to his knees without firing a shot. He let his rifle fall and reached for his throat, making strangling noises before he fell over on his face.

Two more white-eyes foolishly rushed outside, directly into the line of fire from Naiche's warriors. Guns banged at them from the creosote bushes.

One slender man went spinning around, slammed into the wall of the cabin by force of impact from a lead slug. The other fell back into the cabin. When he landed, a thundering roar from his shotgun sent bits of dried mud and sticks flying from the roof.

"Ayiiii!" Chokole cried, rising up in a crouch to rush the door. Others let out the Apache war cry as Naiche began running behind Chokole toward the cabin.

He could hear the white women's screams, and the sound was like sweet music to his ears. He would enjoy torturing the survivors, even the women, for their shrill cries satisfied some inner need he'd learned during his training as a warrior under the greatest of all Apache war chiefs, Cochise.

A boy of less than sixteen years lay on the blood-soaked dirt floor of the cabin, whimpering, holding a mortal wound in his side, blood spilling between his tightly clasped fingers. Naiche stood over him, his knife poised about the white-eye's skull.

In the few words of the white man's tongue he'd learned at Fort Thomas while he was a prisoner there, he spat, "This Apache land!"

One slashing sweep of his knife blade passed across the scalp of the boy while Naiche held an iron grip on his yellow hair. The sound of tearing flesh, of a razor-sharp blade passing across bone, was quickly drowned out by a scream so loud it filled the cabin walls. Blood sprayed from the torn scalp lock as Naiche held it high, showing it to Chokole and the others before he shook the blood from it.

Across the room, Taza sliced off the scalp of a whimpering girl with one swift motion. She shrieked as Taza shook blood off her torn scalp so that she was covered with crimson droplets from head to toe, as though she'd been outside in a red rain.

Then Taza drove his knife into her belly, and the girl passed out. The blade opened her stomach with ease. With his free hand he pulled the white girl's intestines and organs through the wound, making a grisly popping sound, scattering coils of purple intestine across the floor. Taza held the liver in one fist, squeezing blood and bile from it. Then he let out a war whoop and threw it against the cabin wall.

Chokole knelt over an older man whose chest still rose and fell slowly. With practiced skill she cut off his eyelids so it appeared he was staring at her, even though pain had rendered him unconscious.

Otoe, a seasoned warrior of many battles with the bluecoat soldiers, pulled another dying white man by his hair over to the fireplace, where an iron pot held boiling beans. He swung the pot hook out of the way quickly, so as not to burn his hands, for like Naiche and the others he was hungry, and the beans would be eaten as soon as the killing was finished.

Otoe dropped the unconscious white man's head into the hot coals and flames. He looked over at Naiche and grinned as the man's hair and face burst into flame, evoking a moan from what was left of the dying man. In Apache he said, "We will eat the brain of our enemy along with his pot of beans."

"It is good," Naiche muttered, searching the cabin floor for a final victim.

A soft groan from outside reminded him of the boy who fell at the base of the cabin wall. He strolled through the doorway, his knife tip dripping blood, to slice the scalp from the last of the enemy.

The white boy was conscious, watching him as he seized a fistful of his curly blond hair.

"No, please no!" the boy yelled.

Naiche's wicked grin was his only reply as he swept his blade across the wounded boy's forehead. Blood squirted all over Naiche's arms and hands, and the scent of it, even the feel of it, was good. The warm liquid steamed in the chilly night air as he held his hands up to the sky and gave a harsh cry of joy.

Chokole came outside. "All are dead," she said in the softest of voices, with no hint of the ferocity revealed by her actions only minutes before. "These white-eyes are like all the others. They die like cowards, screaming, trying to hide under their wooden beds. Geronimo speaks truth when he tells us the white-eyes have no stomach for fighting. We will drive them from our lands when Geronimo gathers more warriors and guns."

It was true, Naiche thought as he shook the bloody scalp dry and hooked it through his belt. He spoke to Chokole in the darkness while the others began carrying flour and sugar and other foodstuffs outside to be loaded on the settler's horses and mules. "The repeating guns are what make the white soldiers strong," he began. "When we raid the fort and take these guns for our own, the bluecoats will stand no chance against us. They are not brave men. Their repeating rifles give them the strength of ten men. We must have Winchesters and many bullets, and more brave warriors who are not afraid to slip away from the reservation to follow us in a fight to defeat the enemy. As we speak, Isa is moving from one lodge to another at the fort, talking to warriors who want freedom, to live in the old ways. Isa promises many will follow him, and they will bring repeating rifles and bullets into the Dragoons to our secret place.''

"It will be good," Chokole agreed. "With many-shoot guns, we will defeat these white-skinned cowards easily.''

Naiche watched Taza bring haltered mules and horses from the corrals behind the cabin. "Do not forget Geronimo will return with warriors hiding in the Sierra Madres in Mexico, and he will steal many strong ponies from the Yaquis so our movements will be swift.''

Otoe came to the cabin door to speak to Naiche. His arms and chest were drenched in blood. "Let us eat the white man's beans, for I am very hungry.''

Naiche pointed to the animals being taken from the sheds and corrals. "As soon as everything is lashed to the horses. We must be ready to escape quickly if the soldiers come. When all is finished, we eat. Chokole and I will gather the white mens' guns and ammunition. One is a Winchester, a gift from the Great Spirit. With even one repeating rifle, we will kill many more of the enemy until Isa comes to the mountains with more warriors and Winchesters.''

Otoe gave what might pass for a smile. "It is good, Naiche, to kill our enemies again. For too long we have been like dogs, kept in cages at the fort. My heart is happy to be free, killing the whites who have driven us from our lands.''

Naiche turned toward the dark outlines of the Dragoons high above the settlement. "Very soon, the land will be ours again. We will take it back and cover Apacheria with the blood of those who took it from us.''

"The Spirits have answered Geronimo's prayers," Chokole said with a glance toward the sky.

"It is not only his prayers the Spirits hear. When Geronimo kills, the cries of his dying white enemies reach the

Moon, the Winds, Mother Earth, and the Sun. It is his courage the Spirits reward."

"As well as our own," Chokole said.

Naiche stared into her black eyes. "As well as our own, my warrior woman. We have only begun to fight."

Chapter 5

Naiche sat under the stars, admiring the Winchester, turning it over in his hands. He understood only a little of how the gun worked. With a box of cartridges between his folded knees he kept watch from a ridge above the Chiricahua's hidden canyon where the wickiups of the women and children sat in an uneven line along the bare banks of a spring-fed stream high in the Dragoons.

Roasting a mule carcass on a firepit below, several woman attended to the cooking, turning it often on a spit above dry pinyon limbs, giving off no telltale smoke that would alert the soldiers to their presence. Now the starving children would have something to eat—the mules and flour and sugar and salt pork taken from the settler's cabin. It would serve to put some meat on their bones to help them survive the winter months ahead. The Spirits had indeed smiled on their successful raid tonight.

Chokole walked softly up the ridge, balancing her Spencer in one hand. He gave her a single nod to acknowledge her presence and continued to examine the many-shoot rifle.

He understood how the cartridges were fed through a

metal loading gate into a tube below the barrel, counting five, and a sixth fit into the firing chamber. By working the lever under the stock, a shell was ejected while the hammer was drawn back in firing position, then another was somehow magically pushed into the chamber. By lowering the hammer gently with his thumb he did not have to waste a cartridge by firing it to see how the weapon worked.

At last, he thought, *I understand the white man's deadly gun and I am ready to go to war with it.*

Chokole squatted beside him. "The meat is almost ready," she said, also admiring the rifle. "Do you know how to make the bullets shoot?"

"I will teach you its ways," he promised. "But we must have many more, one for each warrior in our band."

Chokole watched the distant desert floor many miles to the north, in the direction of Fort Thomas. "It will be a long war," she said, "even with many-shoot rifles. The white-eyes are so many, and we are so few. They are like ants moving across the land."

"More will join us," Naiche told her, even though her wisdom was as great as any member of the tribe, she having lived for more than thirty winters. As a young girl she had been chosen to be a sixth wife of Cochise, before the old chief died. She had never taken a husband or given birth to children, preferring war over the traditional life of an Apache woman.

"Many are afraid, Naiche. The soldiers and their cages have broken their spirits."

"It is true. Some of our bravest warriors no longer have the will to fight. Even Geronimo cannot reach them when he begs them to join us. They are dead in spirit, and only their weary bodies live on at the stinking white man's reservation."

Chokole nodded, the copper scent of blood still strong on the scalps tied to her belt. "Geronimo tells them this place called San Carlos is the worst. They dug a hole in the ground and covered it with logs, tossing scraps of food to him like a dog, forcing him to live in his own excrement. I was with the Chiricahuas on Salt Creek when the soldiers brought him there in chains, covered with his own filth, starving, blood dripping from his wrists and ankles where the chains cut into his flesh. But when he looked at me, even though his head was bowed, I saw the same fire in his eyes. They could not break his spirit, and they could not break yours while you were in the cages. You are a brave chief, Naiche."

He accepted her compliment in silence, for deep inside he knew he would never be the fighter Geronimo was "I fight for my people, Chokole. More will join us soon. Until that time comes we must continue to raid the white-eyes and take their repeating rifles and bullets. When Isa comes with warriors and guns from Fort Thomas, we will be much stronger. Then we will attack the larger ranches and white man's villages, until we burn them all from the face of Earth Mother. It is The Way."

The call of an owl came from a distant mountaintop, a signal from Otoe that no one was following them. The tracks made by the white-eyes' iron horseshoes were hard to wipe away from the earth with a mesquite or pinyon branch, and Naiche had worried that someone who could read sign might lead the soldiers to them. Without iron tools other than simple knives there was no way to remove the iron from the stolen mules and horses.

"No one comes," Chokole said needlessly, for she knew Naiche recognized the call of the owl made by Otoe.

"The Four Spirits are smiling. We have food and strong horses, and mule meat, and the cattle will keep the children and women alive in spite of their bad taste."

Chokole grunted her agreement, taking the Winchester when Naiche offered it to her.

"I will show you how to load and fire it," he said, "but we have no bullets to waste, only three boxes. Once you understand how the bullets travel in and out of the barrel, and the way it must be loaded, it will be enough until we engage the enemy in battle."

"Will we fight again soon?" she asked, peering down at the rifle and its strange loading gate.

"As soon as our warriors' strength returns. They have been hungry for many suns, and now we have plenty. Before the new moon comes, we will strike again near the white mans' town they call Tombstone. There is a ranch to the south. I have watched it for two suns, and there are few white-eyes to guard it. I counted only five."

She held the Winchester to her shoulder, looking between its sights. "With this I can kill six of the enemy without reloading. I must have one, and we must find more for the others very quickly."

Isa led fourteen silent shadows among the barracks at Fort Thomas. Only three, including Isa, carried knives, while the rest had no weapons.

They crept to a corner of the building where rifles and ammunition were kept under the watchful eye of two soldiers.

Isa whispered to a young warrior beside him. "I will kill the one on the left. You kill the one on the other side, and be sure to cover his mouth so no one will hear his death screams."

The warrior named Sola gave the sign for agreement.

Isa readied his blade, inching forward. Sola came soundlessly behind, a crude knife made from a rusted plowshare in his fist.

Isa lunged around the corner of the small building, thankful there was no moonlight to make him an easy target.

A shadow stirred on one side of the door. The gleam of a rifle barrel was dull, hard to see in dim starlight. Isa's lunge sent him crashing into the soldier's chest while Sola made a similar dive to reach the other guard.

"What the hell—" the soldier gasped, bringing his rifle up just as eight inches of iron entered his belly.

Isa jerked the blade upward, hearing the crack of bone

and pop of gristle as blood shot all over his right hand. His free hand clamped the guard's mouth shut as he slumped against the wall, dropping his rifle to reach for the pain racing through his body.

Isa twisted the knife into the soldier's heart and felt him grow slack, muscles quivering while more blood squirted from his mortal wound.

Sola drove the second guard against the armory wall and pinned him there, ripping and tearing into flesh with his rusted knife, a hand covering the soldier's mouth.

"Arrrgh!" the bluecoat blubbered between Sola's powerful fingers. He slid to the ground on his rump, his Winchester tumbling from his grasp.

Isa jerked his knife from the soldier's body and took the unfamiliar iron key from a ring attached to the guard's belt. As he had seen the soldiers do so often, he put the key into the lock and twisted it.

The door opened into a dark room filled with rows of rifles in wooden racks.

"Tell the others to come quickly," Isa whispered to Sola as he hurried to a wall lined with repeating rifles.

More shadows rushed into the armory. Without a word Isa directed them to the rifles, four for each man, while he took down cardboard boxes of cartridges and began stuffing them into burlap bags, two tied together so each warrior could carry a pair over his shoulder.

"There are so many," Sola whispered, helping Isa gather boxes of shells.

"It will not be enough," Isa replied. "We will hide the ones we cannot use in the cave where Naiche waits for us. When more of our people slip away from the reservation, they will have rifles and bullets."

One of the guards groaned outside, and the sound made Isa's heart labor. He ran to the door, jerking his bloody knife from his belt, and made a slashing motion across the throat of the soldier making the noise.

Isa gave the fort compound a sweeping glance. It was late and all, but a few soldiers would be asleep. It would be an easy thing to slip past the few who paraded back and forth in the night near the horse stables and kill two more who watched the back of the barns.

He raced back inside to finish loading the rifles and sacks of cartridges.

Henry Peters was rolling a smoke, his rifle resting against the rear wall of the stable. He hated night guard duty, for the boredom often got to him. Dave Watkins was asleep inside the barn atop a mound of hay, a serious violation of regulations.

In the flare of the match he held to the tip of his smoke he thought he saw a snarling face very close to his, and he blinked to be sure he wasn't dreaming.

Pulling the match away from his face, flicking it out so he could see clearly, he felt a powerful blow to his stomach.

In a sudden rush of understanding he saw an Indian, an Apache, staring into his eyes as a white-hot pain shot through his belly, spreading like fire.

"Jesus!" Peters grunted, feeling one of his ribs snap in two.

The pain was more than he could take, and his vision clouded. He thought he heard Dave Watkins give a muffled yell from the hallway into the stable.

Then all was black around him, and he felt no more pain and heard no more

Fifteen mounted Apaches under the leadership of Isa rode quietly away from Fort Thomas burdened with more than fifty Winchester .44 caliber rifles and three hundred cartons of shells. Isa led them south, often riding back and forth or in apparently meaningless circles until the desert floor provided a slab of rock where the iron-shod cavalry horses would leave very little sign.

"It is good," Isa told Sola. "Now we are ready for a war with the white-eyes."

"Naiche will be pleased," Sola answered, glancing over his shoulder.

"Yes. And word will reach Geronimo in Mexico that we have many-shoot guns. He will bring more Mimbres warriors across the mountains to join us."

"I do not think so," Sola said. "Geronimo is like the big mountain cat. He prefers to fight with only a few warriors, to strike quickly and then disappear. I do not think he will come to our camp in the Dragoons."

Isa wondered if Sola could be right. It made little difference, for when it came to shedding the white man's blood, Naiche had few equals.

Heading toward the Dragoons by starlight, Isa changed directions often to throw off pursuit. No one must find them until they were fully prepared for the war that was sure to follow.

Chapter 6

...on his traveling clothes and walked to the ... saloon. He found Doc still sitting at his favorite table playing poker. His friend looked like death. His face was pale and covered with sweat, the skin stretched taut over bulging cheekbones and sunken eyes that held only the tiniest spark of life. He had been playing poker steadily for over twenty-four hours, since the gunfight at the corral, his only sustenance, cigarettes and whiskey. Falcon could see the man was dying a little more every day. Perhaps that was why he refused to sleep until he passed out—fear that the man with the scythe would come to him in his slumber.

Falcon looked into Kate's eyes as she sat next to her man. The people in town called her Big Nose Kate, but Falcon no longer noticed her features. He saw only her love and devotion for Doc. She looked as if she had been crying—probably after trying to get him to eat or sleep, which always made him angry with her. He didn't like to be babied.

"Hey, Doc," Falcon called as he approached the table. Tired eyes flicked his way, then seemed to come a little more alive as Doc smiled. "Hello and good morning, Master MacCallister."

Falcon stood there, his hands on his hips and a stern look on his face. "I'm fixing to head on down the road. Are you going to let a friend leave town without letting him buy you breakfast?"

Doc's eyes narrowed even as his lips curled in his ever-present sarcastic grin, as if he knew what Falcon was trying to do. "I would never be so rude as to do that, Falcon. Just give me a few more minutes to finish teaching these young men the rudiments of poker, and I shall join you at Campbell and Hatch's."

As Falcon turned to go, he caught Kate's grateful smile of relief. She gave him a quick wink before she turned back to Doc and the poker game.

Campbell and Hatch's Saloon was a combination bar, dance hall, billiard parlor, and eating establishment. As such, it was just as busy at this time of morning as it was at night. The crowd consisted mostly of businessmen getting a bite to eat prior to opening their doors, red-eyed cowboys trying to get some coffee into them before riding back out to punch cattle, and a few dance hall women taking a break before going to bed for the rest of the day.

Falcon grabbed a table and sat facing the room, as was his habit. When the waiter came he ordered two breakfasts and told the man to keep the coffee coming when his guest arrived.

Doc walked in a few moments later, and Falcon noticed he was limping slightly from the bullet wound in his right hip. He could still see the bullet hole in his pants and the bloodstains on the cloth. Evidently Doc hadn't even changed clothes before he began his nonstop poker playing.

Doc took a seat next to Falcon, so he, too, could watch the other men in the bar. When the waiter brought their cups of coffee, Doc took out a silver flask and poured a dollop of amber liquid into them.

Doc held up his cup toward Falcon. "A toast," he said,

a strange look in his eyes. "A toast to the man behind the scenes."

Falcon clinked his cup against Doc's. "What do you mean?"

A sly smile crossed Doc's lips. "Don't think you went unobserved in your little altercation with Johnny Ringo." He took another drink, and added, "Your timely interference was much appreciated. The man might have gotten lucky and actually hit one of us with that rifle."

Falcon laughed. These last few years, there had not been many men he enjoyed being with. Billy the Kid had been one, and Doc Holliday was another. The man's sense of humor, and his loyalty to his friends, caused Falcon to feel a kinship with him that was rare for a man who spent most of his time alone.

"What are you going to do now, Falcon?" Doc asked, as the waiter piled plates of scrambled eggs, bacon, sausage, tortillas, sliced tomatoes, and potatoes in front of them.

Falcon shrugged. "Mosey on down the trail, I guess. I've still got a lot of country to see."

"Why not stay here in Tombstone? It is a growing town, and given enough time I might be able to teach you how to play poker.

"That'd be the day," Falcon said. "In the little time I've watched you, I've noticed you have a tendency to go against the odds. In the long run, that's a no-win strategy."

"Ah, but that is the key, my friend. For me, there is no *long* run, only the here and now."

Doc bent his head and began to nibble at his food, but Falcon could tell his heart wasn't in it. He knew consumption took away the appetite, but he wished Doc would at least try to take better care of himself. Of course, he didn't say that, for he respected him too much to try to tell him how to live what was left of his life.

After they finished eating, Doc said he was going home to take a nap, and Falcon went to Morgan Earp's house, where both he and Virgil were recovering from their wounds.

Wyatt answered the door, a pistol in his hand. "Oh, it's you, Falcon. Come on in."

"Expecting trouble?" Falcon asked as he took his hat off and entered the room.

Morgan was lying on a sofa, propped up on several pillows, bandages on both shoulders. Virgil was across the room with his wounded leg stuck out in front of him on an ottoman, a shotgun cradled in his arms.

Wyatt peered out the door for a moment, then closed and bolted it. "Yeah. Sheriff Behan has been making noises about arresting us for murder."

"But he has no authority in Tombstone. He's the county sheriff," Falcon said.

Virgil nodded. "That's correct, Falcon, but he still has plans to haul us in to stand trial."

"How do you think it'll play?"

Morgan gave a short, harsh laugh. "There's no tellin'. Half the people in Tombstone make a lot of money off The Cowboys' trade. They're gonna be plenty pissed off that we've shut them down."

"Well, I just came to say good-bye, and good luck," Falcon said, walking around the room and shaking hands with each of the brothers. "But if you need some help—"

Wyatt shook his head. "No, Falcon, you've done enough. This is our battle now, and we'll see it through."

Falcon took Wyatt's hand. "I'll keep watch in the newspapers. If I see that the trial is going against you, I'll be back."

"Thanks Falcon. *Vaya con Díos,* partner," Wyatt said.

Falcon climbed on Diablo and began to ride to the southeast out of town. Just as he got to the city limits he saw three men on horseback followed by two buckboards coming toward him.

As he pulled abreast of the wagons, he glanced inside and his stomach went cold. There were several bodies laid out in a row. All had been scalped, and one's head looked as if it'd been cooked in a fire, then its skull split open.

"Hold on, there!" Falcon called as he wheeled Diablo in a tight turn. "What's happened here?"

One of the men—they were miners by their looks—shook his head. "We found these poor folk at a cabin up in the foothills of the Dragoon Mountains. Looks like the Apaches had quite a time with them."

Falcon climbed down off Diablo, his heart aching at the sight of the slaughtered settlers. There were two women, their naked bodies covered with blood-soaked blankets. Falcon pulled back the blanket and felt his gorge rise at the sight of the gutted woman, her entrails hanging loose. Noonday sun glinted off her bare skull where the scalp had been hacked off. Her face, even in death, still wore a look of horror at what had befallen her.

Falcon brushed flies off her face and gently closed her eyes with his fingers. Then his fist clenched as he felt the familiar killing rage sweep through his body. In his mind's eye, the woman's face became that of Marie, his wife, who had been crucified by renegade Indians in the not too distant past.

He forced his voice past the knot in his throat. "Do you know who did this?" he asked.

The miner shrugged. "Some soldiers came by our claim the other day and said Naiche and a small band of followers was on the warpath in this area, but the blue-bellies was havin' trouble locatin' 'em."

"Naiche, huh? I've heard of him. Some people call him the human tiger, because of his thirst for white man's blood," Falcon said, turning away, unable to look at the woman's body any longer.

"Yeah," one of the men on horseback added, "they also said another band of 'bout twenty or so Injuns escaped from Fort Thomas last week with over fifty Winchester repeatin' rifles and a whole load of ammunition." He leaned to the side and spat a stream of brown tobacco juice onto a cactus beside the road. "I plan on stayin' in town fer a while to give those soldiers a chance to catch them redskins.''

"That's fer sure," another of the miners said. "They bad enough with bows an' arrows, but they gonna be plumb hell with repeatin' rifles in they hands.''

"Looks like they took off with some horses and mules belongin' to these folks, an' whatever weapons they had. There wasn't much left of the cabin that hadn't been trashed," said the man driving the buckboard.

"There was blood everwhere," another said, shaking his head. "Poor devils must've suffered somethin' fierce. 'Couple of 'em looked like they'd been scalped while still alive, and we never did find one of the heads that'd been cut off.''

Falcon slammed his fist into the side of the wagon, making the driver jump and almost swallow his cud of chewing tobacco. As he choked and spit, Falcon turned to him. "How do I find this cabin?''

"Take the north fork of the road headin' up into the Dragoons, 'bout three mile up ahead. You can't miss it. But mister, I gotta tell ya, yore crazy if you go up there.''

Falcon climbed into the saddle and rode off, his back stiff and his neck thick with anger. He'd be damned if he was going to let this happen to anyone else's wife. Not if he had any say in the matter.

Chapter 7

On the trail up into the mountains, Falcon tried to calm himself down. He knew he was traveling into dangerous territory, and he needed a clear head. It was a strange fact, but true, that the surest way to get killed in battle was to be angry. The mind had to be calm and settled, or the body would die.

He took a deep breath of the cool, crisp autumn air, glancing around at the mountain forest he was heading into. The pinyon trees were a deep emerald green, while some other trees Falcon didn't recognize had already started to change their leaves into brilliant patterns of gold and scarlet. It was the best time of year in some of the prettiest country God ever made.

He let Diablo find his own pace up the mountain, while he sat back against the cantle and lighted a cigar, letting his mind roam back to happier times.

After a while, he felt better. His heart had slowed to its normal beat, and his mind was focused. As he neared the spot where the cabin was supposed to be located, he began to search the trail and surrounding brush for Indian sign.

Finally, he came to a small clearing in the trees off to

the side of the trail. He could see a wooden cabin about
fifty yards into the forest, with a cleared area around it
containing a couple of corrals and outbuildings.

He eased out of the saddle and pulled his Colt, holding
it ready at his side. There was a chance the Indians might
have come back for something they missed, and the smell
of blood could have drawn wolves or a bear to the spot.
In any case, it was wise to be prepared for anything.

In front of the cabin door he found where two or three
people had died. Their blood had soaked into the already
reddish-brown dirt, making it a deep crimson, almost black,
color. From the way the ground was torn up, he could see
they hadn't died easy.

Earing back the hammer on his pistol, he slipped in the
door of the cabin, standing with his back against the wall
until his vision adjusted to the gloomy interior.

His nostrils dilated, and his stomach churned at the
smell of dried blood, excrement, and seared flesh that still
hung on the air like a malevolent fog. Blood and body
fluid stains were splattered on walls and floors and wooden
furniture all about the cabin. The place had the appearance and odor of a slaughterhouse.

As he walked through the tiny room he found two
dresses, one adult and one child size. They had been torn
off the females of the family. In the corner against a far
wall was a reddish clump of meat. Falcon squatted before
it and poked it with his Arkansas Toothpick, a knife with
a long, stiletto-type blade ten inches long and razor-sharp.
He almost lost his breakfast when he realized it was a
human liver.

He whirled away from the grizzly find and searched the
rest of the cabin, finding nothing of interest except that
all of the cabinets were emptied of foodstuffs and supplies
and a crude gun rack nailed to the wall was bare, with two
empty crushed boxes of .44 cartridges on the floor nearby.

As he stood there, hands on hips, looking at the empty
cupboard, the door behind him gave a tiny creak. He
whirled, bringing his pistol up.

"Hold on there, Sonny Jim," said a man standing in the doorway. He was dressed in buckskins, with knee-high leather moccasins on his feet, a bushy beard on his face, and he held what looked like a Sharps .50 caliber rifle cradled in his hands pointing at Falcon.

"Just what're you doin' in this here cabin?" he asked.

"I'm looking around," Falcon answered, his pistol still pointed at the man's gut.

The figure leaned to the side and spit a wad of tobacco out of his mouth onto the floor. "What say we both put these guns up and palaver fer a spell?"

Falcon holstered his Colt. "All right, but outside if you don't mind. I need some fresh air."

"It is a bit ripe in here, ain't it?" the man said as he backed out the door of the cabin.

Outside, Falcon took a deep breath, trying to clear the stink of death from his lungs.

The man in buckskin walked to a fallen tree on the edge of the forest and sat, resting his Sharps on his lap. Falcon sat next to him and stared at the cabin, trying not to think of the unendurable agony the settlers must have gone through a few nights ago.

"My name's John Henry Hawkins, but most just calls me Hawk," the man said, also staring at the cabin.

"I'm Falcon MacCallister."

Hawk glanced at Falcon, his eyes narrowed. "What's yore interest in this cabin, Falcon?"

Falcon's eyes clouded, his mind returning to the story his father, Jamie Ian MacCallister, told him about the death of his wife. Marie Gentle Breeze, as she was called, was captured by a band of Indians who tried to take her north with them as a slave. She fought them all the way, until they killed her. They crushed her head with a war axe, raped her many times, and threw her body in the Colored River. Jamie MacCallister rode and walked for miles on either side of the river, searching for Marie. He finally found her body wedged between a large rock and a tree, a few feet away from the west bank of the river.

Jamie gathered what was left of Marie's body and buried it nearby, piling a mound of rocks over the grave and marking it carefully. He rode over to the mining town of Georgetown and got himself a room at Louis Dupuy's fancy Hotel De Paris and sent word to Falcon. (Scream of Eagles)

For all intents and purposes, Falcon's world had ended that day. His gentle Marie, the love of his life and mother of his children, was gone forever. She had been taken from him the same way these poor folks had been taken, violently and horribly, suffering as no one should ever be made to suffer.

Falcon looked at Hawk and said simply, "My wife was killed by renegades a while back. I don't intend to let this massacre go unanswered."

Hawk nodded. He pulled out a twist of tobacco from his shirt pocket and cut a piece off with a large Bowie knife from a scabbard on his belt. As he chewed the tobacco, he watched the cabin.

"One of the men killed here was my baby brother. I sent word to him a few months back an' tole him how much silver was to be had out here in the Dragoons."

Hawk's head dropped and he stared at the ground between his feet. "Damn fool brought his wife an' daughter an' two other pilgrims with him from back east."

He looked up at Falcon with red-rimmed eyes. "I tried to tell 'im to leave the womenfolk in town an' let me teach 'em somthin' 'bout livin' out here in the wilderness 'fore they tried to settle in, but they wouldn't listen."

Hawk waved his hand in a circle, "This is mighty purty land, but it's wild, like the beasts that live here. Ain't no place for pilgrims an' women." He shook his head, "I shore wish they'd listened to me."

Falcon studied Hawk as he talked. The man didn't look like a typical miner. "How long have you been mining out here, Hawk?"

Hawk spat, wiping his mouth with the back of his hand. "Fer 'bout a year, more or less. I scouted fer the army for a spell, then tried my hand at huntin' buffalo." He looked at Falcon. "When the buffalo got scarce, I heared 'bout the silver strike near Tombstone and just kind'a drifted this way."

He glanced at the cabin. "God knows I wished I'd never have come here."

"What are your plans now?" Falcon asked.

Hawk turned eyes full of hate on Falcon. "I plan to hunt down the murderin' bastards that did this an' do to them what they did to my kin. I ain't gonna rest 'til my hoss is carryin' they scalps."

Falcon glanced at the cabin and the dark stains in front of it. He got up and walked to the place where the dirt was soggy with blood. Squatting, he dipped his finger in the soil and rubbed a horizontal crimson streak across each of his cheeks, like warpaint.

"You want some company?" he asked.

Hawk pulled out his knife and stuck the point into his thumb. When blood welled up, he wiped his thumb across his cheeks as Falcon had, then stuck out his hand. "To the death."

"To the death," Falcon repeated, taking his hand.

"Then let's git movin', partner. We're burnin' daylight, an' I got me some Injuns to kill."

Hawk's words and the hate in them gave Falcon a chill. He wanted to go after the men that did this, but he knew they had to have clear heads. He wondered if Hawk's anger was going to get them both killed.

Chapter 8

After sealing their agreement to ride together after the Indians that had killed the settlers, Falcon took a weathered set of buckskins of his own out of his saddlebags and changed into them. When Hawk gave him a questioning look, Falcon explained, "These are my going to war clothes."

Along with buckskin trousers and shirt and Apache-style moccasins that rose to his knees, Falcon added a brace of Colt .44 caliber pistols and his Arkansas Toothpick to his belt. He loosened his Winchester .44/.40 carbine in a rifle boot on the right side of his saddle and tied a Standard ten gauge sawed-off double-barrel shotgun to the pommel with a braided rawhide strap, where it would be within easy reach should they be attacked without warning.

Hawk stepped up to his horse, a buckskin, tan with black mane and tail. He took from his saddlebags a belt and single holster holding an old Colt Army .44 and strapped it on, then stuck an extra pistol in the left side of his belt, butt first for a cross-hand draw. He pulled a small canvas bag full of shells for his Sharps and attached it to his belt next to the scabbard for his Bowie knife.

While he swung into the saddle, Falcon walked over to the corral and bent close to the ground, studying the tracks that led away from the cabin and into the woods.

"I make it about ten or eleven Indians, leading another five or six horses and mules, which are riderless. The Indians are all riding horses with shoes on, so they must be stolen from either the army or others they've killed," Falcon said.

Hawk cut another piece of tobacco from the twist in his shirt. He stuck it in his mouth and chewed for a moment before shifting the cud to his left cheek. "That figures. The Injuns never did figure out how to remove horseshoes from their mounts. One thing, though, it'll shore make it easier to track 'em crost the mountains. Those shoes'll leave marks on hard-packed ground an' rock, whereas Injun ponies wouldn't."

Falcon swung into into the saddle and reined Diablo's head around until he was heading in the same direction as the Indian band.

"Since you used to be a scout for the army, you want to lead the way?" Falcon asked.

Hawk spat, hitting a scurrying ground squirrel dead center. "Don't mind if'n I do. Might be a mite rusty, though. Hadn't done this for a lotta years, partner."

Letting his horse walk at an easy pace, leaning his head to the side to watch the tracks, Hawk led the way into the forest. The Indians had not taken the trail, but ridden straight up the side of the mountain through scattered cacti and creosote bushes and small stands of pinyon trees, as if trying to hide their trail.

After they had traveled about a hundred and fifty yards into the thick overgrowth, Hawk's horse suddenly whinnied in a harsh squeal and reared up on his hind legs, almost throwing Hawk to the ground.

"What the—" Hawk exclaimed, fighting the reins.

Falcon filled his fist with iron and rode up beside the man, fearing an attack.

He slowly holstered his gun and blinked startled eyes at what he saw facing them.

One of the settler's heads was impaled on a spear, stuck into the ground, facing the Indians' back trail with a leering stare, blood trailing down the spear. The eyes were black with flies and a trail of red ants were making their way up the wood from the ground.

"Damn," Hawk said in a husky voice. "I ain't never seen nothin' like that."

"I haven't, either," Falcon said. "But I heard that the soldiers over at Fort Grant, the prison fort for Apaches and other lawbreakers in Arizona Territory, once did that to an Indian as an example for the others not to try to escape. His name was Delshey, and it was said that his grinning, fleshless skull stood in the entrance to the fort for months, greeting all who entered."

"You think maybe the ones done this is from Fort Grant?"

"Could be, or it just might be their way of warning anyone who tries to trail them what is waiting for them up ahead."

Falcon and Hawk took the head and buried it in the soft sandy loam of the mountainside. As they walked back to their horses, Falcon picked up the spear and wiped the blood and insects off, sticking it under his saddleskirts alongside Diablo's flank.

"What you want with that old spear?" Hawk asked.

"The same thing the Indians used it for."

"I don't get ya."

"We're going up against at least ten Indians, who've already proven they're vicious killers. I've heard there's another fifteen or twenty headed this way who may join up with the ones we're after. The only chance the two of us have to come out of this with our hair is to spread a little fear into the men we're hunting, perhaps make them careless."

"Go on."

"That means we've got to be every bit as ruthless as they

are, and this spear is going to let them know that we're on their trail and we mean to give them no quarter."

Falcon stepped into the stirrups and swung into line behind Hawk as he followed the Indians' trail. As the old scout rode along, Falcon could hear him talking to himself in a constant monotone. He guessed his many years of being alone had affected him in some way. *I just hope he's good with that Sharps,* Falcon thought, his eyes searching the forest on either side of them for ambushers as they rode.

When dusk began to fall, they made a cold camp, unable to build a fire that would give their position away. Falcon took out some biscuits and roast meat he'd bought at Campbell and Hatch's before leaving Tombstone. He gave a couple to Hawk, and they sat on their saddles under a pinyon tree and had supper.

After he took a deep swig from his canteen, Falcon glanced at Hawk. "One of our problems is going to be water. From what I hear, the Dragoon Mountains are damn near as dry as the desert."

Hawk chuckled. "You're shore right there, Falcon. That's one of the things that keeps the army from bein' able to track the Injuns. Most of the blue-bellies are too dumb to find water to conform out here. They ain't taken the time to learn how to find the hidden springs, or to mark on their maps where the few streams are located."

"You figure you can do that?"

Hawk shrugged. "Been doin' it for years. They's certain signs you look for, and you can dig down a foot or two and find water ever time. It ain't tasty, but it's wet, an' it'll keep you alive."

"Good," Falcon said. "That's one less thing we have to worry about."

"How do you think we ought to handle it when we find the Injuns?" Hawk asked around a mouthful of meat and bread.

"If we knew they had only single-shot rifles or bows and

arrows and if we caught them by surprise we could probably take on ten at one time."

"What makes you think otherwise?"

"I can't see four men and their womenfolk trying to settle out here without weapons. I didn't find any at the cabin, so the Indians have whatever the settlers had, plus whatever they got from the men whose horses they stole." He shook his head. "I think we've got to assume they have repeating rifles and act accordingly."

"That means followin' 'em to their camp an' then pickin' 'em off by ones and twos," Hawk said.

"Uh huh."

"You think we're good enough to do that and stay hidden where the rest of the band cain't find us?"

Falcon leaned back against his saddle and pulled his hat low over his eyes. "I guess we'll soon find out."

Hawk looked around at the darkness surrounding them and grunted. "I was afraid you was gonna say that."

From underneath his hat brim, Falcon answered. "Of course, if the leader of this band is Naiche, his name's going to be a powerful draw to the other young bucks in the territory. I figure word will have gotten out by now that he's on the warpath, and others will be straggling in to join him in twos and threes from just about every direction. One thing's certain, we're going to have plenty of targets long before we catch up with the main band."

Hawk drew his pistol and laid it on his chest as he lay back to sleep. "You're just full of good news, Falcon." He pulled his hat down low, murmuring, "An' I thought it was gonna be easy."

Chapter 9

Falcon and Hawk were up and on the trail before dawn. They rode slow, taking their time and watching both their back trail and the land in front of them.

The band of Indians they were following were headed generally due northwest, though they cut back and forth often, changing directions to make their tracks harder to follow.

Just before noon, as they approached the crest of a hill overlooking a valley below, Diablo's ears perked up and he gave a soft snuffle, wagging his head back and forth. Falcon quickly covered his nose to keep him from nickering, for it was obvious he either smelled or heard other horses.

"Yo, Hawk," Falcon called softly.

At the sound of Falcon's whisper, Hawk immediately reined to a stop and picked his Sharps up from where it was resting on his saddle horn. He glanced back over his shoulder, and Falcon held a finger up to his lips and slipped out of the saddle to the ground.

Hawk did the same, anxiously peering back and forth, looking for whatever it was Falcon had heard.

Falcon got down on his belly and crawled to the top of the hillock and peered over. Entering the valley below, at a distance of about three hundred yards, were four braves. They were riding bareback, and two were carrying what appeared to be single-shot rifles, while one had an old musket cradled in his arms.

Falcon waved Hawk up beside him and pointed, a questioning look on his face.

"They must be some renegades on their way to join the ones we been trailin'," Hawk said in a low voice. "They're comin' from the wrong direction to be a part of Naiche's group."

"You think you can pick one or two off with that long rifle of yours?" Falcon asked.

Hawk showed his teeth in a nasty grin, licked the end of his finger, and wiped off the front sight of the Sharps.

He spread his feet out, digging his toes in the sand, his elbows in the dirt holding the Sharps up to his eye to take aim while Falcon backed out of sight then sprinted to his horse.

He climbed into the saddle and got his Stevens shotgun ready, holding it in his left hand, the reins in his teeth, and his Colt in his right hand.

When Hawk's Sharps exploded, knocking the big man back against his braced feet, Falcon spurred Diablo into action, guiding the stud with his knees as he raced over the hill and down toward the valley floor below.

Another explosion from the Sharps, and he saw a brave go flying, knocked off his pony with his arms flung wide, to land next to the body of another buck.

The remaining two Indians leaned over their horses' manes and yelled and whooped as they kicked them into a gallop down the valley toward Falcon.

One put his rifle to his shoulder and fired, the bullet singing a death song as it buzzed by Falcon's head.

Falcon eared back the hammers on the Stevens with his left hand and fired from the hip, taking the lead buck full in the chest with a double load of buckshot. The molten pellets tore the man in two, flinging his lifeless body to the ground and splattering his companion with blood and gore as he rode by.

Falcon fired with his Colt, but missed as the brave waved a tomahawk and leapt from his horse onto Falcon, knocking them both to the ground.

Falcon's shotgun and Colt were knocked from his grasp, and he wrapped his arms around the Indian as they rolled over and over in the dirt.

He twisted his head to the side just in time and received only a glancing blow from the tomahawk as he frantically reached for his Arkansas Toothpick.

Falcon managed to wrap his fingers around the handle of his knife as the buck reared back for a killing blow, his eyes wide and reddened with killing fever. The twelve-inch blade of the Toothpick flashed in the sun as it slid under the Indian's ribs and pierced his heart, killing him instantly.

With a bloodcurdling scream he collapsed on top of Falcon, pinning him to the ground. Falcon lay there, every muscle in his body aching and his head pounding as he tried to catch his breath. That had been too close. He reminded himself not to underestimate the Apache. They were fearless riders and fierce warriors. It was not going to be easy to go to war with them and survive.

After a few moments, Hawk came riding up, his Sharps resting on his thigh.

"You alive under there, Falcon?" he called in a lazy voice, as if asking about the weather.

With a mighty heave, Falcon pushed the dead man off his chest and struggled to his feet. "Yeah, but just barely," he answered.

Hawk grinned, leaning to the side to spit tobacco juice onto the dead Indian. "Good, 'cause I was just gittin' used to havin' company along."

Falcon picked up his Stevens and Colt, brushing dirt

and grass off them before putting them away. "That was mighty good shooting back there," he said, pointing to where the first two Indians lay.

Hawk patted the Sharps. "Hell, t'was easy with Baby here. She don't hardly ever miss."

Falcon looked around at the dead bodies and pulled his knife. "Well, time to leave a little message of our own."

Two hours later, he stepped back from their handiwork. One of the braves' heads was on a spear, stuck in the middle of the trail through the valley. The other three, minus their scalps, were hanging upside down from a cottonwood tree, with empty holes where their eyes should have been.

"You think them Injuns'll git the message?" Hawk asked, wiping his bloody blade on one of the bodies.

"Yeah. One of these boys is going to wander through the happy hunting ground without a head, and the others will be forever blind. For all their ferocity, Indians can't stand the idea of being mutilated after death, because they think that's how they'll stay in their afterlife."

"Do you think it'll make any of the ones comin' to join Naiche change their minds?"

"I doubt it, but it will send a message to Naiche that someone's coming after him. He'll know the army didn't do this, so it'll give him something else to think about, maybe even worry him a little until he knows just who it is on his backtrail."

Hawk looked up from tying the four scalps to his horse's mane. "Well, I think it must be gittin' on toward noon. How 'bout we make a noonin'?"

Falcon glanced over his shoulder. "All right with me, but do you mind if we head on up the trail for a ways first? I don't particularly relish the view here while I'm eating."

Falcon made a fire of very dry wood, putting it next to a large boulder under a slight overhang so the smoke would be dispersed by the time it rose into view above them. While he brewed coffee in a pot and fried some fatback and beans, Hawk gave him his first lessons in finding the hidden springs and underground water in the high desert regions of the Dragoons.

"First, you look for any kind of bird activity, 'cause they knows where the water is. If'n you see some doves flying toward a particular spot, 'specially at dusk when they come in to drink after feeding all day on grain, you can be fairly sure they's water somewhere's nearby."

Falcon used a fork to turn the bacon in the skillet, paying close attention to the pearls of knowledge Hawk was sharing with him. He knew it might well mean the difference between life or death in the coming days.

"Now, to find the underground water, you look fer a place that has some shade to it, like near some rocks or in the bottom of an arroyo or dry wash. If'n you see some green to the weeds there, or a small tree or brush, chances are there's water not too far 'neath the surface."

"I've heard, though to tell the truth I've never had to try it, that some of the cactuses have a lot of liquid in them that's drinkable."

Hawk nodded as he plucked a still sizzling chunk of meat from the skillet and bounced it back and forth between his hands until it cooled enough to pop it into his mouth. He spoke around the mouthful of food as he chewed. "That's correct, partner. The one you want to try is the barrel cactus. They's short and squatty and round on top. Best way to get the water out of 'em is to cut 'em off at the base and hold 'em up over your head and let it run right on down your gullet. Got to be careful, though. Them thorns is murder on your hands."

Finally the meal was ready, and Falcon piled heaping helpings of beans and fried bacon onto plates while Hawk poured them both coffee into tin mugs.

They sat on the ground, leaning back against their saddles, and enjoyed the first hot meal they'd had in several days. Neither talked until their plates were picked clean.

Hawk scrubbed his plate with a handful of sand and wiped it dry with a dirty bandanna. He leaned back and took out a cloth sack of tobacco and built himself a cigarette, then offered his fixin's to Falcon.

As they smoked, Falcon asked, "What do you plan to do after we finish with the Indians, Hawk?"

Hawk shrugged, as if he hadn't given it much thought. "I dunno. Go back to minin', I guess." He looked up from his cigarette to stare at Falcon. "To tell you the honest truth, I really don't 'spect to come out of this fracas without attracting some lead."

"Oh?"

"I just don't think it's in the cards for us to go up against this many redskins an' come out of it with our skins intact."

"Why do you say that?"

"Injuns ain't like white men. They don't think like us, an' they sure as hell don't act like us."

"What do you mean?"

"Well, if'n a white man is up against long odds, 'specially if his fight is with someone armed a lot better'n he is, he'll most likely run away and live to fight another day."

As he smoked, the cigarette dangling from the corner of his mouth, Hawk absentmindedly picked up a stick from the ground and began to whittle on it while he talked. "A redskin, on the other hand, thinks it's a mark of bravery to go up against a superior force. Hell, I've seen a lone brave armed only with a tomahawk charge a squadron of men with repeating rifles, an' never flinch 'til he was blown outta the saddle."

He shook his head. "Won't see no white man doin' nothin' like that."

Falcon laughed, "No, and I don't blame him, either."

"My point is, Falcon, that once these Injuns find out we're on their backtrail, they ain't gonna just go on about they business and pay us no nevermind. They is gonna come lookin' for us with a vengeance, an' they won't stop 'til either we're dead, or they is. There just ain't no backup to Injuns. It ain't in they character."

"I know what you mean," Falcon said. "My father, who was out here before most other white men, told me a story once about an old mountain man friend of his, man named Preacher. Seems this Preacher was once taken prisoner by some Indians—Pawnee, I think. These Indians took turns torturing him with what they called games. Making him run across hot coals barefoot, passing him between a line of braves who all took little swipes at him with their knives until he was bleeding from a hundred cuts, and then burying him up to his head and rode by at full speed, throwing spears at him."

Hawk stared at Falcon, interested in his story. "What ever happened to the old man?"

"The story goes, they couldn't make him scream or cry out for help, and that so impressed them with his courage they let him go." Falcon flipped his butt into the fire. "Of course, they couldn't make it too easy for him, so they set him free naked as the day he was born, without boots or shoes, and he had to walk across twenty miles of mountain peaks that were covered with snow, without any weapons or food."

Hawk looked dubious. "And you mean to tell me the old codger made it?"

Falcon nodded. "Yeah. My father said he saw the scars from the knife wounds and the stubs where some of his toes froze off, but he made it. The old man must have been tough as an armadillo's hide to survive that trek through the mountains."

"Heck, they's lots of stories 'bout Injuns, an' truth be told most of 'em won't stand the light of day, but there is no doubt they be strange creatures, all right."

He pitched his stick in the fire and rolled over on his side, pulling his hat down over his eyes. "I think I'm gonna take me a little after noonin' nap."

Falcon stood up, pulled his rifle from its boot, and started to walk away toward a clump of boulders nearby. "I'll just mosey on over there and keep an eye out for uninvited guests. I wouldn't want you to wake up without your hair."

"Much obliged," Hawk mumbled, and started snoring almost immediately thereafter.

Chapter 10

Major Wilson Tarver felt an odd mixture of anger and fear. More than fifty Winchester rifles in the hands of Apache savages would be enough to turn all of southern Arizona Territory into a river of blood, and they'd been stolen right under his nose from the Fort Thomas arsenal. This was not going to look good in his personnel record. He sleeved fear-sweat off his forehead, thinking he might have seen his last promotion.

He spoke to Sergeant Boyd while staring down at the corpses of four soldiers arranged in a row behind the armory.

"Jesus. The redskinned bastards cut Watkins and Peters to pieces. I've told Washington all along I agree with General Crook's policy of utter extermination of every Indian on this continent. We ought to line them up and shoot every goddamn one of 'em."

"Things were too quiet, Major. I had a feelin' somethin' was about to happen. I should have doubled the guard on the armory. Without them repeatin' rifles they'd be a helluva lot easier to capture." Boyd gave the parade ground and fort walls a lingering stare.

Corporal Collins, a new recruit from Ohio, turned away from the blood-smeared bodies, his complexion gone pale. "These damn Apaches ain't human, Major. Only an animal would do something like this to another human being. See how they cut them up like they was hogs at butchering time?"

Sergeant Boyd grunted. "I been fightin' the red bastards out here in the west for nearly twenty years, but these Apaches are the worst. It's on account of that crazy one, Geronimo, that they stay stirred up like this. Then there's Naiche, probably the worst of the Chiricahuas. He escaped last month with eight or nine young bucks. He's every damn bit as bloodthirsty as ole' Geronimo ... maybe worse."

Major Tarver turned his attention to the Indian roll call being conducted inside the reservation. Braves dressed in ragged buckskins and dirty cotton trousers were lined up in front of the barracks showing soldiers their identity tags. "Any idea yet how many broke away last night?" he asked, his voice hard as nails.

"Best we can tell, wasn't but about a dozen, only Private Newman ain't done with the countin' yet. Worst is, they got enough rifles for fifty more. Won't be long 'til more of 'em start slippin' off at night to join Naiche an' Geronimo. Then we'll have us a real Indian war on our hands." Boyd said this as though certain of it.

"Against savages armed with repeaters," Tarver added in a dull tone, fully understanding the potential consequences. "There will be a considerable amount of bloodshed, if I'm any judge of the matter."

"They stole seventeen horses," Collins added. "They'll be hard to ride down. Took some of our best Remount Thoroughbreds, too. Catching up to them won't be easy. Instead of riding them half-starved Indian ponies, they're mounted on some of our best saddle stock."

Tarver turned to Sergeant Boyd. "Assemble two mounted troops. Make sure they're heavily armed and well-provisioned. Get three of our best Pawnee scouts . . . if they're sober enough to sit a horse this morning.''

"Yes, sir," Boyd said, turning on his heel.

Corporal Collins spoke. "I don't trust our Pawnees, Major, if you'll pardon me for saying so. That old Shoshone, the one they call Tomo, is the best tracker we've got, and he don't drink nearly so much."

"Find him, then," Tarver snapped. "If all four scouts are dead drunk, tie them across their horses until they sober up. We must get those rifles back and corral this batch of renegades, or every goddamn Apache on this reservation will take off into the mountains to join up with them when Naiche and Geronimo hear about this."

Tomo, a slope-shouldered man of fifty in buckskins with long gray hair in a single plait hanging between his shoulder blades, gave the desert floor a lengthy study. Major Tarver waited impatiently for the Indian to say something.

"Go this way," Tomo finally said, pointing to the south. "Ride many circles to hide direction they go. Maybe so they go to Dragoon Mountains. Rock there be plenty hard to track horse. Easy to hide in Dragoons."

"That's the way I had it figured," Sergeant Boyd said with a mouthful of chewing tobacco filling his right cheek. "May as well give up followin' their tracks an' head straight for them there mountains."

"Isa is leading them to some place he knows," Tarver said. "I figure he aims to join up with Geronimo and Naiche somewhere up yonder."

"Let's hope we find these runaways before that happens," Major Tarver said.

Entering a narrow ravine winding through solid rock, Tarver had an uneasy sensation. "Where the hell is that Shoshone?" he demanded of Sergeant Boyd.

"Can't say fer sure," Boyd replied, giving the rock walls

on both sides a closer examination. "I seen him ride around that bend yonder. Can't say as I've seen the ole' bastard since then, not to my best recollection."

A gunshot thundered from a rocky bluff above the mounted troopers and a soldier screamed, clutching his chest as he toppled off his horse. Major Tarver and Sergeant Boyd were reaching for their rifles before the noise from the gunshot died to silence.

Mounted soldiers were moving all at once, and in every direction.

"Take cover!" Tarver shouted.

Sergeant Boyd was down off his horse in an instant, knowing he'd make a smaller target.

A rifle shot from above lifted Corporal Collins out of his saddle, spinning him like a child's top with blood squirting from a hole in his back.

Major Tarver watched Collins fall. Then, he too, jumped out of his saddle to seek shelter behind a pile of rocks.

Suddenly, the ravine was filled with the roar of gunfire from high on the rim on both sides. Soldiers began falling to the ground, bleeding, crying for help, as their horses bolted away from the noises.

"Son of a bitch!" Tarver bellowed, when he saw puffs of smoke billowing off the top of the ravine. "They've got us surrounded!"

"Tomo led us into a trap!" he heard Sergeant Boyd shout from a pile of fallen boulders. "We shoulda killed that rotten ole' son of a bitch an' taken the Pawnee!"

"The Pawnees were drunk!" Tarver replied at the top of his voice, to be heard above the roar of guns and the whine of spent bullets bouncing off stones.

Seven cavalrymen fell to the floor of the ravine with mortal wounds. Then three more went down, and finally another was shot from his saddle.

"They'll kill every damn one of us!" Sergeant Boyd yelled from his hiding place behind a pile of rock. "They got us caught in a cross fire!"

This wasn't news Major Tarver wanted to hear right then.

It was evident a slaughter was about to take place in the ravine, and the dead would be U.S. Cavalrymen . . . unless he could figure a way to get out of this trap.

"Sound the retreat!" he cried. "Pull back! We'll get around behind them somehow—"

As the words left his mouth, four more soldiers were cut down in a volley of repeating rifle fire. Tarver knew his own men were being killed by weapons stolen from the Fort Thomas armory.

"Pull back!" he shrieked again. "Have the bugler sound the retreat!"

Only then did he notice a young private with the company bugle tied around his neck lying face-down on the floor of the arroyo. Only a fool would have run out in plain sight to grab the horn in order to follow his command.

"Withdraw!" he shouted as loudly as he could, hunkering down to move cautiously away from the fusillade of gunfire from the top of the canyon.

A bullet struck Private Newman between his shoulders and sent him tumbling to the dirt, blood pumping from the hole just above his coat collar.

"Damn!" Tarver hissed. "That goddamn Shoshone led us right to 'em. I'll have him shot by a firing squad the minute we get back to the fort."

Loose horses galloped down the ravine, and Major Tarver knew they would quickly fall into the hands of the renegade Apaches unless something was done.

"Send some men after our mounts!" he said, when he saw Sergeant Boyd slipping carefully along one wall of the ravine while leading his nervous horse.

"It'll only get the men killed," Boyd shouted above the din of more rifle fire. "Better to lose a few horses than to get your ass shot off."

"Are you disobeying a direct order, Sergeant?" Major Tarver demanded.

"Damn right I am, Major, if it means gettin' killed to save a few lousy horses!"

"I can have you court-martialed!"

"Maybe," Boyd replied, "only you gotta be alive to file the charges against me. We ain't got out of this with our scalps just yet."

A singsong bullet slammed into a rocky ledge above the major's head and he ducked down quickly. Perhaps Sergeant Boyd was right about letting the horses go.

Major Tarver bit the end off a long black cigar and stuffed it into his mouth as he listened to the casualty report.

"We got sixteen men dead, Major, an' three more missin'. We got twelve wounded, an' four of those'll probably die 'fore mornin'."

"How many horses do we have left, Sergeant?"

"Only got nine that can carry a rider. Some's wounded so bad we'll have to put 'em down with a gun."

"And where is the scout, Tomo?"

"Ain't seen him since the shootin' started. I figure he rode off when the first gun banged."

"I want him tracked down and arrested."

Sergeant Boyd shrugged. "How the hell are we gonna track him down, Major?" He leaned to the side and let loose a brown stream of spit from his tobacco. "Far as I can tell, he didn't leave no tracks when he lit out of here."

"I intend to have him shot."

"First thing you gotta do is find him, Major, an' that ain't gonna be easy in these here Dragoons."

"A man can't simply disappear. Send out a detail to look for him."

"Them Apaches are liable to be expectin' us, an' they'll kill the men we send out."

Tarver's impatience was almost at a breaking point. "I gave you an order, Sergeant."

"I'll follow it, sir, only I damn sure ain't gonna go out there myself. You can have me court-martialed soon as we get back to the fort, but I won't go ridin' up this here canyon to look for Tomo."

"And why not?"

"Be the same as committin' suicide. Them Apaches have left a rear guard to see if we follow 'em. They'll shoot me deader'n pig slop"

"I intend to put your refusal in my report to General Crook, Sergeant Boyd."

"Put anythin' in it you want, Major, only be sure to write down that, so far, I'm still alive ... which is more than you'll be able to say 'bout any other poor bastards you send into that canyon."

Chapter 11

Isa followed the stars unerringly toward the hidden spring in the Dragoons. Using rawhide thongs he was able to bind the rifles together in less cumbersome bundles, making travel easier. By dawn the soldiers would find their tracks using Indian scouts, and only the rocks at higher elevations in the mountains would throw off pursuit, hiding the tracks made by the cavalry's shod horses.

"They will be coming soon," an older warrior named Nana said as he looked behind them.

"They fear what will happen when we arm ourselves and many more with these rifles," Isa agreed. "They must follow us and try to get them back."

The clatter of iron-shod horses was annoying to Isa, and he wished for the metal tools white men used to remove them, for the sound was like the beating of a drum at the Sun Dance ceremony. It echoed across the desert like a beacon, pointing to their progress.

"Many more young fighters will come when they hear we have the many-shoot guns." Nana sounded sure of it, and he had seen many more years of war than Isa, more than a dozen, when Cochise was alive.

"Naiche is a wise leader, Nana. He will show us where to strike and where to hide."

Nana appeared to frown. "He is wise in the ways of war, but he is foolish and reckless in battle when he seeks enemy scalps. Geronimo is far wiser, always the cautious one, being careful to strike when he is certain of victory."

"But Geronimo is in Mexico with only a few warriors. One of us must ride into the Sierra Madres to tell him of our good fortune, that we have many-shoot rifles and bullets, enough to kill all the white-eyes."

Nana shook his head. "Geronimo will not join us. He will lead his own warriors. He spoke once at the council, saying that too many warriors would lead the soldiers to him. He prefers to strike in his own way with only a few. Naiche wishes to gather all Apaches together in one big war against the white man, and I think this is foolish. There are too many white soldiers, and we cannot equal their number. No matter how many we kill more come behind them, swarming like bees do when their nest is disturbed."

Somewhere out on the desert floor, a coyote barked four times and then howled at the sky. Isa heard the coyote and stiffened.

"It is only a coyote," Nana assured him. "The coyote barks four times, while the Apache signal for danger gives five barking noises before the howl. You are wise to The Way, and you should know this."

"It is true," Isa said softly, leading his warriors across a gentle rise in the sand and rock, weaving between saguaro cactus and yucca spines. "We have been prisoners at the reservation for so long I sometimes forget the old ways."

"It is time to remember them now, Isa. We will need all our skill to outrun the soldiers behind us."

Isa gave the old man a look, his lips turning up for the first time in a small grin. "I not try to outrun them, grandfather," he said, using the Indian term of respect.

* * *

The narrow ravine wound and twisted into the foothills of the Dragoons. Isa studied it from above.

"It is a perfect place to ambush them," he said, scanning the horizon where a cloud of dust rising from a line of horsemen marked the advance of the cavalry.

"They found our tracks too easily. One of the People is showing them the way."

"Pawnees," Nana spat. "They sold themselves to the soldiers for a few bottles of whiskey."

"It is the old one who guides them, the Shoshone. See how he brings them straight toward us? The old man is wise to the ways of nature."

"He was our friend."

"We have no friends among the white men. The Shoshone hears the voice of *boisa pah,* the white man's whiskey, and for this he will betray us."

"He is called Tomo. He is friend to the Comonses, the Comanches, and I do not believe he would betray us."

"The power of *boisa pah* is very strong, Nana."

"I spoke with him many times. He hates the white-eyes as much as we do."

"Then why does he bring them along our tracks?"

"Perhaps he does this so we may kill them. If he brings them to this canyon, killing them will be easy with the many-shoot rifles."

Isa thought about this. Was Tomo guiding the soldiers to a place where they could be killed?

"I do not trust him. He has been among the white-eyes too long."

Nana wagged his head side to side. "He is like the rest of us on the stinking reservation . . . he has no choice but to accept what we are given by them."

"But now he brings them along our tracks," Isa protested as the line of solders became clearer.

"He knows we have the many-shoot rifles, and he brings them to us so we may kill them easily."

"I do not trust the Shoshone," Isa said, backing away from the rim of the arroyo.

"Wait and see," Nana assured him. "He brings them to us for a killing time. He hates the white-eyes as much as we do, only he must take what the reservation gives him . . ."

A line of mounted cavalrymen rode into the ravine. The old Shoshone, Tomo, rode his horse quickly out in front and went around a bend.

Isa wondered if Nana could be right . . . had the old man brought them the soldiers to kill as a gift?

"They come as if they were blind," Nana whispered. "They do not even look up here where our warriors are hiding with the rifles. Tomo has given them to us . . . he is not our enemy."

"Spread the word," Isa said quietly. "Wait until they are all in the ravine, so few will be able to escape when we shoot down at them."

Nana crept off on the balls of his feet to alert a line of warriors hidden behind rocks across the canyon rim with Winchester repeating rifles.

Isa watched the soldiers. Could Nana be right about the old Shoshone? Were the soldiers being led into a killing place from which only a few could escape?

Then it became clear Tomo understood what was about to take place in the arroyo . . . he heeled his pony to a lope and galloped far to the south along the bottom of the draw.

"May the Spirits smile on you, old man," Isa whispered as the soldiers followed Tomo into the most narrow place in the winding ravine. Tomo was handing them the lives of the bluecoat white-eyes as surely as the rising of the sun.

Isa shouldered his rifle, thumbing back the hammer, taking careful aim at the soldiers riding at the rear of the column. His warriors farther to the south would cut down the other white-eyes.

He waited until he was certain of his aim, casting a glance

across the canyon at his warriors carefully placed on the far side.

"It is good," he grunted softly. Then he squeezed the trigger gently.

Solders fell, screaming in agony, as horses bolted away from the explosions from above. Isa worked the lever to put another cartridge into the chamber, smiling inwardly. They would take a deadly toll on the bluecoats this afternoon.

A soldier flipped out of his saddle with blood squirting from his back, arms windmilling as he tossed his rifle and pistol to the ground.

Another soldier yelped and reached for his throat when a bullet from the far side of the arroyo went through his neck amid the loud crack of exploding gunpowder.

And now more bluecoats were falling underneath the churning hooves of their frightened horses. Noise filled the canyon—the bang of rifles, and the nickering of terrified animals, the cries of wounded and dying men.

Nana rushed over to him, smoke curling from the muzzle of his rifle. "It is a good day for white-eyes to die!" Nana cried at the top of his lungs.

Isa continued to fire into the milling, swirling mass of horses and downed cavalrymen. It *was* a good day for the blue-coats to die, and the old Shoshone named Tomo had given them this opportunity for revenge against the white men. . . .

The smell of blood filled the arroyo. Three dead horses lay among the fallen bodies of soldiers. Isa walked among the corpses to inspect the careful removal of pistols, ammunition, and food from the fallen enemy. Black flies rose in a buzzing cloud as he nudged a body with his foot.

"A victory for the People," Nana said, picking up more of the soldiers' guns and bullets.

76   *William W. Johnstone*

"Naiche and Geronimo will be pleased," Isa told him as he took a pistol from a dead soldier's belt.

"We must make a gift of a gun to the Shoshone," Nana said as he, too, walked among the dead, salvaging whatever they could use.

"Yes. Find Tomo. Tell him we have presents to give him for the victory he gave us today."

"I sent Taoyo, and he cannot find the old warrior. Tomo rode away, into the mountains."

"Perhaps he wishes to join Naiche," Isa said aloud, taking the last pouch of ammunition from a dead soldier.

He is not Apache. He told me this was not his war. His people have already been made into slaves for the white men far to the north."

Isa looked down the canyon, in the direction Tomo had ridden just before the battle. "Find him. His kindness must not go unrewarded."

"Taoyo is looking for him now.

"Find him!" Isa snapped. "He could just as easily have given us away to the enemy. It is The Way, to repay a debt to another warrior."

Chapter 12

Late in the afternoon, Falcon and Hawk came upon the remains of an old campfire, surrounded by the tracks of the Indian band they were following.

Off to the side was what was left of a mule carcass. It'd been gutted and cleaned like a deer, and there wasn't a scrap of meat left on the bones. All of the internal organs had been eaten except the entrails.

Hawk had a look of disgust on his face. "I swear to God, Injuns'll make a meal of anything that walks or crawls." He glanced at Falcon. "Can you imagine eatin' a mule?"

"I guess if I was hungry enough, maybe."

"I heard tales of redskins eatin' a man's heart or brains, if'n they respected him."

"Yeah, me too. Matter of fact, my father stayed with a tribe one winter, and he said they killed some raiders from another tribe and offered to share the heart and brains with him."

"What'd he do?"

Falcon looked away, staring at mountain peaks in the distance. "My father was an educated man, and he told me about a book he once read that said, 'when in Rome do as the Romans do.' ''

He looked back over his shoulder at Hawk. "So I suppose he joined right in."

"Jesus," Hawk whispered, stirring the bones of the mule with his foot. "I *might* manage to swallow mule meat, if I was starvin', but no way I could stomach eatin' another man's flesh."

"You might be surprised at what you're capable of," Falcon said, climbing back up on Diablo. "We better get on the trail. We're burning daylight, and I don't want to be out in the open come sundown."

As they followed Naiche's band of Indians the trail slowly rose into the Dragoon Mountains, winding through pine, mesquite, and even some aspen at the higher elevations. The colors were breathtaking, and the sweet scent of late-blooming wildflowers contrasted with the tangy bite of pine smell in their noses.

Neither man took much notice of such things. They were too busy watching every copse of trees or gathering of boulders for possible ambushers. They both knew enough of the Apache adeptness at camouflage to realize it would be difficult to know of their presence until the bullets or arrows came flying.

Frank Curry stepped out of his cabin and took a deep breath of the crisp, cool fall air. With any luck, he thought, they'd be able to collect another few hundred dollars worth of dust today. The runoff from the fall rains was bringing more and more gold down the small rivers and streams from the mountain tops, and he and his partners planned to pan their share of it. Every one else in the area was so busy mining for silver—they hadn't thought to look for gold—but Frank and his partners were going to show them what a really big gold strike was like.

Johnny Brown and William Duke walked out of the

cabin, stretching and yawning. Johnny handed Frank one of the two cups of coffee he was holding.

"Looks like it's gonna be a good day for pannin'," Billy Duke said, glancing at the clear sky overhead.

"Yep," Frank answered, taking a sip of his coffee. "God-damn," he said, making a face. "Didn't you put no egg shells in this brew? It's full of grounds."

"If'n you don't like it, pardner, go in there an' make your own," Johnny said, scowling. "I don't know who appointed me chief cook and bottle washer, but I'm kind'a gettin' tired of havin' to do all of it myself."

"Quit your bitchin'," Billy said. "We're gettin' plumb rich up here. When the snows come in another few weeks, we can shut down and go down into Tombstone and winter over in style 'til the spring."

"Yeah," Frank said. "I ain't seen a woman in so long I 'bout forgot what they look like."

"Not me ... I 'member real good what they's like," Johnny said with a leer.

"By the way, where's Cal?" Frank asked.

"He left a little while ago," Johnny answered. "Said he'd found a small cave betwixt two boulders yesterday an' he wanted to see if it might have a vein in the back of it."

Frank couldn't believe it. "You mean we got all the dust and nuggets we can pick up out here, and that fool's goin' lookin' for a vein in a cave?"

From behind them, there was a sound like a face being slapped, and Billy gave a grunt. He staggered a step or two and turned around, his hands up to his face holding the shaft of an arrow sticking out of his left eye.

A rifle shot rang out and Johnny took a bullet in his right shoulder, spinning him around and dropping him to his knees.

"Goddamn!" Frank cried, ducking just in time for the shot aimed at his head to buzz by inches from his face. He grabbed Johnny by the arm and jerked him to his feet as Billy finally collapsed onto his back in the sand.

Frank and Johnny half stumbled and half ran into the

cabin, slamming the door and putting the wooden brace across it to lock it. As Johnny wrapped a towel around his arm to stop the bleeding, Frank shut wooden shutters on the windows, using small pegs to bolt them shut. They had made the shutters with small openings cut out for gun ports, just in case of attack by Indians.

Several more shots peppered the door and walls, as if the Indians were testing the thickness to see if the shots would penetrate.

"Damn . . . did you see how many there were out there?" Frank asked.

"Hell, no," Johnny replied. "I was too busy gettin' shot an' bleedin' to take much notice."

Frank threw him a Henry Repeating rifle and a box of cartridges as he took down an American Arms 10 gauge shotgun and a Winchester for himself.

As he shoved shells into the loading chamber of the Winchester, Frank peered through the gunport of his window. "You think I ought'a make a run out there an' see if I can get Billy in here?"

Johnny looked up from loading his Henry and shook his head. "You wouldn't get ten feet out that door 'fore they'd blow your head off, Frank. Besides, ain't no way Billy can survive that wound."

"But I can see him movin'. Looks like he's tryin' to crawl toward the cabin."

"If he makes it, we can let him in, but don't even think 'bout goin' out there yet."

Frank put the barrel of his Winchester out the hole in the shutter and took careful aim. He saw an Indian crawling on his belly toward Billy, his knife in his teeth, warpaint on his face and an Eagle feather in his hair.

"Sons of bitches," he muttered as he squeezed the trigger. The Winchester exploded back against Frank's shoulder, the sound loud in the small room.

A sharp cry of pain was heard from outside, and Frank

saw his shot take a chunk out of the left shoulder of the brave, spewing blood and tissue all over his face. He dropped his knife and grabbed his arm, squirming back around to crawl away from where Billy lay, no longer moving.

"Looks bad, partner," Johnny called softly from the other side of the room. "When you fired, I saw at least five of the bastards movin' over on my side of the cabin. Looks like they're trying to circle around and come at us from behind."

He scrambled over to a window on the other side of the cabin and pointed his Henry out the gunport. He fired, cursing under his breath as his shot went wide, chipping stone off a boulder but missing the man he was aiming for.

Luckily, they had planned their cabin well. It was located in a clearing, at least fifty yards from the nearest cover. There were no overhanging rocks or nearby elevations, and they always stocked plenty of water and food inside. Their only problem was that the house was designed for four men to defend it, and with Billy's death and Cal's absence, it would be difficult to watch all sides of the structure.

Only a couple of shots answered Johnny's, and they buried themselves harmlessly in the thick wood of the wall next to his window.

"You think we got a chance, partner?" Johnny asked, his eyes flicking back and forth, searching for another target.

Frank paused before answering, the words bitter on his tongue. "Not unless there happens to be an army squad nearby. All they got to do is wait for dark. Then they can rush us from all sides or fire the cabin. Either way, we're done for."

Johnny glanced over his shoulder, his jaw set, eyes hard. "At least maybe we can take some of the bastards with us."

"Yeah, but don't forget," Frank said, patting his Colt in

his holster on his hip. "Save at least one bullet for yourself. No way you can let 'em take you alive."

Frank's skin crawled as what sounded like screams of wildcats and eagles and other animals came from the area around the cabin. Interspersed with these were yells and whoops and hollers of braves who ran out into plain view, loosed an arrow or a shot from a rifle at the house, then disappeared just as Frank or Johnny was drawing a bead on them.

Glancing back over his shoulder, Frank saw a small puddle of blood forming on the floor on Johnny's right side. Evidently his arm was still leaking blood from the wound. *Damn,* he thought, *we've got to do something. I ain't just gonna sit here an' let them heathens wait to kill me.*

He scurried over to Johnny, keeping low and out of the line of fire through the windows in case one of the Indians got a lucky shot through the gunport.

"Partner," Frank said, "we got to make a move, otherwise they're gonna kill us for sure."

Johnny squeezed off a shot, kicking up dust next to running feet of a brave a hundred yards away.

"Just what do you want to do, Frank? It don't seem to me we have a surplus of choices."

"Let's make a run for the corral. Maybe we could get to our mounts and manage to get away 'fore they got to us."

Johnny turned skeptical eyes on his partner. "It'd be suicide to try that. Besides, them 'Pache are the best riders around. They'd ride us down 'fore we got a mile, even if we could get to our broncs, which I doubt."

"Anything'd be better than holein' up here waitin' for 'em to burn us out."

"You do got a point there, partner. Let's do it."

Johnny positioned himself next to the door, his rifle and pistol fully loaded, while Frank fired several shots out the window on the far side of the cabin, hoping to draw the Indians' attention away from the other side.

After his last shot, he turned and sprinted for the door

as Johnny opened it and began to run toward the corral, forty yards distant.

One brave stepped out from behind a boulder and let an arrow fly toward the men. Johnny fired from the hip, his Winchester blowing a hole through the Indian's mid-section and flinging him backward to lie dying in the dirt.

A man off to one side aimed a rifle and fired, the bullet catching Frank in the thigh, making him stumble and stagger a few steps until suddenly he was at the corral fence.

He flung the gate wide, yelling, "Scatter the rest of the horses. Maybe it'll keep 'em busy for a few minutes!"

With no time to try to saddle the horses, Frank grabbed the mane of his favorite ride and swung himself up on the animal's back, holding his rifle in his right hand.

Johnny did the same. Then the two men flapped their arms and leaned low over the broncs' necks and rode out the corral gate, sending the other five animals stampeding ahead of them.

A young brave who looked to be no more than fifteen years of age stepped in front of the horses, an arrow cocked in his bow, and took aim.

He was knocked to the ground and trampled by several of the crazed, frightened animals as they bolted out of the fenced area.

Spurring his mount for all he was worth, Frank headed up the mountain away from the cabin while Johnny turned his animal south to ride down the trail toward Tombstone.

Frank heard several shots ring out in unison and looked back over his shoulder to see Johnny go flying from his horse, his rifle spinning out of his hands. Frank saw three Indians, one of them a skinny female with wiry muscles who had a furious scowl on her face and a large knife in her hands, running toward his friend.

"Aw, hell!" he muttered and jerked his horse's head around. He rode as fast as he could toward the fallen man, guiding his mount with his knees as he sprayed rifle fire at the Indians. The two males went down, mortally wounded, and the woman stopped her advance and stood defiantly, waiting for him to kill her.

Frank's rifle clicked on an empty chamber, so he grabbed it by the barrel and swung at the woman's head as he rode past. The butt of the gun took her on the shoulder as she threw herself to the side.

An Indian wearing paint and a headdress of eagle feathers, showing him to be the leader, stepped into view and aimed a Winchester at Frank, shooting him in the chest at point blank range.

Frank was knocked off his horse to land several feet from Johnny, who was lying dazed and bleeding from three separate wounds to his chest and abdomen.

As a group of Indians ran toward them, Frank drew his pistol and took careful aim. "I'm sorry, partner," he whispered hoarsely, "Adios." He fired, hitting Johnny in the forehead and killing him instantly.

The female Indian screamed something in Apache and rushed Frank, her knife held high and her eyes red with fury.

He smiled, knowing he was going to disappoint the bitch, and put the barrel in his mouth and pulled the trigger.

Cal Franklin, from his hiding place in a small cave formed by the juxtaposition of several large rocks, lowered his head to his crossed arms and began to cry silent tears. He'd seen what had happened to his friends and partners, and knew that he could do nothing to help them. He'd crawled far back in the space last night, more drunk than sober, and fallen asleep.

He'd only awakened when the sound of gunfire had startled him awake just an hour before. Armed with only an ancient Walker Colt and no extra ammunition, he knew he was as good as dead if he tried to fire at the overwhelming number of Indians surrounding the camp.

He slowly pulled a small creosote bush tight to the entrance to the cave, deciding he didn't want to watch what the Indians were going to do to the bodies. As he hunkered down in the damp earth on the floor of his hiding place, he gave a short prayer the heathens wouldn't think to search for him.

Chapter 13

Falcon and Hawk slowed their horses to a walk as they got closer to the place where they'd heard the rifle shots coming from.

Through the trees, they could make out clouds of gunsmoke hovering in the air like new morning fog off a freezing river. Falcon held up his hand and pulled Diablo to a halt, tying his reins to a nearby pinyon tree.

He pulled his Winchester .44/.40 out of its saddle boot and motioned for Hawk to circle around the other way as he crouched down and moved to the right through heavy brush.

At the edge of a clearing in the forest, Falcon stopped to peer though the leaves of a hackberry bush, careful not to let the thorns pierce his eyes.

He could see what looked like the aftermath of a battle royal. There were at least five or six Indian bodies lying around small, cedar-sided cabin in the center of the clearing, and a makeshift corral stood empty, its gate hanging cockeyed by one hinge.

Off to one side, two white, naked bodies lay next to each other. Both had been scalped, and their abdomens were torn open and entrails pulled out to form a grisly portrait of suffering and death. The sand had soaked up enough blood to make the area around the bodies soggy with scarlet-tinged mud.

Most of the Indian bodies had no moccasins or weapons, and it looked as if the remaining attackers had stripped their corpses of anything that might be useful as they fled the scene.

The smell of blood and excrement and cordite was heavy in the air, and Falcon heard Diablo's nervous whinny behind him as the stud caught the scent.

Falcon gave a low trilling whistle such as a whippoorwill might make, his and Hawk's prearranged signal that all was clear.

He levered a shell into the chamber of his rifle and slowly, eyes flicking back and forth for any sign of movement, walked into the clearing.

Hawk could be seen doing the same from the opposite edge, a bulge in his cheek from the tobacco he was chewing furiously—the only sign of his nervousness.

They met in the center of the open space and stood together over the white men's bodies.

Hawk squatted on his haunches and examined the dead men closely. "One good thing. Looks like they was already dead when the Injuns went to work on 'em."

Falcon agreed. "Yeah. It appears this one shot himself in the face as they approached. You can see the powder burns on what's left of his cheeks."

Hawk stood up, wiping his hands on his trousers. "Cain't say as I blame 'em much. There ain't no worse way to die than at the hands of an Apache, 'specially if'n he's pissed off."

As a cry and sounds of footsteps came from a small group of boulders across the way, both Hawk and Falcon whirled around, their rifles cocked and aimed.

"Hold your fire . . . hold your fire!" a disheveled man screamed as he came running down the slight incline from his place of concealment.

Hawk leaned to the side and spit a stream of tobacco juice on the forehead of a brave lying near the two dead white men.

"Looks like we got a survivor," he drawled.

Falcon wagged his head. "That's not like Apache, to leave someone behind still breathing."

The man stopped in front of them and leaned over, breathing heavily, his hands on his knees. "My name's Calvin Franklin," he gasped, his chest heaving. "Thank God you've come."

Falcon eased the hammer down on his Winchester and laid it back over his shoulder. "What happened here, Mr. Franklin?" he asked.

Franklin ran his hands over his face, then his eyes widened and his face paled as he saw what lay on the ground behind Falcon. He brushed by Falcon and staggered over to stand above the bodies of his friends. He stared down for a moment, swaying as if he might faint, then he leaned over, gagging, and vomited on his boots at the sight of what the Indians had done to his partners.

When he was done retching, Falcon took him by the shoulder and led him away from the bodies.

Again he asked the man what had happened.

"I don't rightly know," Franklin mumbled, his eyes shifting from corpse to corpse. "I was sleepin' in a little cave over there," he said, pointing over his shoulder to a group of boulders near the cabin, "after a mite too much redeye last night, when I woke up to the sound of gunfire."

"What did you see when you looked out?" Hawk asked.

"Billy was lyin' dead over yonder with an arrow through his eye," he said, pointing toward where a body lay that was so mutilated it was hard to tell if it was a white man or an Indian "and Frank and Johnny were holed up in the cabin, grin' back at a whole bunch of redskins that had surrounded the place."

"Why didn't you help them?" Falcon asked, his voice soft, not accusatory.

Franklin held up the pistol he was carrying. "You see

this? It's all I had. Six shots, an' no cartridges to reload with." He hung his head, looking at the ground as he mumbled, "It would've been suicide."

"I see your point," Hawk said, spitting again into the dirt.

"I was wondering why the Indians left you alive," Falcon said. "I guess they didn't notice your hiding place in all the excitement."

He stepped over to the cabin and examined the many holes in the walls. "Hawk, take a look at this."

"Yeah?"

"From the number of bullet holes, I'd say the Indians had at least one or two repeating rifles. Otherwise there'd be more arrows used."

Hawk nodded, chewing slowly as he thought over the implications of Falcon's discovery. "It's gonna make trackin' the bastards a mite more dangerous if they got Winchesters or Henrys."

Falcon opened the cabin door and led the other two men in. Inside, it looked as if a wild bear had been there. The contents were scattered around the room, all of the foodstuffs were gone from the shelves over the sink, and the furniture had been hacked at with tomahawks and knives until it was all useless. Muddy red footprints of moccasins were all over the floor, and a fragment of half-eaten liver was lying against one wall.

"Jesus," Franklin whispered as he looked around at the mess. "They're like wild animals."

"Worse," Hawk opined. "Animals only kill for food, not for fun."

"How many weapons did your friends have here?" Falcon asked.

Franklin rubbed his stubbled face as he thought for a moment. "Three rifles, two Winchesters, an' an old Henry. An' three or four pistols, single-shot Colts, as I recall."

"Damn," Falcon said.

Franklin walked to a far wall and bent down, removing

a section of board that'd been cut. "I wonder if they found our stash of gold."

"Wouldn't matter if they did," Falcon said. "Indians don't have any use for gold or silver, other than as decoration. They wouldn't take it even if it was lying on a table right in front of them."

Franklin sighed as he removed several canvas sacks of gold dust, and turned, holding them up. "You're right. Here it is."

Hawk snorted. "I hope it was worth it," he said, turning and walking out of the room.

"What are your plans now, Mr. Franklin?" Falcon asked.

Franklin shrugged. "I guess I'll mosey on down to Tombstone and winter over, then git me some more partners an' come back in the spring to finish minin' this here creek."

Falcon pointed at the bags of gold dust. "You're already a rich man, Franklin. Why come back here?"

The man turned feverish eyes on Falcon, " 'Cause there's still gold here to be found. I ain't leavin' 'til I've gotten it all."

Falcon shook his head, wondering at the greed the yellow metal instilled in men, causing them to risk everything to attain more than they could ever spend.

"Do you fellows think you could take me down to Tombstone?" Franklin asked, holding up the sacks of gold. "I'd be willin' to pay you for your trouble."

Falcon shook his head. "Sorry, can't help you. We're on the trail of the Indians that attacked your place. But you shouldn't have any trouble making it there on your own."

"But what if they come back?"

"They took off up into the Dragoons," Falcon said as he walked out of the cabin. "You'll be safe if you stay on the main trail into town."

"I'll give you one piece of advice," Hawk said as the two men approached where he was standing staring up into the mountains. "When you get to Tombstone, don't go flashing that gold around too much. There're men there who'd cut your throat for half of what you got in them sacks.''

After helping Franklin bury his friends, leaving the Indian bodies where they lay, Falcon and Hawk got their horses and climbed into the saddles. "Adios, Mr. Franklin," Falcon said "You take it easy when you get to town. Don't try to spend all that money the first night.''

Franklin grinned. "Thanks, fellas. I'll be seein' you.''

As they rode off Falcon said to Hawk, "I wonder how many lives have been lost in the search for gold and silver?''

"Too many to count, I reckon," Hawk answered. "It seems some men just cain't get enough money an' riches, an' sooner or later the gettin' takes over their lives 'til it's more important than the havin'.''

"Greed can be a sickness, all right," Falcon said. "And like with most illnesses, a severe case can be fatal.''

Chapter 14

Isa darted among lengthening shadows spread across the floor of the ravine, picking up pistols, woolen army coats, ammunition pouches, anything of value. All around him the shapes of his warriors moved among the dead and dying soldiers. A few were high on the canyon rim keeping watch in case the bluecoats returned.

A soldier screamed.

"I take his scalp," Nana said, looking down the arroyo at the distant bluecoat survivors assembled in a tight circle to talk things over.

"Take all their scalps," Isa told him. "Make sure you take all their guns and bullets."

Off to the south a wounded horse floundered in the sandy bottom of the dry stream. An Apache warrior quickly silenced the bleeding horse with his knife.

A soldier with a gaping hole in his chest struggled up on his elbows. "You red bastards!" he cried, reaching feebly for his empty holster.

The words had no sooner left his lips then Isa was standing over him with a knife. . . . he made a slashing motion across the soldier's throat and then there was a gurgling sound like that of a brook after heavy spring rains.

"Here is one with many stripes," a voice cried out in the tongue of the Apache. "He still lives."

"Kill him," Isa commanded. "Take his scalp and his coat with many stripes. Wear the blue coat as a sign of our victory here today!"

An Apache boy named Watoso seized the soldier by his hair and sliced his scalp lock away, and as the soldier fell back on the sand Watoso sliced the unfamiliar buttons off the front of the trooper's tunic and jerked it over his shoulders.

Nana came running over to Isa. "It has been a good day for war against the white-eyes!" he said, holding a bloody scalp lock in one hand.

"Yes, it is good," Isa agreed. "The many-shoot rifles give us their magic."

Nana looked north. "The bluecoats are talking. They will come back."

"Let them come," Isa hissed, glaring angrily at the shapes of mounted men on the desert beyond the arroyo. "We will be gone to take the rifles to Naiche."

"Let the great war between red men and white men begin soon," Nana growled.

"Yes," Isa said, taking a cartridge belt off a dead soldier. "We are ready for them now."

"We must send word to Geronimo in Mexico."

"Naiche will send someone. Naiche is war chief of the Chiricahuas."

"We are still so few," Nana said, pulling the boots off a dead cavalryman.

"More will come," Isa assured him, tucking a pistol into the belt around his waist. "The others are afraid of the many-shoot rifles."

"And now we have them," Nana said as Watoso pulled a rifle from a boot below the saddle of a dead cavalry horse. The boy's arms were laden with weapons and ammunition and three pairs of stovepipe cavalry boots.

"The Spirits are smiling now," Isa told Nana. "See how easily the bluecoats die?"

"Their magic is in the rifles," Nana said, cradling three Winchester repeaters. "Now we have the white man's magic ourselves."

"Yes," Isa said quietly, giving the arroyo a last look as his warriors began a climb back to the rim where their horses were tied. "Let the great war begin between us now, for we have their deadly rifles."

"They will never defeat us," Nana said, starting his own climb up the rocky sides of the ravine laden with weapons and ammunition. "They are not brave warriors, only men who fight us when they are many and we are few."

"Word will reach the others at Fort Thomas," Isa said, scrambling toward the lip of the canyon. "Many more will leave the reservation soon to join the fight with Naiche."

"Geronimo will come also, with Mimbres hiding south of the great river."

"Perhaps," Isa said. "Geronimo has counsel with the Four Spirits. If they tell him to join us, he will, and if their voices are as one that we should fight alone, it is his way and he will not come."

"He has the heart of the mountain lion," Nana said, making slow progress around a rock slide.

"And so does Naiche. We follow Naiche, for he has been given the power of war chief. If Geronimo joins us it will be because the Spirit Father wishes it."

Nana and Watoso crawled over the arroyo rim with their burdens of weapons and bullets and boots. Other warriors who guarded the entrance into the ravine rushed over to help load the bounty onto the backs of their stolen cavalry horses.

Watoso came over to Isa with blood dripping down both arms after scalping three soldiers. "Tell us how far we must ride to reach the hiding place where Naiche waits," he said, out of breath from a steep climb.

"Two suns," Isa answered, tying the rifles and pistols he

carried into bundles that could be placed across a horse's withers.

"The bluecoats will follow us," the boy said as though he was certain of it.

"We will cross the rocks higher up, and only another Apache will be able to see our tracks."

"What of the old Shoshone? Should we follow him and kill him?"

"No. He has given us the gift of these dead bluecoats by leading them into our trap. We owe him a great debt, but he will not return."

"You are wise in many things, Isa. How is it you know all of this?"

Isa gave the boy a shallow grin. "The Shoshone rode west as fast as his pony could travel. He knew what was to come. He asks for nothing, for he, too, hates the white-eyes and the way they treat our people. They killed many of his people in the north country a long time ago, and he wanted nothing in return, only to hear the bluecoats cry out when our bullets pass through them."

Watoso glanced out on the prairie where the soldiers were gathered to have their talk. "More bluecoats will come, Isa. I am sure of this."

A savage look passed across Isa's face. "Let them come like drops of rain!" he growled, swinging aboard his horse, adjusting the bundles of rifles and cartridges. "We are ready for a war with them now. . . ."

As Isa spoke, the harsh cry of an eagle came from the valley floor below.

Watoso walked back to Isa, pointing to the soldiers, who were beginning to move. "It is a danger signal from Yassa. The bluecoats are moving toward the valley once again."

Isa narrowed his eyes and shaded the sun with his hand as he stared at the calvary troops in the distance. "I do not believe even the white-eyes will be so stupid again. Let us spread out over the approach to this high place and wait. It is my feeling the bluecoats will not enter the valley, but will try to come to us up the back of the mountain."

Watoso held up the Winchester he was carrying. "We will welcome them with their own many-shoot guns."

Isa's lips curled in a tight smile as he glanced at the sky. "It is still a good day for bluecoats to die."

Chapter 15

Major Wilson Tarver was badly shaken, uncertain what to do next. The thunder of rifle fire from all sides was still ringing in his ears, and the screams of his wounded and dying troopers in the canyon left him chilled to the bone in spite of the unusual warmness of the day.

"Sergeant Boyd is dead, sir," Private Newman stammered, nursing a minor flesh wound in his right shoulder. "I saw him go down with this huge hole in his head. Blood came pouring out the back of his skull like it was a wooden bucket that sprung a leak."

"Spare me the details," Tarver replied, staring up the arroyo where the deadly ambush had taken place. "I can see he's among the missing."

Corporal Collins rode his limping bay gelding up beside the major. "Looks like we lost almost twenty men, sir. No telling how many are lying in that ravine badly wounded, needing medical attention. I can hear some of them moaning, crying out for water."

"If we ride back in there to render aid, they'll slaughter the rest of us," Tarver snapped. "What we need is a flanking maneuver. We must find a way to get up on that rim behind them, somehow.''

"Sure will be hard to do on a horse, sir, and my horse has gone lame in a forefoot. I don't see any way a horse can make that climb.''

"Then we'll proceed on foot. Dismount!'' Tarver shouted the order as though he felt sure of his decision.

Tarver shouted the even though he had serious reservations about it. He hated this dry desert country, and above all else, he hated Indians. The Apaches at Fort Thomas were a filthy lot, beneath contempt, and not a single one could be trusted, in his experience.

Private Newman seemed nervous. "If you'll pardon me for saying it, sir, we need to leave plenty of men to guard our horses or those Apaches are liable to steal 'em and leave us out here on foot.''

Tarver gave Newman an angry glare. "I don't need anyone to remind me of proper military tactics, Private. Now dismount and prepare a picket line for the horses.''

"Yes sir,'' Newman replied meekly, swinging down from his McClellan saddle with his ammunition pouch and rifle. "Sorry I said anything, sir.''

Men climbed down from their saddles. A young private from New Jersey began driving stakes for picket ropes in the sandy desert soil.

"I want a six man squad around our mounts,'' Tarver said as he stepped to the ground. "Corporal Collins, pick five good marksmen and form a circle around our animals. The rest of us will climb that west ridge from the rear. Spread out in a line and stay behind cover whenever you can find it. Surprise will be our advantage.''

"You don't figure they'll see us coming?'' Private Newman asked. "I figure they're watching us right now, just waiting to see what we'll do. They'll know what we're up to.''

"Not if we employ every precaution and proceed slowly. I assure you these red savages are mere mortal men who die just as easily as anyone, when taken by surprise.''

Tarver motioned to a private named Hiram Walker. "Lead the way up the side of that ridge, Private, and stay down as low as possible."

Private Walker lost most of the color in his face. "Yes, sir, Major," he answered, leading off toward the craggy slope west of the ravine.

Nervous sweat poured down Wilson Tarver's face from the band of his cavalry hat. Climbing long stretches of impossibly steep slabs of limestone, he had his rifle at the ready and the flap on his pistol holster unfastened. Yucca fans and all manner of desert plants offered the Apaches hundreds of places to hide as the soldiers ascended the west slope leading to the ravine. Extreme caution was called for by the terrain.

"Maybe they pulled out," Private Newman whispered off to Tarver's right.

"We'll know soon enough, so please refrain from doing any more whispering. This wind will carry the sound of your voice straight toward them . . . if they're waiting for us to try to ambush us again."

One of Tarver's boots made a crunching noise when he stepped on a pile of loose rock. He cursed his carelessness silently and kept on climbing.

Private Walker knelt down suddenly behind a clump of yucca and signaled the others to halt.

"What is it?" Tarver asked softly.

"Can't say for sure, Major, but I think I heard a noise right up yonder."

"Where? Point to it."

Walker pointed to a spot slightly south of their present position.

Tarver couldn't see anything amiss. "It's probably nothing. Continue forward, Private."

Private Walker came up in a crouch, still wary, taking small steps around the yucca fans with his Winchester held tightly to his shoulder.

Tarver waited until Walker had moved on a few paces before he continued his own climb up the rocks.

Then he saw a sight that froze him in his tracks. The men on either side of him stopped to stare.

A blue-uniformed trooper from Company C came staggering toward them . . . Tarver seemed to remember the boy's name as being Longworth. Blood covered the front of his blue tunic and the legs of his pants. His arms were folded in front of him as though he was cradling an infant, but what he held in his hands was no child.

Longworth was doing his best to hold his intestines in place, to keep them from dragging across the sand and rocks. A huge gash in his abdomen allowed his innards to spill from his body like bloody coils of slippery purple rope, squirming with each step he took.

"Dear God," Private Newman croaked, sinking to his knees when he saw Longworth. Then he began gagging on the contents of his stomach.

"His throat's been cut, too," Walker said over his shoulder, "and it looks like they cut out his tongue. I can see the stump of it waggin' inside his mouth, only he ain't making any words, just noises."

Major Tarver felt his legs tremble. *How could another race of human beings do such an animalistic thing?* he wondered. It was clear these Apaches were not a part of the human race, more like wild animals than men.

Longworth continued to stumble toward them, loops of his intestines dragging in the sand, his mouth opening and closing as if he meant to talk, but only a fountain of blood came forth and strange, muffled sounds.

"The bastards," Tarver hissed.

"You want me to fetch him and help him to some shade?" Private Walker asked.

"Yes. Please. One of you men go with him," Tarver replied, finding he was unable to move or take his eyes from the ghastly sight.

As Private Walker started toward Longworth, a gunshot

rang out from a clump of cactus higher on the ridge. The back of Walker's shirt exploded in a shower of crimson.

"Everybody down!" Tarver screamed, throwing himself flat on a slab of limestone.

Another gunshot lifted Private Collins off his knees, sending him tumbling backward. A bullet had entered his skull through his right eye socket, blowing the rear of his skull away, killing him instantly.

More gunfire erupted from the top of the slope, and more of Major Tarver's troopers began to fall. The rattle of rifle fire grew so heavy it became a single sound.

Private Walker, blood pumping from his back, came crawling toward Tarver.

"Help me, Major! I'm shot!"

Tarver had no idea how he could help. He found he was too frightened to even raise his rifle and return the hail of heavy gunfire.

"Please help me, Major!" Walker pleaded, still crawling, leaving a trail of blood in his wake.

At that precise moment, Wilson Tarver did the unthinkable for a trained military commander. When duty required that he make a decision in hopes of saving the lives of his remaining soldiers, he simply urinated in his pants and began to weep uncontrollably.

"You gotta help me, Major! I'm dyin'!"

Tarver heard the dying man's plea and did nothing, feeling the wetness creep down his pants leg as a stream of tears flooded his cheeks.

Another soldier's voice sounded from his left.

"Pull back, boys! They're gonna kill every one of us if we keep lying here!"

It was an order Tarver knew he should have given, yet at the moment he was unable to speak.

All around him, soldiers began creeping backward, and Tarver knew he must do the same. He raised his head just long enough to catch a glimpse of Longworth falling headfirst into a bed of prickly pear cactus. He lay there among the cactus needles, his feet still kicking.

"Withdraw!" Tarver cried weakly, pushing himself backward with all his might.

A trooper to Tarver's left let out a yelp and tumbled down the slope, a puddle of red shining in the sun where he had been hiding behind a fan of yucca spines.

Then another sound reached Tarver's ears—gunshots coming from behind.

He glanced over his shoulder as he was inching backward, and saw a band of Apache warriors armed with repeating rifles attacking the men guarding their horses.

Corporal Collins was the first soldier to go down, clutching his belly after he dropped his rifle. Spooked horses broke free of the picket ropes when the explosions started, and most of their mounts took off in a gallop in every direction.

It was the massacre of his troopers that held Tarver's attention. Half a dozen Apaches fired endless rounds of ammunition into the five remaining troopers, cutting them down one or two at a time.

"We're doomed," he said aloud, for now they were afoot in the desert foothills of the Dragoons, surrounded by Apache warriors armed with Winchesters.

Tarver managed to struggle to his feet, not to race downhill to aid his fellow soldiers, but to run west toward a jumble of rocks where he hoped to hide until the killing was over. He knew he was abandoning his command, and that was certainly grounds for a court-martial, but right at the moment all he cared about was getting out alive.

He ran toward the rocks in a low crouch, the stains of his urine darkening his pants, ignoring cries for help coming from the men he was leaving behind.

Tarver had almost reached the safety of the boulders when a blow struck him in the back. At first he thought someone had hurled a stone at him due to his show of cowardice.

And then a flash of white-hot pain shot through his body, running down his spine, and he understood he'd been hit by a bullet.

He tripped over a rock and fell on his face, whimpering, wishing this was only a bad dream.

Moments later someone seized him by the hair and turned him over on his back. He stared into the hate-crazed eyes of a huge Apache warrior holding a knife.

The last thing he felt before he lost consciousness was a searing pain across the top of his skull as his scalp was sliced off his head. Blood rained down on his face . . . his own blood, and then he felt nothing.

Darkness hid them from all but the most watchful eyes and Isa knew this, guiding his warriors up an ancient trail to the highest mountaintops in the Dragoons. He had ridden the trail hundreds of times when he was a boy, before the white men came to take them prisoner at Fort Thomas. It still bothered him that the iron horseshoes made so much noise, yet it was all but impossible to pull the shoes off without crippling an animal. Thus he listened helplessly to the grinding of metal against rock.

"We are close now," Nana said, riding his horse up beside Isa's.

"Yes," Isa agreed.

"By the time the sun rises, we will see the valley and the stream."

Isa halted his horse long enough to give their starlit back trail a careful examination. "The bluecoats have not found our tracks, and that is good. Without the old Shoshone, they are as helpless as children."

"Perhaps they will bring the Pawnees," Nana suggested when they heeled their horses forward again.

"Let them come," Isa whispered, his jaw clamped in an angry line. "We will kill their Pawnee scouts at the high pass above the stream and hang their scalps from the limbs of the pinyon pines on the slopes."

"They will surely come with many more soldiers," Nana warned.

Isa grunted, guiding his horse around a pile of rocks.

"It will give us many more enemy scalps," he said. "We have their magic rifles."

"But we have only a handful of warriors to shoot them at the enemy."

"Word will reach the others at Fort Thomas and San Carlos. All the older warriors know of the hidden spring in these mountains and the meeting place."

"Too many of them are dead in spirit, Isa," Nana said in a grave voice. "They are ready to die on the white man's reservation."

"They need a leader who has courage. Naiche is as brave as any Apache upon the face of Earth Mother."

"But will the others have the courage to slip away to join us?"

Isa glanced down at his bundles of rifles. "When they know we have the white man's magic guns, they will come. Naiche has seen this in a peyote vision."

Nana still seemed doubtful. "We have been prisoners at Fort Thomas for many winters. The old ones who fought so bravely are now nothing more than broken-spirited men. I do not think they will have the heart for battle."

"It is the bluecoats' whiskey that makes them weak. When they hear about the rifles they will come, and we will drive the white men from our land."

"You are sure of this?"

"Naiche has seen it in a dream."

Nana reined his horse to a piece of high ground with a view of what lay behind them. "It will be good," he said softly, "to have our homeland again."

Isa frowned as he rode his horse over the ridge. "The price will be high. Some of us must die in battle . . . but in the end we will drive them from our ancestral lands, and the buffalo will return. We will live in peace again. Naiche told me this as it came to him in his vision."

The Apaches rode down a rocky ledge, moving deeper into the Dragoons carrying an arsenal of repeating rifles and ammunition. Isa could feel the drumbeat of a war dance pounding in his heart as he led his men toward

Naiche. Putting on warpaint had made him feel powerful before, but it was nothing compared to the feeling of seeing the white-eyes soldiers fall when he aimed and fired the many-shoot rifles. There was nothing the Apache could not do, no enemy they could not defeat, now that they had the weapons that once had made the bluecoats invincible.

This dry, arid land the Apache called home was soon going to run with the white man's blood.

Chapter 16

Falcon was gathering wood for the campfire when he heard the unmistakable sound of a horse walking toward the camp through the forest.

He laid his bundle of sticks and branches down and pulled his Colt, stepping behind a nearby tree as the sounds came closer. He could see Hawk in the distance, digging a small hole next to a boulder and piling rocks around the edge of it, so the smoke from the fire wouldn't be seen by unfriendly eyes.

As the horse walked by, the rider ducked to avoid a low-hanging branch. Falcon stepped over to him and put the barrel of the Colt to the back of the man's head.

"Skin that smokewagon out of your holster and pass it back here, mister," he said in a low tone as he grabbed the rifle from the saddle boot with his left hand.

The stranger drew his pistol and held it out behind his back. "Falcon, is that you?" the man said, his voice quivering a bit with evident fear.

Falcon stepped around the horse's flanks to get a look at the man's face. "Cal Franklin. What the devil are you doing out here? I thought you were on your way to Tombstone," Falcon said, handing him back his weapons.

"Well!"

"Hold on, Cal. I'm sure Hawk'll want to hear this, too. Help me grab some firewood and we'll get supper started, and you can explain what's going on then."

Soon they were eating fried bacon and beans and skillet biscuits, washing it all down with strong, hot coffee as the temperature in the mountains fell.

As they ate, Franklin filled them in.

"I had walked 'bout halfway down the mountain, doin' some heavy thinkin' the whole way, when this group of miners caught up with me. They hadn't had any luck findin' silver or gold, an' were headin' into town to get more supplies 'fore the first winter snows came."

"That's the story of most men who come into the Dragoons seekin' their fortunes," Hawk said, staring at his hands as he built a cigarette. He stuck it in the side of his mouth and lighted it off a twig from the fire. "It ain't easy, findin' a strike rich enough to mine. You and your friends were mighty lucky."

Franklin's eyes clouded, and his expression sobered as he thought of his partners. "No . . . we weren't lucky. We worked hard, damn hard. Every day for more than a year, rain or shine, we were diggin' an' movin' rocks and dirt and panning every stream we could find 'fore we finally hit pay dirt."

"What happened after you met the miners?" Falcon asked, hoping to change the subject.

"Like I said, I'd been doin' some thinkin' on that long walk down the mountain. Frank an' Johnny and Billy an' me go way back." He cut tortured eyes toward Falcon. "We fought in the war together when we wasn't no more'n pups. Anyhow, wasn't no way I was gonna take the gold all of us dug outta that mountain and go to Tombstone and live the high life after what happened to my friends."

He stopped, his voice choking, and reached over to stir

the fire with a long branch for a moment, silent tears glistening in the firelight on his cheeks.

"So, I gave those miners enough dust to see 'em through the winter in exchange for that bronc over there, a rifle, a couple of pistols, and some ammunition. Then I went back to our camp and gathered up that sack full of dynamite and followed you boys on up the trail."

Hawk grunted, throwing his butt in the fire. "So you want to hunt Indians, huh?"

"No, Mr. Hawkins. I want to kill Indians."

"You know how to use that hogleg on your hip?" Falcon asked.

Franklin shrugged. "I can usually hit what I aim at, though I ain't no fast draw."

Hawk looked over at Falcon. "Another gun or two wouldn't hurt nothin'."

"Yeah," Falcon answered. "And that dynamite'll come in handy, too."

He looked up as a few heavy snowflakes began to fall, dancing like fireflies in the light of the campfire.

"You boys better bundle up. Looks like it's going to get a mite cold tonight. I'll take the first watch," Falcon said, wrapping his furlined coat tight around his shoulders and edging closer to the fire.

The next morning, with hoarfrost covering the ground, the three men packed their horses and got ready to ride.

"We'll go in single file, about fifty yards apart, with Hawk leading the way," Falcon said. "That way, if we come upon an ambush, maybe they'll only be able to get one of us."

"You think that's likely?" Franklin asked.

Falcon shrugged. "Who knows? Apaches seem to know when someone's on their back trail. I wouldn't be surprised if Naiche didn't leave a few braves behind to make sure no one follows him to their camp."

"So, we make as little noise as possible, an' we ride with

our guns loose,'' Hawk added, jacking a shell into the Henry he carried slung across his saddle horn.

"Gentlemen,'' Franklin said as he swung into the saddle, "you've made my day.''

Falcon smiled as he climbed on Diablo. "The Chinese have a saying, Franklin. When you start out on the revenge trail, dig two graves . . . one for your enemy, and one for yourself.''

"I prefer the bible version,'' Hawk added, pointing to the scalp locks hanging from his horse's mane. An eye for an eye, a tooth for a tooth, an' a scalp for a scalp.''

Chapter 17

It was a small group of covered wagons, only five, with half a dozen men and boys on horses serving as outriders flanking the oxen and mules pulling the wagons. A few women wearing sunbonnets and heavy woolen dresses walked beside or behind the larger rear wagon wheels in a cloud of chalky dust.

Naiche watched from a high rocky outcrop, taking note of a man with long silver hair, dressed in buckskins, riding out in front of the wagon train.

He spoke to Chokole sitting beside him on her pony. "The old one is their guide, taking them west to build a new village where more white men will come to settle and build their houses of mud. We have all seen these groups of wagons, and they stop near water to build their villages and claim the land for themselves. The old man is showing them the way."

"The old one is very watchful," Chokole said. "He looked at this mountain for a long time, even though we are far away. He may have Spirit powers telling him that we are here."

Naiche grunted. "White men do not hear Spirit voices.

They do not know where we are hidden, or that we are watching them from this place."

"Do you think we should attack now?" Chokole asked.

Naiche looked far beyond the wagons to a narrow pass through the Dragoons where the wagons must travel. "No," he answered. "We wait for them at the pass, hiding high among the rocks. Then, we will kill them all."

Chokole looked north. "Toza has not returned to tell us if the soldiers are coming."

Naiche was not worried. "The bluecoats move slowly, and they stop often to rest. There will be plenty of time to kill the white-eyes in those wagons and ride back to our camp with whatever we take from them. The mules will give us meat. The oxen will be old and tough, and the meat will not taste as sweet as the mules."

"Perhaps we should wait for Toza," Chokole warned.

Naiche ignored her. "Tell the others to mount. We ride around the wagons and take our hiding places above the pass. There will be no soldiers for many suns. Their Pawnee scouts drink the white man's crazy water, and they see nothing. Now is the time to strike."

Naiche and Chokole left their lookout spot on the side of the mountain to enter a twisting arroyo where the other Apaches waited with the horses.

Chokole told the young warriors of Naiche's plan as she was mounting her horse. Naiche swung aboard the back of a stolen army horse and swung south, leading the others down from one winding ravine to the next, angling southwest to move around the slow wagon train in time to prepare their ambush.

The Apaches rode single-file, and as they began a wide circle around the wagons, each warrior carefully loaded his Winchester and pistols.

Jasper Meeks didn't like the smell of things. Although he hadn't seen an Indian, he could almost feel their presence close by. After years of scouting for General Crook and

Phil Sheridan he had a sixth sense when it came to the close proximity of an Indian war party.

He spat tobacco juice over his right shoulder and spoke to Billy Clements. "We's gonna have to move through that tight pass up yonder, Billy, an' that'd sure as hell be the right spot fer an' Injun ambush."

"But it's the only way through these terrible mountains," Billy protested.

Jasper wagged his head. "There's other ways around, only it'll take a few extra days to swing so far north."

"I say we drive through the pass," Billy replied. "We have two sick women down with the fever, and we simply must get them to the closest doctor."

Jasper shrugged. "Fever won't matter much if they get shot dead movin' through that tight spot, but it's up to you. You're doin' the payin', and I'm only givin' you my advice on that sort of thing."

"Do you really think Apaches would attack so many of us?" he asked.

"If there's enough of 'em."

Billy seemed undecided for a moment. "I say the risk is worth taking. Doris Taylor is very ill, and so is Miz Roberts. We need to get them medical attention as soon as possible. Take us through the pass, Mr. Meeks."

Jasper spat again and gave the rocky peaks ahead of them a closer look. He could all but smell the presence of Indians close at hand. "Tell all your menfolk to git their rifles out an' loaded. Just in case."

Billy swung his horse away to inform the other outriders of Jasper's warning.

The first volley of gunfire from the top of the pass sent Jasper diving off his horse to the ground with his rifle. His red roan gelding was spooked by the noises and took off up the pass at a gallop, leaving Jasper afoot.

He belly-crawled to a spot behind a slab of limestone

fallen from the rim and kept his head down, waiting, listening to the sounds.

Men were crying out in pain. Women shrieked, and children cried out for their mothers. A wounded horse fell not far from the rocks where Jasper was hiding, a bullet hole though its shoulder. The pounding of rifles filled the pass with a wall of noise.

A team of oxen bellowed, and one collapsed in its yoke with blood pumping from a hole in its side. A screaming woman ran a few paces toward one of the wagons when a bullet struck her down, turning her pale blue blouse into a patchwork of crimson stains and faded fabric.

Billy Clements was shot off his horse, with a bullet through his neck. He landed hard, choking, trying to yell a warning to the women and children.

A slender boy of eight or nine, one of the Taylor twins, raced toward the back of a wagon when a .44 caliber rifle slug lifted him off his feet, spinning him around with his arms outstretched until he landed on his back with blood pooling around him.

Jasper had tried to warn Billy Clements and the others, but no one would listen. They were farm families, defenseless, knowing almost nothing about guns or how to fight Indians.

Jasper had only one thing on his mind . . . getting out alive, somehow.

A slug ricochetted off the rock where he was hiding, singing off harmlessly down the pass. Jasper eyed his escape route, a way to move up the pass to fetch his horse if he stayed close behind the shelter of fallen boulders.

Crawling, moving only a few feet at a time, he moved from rock to rock, leaving the settlers to fend for themselves. He felt no remorse for leaving them behind. He'd tried to warn them and no one would listen.

The clap of exploding gunpowder came from both sides of the pass. Jasper continued to crawl, worming his way as far from the wagons as possible.

He spotted his roan less than a hundred yards up the

pass where it had stopped, ears pricked forward, listening to the guns and the bellowing of wounded animals.

"If only that damn roan will stay still," he whispered as he crept onward as quickly as he dared.

"Help us, Mr. Meeks!" a voice cried behind him. The voice belonged to Luther Taylor.

"I warned you," he said to himself, still moving steadily but carefully toward his red roan gelding.

"Where are you, Mr. Meeks?" the same voice asked, shrill amid the banging of guns.

For a moment Jasper felt a touch of shame, abandoning these helpless people like he was, but he aimed to get out of this pass with his hair at any cost.

"Help us—" The crack of a rifle silenced Luther Taylor forever.

Jasper took a terrible risk. He came to a crouch with his rifle cradled in one arm and took off in an awkward run, staying as low as he could.

A gun roared from the top of the pass and a slug plowed up a spit of sand and dirt near his feet. He dove behind a rock and lay there, panting, collecting himself.

He glanced back down the pass and saw a sight he fully expected. Apache warriors were already running between the wagons with bloody knives, slicing off every scalp they could find.

Jasper jumped up again and took off in a zigzag run toward his gelding, praying that the Indians were distracted with their scalping just long enough for him to reach his mount. Once he was aboard his roan, he'd challenge these Indians to a horse race.

He made it to his roan just in the nick of time, for suddenly two rifles began firing at him from the rim of the pass. He swung over his saddle and gathered his reins, drumming his heels into the gelding's sides.

His horse was eager to escape the exploding guns and ran as hard as it could across rough ground, pounding out a rhythm with its hooves.

Jasper risked a glance over his shoulder, and what he saw made the short hairs on the back of his neck prickle.

An Indian mounted on a pinto pony was charging up the pass close on his heels. The warrior had a rifle to his shoulder as though taking aim, but Jasper Meeks knew a thing or two about shooting from the back of a moving horse. He quickly brought his Winchester up, turning back in the saddle, aiming carefully.

The Indian's rifle popped. The whisper of hot lead brushed close to Jasper's left cheek.

He took his time, steadying the muzzle of his rifle until he was certain of his target. Then he gently squeezed the trigger as his horse carried him headlong toward the west end of the pass where the ground was level.

The rifle slammed into his shoulder, and a young Apache went flying off the back of the pinto, flinging his rifle away to grab a wound in his chest.

"Gotcha," Jasper growled, levering the empty cartridge casing out, sending another into the firing chamber just in case more Apaches were following him.

His roan reached the end of the pass, and Jasper found himself in open desert country. The red roan was a thoroughbred cross he'd purchased from the army a few years back, and it had plenty of speed and stamina.

"Come git me, you red bastards!" he cried, turning his horse north to head for Fort Thomas.

To Jasper's surprise no more Indians were following him, and after a quarter mile of hard galloping, he slowed his roan down to a short lope.

Still watchful, he pushed toward Tombstone and Fort Thomas to inform the post commander of the ambush. One thing he was sure of . . . none of the settlers accompanying Billy Clements to California would make the journey. All of them would be dead by now.

He celebrated silently that he had escaped a close call and not lost his scalp. Reaching into his saddlebags, he pulled out a bottle of red-eye whiskey and took a healthy swallow while his horse loped toward Tombstone.

Jasper Meeks prided himself on being a survivor. This had not been his first close scrape with death at the hands of a tribe of warlike Indians. The settlers had paid dearly for ignoring his advice.

Chapter 18

Naiche stood near the spring, well beyond the wickiups, to watch Isa and the others ride into the mountain valley. Word had come from a lookout that more than a dozen of the People were climbing the secret Apache trail into the Dragoons with over forty horses and mules Naiche smiled inwardly. More warriors were coming to join them in the war against the white men. Soon his people would be free.

Chokole waited beside him, and she spoke softly when the first of the riders came down a narrow game trail leading to the valley floor. "Look, Naiche! The horses are loaded with bundles of many-shoot rifles."

Naiche noticed several of the braves with Isa were wearing bloody, torn uniform coats of the soldiers around their shoulders. "It is Isa who leads them. He has won a great victory against the bluecoats and taken their weapons and horses. We are much stronger now."

"Yes. And I see old Nana with them. He is wise, and a brave fighter."

"We must send word to Geronimo in Mexico. He will be pleased."

"Now we can strike the white settlement south of the town the white men call Tombstone."

Naiche said nothing as Isa galloped his horse away from the line of warriors. He rode up to Naiche and gave the sign of friendship before he jumped to the ground.

"We have killed more than forty of the bluecoats," Isa began. "And we took rifles from the locked room at the stinking fort, along with many horses and bullets. See how many warriors have come to join you? I bring all this to you, Chief Naiche, so we may begin war against the white-eyes."

"It is good," Naiche said, seeing so many bundles of the repeating rifles tied across the empty saddles of the soldiers' horses.

"We took many scalps," Isa continued. "We killed all the bluecoat soldiers who followed us, and have brought their guns, bullets, and food, along with the horses. More warriors will slip away from the reservation when they hear of our great victory."

The fat cavalry horses would carry them swiftly to the white settlement, Naiche thought, and with repeating rifles they could wipe out the entire group of white settlers quickly. "You are a brave warrior, Isa," Naiche said. "You will tell the others of your victory at a council fire tonight. We have roasted mule meat, and bags of flour and sugar. Tonight, the People will celebrate the courage of you and your warriors."

"We bring many rifles, more than seventy, and pistols taken from the dead soldiers who followed us. There are boxes of bullets, so many I could not count them, along with bags of the bluecoat soldiers' strange food. Some of it has a terrible taste, but no more of our women or children will be starving, as they did at the stinking fort. It has been a good day for the People. The spirits smiled on us."

Naiche frowned, thinking of the days ahead. "More soldiers will come. We have also drawn the blood of the white-eyes by attacking a group of the wagons that bring the settlers like locusts to destroy our land. The war with them will be long, and many of the People will die. But the spirits are with us now, and we will drive the whites from our homeland forever."

Nana and the other warriors led dozens of horses and mules loaded with rifles past the spot where Naiche, Chokole, and Isa stood. Nana looked at Naiche and gave the sign for a brave heart in battle. Then he rode toward the wickiups where the women and children were gathered at the spring pool to watch the arrival of Isa's war party.

Chokole spoke. "All the warriors must be trained in the use of many-shoot rifles . . . how to load and fire them. Tonight, at the council fire, we must begin their training."

Naiche agreed with a silent nod. "There is little time before more soldiers are sent to follow your tracks, Isa. We must be ready to strike the settlement near Tombstone in two or three suns."

"We will be ready," Isa said. "Most of the warriors who followed me know the ways of the new rifles. Only the youngest have not learned how to use them."

"I will instruct them," Chokole promised. "With these guns our warriors will have the strength of five times their number. I will give each warrior a rifle and a box of bullets before we gather at the council fire."

The rhythmic beat of deerskin drums accompanied chants coming from the dancers circling the fire. Warriors sat on the ground, Apache-fashion, each holding a Winchester rifle, as Chokole instructed them in the loading of bullets into the cartridge tube through a metal loading gate.

Naiche watched with satisfaction in his dark eyes. The new rifles were surely a gift from the Great Spirit, a sign that the time had come to drive the white men from traditional Apache lands.

Sitting beside Naiche, Nana spoke. "The young men are ready for war. I can see it on their faces."

"Geronimo promised all Apaches the time would come, when it is time for war."

"We have been like sheep on the reservation."

Naiche agreed. "There will be much suffering, and much bloodshed, but our Earth Mother's skin will be red with the blood of the white man."

"Will Geronimo join us?" Nana asked.

Naiche wagged his head. "He will fight his own fight. He is guided by a powerful spirit voice that tells him where to hit the enemy, and when to hide."

"But you are war chief of the Chiricahuas. It is The Way of the People that he must follow you."

Naiche knew Geronimo would never follow him into battle unless his spirit voice ordered it. "Geronimo has no chief. Since the white men killed his wife and children, he listens only to the Spirits. He seeks vengeance, and he will do it in his own way."

"Then we must strike the settlement near Tombstone quickly, and return to these mountains. After they find the remains of the wagons with the dead white-eyes, soldiers will be everywhere looking for us very soon."

"We will leave with the rising of the sun," Naiche said. "Along the way, our young warriors can learn more about the rifles. Chokole will teach them."

Nana listened to the beat of the drums a moment. "It is good, like in the old days, to hear the war drums and the war chants. I am remembering now what it was like to be free of the reservation."

"We will never return to the fort, Nana. Some of us will die so the others may remain free Apaches, but this is the Way of our people."

More young warriors stood up with their Winchesters to join the dancing and chanting, shaking the rifles above their heads as they circled the council fire.

Nana smiled. "My spirit is happy now. If I must die to keep our people free, then I am ready."

Naiche stood up, folding his muscular arms across his chest to watch the dancers. Deep inside, a feeling of pride began to swell within him. He longed to hear the screams of dying white men, to see their blood shed, to take their scalps.

It was a collection of adobe mud huts and corrals filled with goats and cattle and horses. At night, lantern light made golden squares of the windows across the settlement known to the white man as Bisbee.

Naiche and twenty warriors moved silently toward Bisbee in the dark of a moonless night, spreading out, forming a circle from which no one could escape.

A dog began to bark somewhere in the village when it heard the Apaches' horses moving through the brush, and Naiche knew it was time.

"Ayiii!" he cried, heeling his horse into a run.

The other Apaches came toward Bisbee at a gallop, leaning low over their horses' necks, readying their rifles.

Chokole led five young warriors charging into the village, and in an instant the booming reports of Winchester .44s filled the night.

White men and women came shouting and screaming from their adobes, some firing shots at fast-moving shadows darting among the houses.

Naiche rode toward a white man firing a shotgun at the raiders, and when he was very close he pulled the trigger on his Winchester.

The rifle stock slammed into his shoulder as the gun blasted its deadly load. The farmer with the shotgun was lifted off his feet and sent tumbling to the ground, yelling with pain, calling out a woman's name.

Naiche worked the lever, sending another cartridge into the firing chamber as his horse carried him swiftly toward another target, a man firing two pistols at the Apache intruders.

Naiche fired again, and he was rewarded by another victim when the white man collapsed in front of his adobe holding a wound in his belly.

The banging of gunfire sounded everywhere, along with the shrill war cries of Naiche's warriors. It was like the time before the bluecoat soldiers defeated them and forced them onto the reservation, a good time to be an Apache.

Naiche, thirsting for the feel of a white man's blood on his hands, jerked his horse to a sliding halt and jumped down with his knife drawn. He raced over to the farmer who had been firing the shotgun and sliced off his scalp with a single motion of his blade.

"Ayiii!" he cried again, shaking the steaming, bloody trophy above his head so all the other Apaches near him could see it. "Kill them all!" he shouted in the guttural Apache tongue. "Leave none of them alive!"

Apaches began jumping off their horses to scalp their victims, and now the shrieks of women and children grew louder. Fewer gunshots echoed through Bisbee as its citizens died in a hail of bullets.

Chokole was off her horse, dashing among the fallen whites, taking one scalp, then another. Naiche saw Nana's shadow move to a door into one of the adobes where he lifted a fallen white man by the hair and cut off his scalp.

Toza came running up to Naiche, his Winchester in one hand, a pair of bloody scalps in the other. "It is the magic of the many-shoot rifles, Chief Naiche!" he gasped. "See how easily the white-eyes die when we have their magic guns?"

"The power of the Spirits is with us now," he told the boy as he turned for his horse, tucking the farmer's scalp into his belt.

Toza threw back his head and gave the Apache war cry, holding his scalps and rifle high above his head.

Across Bisbee, more war cries answered Toza and Naiche, and soon the entire village resounded with whoops and yells.

Naiche swung over his horse's withers, filled with satisfaction. Before they left the settlement they would leave their mark upon every dead body . . . disemboweling the men and women, taking every scalp before they looted the houses for food and weapons. And when the bloodletting and looting were finished they would drive off all the livestock. The cattle and goats could be hidden in high mountain canyons. Their meat would make plentiful food for many moons, and their skins could be made into blankets and coats against the winter storms.

Nana rode over to Naiche as the last victims of the raid were being scalped and gutted.

"They are all dead, Naiche, and not a one of us has suffered any injury. It is a sign from the Spirits that this will be a good war. We will defeat the white soldiers and drive them back to the east."

Naiche glanced at the dark horizon. "Open the gates of all the corrals and drive the cattle and goats and mules to the south. We must be careful to hide our tracks, for the soldiers will hear of this and they will come after us."

"Let them come!" Nana said savagely, shaking his rifle. "They will all be killed, for now we have their magic!"

Chapter 19

It was just after dawn, and Falcon and his men were breaking camp, a light snow fall obscuring the rising sun.

Hawk rummaged in his saddle bags as he prepared to mount his horse. "Yo, Falcon. I'm gettin' a mite low on provisions, how about you?"

Falcon checked the canvas sack he had tied to his saddle and looked up. "Me, too. Now that there are three of us to feed, it might be wise to see about stocking up before we head farther into the mountains. Is there any place close by where we could buy some supplies?"

Hawk shrugged, "I don't know right offhand. How about you, Cal?"

Cal scratched his beard for a moment, thinking. "There's Bisbee Corners. It ain't much, just a few settlers and goatherders, but there's a store there that my partners an' I used to use when we didn't want to go all the way into Tombstone."

"How far is it?" Falcon asked.

Cal thought for another moment, then pointed off to the west. "I figger it's 'bout six, maybe seven miles in that direction."

Falcon glanced at Hawk. "It wouldn't hurt to make a run over there and get some more food and cartridges. If we're going to make war on the Apache, we're going to need all the ammunition we can carry."

"Could be they might have some news from somebody whereabouts the 'Pache were last seen, too," Hawk added.

"Cal, why don't you lead the way to Bisbee? I wouldn't mind a hot bath if they have one," Falcon said.

Cal grinned. "Don't get your hopes up, Falcon. It ain't all that big a place, an' from what I seen of the settlers there, don't none of 'em appear to have much of a cravin' for bathing."

After the three men had been traveling for about an hour, Cal held up his hand and reined his horse to a stop.

Falcon rode up next to him. "What's going on, Cal? Why'd you stop?"

"You hear that?" the miner asked, cupping his hand to his ear. "Sounds like a bunch of riders coming this way."

"Get off the trail, quick!" Falcon said, jerking Diablo's reins to the side and spurring the big black bronc into the forest to the side of the path.

Hawk and Cal followed him, just barely managing to get out of sight before a band of twenty or thirty Apache braves came galloping over the ridge. They were driving a few head of cattle and horses in front of them, and all were carrying Winchester rifles in their hands.

Cal jacked a shell into the chamber of his rifle, his face a mask of hate and fury when he saw the bloody scalps hanging from the manes of the Indian ponies.

Falcon reached over and put his hand on the rifle, shaking his head. "They've got us outnumbered eight to one, Cal. We wouldn't stand a chance in a face-to-face fight now."

"But they'll get away."

"No they won't. They'll be easy enough to trail if they keep those cattle with them."

"Damn! Most of those bastards've got blood all over their bodies," Hawk said in a hushed tone.

After the Indians rode out of sight over the next ridge, whooping and hollering to drive the beeves ahead of them, Falcon and the others came out of hiding.

Falcon could see Cal's hands shaking, his knuckles white as he gripped his rifle.

"Cal, the only way we've got a chance against the Apaches is to pick our fights. We have to hit and run, picking them off a few at a time. They're too good fighters for us to go up against a superior force and hope to come out on top," Falcon said.

"I know," Cal said, his voice husky with hate. "It's just that when I saw them all covered with blood, I couldn't think of nothin' 'cept what they done to Billy and Johnny and Frank."

"It looks like they were coming from the direction of Bisbee. You don't think they had the nerve to attack an entire town, do you?" Hawk asked.

"Apaches have never been accused of not having nerve," Falcon answered. "We'd better ride on over there and take a look."

"Yeah, there might be somebody left alive who needs our help," Cal said.

Falcon gave Hawk a look, both knowing if the Apaches had indeed hit Bisbee there'd be no one left alive to tell the tale.

As they rode through what was left of the small settlement, Falcon could feel his stomach turn at the grisly sights that surrounded them. After finding a small female child with her stomach sliced open and her entrails in her hands, her bloody skull gleaming in the sparse sunlight, Cal leaned to the side in his saddle and emptied his stomach on the ground, retching in disgust.

Falcon turned his head from the gruesome sight, and saw a figure riding slowly down the street toward them on a roan horse. The man had long, flowing silver hair and was wearing buckskins. His Winchester was cradled in his arms, the barrel pointing toward Falcon and his men.

"Looks like we're not alone after all, boys," Falcon said in a low voice.

Hawk twisted in his saddle, his hand automatically moving toward his pistol.

"Hold on, Hawk. He's just riding in, like us. He didn't have anything to do with this massacre."

"No white man could do anything like this," Cal added in a husky voice.

The man walked his gelding up to them, his eyes narrow and suspicious. "Howdy, gents," he murmured, his eyes darting back and forth as he surveyed the carnage all around them.

"Hello," Falcon answered. "My name's Falcon Mac-Callister, and this is Hawk Hawkins and Cal Franklin."

"I'm Jasper Meeks," the stranger said. He waved his hands. "Looks like the Apache got here ahead of me."

"Oh?" Falcon said.

"Yeah. Two day ago I was leadin' a wagon train across the desert an' we was hit by a bunch of Apache renegades. They had repeatin' rifles an' ambushed us in a mountain pass." He lowered his eyes and added, "we didn't stand a chance."

He pulled an almost empty bottle of whiskey out of his saddlebags and took a deep drink.

Hawk spat on the ground and wiped his lips with the back of his hand. "You say you was leadin' this group?"

"Uh huh."

"Then how is it you managed to escape an' the others didn't?"

"Just what do you mean by that, mister?"

Hawk shrugged, but his face looked as if he was tasting something bitter. "Don't mean nothin' by it, stranger. Just wonderin', is all."

"The first volley spooked my horse an' I was throwed to the ground. By the time I was able to chase 'em down, it was all just about over, so I climbed on an' rode like the devil hisself was after me.''

"You mean you left the others to be killed?" Cal asked, his expression incredulous.

Meeks lowered his eyes and looked at the bottle in his hand, but he didn't take another drink. "It wouldn't have made no difference. Like I said, they had us outnumbered three to one, an' they had repeatin' rifles. Most everybody was already dead by the time I got back in the saddle.''

"How come it took you so long to get here?" Falcon asked.

Meeks looked at him like he was crazy. "After that, I didn't dare to ride on the trail. I went into the brush and heavy forest and kept to the back side of the mountains, where there wasn't no chance of another ambush. It was slow goin', but a lot safer than ridin' out in the open.''

"An' a hell of a lot safer than stayin' an' fightin' side your friends," Hawk added.

"Listen, Hawk, or whatever your name is, I tried to warn those crazy pilgrims not to go through that pass, but they wouldn't listen to me . . . I tried to warn 'em . . ." Meeks said, his voice choking with emotion and shame.

"You don't have to explain anything to us, Mr. Meeks," Falcon said. "It's not up to us to judge you, especially since we weren't there. Now, let's separate and comb the town," Falcon said, giving a warning glance to Hawk to lighten up on Meeks. "There might be someone they missed, hiding somewhere waiting for help to arrive.''

Two hours later, the men met back at the general store in the center of town. Their faces were grim. They'd found not a living soul in the entire settlement.

Falcon got down off Diablo and walked into the store. The shelves and cabinets were destroyed, and foodstuffs were scattered all over the floor, but many were still in good enough shape to eat.

"They must have been in a hurry. They didn't ruin what they didn't take with them. Let's gather up what we can salvage and get on our way," Falcon said. "I have a feeling the army's going to be coming this way, and I don't particularly want to have to explain what we're doing out here.''

"Why not?" Cal asked.

"Because they'll order us back to Tombstone. Army officers like to throw their weight around, in spite of the fact that most of them are political appointees who don't know the first thing about Indian fighting and are too dumb to listen to men who might help them win against the Apaches."

Hawk tipped his head to the side and spit a brown stream onto the muddy ground. "That's fer damned sure!" he echoed.

After they'd loaded up as much food and extra ammunition as they could carry, Meeks asked, "What are you gents gonna do now?"

The muscles in Falcon's jaw tightened as he answered, "On the way here, we passed the band of Indians that did this on the trail. They were driving some cattle and livestock they rustled from the town. I figure they'll spread out soon, leaving a few braves to drive the cattle while the rest of them hurry back to their main camp with the rifles and guns they stole from the town. I don't plan on letting them get those cattle to the camp."

He hesitated a moment, then asked, "How about you?"

Meeks pursed his lips, then took a deep breath. "I was plannin' on headin' on into Tombstone, but if it's all the same to you men, I think I'd kind' a like to come with you."

Hawk spat again, his eyes on Meeks. "You sure? It ain't exactly the safest thing to do."

Meeks nodded. "I'm sure. I ain't felt so good 'bout myself since I left those pilgrims an' lit out. Maybe if I kill some of the Injuns that done it to 'em, I'll be able to sleep without seein' their faces in my dreams."

"That's good enough for me," Falcon said, jerking Diablo's head around and spurring the big stud into a gallop down the main street of Bisbee.

* * *

It took them until just before dark to catch up to the Indians driving the cattle and to ride around their flanks and get ahead of them on the trail.

Falcon positioned Hawk and Cal and Meeks on ridges on either side of the road while he prepared himself for a frontal assault. He loaded both barrels of his express shotgun with 00-buckshot, unhooked the rawhide hammer thong from his holstered pistol, and stuck an extra Colt in his belt where he could grab it with either hand.

He walked Diablo to a spot in the middle of the path just around a bend, and waited.

As the Indians rounded the curve in the road, they pulled on their rope halters and halted their ponies at the sight of a lone white man waiting for them.

They talked among themselves for a moment, letting the cattle walk on ahead. From their mannerisms, it was apparent they couldn't understand why the white man didn't turn tail and run when he saw the seven braves coming toward him.

When he suddenly leaned forward and spurred his horse into a gallop toward them, their expressions changed from astonishment to fury. If the crazy white-eyes wanted to die, they were ready to accommodate him.

With war whoops and yells, they cocked their rifles and kicked their ponies into action, running right at Falcon.

Reins in his teeth, his Greener in his right hand and a Colt in his left, Falcon heard the booming sound of the big Sharps fifty-caliber rifle as Hawk fired from the left side of the road. The lead brave was blown off his horse, his chest blossoming blood as he fell beneath the hooves of his friends.

The lighter cracks of Cal's and Meeks's Winchesters followed, knocking another red man off his mount and doubling another over his pony's neck. Then they were right in front of Falcon.

He stretched his arm out and fired the shotgun, one

barrel blowing the head off a brave and the other barrel cutting another almost in two as they passed close enough to spit on. The closeness of the action saved Falcon's life. The Indians were so close, and Falcon was approaching so fast, that they didn't have time to aim their rifles, and fired from the hip. The bullets sang by Falcon's head like a swarm of angry bees.

One of the remaining Indians jerked his pony to a halt, aimed, and fired his rifle at Falcon, cutting a groove in the meat of his thigh but missing the bone. He jacked another shelf into the rifle and kicked his mount into a dead run right at Falcon, firing again from the hip and missing.

Falcon answered with his left-hand Colt. His first shot missed. The second hit the Indian's horse in the forehead. As the pony fell the brave was thrown headfirst into a tree next to the trail, smashing his head into bloody pulp against the bark.

The last two braves reined to a halt, uncertain what to do next. As they sat there, watching Falcon and trying to decide what to do, two shots from the forest rang out. The Sharps and the Winchesters sent them both to hell, knocking them out of their saddles to the frozen ground below.

Falcon walked Diablo around the battle scene, looking at the crimson splotches dotting the sparse patches of melting snow, letting his battle fury calm down a mite.

As his heart rate slowed, he took a cigar out of his pocket and lighted it. He sat and smoked, wondering why the Apaches were so different from other humans, even other Indians, as he waited for Hawk and Cal and Meeks to get down to him.

When they rode up, Cal was grinning from ear to ear. "Goddamn!" he said, his eyes bright with excitement. "I never seen nothin' like that, Falcon. You just charged right into the thick of them Injuns like it weren't nothin'!"

Falcon gave a tight grin. "It wasn't as brave as it seems, Cal. The only way to fight the Apaches is to surprise them.

If I'd sat on my horse and traded rifle shots with them, I'd be dead now. I had to do something they didn't expect, and that was to charge them and get in close before they were ready for me. That's why those rifles they were carrying didn't do them any good. You need a pistol or shotgun for close-in fighting."

Hawk nodded and spat, his stream hitting a dead Indian in the forehead as he lay next to Hawk's horse. "Still, you did go through them Injuns like Grant went through Richmond, Falcon," he said, an approving look in his eyes. "No matter how you explain it, you got to have *cojones* as big as melons to do that."

"That's right, Falcon," Meeks added. "I never seen anyone charge a band of Injuns like that."

Falcon stepped down from his horse and slipped his Bowie knife out of his scabbard. "Come on, Hawk, Meeks. We've got work to do."

Cal raised his eyebrows. "What do you mean, Falcon?"

Falcon didn't answer, just knelt next to a dead body and cut its eyes out, then grabbed the hair and sliced it free of the skull, holding the bloody scalp lock up for Cal to see.

"Oh Jesus," Cal said, covering his mouth as if he were going to vomit again.

Hawk looked up from nearby where he was doing the same thing. "It's not like that, Cal. We're gonna send a message to the men that ride with Naiche. Injuns have some funny notions 'bout not bein' able to see or find their way to their heaven—the Land of the Shadows they call it—if'n they eyes is cut out."

Meeks didn't say anything. He was too busy peeling the scalp off a dead Indian.

Falcon nodded as he walked toward another corpse. "When Naiche sends a scout back to see why the cattle didn't arrive, we want him to see this and carry the word back to his chief that some crazy killers are on his trail. He'll know from what we do to the bodies that we're not army, and he'll wonder just who the hell is after him."

Hawk paused from tying a pair of bloody scalps in his horse's mane and called to Cal. "Why don't you round up those ponies, take their rope halters off, an' use 'em to string these bodies up in some nearby trees? Wouldn't want coyotes or wolves to get at 'em 'fore Naiche's scout sees 'em."

Cal nodded, sweat forming on his forehead in spite of the cold, crisp fall air that blew in from the north. "I'll do it, but that don't mean I approve of what you're doin'."

Falcon, scalping another Indian, didn't look up. "You've got to look at this like it is, Cal. This isn't a nice duel between a couple of gentlemen on a riverbank, or a gunfight in the middle of a dusty street. This is war, plain and simple. When we took out after Naiche and his band of killers, we set out on a course that has only one possible ending. Their death, or ours. There is no in-between. So, I'm going to do anything that might give us an edge, that might make Naiche look over his shoulder when he rides, that might make his warriors a little fearful or hesitant when they go into battle against us. I want them all to know what's going to happen to them if they lose, and I want them to think about that when they see us coming."

Meeks looked up, his arms bloody all the way to his elbows. "My old pappy would say it's givin' 'em a taste of they own medicine."

Cal tied a rope around the neck of a brave, threw the rope over a branch, and hoisted him up off the ground until his feet were dangling in the air. "Okay, Falcon, I understand, but that don't mean I gotta like it."

Hawk spat, making a field mouse break from its burrow and run along the ground. "Don't none of us like it, partner. It's just somethin' we gotta do."

Chapter 20

Colonel Thomas Grant surveyed the grisly scene from the back of his sorrel horse. Buzzards circled high above the sun-bloated corpses of Major Wilson Tarver's command. Dead troopers were lying all along the bottom of a ravine, and to the west on the rocky slopes of an incline leading up to the rim of the canyon where more bodies lay.

He spoke to Captain Buford Jones. "Worst damn thing I've ever seen. Hell, it wasn't enough that they killed them, but the way they mutilated them. It's senseless."

"It's that damn Naiche an' the bunch that run off with him. You can be sure of that, Colonel."

"How can a human being do such butchery to another? These men are cut to pieces."

"Sir, there's some in this army who don't think a god-damn Apache is a human bein'."

Grant took a deep breath. "After seeing this, I'm inclined to agree."

"Do you want me to form a burial detail, sir?"

Grant thought a moment. "It seems a shame to bury

them way out here, without proper grave markers or any type of ceremony over their bodies.''

"Only other thing we can do is ride back to the fort an' send back wagons so we can bury 'em in the post cemetery at the fort.''

"That sounds more humane, Captain. Send a messenger to Fort Thomas with orders to bring back three wagons and a squad of men to load the bodies.''

A sergeant by the name of Skinner came riding back from the slope where twenty more troopers had died. He rode up to Colonel Grant and halted his horse. "We found Major Tarver, sir. Like the others, he was scalped and his belly was cut open. Found him over near this big rock pile.''

Grant shook his head in disgust. "That accounts for all of them, I think. Too bad about Sergeant Boyd. He was a good soldier with plenty of Indian fighting experience. I'm a bit surprised they got him, although it appears they were ambushed from above.''

"I'll send for the wagons," Captain Jones said, turning his horse away to summon a messenger.

Grant glanced over to Sergeant Skinner. "See if those half-drunk Pawnees have picked up any of the Apaches' tracks. I have my doubts they're sober enough to find a pair of railroad tracks at the moment, but ask them anyway.''

Skinner rode off up the canyon to look for the two Pawnee scouts accompanying the detail. Grant felt helpless, and let his shoulders droop. Finding Apaches out in these wilds was like trying to grab a feather in the wind. They knew how to disappear without leaving a trace.

A trooper struck a gallop on his bay gelding, heading north toward the fort to bring back burial wagons. Grant knew his report to his superiors regarding this affair would look bad on his record. As commanding officer at Fort Thomas, the men and their safety was his responsibility.

From the looks of things, despite having the old Shoshone scout with them Major Tarver had led his men blindly into this canyon where a death trap awaited them. Grant wondered idly what had happened to the old Indian ... no one had reported finding his body among the others.

A young cavalryman trotted his horse up to the colonel and saluted. "They even took most of their boots an' shirts, sir. Every pistol and rifle is gone, too, along with all the ammunition pouches. The buzzards have been eatin' on them for a couple of days, an' even with the cold the stink sure is hard on a man's belly. I was wonderin' what you wanted us to do with the bodies."

Grant's stomach was also a bit queasy after seeing the end result of the massacre. "Bring down the bodies that are up on the side of the canyon. I've sent for wagons. Place all the bodies in a row so they can be loaded in the wagons. I fully understand it won't be a pleasant chore, Corporal, but it must be done, anyway, out of respect for our fellow soldiers, so they can be given a decent burial."

"Yes sir," the corporal said, urging his horse around to ride up the canyon with the colonel's orders.

Grant swallowed back bitter bile as Captain Jones returned from dispatching the messenger. He gave Jones a sideways look. "We'll make those red bastards pay for what they did here. If it takes every man under my command, we'll scour the countryside until we find Naiche and his runaways and bring them to justice. I intend to give the order to have all of them hanged."

"We gotta find 'em first, Colonel. That ain't gonna be no easy job in the Dragoons. This is their home range. They'll know every back trail, every cave, every hidin' place there is to be had."

"We need to find competent scouts, Captain," Grant replied. "Those Pawnees are utterly useless. If we could find just one man who knew what he was doing, he could track these savages down for us."

Jones scowled a moment, thinking. "Somebody told me there was this feller who rode into Tombstone right about the time they had that shootout at the OK Corral. He's supposed to be some sort of expert on huntin' and killin' Indians, or so they say."

"What was his name? Do you remember?"

"Seems like he was named after some bird, like an eagle, maybe. When we get back to the fort I'll ask old man Sudderth. He was the one who told me about him."

"One good tracker can save us valuable time, and we won't have to put up with these-drunken Pawnee scoundrels. Remember to ask who the fellow is who showed up in Tombstone. I'll make him an offer he probably won't refuse."

As the bodies were being arranged in a row to await the arrival of the wagons, a soldier on a badly lathered chestnut gelding came riding at a gallop toward Colonel Grant's temporary campsite.

He saw the colonel standing in the meager shade of a slender mesquite and rode over to him, jerking his winded mount to a halt.

"More bad news, Colonel," he said, sounding as out of breath as the horse he rode.

"Speak up, Private," Grant demanded, growing impatient with the soldier's hesitation.

"The entire population of Bisbee's Corner has been wiped out, slaughtered by Indians."

"The women and children, too?" Grant asked, dismayed.

"Every last one of them, sir. They were all scalped and cut up something awful."

"Did you see this for yourself?"

"No sir, but an old prospector who hangs around the Sutler's store sometimes came upon it, and he headed straight for the fort to report it."

Grant's stomach was in knots. "How many lives were lost? I haven't been to Bisbee's Corner since last spring."

"Thirty-four in Bisbee, sir, includin' the women and kids." The man hesitated, as if fearful of imparting even more bad news. "There's more, sir."

"Out with it, man," Grant snapped.

"On the way to the fort, the prospector came across another massacre. A wagon train filled with settlers and their wives and children was also hit by Indians. There were no survivors there, either."

"Naiche," Captain Jones said needlessly. "He's gone on a killin' spree, now that he an' his bucks have Winchester rifles an' fresh horses. He's killin' us and every white man, woman, and child he can find with guns they stole from our armory, and they're ridin' some of our best remount horses they took from the stables."

"Dear God," Grant sighed. "There's no telling where this will end unless we find Naiche and his Apaches quickly. He could go on raiding and killing for months."

The newly arrived messenger glanced at the row of soldiers' bodies. "Looks like he took a mighty heavy toll on Major Tarver and his troops."

"They're all dead," Grant said, his mind racing, thinking of what this would look like when his superiors heard about the Bisbee massacre. Grant could envision himself being relieved of his command in short order.

"What shall I tell Major Evans, sir?" the messenger asked, sensing Grant's growing anger.

Grant had left Major Carl Evans in command of the fort while he rode out to look for Major Tarver's missing troops. "Tell him I will be back tomorrow, and to prepare every able-bodied man and horse for a major campaign against the runaway Apaches. Take a fresh horse from one of ours and return to the fort immediately with my message."

"Yessir," the private said, saluting smartly before he wheeled to find himself another mount.

Jones toed the soft sand with his boot. "There's another thing to think about, Colonel, an' it could be the worst news yet."

"And what might that be?" Grant asked, mopping his sweating face with a neckerchief.

"Naiche, now that he's got maybe twenty or thirty fightin' men and twice that many rifles, might join up with Geronimo. If that happens, we're in for a helluva fight."

"Geronimo seems to have disappeared since he left the San Carlos reservation. No one has heard of him or seen him since, and until now, things have been quiet."

"Word is, Geronimo is down in Mexico raiding rancheros for horses and attacking small Federale patrols to get their rifles and ammunition."

"Where did you hear this?" Grant asked.

"Same place . . . old man Sudderth. He heard it from a *vaquero* who works cattle in Sonora for one of the big ranchers. They say Geronimo is hidin' out in the Sierra Madres, buildin' himself an Apache army."

"That is troublesome news, if it's true, Captain. If Geronimo comes across the river to join forces with Naiche, we'll have a full-fledged Indian war on our hands."

Jones nodded. "Apaches are hard to kill or capture, because they break up into small groups after a raid. Our scouts never know which tracks to follow, and when they do find several sets of tracks, the Indians split up again into twos and threes. It gets mighty damn frustratin'."

"We simply must find a good scout, a man who understands the ways of these savages."

"I'll inquire about that feller up in Tombstone as soon as we get back to the fort. Sudderth will remember his name, an' maybe somethin' about his past."

"Make that your top priority, Captain. Leave now for the fort, and find out who this newcomer is. I want to know his name and where to find him."

Jones saluted and wheeled his horse, then he pulled back on the reins. "Seems like Falcon was his name. He isn't from this country. Up north, I think. Maybe Colorado Territory is where he's from."

"Find out where he is," Grant said impatiently, listening to the buzz of swarming blowflies hovering over the decaying corpses at the mouth of the ravine. On the eastern rim of the canyon he saw the pair of Pawnee scouts riding back and forth, studying the ground. One of the Indians was holding a pint bottle of whiskey as he went about searching for tracks. "As you can see, we've got a pair of drunks serving as our guides out here. We might as well give up."

"I'll talk to ole' Sudderth as soon as I get to the fort, Colonel. He'll remember the stranger's full name."

"Get going," Grant said, turning his attention away from the Pawnees. "I'll be back at the fort by noon tomorrow, unless we run into difficulties. I plan to ride over to Bisbee's Corner on my return trip to see the carnage Naiche left for us there. And tell Major Evans to send a burial detail to Bisbee so those poor settlers can be buried."

Jones rode away at a hard gallop. Colonel Grant felt a chill run down his spine in spite of the warmth of the desert sun. A huge Indian war was in the making, and he would be squarely in the middle of it, by the looks of things.

Chapter 21

Naiche listened to the wailing women as they prepared the body of Yapo for burial in the cave high on a mountain overlooking the valley. The white man with silver hair had killed the boy with a single shot from the back of a running horse, proof that he was a skilled fighter. There would be more burial ceremonies before the war against the whites was over, and every warrior in Naiche's band knew this.

Naiche turned his attention to the wickiups, where dozens of scalps were hanging from stakes driven into the ground. The whites had paid heavily for occupying Apache land since Naiche first escaped from the fort. And now, with their numbers growing, more scalps would adorn the stakes in the days to come.

Chokole left the women to sit across from Naiche. "Toza has not returned. The soldiers may have captured him or killed him. He has been gone for two suns."

"I sent Isa and three more to look for him. Toza knows the ways of the mountains and desert. He may be watching the fort to see how many soldiers are sent to look for us."

"The soldier horses with iron shoes leave tracks that are

easy to follow," Chokole said. "We have no tool that will cut off the iron without crippling the horses."

It was one of Naiche's darkest fears, when iron-shod horses left sign that was too easy to follow. "We cross the rocks wherever we can," he told her. "Only a man who knows how to read sign like an Indian will notice the tiny scars on the rocks."

"I fear the soldiers will find us here," she said, gazing around the valley.

"We will move south soon, deeper into the mountains, to the steep canyon the old ones called Deer Springs. There is grass for the horses, goats, and cattle, and the trail is very long and narrow, easy to defend if the bluecoats follow us."

"I remember the deep canyon," Chokole said. "It seems so long ago when we made camp there."

"A brave one among us must be sent back to the reservation to tell others where we are, so they will join us. They must be told about our many-shoot rifles, and horses. Word has to be taken to San Carlos, so the Mimbres and other Apaches will know we are preparing for a great war, and where to find us."

"I will go," Chokole said. "The bluecoats will be less suspicious of a woman. I will wear an old deerskin dress, and no one will notice me."

A gust of wind rustled the drying scalps in front of the wickiups while Naiche thought about Chokole's plan. She was as brave as any Apache warrior, and a fearless fighter. "Then you will go with tomorrow's sun. Ride one of the starving ponies, and carry only a knife hidden under your dress. It will be dangerous, but word must reach the others that we have guns and food and horses."

The women carried the body of Yapo out of a wickiup, his corpse covered with charcoal. They started up a steep trail to the burial cave, singing a chant for the dead.

Watching this, Naiche vowed to make the old white man with silver hair pay for killing Yapo if he ever saw the wagon scout again.

* * *

As the women were returning from the burial ceremony, Naiche heard the night cry of a hunting owl, signaling someone was approaching the camp. He turned and watched the trail leading to their camp.

Isa, along with the three braves who had been sent with him, were leading ponies with bodies folded across their backs.

Naiche walked rapidly down to meet the procession.

"Is it Tozo you have found?" he asked.

Isa shook his head. "We found no trace of Tozo. These are our brothers who were left behind after the attack on the white-eyes village to drive the cattle and mules to our camp."

"What happened to them?" Naiche asked.

Isa didn't answer, but pulled the blankets off the corpses.

Naiche sucked in his breath, feeling as if someone had punched him in the stomach. It wasn't fear, for he didn't know the meaning of that, but his heart hammered and his mouth became dry nevertheless.

He stared at the mutilated bodies, their skulls glistening in the moonlight where the scalps had been ripped off. Their empty eye sockets seemed to look right at him, and their throats gaped in gruesome semblances of smiles where they had been cut from ear to ear.

"The white-eyes could not do this!" Naiche gasped.

"Who, then?" Isa asked.

Naiche stroked his mouth as he thought, staring at the stars to take his mind off the bodies of his followers.

"It must be the Kiowa," he finally muttered, "brother to the Comanche, our ancestral enemies from the dawn of time."

"But the Kiowa are all on reservations," said Chokole, who had come to stand next to Naiche.

He glanced at her, scorn on his lips. "So were we less than a moon ago, Chokole, and this has all the earmarks of a Kiowa killing."

She nodded, her eyes thoughtful. "It is true that they do mark their victims as we do, but why would they suddenly make war on us after all the moons of peace between us?"

Naiche shrugged. "If they have escaped the reservations as we have, then it may be no more than hunger for our cattle and mules that caused this attack."

He turned back toward the camp. "Warn the others to be watchful for any sign of our enemy, the Kiowa, when they are away from camp.

Toza entered the valley in darkness an hour later. A lookout had given the owl's call to alert Naiche that one of the People was coming back to camp.

Naiche waited for Toza in front of his wickiup, his face illuminated by the glowing coals of a dying fire.

Toza dropped off his horse. "Many bluecoats came to the arroyo where Isa killed the soldiers. They had two Pawnee scouts with them."

"Did they find Isa's tracks?"

"No. The Pawnees were drinking *boisa pah*, the white man's crazy water, and they only rode a short distance and then went to sleep under a tree."

"Where are the soldiers now?" Naiche asked.

"The soldiers waited until big wagons came. Then they loaded the bodies of their dead and drove away toward the fort. But a rider had come, and some of the soldiers rode off to the white settlement where we killed so many. I watched them from the top of a mountain, and they sent another soldier away in the direction of the fort. Some of the soldiers carried the bodies to a single place and began to dig holes. More soldiers rode out to look for our tracks, but they behaved strangely, riding in big circles, climbing off their horses to talk and point to the ground."

"They did not find the tracks of all the animals we drove away with us?"

"Yes, they followed our trail until they came to the place

where we crossed the flat rocks. They stopped, and went back to the village to bury the dead."

Naiche was pleased. "They know nothing about following the tracks of an animal."

Toza nodded, although he appeared troubled. "More will come to look for us. I saw their dust to the north just before the sun went down."

Naiche glanced up at the stars. "Then it is time to move our camp deeper into the mountains. You have done well, Toza. Sleep, for tomorrow we must leave this place."

Toza led his horse into the darkness. Naiche thought about the dust cloud the boy had seen, wondering how many soldiers had been sent to look for them, and if they had a scout who knew how to read sign. He also wondered if the cloud of dust could be from Kiowas coming to make further war on the People.

He shook his head. It would be most difficult to fight both the white-eyes soldiers and the Kiowa at the same time.

More than anything else, Naiche thought, he needed more warriors to use the repeating rifles Isa took from the fort and from the soldiers he and his warriors killed in the ravine. It was useless to have so many many-shoot guns and bullets when there was no one to fire them at the enemy. Especially if there were to be two different enemies to fight.

Chokole, dressed in a torn, badly stained deerskin dress, rode a slope-shouldered gray Indian pony into the rows of army barracks where Apaches were forced to live. A pair of guards hardly noticed her as she rode in. She carried a bundle of old clothing. Apache women on the reservation were allowed to go down to the river to wash clothes and bathe themselves. Some soldiers watched the younger Apache girls when they were naked in the river, laughing among themselves and pointing at the prettiest women.

Chokole tied the pony behind one of the buildings and

began going from room to room, speaking in a whisper, telling all who would listen about Naiche's plan, the rifles and horses and food, and of their victories at the canyon, the white settlement, and the wagon train.

Some of the younger Apache men listened eagerly, while others waved Chokole away, for they were broken in mind and spirit. As she went from barracks to barracks, more and more warriors paid close attention to what she told them.

"Leave at night, only a few at a time," she said over and over again. "Do not steal horses or guns. Run as fast as you can to the foothills of the Dragoons. We will be waiting for you with horses and rifles and food."

"They will come after us," one boy said to her.

"Leave no tracks for them to follow. Run across the rocky ground, and stay far from the village they call Tombstone. If they cannot find your tracks they will be too late to ride in the right direction. The foothills are not far, and we will be waiting for you there with horses."

For several hours Chokole spoke with Chiricahuas, Mimbres, Mescaleros, and Warm Springs Apaches being held at Fort Thomas. In the wee hours before dawn, she mounted her gray pony and rode quietly past two sleeping guards at the fort gates, carrying her bundle of garments.

Almost thirty Apaches had promised to slip away from the reservation over the next two days, to join Naiche in the Dragoons. Chokole had hoped for more, but many of the People were afraid.

When she was far from the fort gates she kicked the pony to a lope. Naiche had to be told about her promise, to have horses, food, and guns waiting for the warriors who would try to escape and run through the night to the northern edge of the mountains. An Apache warrior was trained from boyhood not to depend on a horse, learning to run for miles without food or water as a test of their endurance.

* * *

Isa and Nana watched the desert as sunrise brightened the flats. In a ravine to the south, more than twenty horses were tethered to scrub mesquite trees. Already, during the night, five Mimbres had come, four young boys and one older warrior named Ulole who had once been one of the most skilled fighters among the Mimbres.

The five had been given food and water, and horses to ride to the camp where Naiche waited for them.

"More are coming," Nana said. "Even with these old eyes I can see them running. There are three."

"Yes, I see them," Isa agreed. "And farther to the north, four more are running single file, staying out of sight in a shallow wash."

Nana grinned. "You have the youthful eyes of an eagle, Isa."

Isa swept the horizon for any sign that soldiers were following the escaping Apaches. "It is good that no soldiers are following them. The bluecoats are lazy and stupid. They do not notice things. The warriors Chokole has brought to us may not be missed until the roll call is taken."

"When the sun is high," Nana remembered. "By then all who are coming will be here."

Isa stepped away from the rock where he and Nana were hiding so the running Apaches would see him. The first three saw him at once and turned in his direction.

Moments later the four warriors running down the dry wash saw Isa and they changed direction, trotting toward him as they looked behind them.

Nana spoke softly. "Chokole said as many as thirty agreed to join us."

"We will be much stronger now, Nana. Thirty more warriors armed with repeating rifles, mounted on good horses, will give us the strength to attack the bigger blue-coat patrols. Naiche has sworn we will paint this land red with their blood."

Nana frowned slightly. "Naiche is a brave war chief, but he can be reckless. His hunger to kill the white-eyes can make him take chances."

"How can there be war without chances that some of our people will die, Nana?"

"You speak true words. Only Geronimo seems to know how to escape the bluecoats without harm. It is said his wisdom comes from our spirit fathers . . . that they speak to him in a voice only he can hear, because the whites killed his wife and his son and daughter."

Isa motioned the running Apaches closer before he answered Nana. "Geronimo will not join us. He has only a few warriors, and this is his way of fighting the enemy."

Nana stood up, watching three slender young men race to the rocks at the entrance into the ravine. "Naiche will lead us to many victories. Let Geronimo fight the white-eyes as he wishes, for we will win many battles now. Our many-shoot rifles will hang scalps on every lodge pole."

Isa greeted the three panting Apaches with sign language and pointed to the ravine where the horses and food were being kept by Toza.

"More are coming," Nana said, squinting in the sun's early glare. "I count five more running among the cactus and brush."

Isa saw them. Before the sun was fully above the eastern hills, twenty-two Apaches would arrive to join them.

Chapter 22

Captain Buford Jones pushed the batwings open and swaggered into Campbell and Hatch's Saloon. Though it was the middle of the day, the popular eating place was already full of cowboys and businessmen of Tombstone. Some had come to drink, some to eat, and some to just get out of the frigid north wind blowing through the dusty streets.

Jones had two privates with him, both as escorts and bodyguards, since the army wasn't all that popular with the miners and cattlemen around the area.

Jones bellied up to the bar and ordered whiskey for himself and beer for the two privates with him. After the bartender placed the drinks in front of him, Jones turned to lean back against the bar, facing the room.

"Attention, people of Tombstone!" he shouted, causing the muted noise of conversation to die down as the diners turned to stare at him with suspicious eyes.

Damn, but he hated civilians. Here he was, living out on that godforsaken desert, protecting their way of life, and still they treated him and the other soldiers like dirt.

He cleared his throat "I'm looking for a man named MacCallister, Falcon MacCallister. He was here in Tombstone last week, and the army is willing to pay for any information that'll help me find him."

For a moment, no one moved. Then everyone turned back to their drinks and food and talk—all except two men. They continued to stare at Jones as they whispered among themselves. Finally, they got up from their seats and approached him.

"This Falcon yore lookin' fer, he a big man, ridin' a big black stud hoss?" the older of the pair asked.

The two men were dressed in old, dirty shirts and canvas Levi pants, indicating they were miners, in town to hole up until the worst of the winter weather passed.

"Yeah. Do you know anything about his whereabouts?" Jones asked.

The younger of the pair, a man in his fifties, licked his lips and held out his hand, rubbing thumb and forefinger together. "First, what 'bout the money you promised fer information."

Jones pulled out his wallet and held it up. "Twenty dollars, *if* what you tell me leads me to Falcon."

The two miners looked at each other for a moment, then nodded and the older man spoke. "Jake an' me was bringin' in some wagons with the bodies of a family kilt by Injuns in it, an' this here Falcon feller stopped us on the edge of town."

"Bodies?" Jones asked. He hadn't heard of any other killings by Naiche and his band.

"Yep. They was five or six men an' women lived in a cabin up in the Dragoons kilt couple'a weeks ago. All cut up and butchered, they was."

"So, what business was that of Falcon's?"

The old man shrugged. "Can't rightly say. But he got real upset when he stopped us an' took a gander at the bodies. Asked where the cabin was, an' then said somethin' under his breath 'bout not letting the Injuns get away with any more killings."

"What did he do then?"

"He hightailed it toward the road leadin' to the cabin, up into the Dragoons."

The old man shook his head. "He must be crazy to go up into those mountains with the Injuns on the warpath again." He shook his head. "Not a fit place to be now, that's fer sure."

The younger miner held out his hand. "Now, mister, where's our money?"

Jones inclined his head toward the private standing next to him. "Private Guttman will take down your names and addresses. If we find Falcon based on your information, the money will be sent to you."

The two men stared at Jones with narrowed eyes, then shrugged and gave Guttman their names. "We don't exactly have an address. We mine up in the Dragoons most of the year, but you can leave the money with the bartender here, an' we'll check back ever now an' then."

Jones turned back to the bar, intending to finish his whiskey, when a man stepped up next to him. The man was short, and his skin was as pale as a woman's, and covered with a fine sheen of sweat even though the room was fairly cool.

"Hello, Captain," the man said, raising his finger to order a whiskey.

"Good afternoon, sir," Jones replied, wondering just what the man wanted.

When whiskey was placed before him, the man upended his glass and drank it down in one swallow. Then he turned sideways, leaned on the bar, and addressed Jones.

"Just what is it you want with Falcon MacCallister?"

Jones glanced at the man, then turned back to his whiskey. "That's the army's business, not yours, mister."

Quick as a flash the man's hand moved, and a pistol barrel was stuck in the left side of Jones's abdomen.

"Captain, do you happen to know anything of anatomy?"

Jones tried to swallow around the lump that suddenly appeared in his throat, then croaked, "Uh, no. Why?"

"I just wanted you to know that my Colt is nudged up against your liver and gall bladder. If I let the hammer down, the bullet will pass right through those organs. If you're lucky, a major artery will be hit, and you will die within minutes. However, if Lady Luck happens to be looking somewhere else at the time, you will live for days to weeks, sweating, puking, and generally being in the most excruciating pain. Do I make myself perfectly clear, Captain?"

"Who . . . who are you?" Jones managed to say.

"My name is John Henry Holliday, but most folks just call me Doc."

Jones's heart began to hammer in his chest, and fear-sweat broke out on his forehead. He'd heard of Doc Holliday, who hadn't?

"What . . . what is it you want?"

"I just asked a perfectly civil question. What does the army want with Falcon?"

"I was asked to try to find him to see if he would do some scouting for us. We're having some trouble locating the Indians that have been killing people all over this region. Word is that Falcon MacCallister is an accomplished tracker who knows the ways of the Apache."

The pressure against Jones's stomach disappeared, and Holliday turned to go. "There now, that wasn't so bad, was it? You army bastards ought to try being move civil and less arrogant, and perhaps people would treat you better when you came to town. Now, Mr. Army Captain, Falcon is a friend of mine. If I find out the army causes him any harm or harassment at all, there won't be a rock large enough for you to hide under. Do I make myself clear?"

Jones nodded his head as Holliday walked off. Then he ordered another whiskey and drank it down as soon as it was poured.

Private Guttman, completely unaware of what had just

happened, asked Jones, "What's the matter, Captain? You look kind' sick."

"Shut up, Private, and mind your own business," Jones growled, ordering another whiskey.

Chapter 23

Ishton, Cuchillo, Tao, and Juh scouted the foothills for any sign of soldier patrols approaching the Dragoons from the east. They had also been instructed by Naiche to keep a sharp lookout for any sign of Kiowa, or other Indians, and to report back immediately if any were sighted. They rode strong cavalry horses stolen from Fort Thomas, and carried Winchester rifles and Colt pistols taken from the dead bluecoats killed by Isa and his warriors. Naiche wanted scouts watching all sides of the mountains in order to be prepared against a surprise attack if the soldiers found their tracks. Naiche had moved the village to the canyon called Deer Springs, where their stronghold would be easier to defend. From Deer Springs they would launch many raids against the white-eyes and bluecoat patrols, before returning to their isolated camp in some of the most rugged terrain high in the mountain range, where water and grass were plentiful and the steep canyon walls were honeycombed with caves providing shelter and hiding places for the women.

Cuchillo suddenly halted his horse as they were at the edge of a thicket of scrub pinyon pines. The others stopped on either side of him, trying to see what had caused Cuchillo concern.

"What is it?" Juh asked. "I see nothing."

"Four white men. Not soldiers. One rides a big black horse and he wears buckskins. One is old . . . I could see his white hair. He rides a bay. He has a gray hat covering his face. Another with silver hair rides a red horse, but he sits straight and does not appear to be old in spite of his hair. One more rides slowly at the rear on a chestnut, slumped over his saddle, dressed like the whites who work with cows. They are being very cautious. The tall man on the black horse looked up at this mountain and quickly led the other white-eyes into a dry streambed, as if he saw us. They are staying out of sight now."

"No white man could see us hidden in these trees," Ishton said. "White men are fools. Careless. They know nothing of stalking an enemy or hiding themselves."

"This tall one is different," Cuchillo promised, for he felt sure the bigger white man in buckskins had seen them, or noticed movement in the pines. "He looked up here and turned his horse too quickly to ride out of sight. He saw something—perhaps only a shadow moving among these trees—and he is taking no chances. He may be a scout for the soldiers, one who knows our ways. His leggings are like those of the Utes or the Arapaho from the cold country to the north. The two with white hair also wear deerskins. These whites are not soldiers or builders of sod houses who plant seeds in the ground. The one on the black horse watches everything."

"What should we do?" Juh asked. "Kill them?"

Cuchillo gave the dry streambed's wandering course a close examination. There were few places where they could ambush men who were careful, watchful, expecting trouble.

Farther up the streambed, where it came down out of the steeper hills from the high peaks, clusters of trees and rocks might offer the right spot if the white men continued to ride along the bottom of the wash.

"One of us must ride back to the village and warn Naiche of these four white-eyes coming into the mountains," Cuchillo said. "Juh, you ride back to the canyon. Ishton and Tao and I will watch these whites to see where they go, and if they start along any of the trails we will find the right spot and then we will kill them."

Juh said nothing and turned his horse, heeling it to a trot back through the pinyons, swinging due south when he was off the skyline.

Cuchillo studied the streambed. He was still sure the tall white man had seen them, for now all four men were staying out of sight at the bottom of the wash, moving slowly, for no dust arose from the hooves of their horses in the still morning air as it would if they were pushing their mounts at a faster gait than a walk.

"I see nothing," Ishton said, a thin young warrior full of courage but with little battle experience—unlike Cuchillo, who had fought the bluecoats for many years.

"This is what troubles me," Cuchillo replied. "Very few white men know how to disappear into the face of Earth Mother like an Apache, or how to move without leaving a trace for an Apache eye to see."

Tao pointed to a group of sparrows suddenly leaving the limbs of a mesquite thicket on the banks of the streambed, flying west as if something had startled them. "There, Cuchillo. The birds tell us where they are now. They fly away from the approaching horses. The white-eyes are coming into the hills by following the dry stream. If they continue along the course of the stream, they will come to the deer trail that will take them to Deer Springs Canyon."

Cuchillo watched the flight of the birds. They flew a few hundred yards westward and then settled into the brush. "Yes, the birds announce their movements. They ride slowly, for the sparrows do not go far. If the birds fly again, we will know these whites are climbing into the mountains looking for us as scouts for the bluecoats."

"Then we must kill them before they return to the fort

when they find our tracks," Ishton said. "If we do not, they will bring the soldiers to our camp at the springs."

"Wait for the sparrows," Cuchillo told him. "If they rise again, we will ride higher and find a place in the rocks where killing them will be easy. Remember your training as warriors in the days before we were taken to the reservation. Patience and surprise will give us the advantage."

Moments passed, and then the sparrows fluttered skyward again as Cuchillo had been certain they would.

"They are looking for us. No one rides into these mountains without a purpose. Follow me. Ride slowly so we send no dust into the air. We will find a killing place where the streambed comes down from the edge of the mountains."

Cuchillo wheeled his horse and led Ishton and Tao off the back of the hilltop. They would ride many extra miles to stay out of sight of these white men, until they found the right spot to lay in wait for a deadly ambush.

Tao lay behind a slab of stone, hidden in its shadow so the sun would not reflect off the barrel of his Winchester, giving the white-eyes a warning of his presence.

Ishton rested on his belly behind fans of yucca spines on a ledge above the creekbed, where he had a view of the rocky bottom of the wash, his rifle barrel covered with a soldier's shirt taken from one of the dead by Isa's warriors.

Cuchillo hid behind a crevice between two jutting outcrops of stone on the other side of the wash, only the top of his head and eyes peering above the cut in the rocks, giving him a clear view of the path the white men were following as they climbed into the Dragoons.

The flight of more startled birds pointed to the progress of the white-eyes as they were climbing into the eastern edge of the mountain range, although Cuchillo was puzzled by their slow movements. It was as if they stopped often. These were the actions of cautious, experienced men who understood the ways of battle.

And, too, these whites were careful never to show themselves, staying close to the edge of the wash in deeper shadows as the sun lowered in the western skies. It was further proof that they intended to enter the Dragoons unseen, tracking Naiche and his band so they could lead the soldiers to their camp at Deer Springs.

Time passed slowly, and now no more birds darted from the brush and trees near the streambed.

They have stopped, Cuchillo thought, pondering it, wondering why. Were they only resting their horses, as white-eyes did so often?

He cocked an ear to a dry desert breeze, listening for the slightest sound. All was silent around him, and the silence became more troubling as it lengthened. Why had the white men stopped? There was no water in the wash for their horses, and very little shade. Were they waiting for darkness to continue their climb? He was sure of one thing . . . these were not ordinary whites, by their dress and their great caution.

A gust of wind swirled down the slopes behind Cuchillo, and for a moment tiny clouds of dust arose from patches of thin soil around them. He blinked to rid his eyes of gritty particles and swept the bottom of the creek again.

A faint sound came from the yuccas where Ishton was hiding, a strange noise, hard to identify. Cuchillo knew the sounds of Earth Mother's creatures well, and he knew at once something was wrong.

Very slowly he raised his rifle to his shoulder, keeping its gleaming barrel in the shadow of the rocks around him. He thumbed back the hammer on the Winchester, tensed, sensing danger was near.

Then he saw movement in the yucca plants. Something was tossed from Ishton's hiding place, an object Cuchillo could not identify at first. It flew into the air, ball-like, and then tumbled down the bank of the wash, landing in the gravel and sand with a soft thump.

The muscles in Cuchillo's cheeks tightened, for now he recognized what had been thrown from the ledge. Ishton's head, severed at the neck, lay in a spreading puddle of blood on the gravel at the bottom of the creek.

In that instant he understood what was happening. One of the white men had somehow been silent enough to slip up behind Ishton, explaining the long silence and the reason why the whites had stopped somewhere farther down the wash. They were stalking Cuchillo and his warriors, as impossible a feat as that seemed for white-eyes, who were known by all the Apache tribes for their foolish blunders in battle. The hunters had now become the hunted.

He glanced over his shoulder, carefully checking every rock and clump of brush behind him. He saw nothing, and quickly turned his attention back to the far side of the stream.

Time seemed frozen. Cuchillo looked again at Ishton's bloody head resting at the bottom of the wash. The white man who killed him so silently was skilled, a true warrior with white skin, but no matter how carefully Cuchillo studied the far side of the cutbank he found nothing, no target for his rifle, no sign of movement anywhere.

A piercing cry came from the rocks where Tao waited in ambush. Then the sound became muffled, a strangling noise, before it faded to silence. Had Tao killed the white-eye with his knife? Cuchillo wondered.

He soon found an answer. Tao's coppery body was pushed off the top of the cutbank, a crimson stain smearing the rocky side of the wash as he slid, head-first, down to the floor of the stream, a huge gash across his throat pumping blood over the smooth gravel where he lay on his back, dying.

Now Cuchillo faced four white men alone. Of far more importance, Naiche and the others had to be told about these white-skinned warriors who fought like Apaches, with cunning and soundless stalking skills unlike anything Cuchillo had ever witnessed in all his battles with white men.

Very slowly, Cuchillo backed away from the crevice and

bent down in a crouch, moving on the balls of his feet, his moccasins whispering across the rocks toward their horses. He moved from one clump of brush to another, darting among the yucca and cacti, pausing briefly to examine his surroundings before he moved again.

He came to the draw where their horses were tethered and swung up on his bay, gathering up the other horses' jaw reins before he drummed his heels into the gelding's sides. Riding at a fast trot, he moved north and west, away from the white men, staying to low ground wherever he could to keep from being seen until he reached a steep trail twisting into the high peaks.

Cuchillo was worried. Naiche would not be pleased to hear of what had happened. At least two of the white-eyes coming into the mountains fought like Apaches. They would be hard men to kill.

Chapter 24

As the last brave in the bunch rode away, bent low over the neck of his pony, Hawk eared back the hammer of his Sharps .50 caliber rifle and drew a bead on his back.

Just before he pulled the trigger, Falcon appeared out of the nearby brush and put a hand on the barrel, forcing it down.

"Hold on, Hawk. Let him go," he said in a low voice.

Hawk let out the breath he'd been holding as he took aim. "Why, Falcon? The bastard's sure to go back to the main camp and warn the others we're on our way."

Falcon nodded, his eyes on the retreating Indian. "I know, and that's just what I want him to do. Like I said, I want Naiche and the others to know someone's on their back trail, someone who can kill just as good as they can."

He gave a tight grin. "I hope he gets an itch in the back of his neck and thinks about who may be behind him every time he ventures out of his stronghold. Maybe, just maybe, it'll distract him from thoughts of killing other whites long enough for the army to get on his trail."

Just then, Cal Franklin and Jasper Meeks walked their horses up out of the old riverbed.

Meeks stared at the tiny figure in the distance as he rode over the horizon. "Why'd you fellers let him get away?" he asked, a worried look on his face.

Hawk spit out his cud of tobacco, a sour expression on his face. "Falcon's got it in his mind to give Naiche somethin' to worry about."

Falcon swung up on Diablo's back in a fluid motion. "I'm going to follow him. With any luck he'll lead us to Naiche's main camp. Y'all follow along behind, and I'll mark the trail as I go."

Meeks stared at Falcon as if he thought the man was crazy to be heading to the main body of Indians. "You ride with your guns loose, Falcon, an' keep a tight rein on your scalp lock, you hear?"

Falcon nodded and pulled Diablo's head around and started out after the brave.

"How about we take a noonin'?" Cal said, rubbing his stomach. "I'm so hungry I could eat a lizard."

Falcon followed Cuchillo at a safe distance, being careful not to stray from thick brush and wooded areas or to reveal himself against a skyline on the horizon. He knew Apaches were expert trackers, but were less adept at discovering if someone was following them, the experience being so rare in their past. As he rode, he occasionally leaned over to break a twig next to the trail, or to blaze a mark on the trunk of a tree so the others would have no difficulty following his lead.

Just before dusk, when the sun was disappearing over distant peaks and the temperature was falling toward freezing, Falcon saw Cuchillo stop his pony and put his hands to his mouth. He heard the faint cry of a horned owl come from Cuchillo's direction.

So that's the signal a friend is on the way in, Falcon thought, nodding to himself as he heard the answering cry of another hoot owl from the ridges directly in front of the brave he was following.

Falcon dismounted and tied Diablo to a tree, leaving him plenty of slack so he could graze on the sweet, green mountain grass growing next to the trail. He unhooked the rawhide hammer thongs on his pistols and positioned his Winchester rifle across his back on its rawhide sling. He knew if he had to use either of these weapons he was as good as dead, for the sound of a gunshot would bring the Indians in Naiche's band boiling out of their camp like a swarm of angry hornets whose nest has been poked with a stick.

He slipped his Arkansas Toothpick out of its scabbard, hoping to be able to find the sentry before he was spotted.

As shadows melded with darkening air and night fell, Falcon began to crawl toward where he'd heard the owl hoot answer to Cuchillo's call. He moved as slowly as molasses in February, making sure not to put his feet on anything that would make a noise and give his position away.

Taking over three hours to travel just a hundred yards, he took a deep breath through his nose. He could smell the pungent aroma of unwashed Indian nearby. Grateful the Apache didn't much believe in baths, especially in the winter months, he put the blade of his knife between his teeth and crawled forward on all fours.

Peeking between the branches of a mesquite tree, Falcon saw the sentry ten feet ahead, his back against a boulder, his arms folded, his head nodding on his chest, as if tired from a long watch.

Falcon hunkered down, deciding the brave must be near the end of his shift on watch and electing to wait for his replacement so he would have more time after killing him to look around before the man would be missed.

It was lucky he did, for no more than ten minutes later a soft call came from the darkness and the sentry jerked awake, his hand on his rifle.

A laughing young man walked up and slapped him on the shoulder, speaking words in Apache that sounded like teasing the man for being asleep on duty. After a couple more jibes, the newcomer took his place with his back to the same boulder, and the first sentry walked down a well-beaten path toward the valley floor below.

When Falcon could no longer hear his progress through the brush, he searched the ground at his feet with his hands in the darkness. After a moment, he found a small rock and picked it up.

Slowly, he stood, staying close to the trunk of the mesquite tree so as not to give the Indian any glimpse of movement. He raised his hand and pitched the stone over the brave's head, where it landed in a briar patch a few yards from the man.

The Indian jerked, his head whipping to the side and his rifle coming up as he turned toward the sound. Falcon felt his body stiffen as he placed his hand over the Indian's mouth and bent his head back, exposing his neck to the blade of the Arkansas Toothpick.

Seconds later, with no sound having escaped the sentry's lips, Falcon lowered his dead body to the ground. He picked up the Winchester rifle, took the deerskin pouch of ammunition the man was carrying, and crept to the ridge overlooking the valley below.

Naiche has picked his campsite well, Falcon thought. The valley was deep enough for several fires to be burning and not be seen from above. There was also a small stream running through the middle of the valley floor which would provide water for drinking and washing without anyone having to leave the protection of the valley.

As he glanced around the walls of the ridges overlooking the campsite, Falcon saw many dark openings in the stone of the cliffs, some with small fires burning inside them. Even though conventional wisdom would say it was foolish to camp in a valley, the presence of sentries could protect against unwanted visitors, and the number and placement of the caves would provide enough hiding places that it would take an army to ferret the Indians out. As bloodthirsty as Naiche's reputation was, Falcon knew he was dealing with someone skilled in the art of warfare, especially as practiced by the Apaches on their home territory.

Pulling his binoculars from his belt, Falcon surveyed the campsite below. He soon found the largest wickiup and saw the brave he'd been following talking animatedly with a man he could only suppose was Naiche. Evidently the brave was telling Naiche of the killings by the white men.

Suddenly, Naiche reached out and grabbed the brave in front of him by the throat. He began yelling at him as he shook him like a dog with a bone. *I guess he's pissed off at that fellow for leaving his friends behind to die,* Falcon thought.

Finally, Naiche pushed the man away and turned his back on him, calling out in a harsh voice and summoning others to gather around him. As he spoke to the group of young braves, he began pointing out certain men and then pointing off in different directions.

Uh-oh, Falcon thought, *looks as if he's going to send out war parties. Probably going to be coming after us for what we did to his men. I'd better hightail it on back up the trail and make sure Hawk and the others get to a good hiding place before those Indians get there. Maybe, just maybe we can arrange a little surprise to be waiting for them when they arrive.*

He backed quietly out of sight of the ridge, then sprinted to where he'd left Diablo. He had to make tracks to get back to Hawk and Cal and Jasper in time to setup an ambush for the Indians.

Chapter 25

Isa, Nana, Juh, and seven more experienced warriors were scattered throughout a pinyon pine forest, along a trail climbing into the western edge of the Dragoons. It was the same trail where the braves had been killed who were driving the cattle, goats, mules, and horses taken from the Bisbee settlement during the raid. Several of the warriors cast angry eyes at the tree where the bodies had been found hanging, mutilated to prevent their entrance to the Land of Shadows in the hereafter.

After Naiche heard the report from Cuchillo, that four white men were approaching from the east and had managed to kill three of his followers even as they lay in ambush, he became furious. He berated Cuchillo for leaving his companions to die without exacting vengeance on the white-eyes, stopping just short of calling him a coward.

He called a meeting of all the young braves and formed them into war parties, sending them out in all directions to ambush any soldiers following trails that would ultimately take them to the Apaches' new stronghold at Deer Springs. Naiche sent over a dozen warriors to the east, led by Cuchillo, to halt the four whites who had killed Tao and Ishton. With narrowed eyes and tight lips, he told Cuchillo not to return to camp without the scalps of the killers on his pony.

Isa led a band of nine warriors to guard the western approaches to higher elevations, fully expecting a blue-coat patrol to return with capable trackers to follow the trail left by so many head of stolen livestock after the Bisbee raid.

Naiche led six seasoned fighters to the north to keep an eye on soldier movements coming from the direction of Fort Thomas. Chokole rode with him, leaving Delshi, Naiche's half-brother who was burdened by an old leg wound that would not heal, in charge of protecting the camp at Deer Springs with seventeen of the youngest Apaches. It was from the west where the chief of the rene-gades believed the greatest danger would come, despite what Cuchillo told him about the stealth of the white men dressed in buckskins advancing slowly into the Dragoons who were able to kill two Apaches at close quarters with a knife without making a sound.

Naiche was correct to assume the soldiers would come first from the west; now, riding in a column of paired cavalrymen, thirty-two heavily armed troopers climbed the steep game trail along distinctive two-toed tracks left by cattle and goats and the prints of other stolen Bisbee live-stock moving toward high grasslands. Isa had spotted the soldiers easily from a lookout spot on the side of a moun-tain. He prepared his ambush where a pinyon forest would hide his warriors until the bluecoats were caught in a deadly cross fire. Picking just the right spot had taken considerable time. He finally decided to attack the bluecoats just beyond the spot where his brothers still hung from the tree. Isa felt it would be fitting to mark their death ground with the deaths of many white-eyes.

An Indian rode out in front of the cavalry, his face to the ground.

Nana spoke softly. "The scout who leads them is one of our own people, the old Mescalero named Jaseh. He betrays his own blood brothers for bottles of crazy water and extra rations of food. I have seen him at the fort many times, at the building where the blue coats get *boisa pah*. He tells the bluecoat chief about Apaches who talk of escaping from the reservation, giving him their names so they will be put in the iron cages and given only moldy bread and water. I am sure he is the one who betrayed Geronimo to the white soldier chief two winters ago.''

Isa did not recognize the old Apache, for there were hundreds of Indians being held at Fort Thomas and more arrived with each passing moon.

"He will be the first to die,'' Nana promised, a savage look crossing his face. "My first bullet will pass through his black heart.''

Isa felt sure of their success. With ten repeating rifles being fired from fortified positions behind pinyon trunks and rocks, the bluecoats would have no escape, even though their number was high. "We must wait until they are between us. Let the first riders pass. The old one, Jaseh, will not see us. He only looks at the tracks. Only once has he looked up at the mountains, and he saw nothing.''

Juh was on the far side of the trail with four more Apache riflemen, spread out, well concealed. When the column of troopers was between Isa's warriors and those with Juh, the killing would begin.

He could hear the click of the soldiers' iron horseshoes on rock clearly now, and see the faces of troopers riding at the front of the column. His heart began to beat rapidly. While a prisoner at the fort, he had dreamed about his days as a free Apache and the wars they fought against the first white settlers and bluecoats.

Isa readied his rifle against his shoulder, taking pains to keep the barrel from reflecting any of the slanted sunlight coming from a setting sun. Shadows cast by the sun would help hide his warriors from the soldiers' eyes.

The rattle of curb chains and the clatter of hooves grew louder.

"Our time has come,'' Nana whispered, sighting along

the barrel of his Winchester, a deerskin pouch of bullets lying on fallen pine needles near his elbow.

Captain Buford Jones felt dizzy, light-headed, at the higher altitude after their hard push across the flatland desert between the mountains and Bisbee. He felt satisfaction after the old Apache drunk picked up the renegades' trail with relative ease. He also secretly despised old Jaseh for being so willing to double-cross his own race for a few bottles of rotgut corn whiskey flavored with tobacco.

Sergeant Skinner interrupted Buford's thoughts. "I don't like the looks of them trees up yonder, Cap'n. They could be hidin' in them pines waitin' for us."

"You worry too much, Sergeant. Those Apaches have gone deep into these goddamn miserable dry mountains. They'll play hide-and-seek with us when we get up there, but there's nothing to worry about while we're down this low. It's when we get up to those mountaintops that we'd best be vigilant and post extra guards at night."

Skinner didn't appear convinced. "That half drunk Mescalero could be leadin' us right where they want us. He could be in on the whole thing, pretendin' to take us to Naiche an' the rest of 'em when he's really settin' us up to get our asses shot off by our own damn rifles they stole."

"You'll die young of stomach ailments if you keep worrying so much, Skinner."

Sergeant Skinner wagged his head. "All I'm doin' is tryin' to stay alive, Cap'n. An' I sure as hell don't like the looks of them trees on both sides of this trail we're followin'. Trees is mighty damn close on both sides."

Buford had become irritated by Skinner's constant whining about the pine trees, and he said so. "If you're so damn worried about riding through that thicket, then you have my permission to find a way to ride around it."

Skinner fell silent, yet his full attention remained focused on the pinyons, searching for anything that might be a hint of a bushwhacking in the making.

Jaseh continued to read the ground as he led the cavalry-men higher up the side of a tree-studded mountain, winding back and forth with the old game trail where the prints of livestock were plain.

Buford turned back in the saddle to inspect his troops, and the terrain behind them. Off in the distance the desert they had crossed stretched to the horizon, empty, only the desert plants casting lengthening shadows eastward as the sun became a fiery ball in the western sky.

Jaseh apparently felt no apprehension riding toward the pine trees Sergeant Skinner was so worried about. The old Apache looked up at the trail ahead now and then, but he continued to lead them upslope toward the forest without hesitation—a good sign in Buford's view that no danger lurked in the pinyons. An Apache, even an old drunk like Jaseh, would know if they were about to be lured into a trap.

Captain Jones's heart hammered when he saw Jaseh suddenly sit bolt upright in his saddle and rein his horse to an abrupt halt. Buford unsnapped the flap over his pistol and warily rode up next to the scout.

"Jaseh, what the hell are you doing stopping? Have you lost the trail?" he asked irritably.

The old scout didn't answer, just inclined his head toward what his eyes had never left.

Buford followed his gaze, and came near losing his lunch. Three rotting Apache corpses were hanging from the lower limb of a tree next to the trail. There were only gaping holes where their eyes had been, and their throats were cut so deep white neck bones could be seen. The feet were just inches from the ground, and scavengers had eaten off the toes and lower part of the legs. The bodies were almost black from the blowflies covering them like a blanket.

"Jesus God Awmighty," Sergeant Skinner whispered from next to Captain Buford, "ain't that a sight?"

Buford tried to speak, but had to first swallow the gorge

rising in his throat at the gruesome sight. "Jaseh, what do you make of that?"

The Indian didn't answer at first, but merely shook his head. After a moment, he turned in his saddle and stared at Buford with frightened eyes. "Evil spirits live in this forest. No white man would kill like this, and the People do not kill their own in this manner, not even in war."

"Maybe these were deserters or somethin'," Skinner said, "An' were killed by Naiche to set an example to others."

Jaseh shook his head. He knew Apaches were casually brutal about killing and mutilating whites, but even in the rare instances where Apache killed Apache, it was done with respect, and the bodies were never mutilated after death . . . never. Something was terribly wrong here, but he didn't know what.

Buford took a deep drink of water from his canteen, hoping it would settle his stomach. He didn't particularly want the humiliation of vomiting in front of his men.

"Go on, keep following the track, Jaseh. We're burning daylight, and I want to get to a suitable place to make camp before sundown."

Jaseh cast a worried glance at Buford, but reluctantly heeled his horse forward.

They rode into the trees without mishap, and Skinner seemed to be relieved. Buford hadn't given the order for his men to draw their rifles, simply because he did not share Skinner's concerns over an ambush at these lower altitudes. It was when they hit the higher parts of the Dragoons that he expected to find Apaches, but most certainly not here.

He relaxed against the cantle of his cavalry saddle and took in a deep breath of pine-scented air, relieved to be climbing away from the horrible sight behind them.

A cracking noise came from Buford's left, just as he was enjoying the smell of pine. The old Mescalero riding out in front of the column was swept from the back of his horse as if he'd been met by a mighty gust of wind.

Sergeant Skinner stood in his stirrups as Jaseh went tumbling to the ground with blood spouting from a hole above his right ear. "Indians!" Skinner cried, jerking his Winchester from its saddle boot.

A series of thundering explosions came at Buford and his troopers from both sides of the trail. Horses nickered, rearing on their hind legs, pawing the air with fright as men shouted and cursed while clawing for their guns.

Sizzling balls of molten lead came flying from every direction amid the booming of guns. Behind Buford, soldiers began screaming with pain, some toppling to the earth clutching mortal wounds as others merely tried to stay aboard their terrified horses.

Buford, thinking as fast as he could despite the confusion and hail of bullets all around him, knew what he had to do. He pulled his rifle, holding a tight grip on the reins to control his plunging sorrel, and yelled, "Retreat!" as loudly as he could.

From the corner of his eye he saw Sergeant Skinner's left tunic sleeve erupt in a spray of blood and shreds of blue fabric. Skinner yelped and dropped his rifle to grab his wound with his free hand, wheeling his horse downslope.

Buford jerked his sorrel around while the banging of heavy bore rifle fire seemed to grow louder. What he saw across the lower part of the trail made him queasy, sick to his stomach, his throat filling with bitter bile. Dead or dying troopers lay everywhere. Spooked horses with empty saddles galloped back down the incline.

A bullet tore through Buford's cavalry hat, lifting it off his head as he was digging his spurs into the sorrel's sides. A burning sensation spread across his scalp just when his horse lunged into a headlong run.

The explosions continued, an endless wall of noise, and the air was filled with speeding bullets. Suddenly his vision blurred, and his surroundings turned an odd shade of red. He felt something wet dripping down his forehead and sleeved it away, then he rubbed his eyes to clear them as his horse charged through the melee. His sleeve was bright red with blood, and his scalp felt as if it was on fire.

Galloping past wounded men lying on both sides of the trail, he tasted fear on the tip of his tongue, wondering if he would get out of this alive.

Sergeant Skinner, gripping his bleeding arm, galloped past him on a faster horse. Skinner leaned over his chestnut's neck to make himself as small a target as possible, and after Buford saw this he did likewise, bent forward in the saddle, making no effort to return the bushwhackers' fire.

"Retreat!" he bellowed again, knowing that any soldier with his wits about him would already be trying to get out of range of the deadly guns aimed at them.

A young trooper from Indiana—Buford recalled his name was Smith—was riding hell-for-leather down the incline ahead of him when a slug struck his horse. The dark brown gelding went down, crumpling underneath Private Smith, tossing him forward into the air as though he'd sprouted wings.

Buford understood that duty required him to stop and give aid to one of his men, yet fear forced him to abandon any notion of helping the boy. He sent his horse racing past Smith's prone form until it galloped to the bottom of the trail behind Sergeant Skinner's mount. Together, along with seven surviving cavalrymen, they charged out onto the desert plain until their winded mounts forced them to slow to a trot, then a halt.

Buford looked back up the mountain slope. He could see bodies lying everywhere . . . some wounded men were crawling toward safety, crying out for help. Loose horses were scattered all over the mountainside.

"Jesus," Buford whispered, his hands shaking.

He heard Sergeant Skinner whimpering with pain. "I just had a feelin' they were in them goddamn trees," Skinner said, his face twisted into a grimace.

Buford glanced up at the mountain trail again. The shooting had all but stopped, and now Apaches were running from one fallen body to the next, scalping some of his men while they were still alive.

Buford heard their screams, and he knew he would hear them in his sleep for the rest of his life.

"I sure as hell wish I'd listened to you," he told Skinner, watching the grisly work of the Apaches from a half a mile away. "Next time—if there is a next time—I'll damn sure pay more attention to your advice," he said, already planning on how to explain this fiasco to his superiors back at the fort. He knew his career hung in the balance, and he would need a good story to keep his stripes.

The shrieks of men being mutilated by Apache knives echoed from the forested slope. "Dear God," he muttered, trying to control the tremors in his limbs. "They're gutting our men while they're still alive. What kind of savages are these damn Indians, anyway?"

"The worst kind there is," Skinner replied in a weak voice. "They ain't human, Cap'n. The army should'a killed every last one of 'em when we got 'em to Fort Thomas."

Although he did not say so aloud, after today's events he wholeheartedly agreed. Total extermination of the Apache race was the only sensible solution.

"Let's head back to the fort," he said. "The colonel isn't going to like what I have to tell him."

Nine survivors of the ambush rode off to the north, leaving the screams of their dying fellow troopers to resound over an empty desert.

As he rode, Captain Buford thought once again of the mutilated Apache bodies they'd found hanging by the trail. Could it be that the army had an ally they knew nothing about? Perhaps some other Indian tribe was making war on the Apaches. It was an interesting theory, one he would have to share with Colonel Grant. It might take the old man's mind off his failure as a leader. At least, it would give the colonel something else to think about besides how many men Buford had gotten killed, and how he had escaped with his life while so many others died.

Chapter 26

It was well past midnight when Buford led what remained of his Company through the gates at Fort Thomas. Sergeant Skinner had lost so much blood he had to be held in the saddle for the final few hours, riding across a starlit desert with a tight bandage around his shoulder to stem the blood flow.

Buford spoke to one of his men. "Take Skinner to the post surgeon at once. I have to awaken Colonel Grant to give him my report."

Troopers riding on either side of Sergeant Skinner assisted him toward the surgeon's quarters while Buford rode across the fort compound to the colonel's small house, set apart from the soldiers' barracks.

He swung down, weary to the bone, his mind dulled by what he had seen when the Apaches attacked. He'd mourned over the loss of so many of his men, angry at himself for trusting Jaseh to warn them of danger ahead and for ignoring Sergeant Skinner's words of caution about a possible ambush.

He climbed the porch steps and rapped softly on Colonel Grant's door, wondering if he would be stripped of his rank for having taken his men into an outright disaster, a virtual slaughter. It was a clear demonstration of failure at military leadership, an end to his dreams of a promotion.

Moments later a lantern flickered to life behind one of the cabin windows. The colonel's wife came to the door clad in a long cotton sleeping gown.

"Yes?" she asked, peering past a crack in the door to see who had disturbed them at this late hour.

"Captain Buford Jones, ma'am. I'm sorry to awaken you so late, but I must speak to the colonel at once."

"Please come in, Captain. Take a chair and I'll wake my husband."

He walked in, hat in hand, and sat in a rocking chair near a window. The lantern glowing softly on a coffee table cast moving shadows on the cabin walls.

"This could be the end of everything for me," he whispered to himself.

Colonel Grant ambled into the front room in his undershorts and socks, giving Buford a sleepy but wary look. "What is it, Captain? Why have you come to see me in the middle of the night when you should be patrolling that region south of the massacre at Bisbee?"

"We were ambushed, sir," Buford began, standing up to give a formal salute before he spoke.

"Ambushed? Where? Do we have casualties?"

"Very heavy casualties I'm afraid, sir. We lost twenty-four men to a surprise attack as we entered the Dragoon mountain range. The old Mescalero, Jaseh, picked up the trail of the raiding party and we followed it to the western edge of a northern section of the mountains. As you know, sir, the Dragoons are at least sixty miles long, and we expected to meet armed resistance once we entered the higher regions. But they laid a trap for us at a wooded spot just as we were beginning our climb. They took us completely by surprise."

Grant came over to a bullhide chair across from Buford and sat down, staring him in the face, wide awake now.

"Did I hear you correctly, Captain? Twenty-four troopers from Company D are dead?"

"Yessir," he replied, dry-mouthed, watching the anger come to life in the colonel's eyes. He hastened to explain. "They shot the old Apache first. They were well-hidden on both sides of the trail in a dense pine forest. There was absolutely no warning."

"The Mescalero . . . Jaseh. Was he drunk?"

"No sir. I kept his bottles of whiskey in my saddlebags to prevent just such a thing. I told him he could only drink after we camped for the night."

"And your Indian scout still was unaware of the renegades' presence before the ambush?"

"Totally. As I said, he was the first man killed when the shooting started."

Grant took a deep breath and closed his eyes for a moment, a pained expression on his face. Buford expected the worst from his commanding officer. Loss of rank. A transfer to one of the cold northern Territories where soldiers froze to death as often as they died in battle. Or a court-martial.

"Twenty-four men," Grant said quietly, blinking, fixing Buford with an icy look.

"Nine of us made it out alive. Sergeant Skinner has a deep wound in his shoulder. He's at the surgeon's quarters now for medical attention." Buford paused long enough to show Colonel Grant the bloody slice across his scalp. "I narrowly avoided death myself, sir," he said, pointing to his wound. "Had the bullet been only an inch or two lower, I would be lying dead on that trail with my men."

"What is your estimate of the number of renegades who attacked you?"

"At least fifty, sir. We were badly outnumbered," he lied, having no idea how many rifles had been firing at them when the ambush took place. "Quite possibly more."

"Fifty," Grant muttered. "Our roll call of the Apaches held prisoner here showed only thirty men were missing. This could mean Geronimo has joined forces with the

Chiricahua chief Naiche. Or it may well be that some of Naiche's renegades are escapees from San Carlos. I will wire the Indian Agent there this morning. If Naiche has fifty armed Indians under his leadership, equipped with our own repeating rifles, I'll be forced to send for reinforcements."

"I would strongly recommend that, sir," Buford said as a way of pleading his own case. "There may have been far more than fifty Apaches shooting at us. It was hard to make an accurate count while we were under heavy fire."

Grant slumped lower in his chair. "Let us pray the other companies we have searching for these runaways have fared better than you did. This calls for a new tactic. I must combine what forces we have into a single unit and drive straight into the heart of the Dragoons to ferret them out and destroy them, or bring them back in chains."

"I wholeheartedly agree, sir. We can put roughly a hundred and fifty cavalrymen afield, leaving a small force to keep a sufficient guard on the Apaches here at the reservation. With one hundred and fifty armed cavalry, we can strike Chief Naiche with overwhelming superiority."

"Yes," Grant whispered, lost in thought. "This calls for a sound strategy and superior numbers when we engage them. I was unaware they had grown so strong. Based on your report, I am quite sure a large number of Apaches have slipped away from the San Carlos reservation. I'll wire them at dawn. Get some rest, Captain. I shall send messengers out to collect the other Companies we have in the field, and preparations will be made to launch a major offensive." He briefly held his head in his hands before he continued. "All these Indian attacks, the tremendous death toll, and the way these Indians carve up their victims will make newspaper headlines all across the country. When my report reaches Washington it will sound as if I've been unable to put down a major Indian insurrection. There will be a hue and cry from all quarters to have me transferred, or demoted. This is the worst possible event a military commander can endure."

Buford allowed himself to relax. The colonel wasn't blaming him for what had happened. He stood up abruptly and moved toward the door. "Goodnight, Colonel," he said, letting himself out.

"Yes, goodnight, Captain Jones," Grant said as Buford was closing the door behind him.

He untied his horse and led it toward the stable, relieved at the colonel's reaction. He hadn't even had to distract the colonel with the tale of the mutilated Apaches, after all. A small white lie had salvaged the career of Buford Jones, a lie no one could dispute since it was truly impossible to judge how many Indians had set upon them on the mountainside. His surviving troopers, even Sergeant Skinner, would not dispute his estimate.

Buford unsaddled his horse and put him in a corral. More than anything else, he was thankful to be alive. He would not think about how he had abandoned his men under fire, at least not now.

He headed for the surgeon's quarters to see if he needed stitches where his hair had been parted by a bullet.

Isa stood with Juh while the others collected every weapon and bullet from the bodies of the dead bluecoats. The night was dark, an inky sky sprinkled with stars above the pine limbs over their heads.

"It was good," Juh said, four ripe scalps hanging from his waistband, blood dribbling down his bare legs. "The white-eye soldiers are stupid. They know nothing about making war. They rode into the jaws of our death trap like men who were blind, and they were easy to kill."

Isa heard mounted warriors coming back with the stray horses frightened away by gunshots, free to run loose when their riders were killed. The horses and ammunition carried behind the soldiers' saddles would be valuable as the war continued. "It was a great victory," Isa agreed. "Naiche will be pleased when we bring back more horses and rifles and bullets."

"And the scalps of our enemies," Juh added with a note of pride in his voice.

In a patch of starlight, sprawled on his back across the trail, lay the traitor Mescalero who brought the bluecoats to them. "We have another enemy now," he said gravely. "The old Apache betrayed us. There will be others, our own blood brothers, who will lead more bluecoats to our village for the price of a few bottles of the white man's crazy water. This will be our greatest danger, that one of our own people who knows the hidden trails and springs in these mountains will bring the enemy to our wickiups."

Juh nodded once. "You speak true words. Even some of the bravest warriors among the People are no longer Apaches in spirit. The reservation has done this to them."

Isa knew how true this was. After years of starvation, rotting food rations on ration day, and brutal punishment at the hands of the soldiers, a growing number of the People had given up in their hearts and minds, adapting to reservation life as little more than shadows of men and women, living in despair, waiting to die. "Some will betray us. More will join us when they hear of our victories."

Juh's grip tightened on the stock of his repeating rifle. "Naiche is a wise chief. He has the courage of a mountain lion. And with the white man's many-shoot guns, we can drive them from our homeland."

"Only if we have warriors to use the magic rifles," Isa warned.

Juh looked at him in the darkness. "Chokole brought us the restless ones from Fort Thomas and San Carlos. More will hear of our battles, and they will come. Naiche must send Chokole back to the reservations, in spite of the danger, to tell our people of this victory, and how strong we are now."

Isa believed this was true. If word could reach San Carlos and Fort Thomas of their success fighting the bluecoats, more Apaches would find hope of returning to the land of their ancestors as free people. "We must go now. Tell the others to ride only where the rocks will hide our tracks.

When we return to the village with horses and guns, Naiche will call for a council fire. Our war drums will beat again. Fresh scalps will hang from lodge poles. It will be as it was before the bluecoats captured us, a time for war and celebration over the defeat of our enemies."

"I can hear the drumbeats and war chants now in my heart," Juh said, walking away to give Isa's instructions to the warriors leading strings of riderless cavalry horses from the forest.

Isa turned to face the east, wondering if Cuchillo had found and killed the four white men yet. From his experience fighting white-eyes, they were no match for the People in combat, and he wondered how Cuchillo had allowed his men to be killed by such as these.

Chapter 27

Cuchillo held up his hand, stopping the twelve riders behind him. "Here is a good place for our ambush," he said, looking left and right at the heavy forest of pine trees on either side of the trail. "The white-eyes who killed our brothers will be coming this way soon. We must seek revenge for the spirits of Tao and Ishton, so they may hunt and fish in the Land of Shadows forever."

Cuchillo had one of the braves lead the ponies off deeper into the forest so their nickering wouldn't alert the whites to their presence. Then he and his band settled in to await the coming of their prey.

Behind Cuchillo and his men, lying flat on their stomachs upslope of the trail, Hawk and Falcon watched the ambush being set through their binoculars.

They had allowed Cuchillo's band to pass by them, knowing it would be easier to surprise them if they came from an unexpected direction.

"How many did you count?" Falcon asked.

"I got it 'bout twelve or thirteen, give or take one or two. How 'bout you?" Hawk answered.

"The same." Falcon took the glasses from his eyes and looked at Hawk. "What do you think? Should we take them out now, or wait and do it later?"

Hawk shrugged, but his eyes were fierce as he replied, "No time like the present. I figure that'll mean twelve less of the bastards to have to worry about later."

Falcon smiled. "A man after my own heart." He hesitated, then asked, "What do you think about Cal and Jasper? Do you think they'll be able to hold their own in a fight?"

Hawk pursed his lips, thinking. "Yeah, if the situation's just right. I know Jasper's had plenty of experience, but Franklin's another matter entirely. I s'pect he'll be all right if the advantage is ours, an' he don't have to do no thinkin'."

Falcon nodded and turned to crawl back up the ridge toward where they'd left Cal and Jasper. Once they got there, Falcon gathered the three men around him as he outlined their plan of attack.

"The Apache are spread out, six men on either side of the trail. Their attention is back toward the east, where they think we'll be coming from. Jasper, I want you and Cal to stay upslope, and have some dynamite ready. Hawk and I will go in silently and take out as many as we can with our knives. When they realize what we're doing and raise the alarm, I want you two to drop a couple of sticks right in amongst them."

"What about you and Hawk?" Cal asked. "Won't you be in danger from the dynamite, too?"

Falcon shook his head. "No. Throw the dynamite as close to the trail as you can. Hawk and I will stay well back from the path, and as soon as we hear any commotion, we'll hit the dirt and get behind something. Any questions?"

Jasper nodded. "Yeah. Why do you and Hawk get all the fun? I'm gettin' kind'a tired of always being on the outside during a fracas."

Hawk glared at him. "Your history in combat don't exactly inspire confidence, Meeks. Last time you had a chance at 'some fun', as you call it, you turned tail and ran."

"Why you—" Meeks began. Falcon stopped him with a hand on his shoulder.

"Settle down, Jasper. It's just that I know Hawk can kill without making any noise. Believe me, you'll get your chance to kill some Indians. Just be patient."

The scout nodded, his face still red from the insult Hawk had given.

Ten minutes later, Falcon was crawling on hands and knees toward the ambushers. He slipped his Arkansas Toothpick from its scabbard and slipped silently around the trunk of a pinyon tree. He threw his left arm around a brave's neck and plunged the knife into the middle of his back, severing the spinal cord and shutting down his brain so fast he didn't have time to make a sound. He lowered the body gently to the carpet of pine needles on the ground, then crept through the brush toward the next Indian.

While moving silently toward his third kill, Falcon heard a scream from the other side of the trail. Evidently one of Hawk's victims managed to yell for help as he was being killed.

Falcon was still five feet from his intended victim when the brave turned at the sound of the yell from nearby. His eyes widened and his face blanched in surprise as he raised his rifle to aim at Falcon.

Falcon reared back and threw his knife as hard as he could, then dived to the side. The Arkansas Toothpick turned over three times and embedded itself in the breast-bone of the Indian, knocking him backward and throwing off his aim just enough to miss Falcon. Though the wound was painful it was not mortal, and the brave levered the Winchester to try and get off another round.

Falcon hit the dirt and rolled once, coming up on his knees with his hands filled with iron. He put his first bullet in the brave's forehead, snapping his head back and flinging him backward into a small bush.

Two more Apaches appeared side-by-side, both firing at the same time at Falcon. He snapped off a shot, but missed as he dove behind a small boulder, the Indians' bullets ricochetting off the stone and showering him with fragments.

Seconds later, a tremendous double explosion shattered the air, the concussion almost rupturing Falcon's ear drums and flattening him to the moist earth below.

An arm and part of a leg landed on the ground next to where Falcon lay, and a fine scarlet mist splattered his clothes. With his ears still ringing from the blast, he peeked over the top of the boulder and saw remnants of the two Indians scattered all over the landscape, next to a large hole in the ground.

He whirled at the sound of a scream from behind him and turned in time to see a yelling Apache running at him with a knife in an outstretched hand.

Falcon had no time to aim his pistol and barely got his hands up in time to block the knife thrust. The two men collided, chest to chest, and went backwards over the rocks. Each grabbed the other's throat and squeezed as they rolled around on the ground.

Falcon had his left hand on the Indian's wrist holding the knife, while his right hand was trying to get a grip on the brave's throat.

After two rolls, the Indian ended up on top, and slowly pushed the knife down towards Falcon's face. He strained, but couldn't stop the knife's slow progress.

Suddenly there was a loud blast and the savage's head seemed to explode, completely disappearing above the eyes, showering Falcon with blood and brains.

He rolled and threw the Indian's dead body off him, and saw Jasper Meeks standing twenty feet away, smoke curling from the barrel of his Winchester.

"Thanks, Jasper," Falcon gasped, aware of how close to death he'd been.

"Think nothing of it, Falcon. All in a day's work."

"Have we got all of them?" Falcon asked as he got to his feet and bent to retrieve his pistols.

"Yep. Twelve are dead, and one's wounded pretty bad."

"Take me to him," Falcon said, sleeving sweat off his forehead.

Meeks walked back toward the trail and stopped next to a body lying on its back, arms flung out, eyes closed.

Falcon nodded, a slow smile curving his lips. "We're in luck, Jasper. That's the leader of this little party, the one we let get away to carry the message to Naiche that we were after him."

Meeks leaned his head to the side, staring at the face of the man on the ground. "If you say so, chief. They all look the same to me."

Falcon pulled his bandanna from around his neck and wrapped it tightly around the bullet crease on Cuchillo's skull, stopping the bleeding.

"I want to keep this one alive if we can. He'll have some mighty interesting things to say to Naiche when they find him."

Hawk and Cal Franklin walked out of the bushes, Hawk holding three scalps in his hand. "You want we should dress what's left of the rest of them up like we did the others, Falcon?" he asked.

Falcon nodded. "Absolutely. It's time we sent Naiche another message. I want him to be convinced that the hounds of hell are on his trail, and won't give up until he's dead. If we can keep him thinking about us, maybe he'll pay less attention to raiding the countryside."

Meeks nodded. "That's so. A man who's worried overly much 'bout his back trail don't always keep his eye on what's up ahead of him."

Chapter 28

Naiche was worried. He had heard thunder in the distance, coming from the direction where he'd sent Cuchillo to find and kill the white-eyes who were following his band. As he glanced skyward, he saw only stars and a half-moon in a clear sky. There were no clouds to account for the sounds he'd heard. He was familiar with the thunder-sticks of the whites, having seen them used to clear tree stumps when he was incarcerated at the fort, and feared it meant Cuchillo and his men were in trouble. He wondered briefly if perhaps Cuchillo might have run into a squad of soldiers, for he couldn't make himself believe for a moment only four whites could give Cuchillo and his twelve braves much of a battle.

He caught Chokole's eye and inclined his head toward a spot near a Juniper tree where they wouldn't be seen by the others milling around the fires.

When she came up to him, a puzzled look in her dark eyes, he bent his head down and spoke in a harsh whisper. "Chokole, I fear Cuchillo may have failed in his mission to kill the white-eyes that murdered Tao and Ishton."

Chokole's eyes widened, but she said nothing, nodding her head to show she understood.

"I want you to take Juh and follow Cuchillo's trail. Find out what has happened." He stopped speaking and looked over her shoulder at the young braves dancing around the fires, smearing their faces with the colored clays and dyes they used as warpaint, laughing and crying out what they were going to do to the bluecoats in their upcoming war.

"I do not want the young ones and the new ones to know of this. I fear it will hurt their spirit if we find Cuchillo's war party has been defeated by only four white-eyes."

Chokole reached out her hand and lightly touched Naiche's shoulder. "Perhaps you are mistaken in your feelings, Chief Naiche. It may be that Cuchillo is merely late in returning and has successfully killed the intruders to our lands."

"I hope you are right, Chokole. But if there are men on our trail who are skilled in the ways of war enough to vanquish a war party that far outnumbers them, then plans will have to be made to remove them from Earth Mother. I will be unable to send out any more raiding parties until this matter is taken care of."

Naiche's head jerked around as a distant coyote howl was heard barking five times, the signal for extreme danger. He turned from Chokole and sprinted to his wickiup, grabbing his Winchester rifle and levering a shell into the chamber as he turned toward the sound.

A young brave could be seen running down the path from the sentry post as fast as he could, looking back over his shoulder as if the devil himself were after him.

Naiche walked rapidly to intercept the brave, having to reach out and grab his arm as he tried to run past.

"Kumo, what is the matter?" Naiche asked, his voice rising in anger at the show of cowardice from his man.

"Up there . . . Jaba has been killed!" the young man shouted, his voice squeaky with fright.

Naiche's eyes narrowed, and his nose dilated at the fear-stink exuding from the frightened brave. "Our sentry has been killed, and you left your post unattended?"

Kumo's face blanched at the tone of Naiche's voice. He suddenly realized he had done the unthinkable: he'd left the camp unguarded.

Naiche backhanded Kumo, knocking him to the dirt. "I will see to your punishment later, Kumo."

Quickly shouting orders, Naiche assembled a group of ten warriors who leapt on their ponies, Winchesters in hand, and galloped up the trail toward the lookout area.

When they arrived at the spot, Naiche posted two warriors to keep watch for intruders, and he walked to the boulder where the sentry was stationed. His stomach lurched at the sight awaiting him, and he realized why Kumo had been so upset.

The young brave known as Jaba was sitting on the ground, his back to the boulder and his legs stretched out in front of him. His head had been cut off, and he was holding it under his arm as one would a melon. The freshly scalped skull gleamed in the weak moonlight. Jaba's empty eye sockets were staring at Naiche, as if berating him for starting the war that had gotten him killed.

Juh stepped to the side of the body and knelt down, examining it closely. After a moment, he stood up and walked to stand next to Naiche. "Jaba's Winchester and ammunition pouch are missing, as is his knife," he whispered in a low voice, watching the other braves as they stood in a small group, eyes wide at the sight of their friend butchered like a beef cow.

Naiche stifled an impulse to scream at the moon, feeling the first stirrings of fear in his breast. What manner of white-eyes could so stealthily approach and kill and mutilate one of the People only a hundred yards from his camp and not be heard? There were a handful of whites, men famous as Indian scouts and trackers, that Naiche had heard of who were capable of such a feat. None of these men were known to be in the area.

It was a mystery, and one that must be solved soon, or

the tales of mutilated, butchered warriors would sow the seed of defeatism among his people. They must believe that the white-eyes and bluecoats were inferior fighters if they were to remain committed to making war on the intruders. If his followers ever began to think mighty Apache warriors could be killed as easily as this, it would signal Naiche's defeat before the war even started.

He grabbed Juh by the arm and pulled him aside. "Take Chokole—I have already spoken to her—and find Cuchillo. Do not let the others see you leave."

Juh opened his mouth to speak, but the fury in Naiche's eyes stopped him.

"No questions. Go!" Naiche spat.

A little over two hours later, Chokole and Juh were riding to the east, Juh bent over on his pony's back as he followed the small signs of Cuchillo's passing.

Chokole, who was watching the trail ahead of them, sucked in her breath and reined her pony to a halt.

Juh, hearing the sound, looked up, and felt the hair on the back of his neck stir at what he saw.

In the middle of the trail, hanging spread-eagled on a cross, was Cuchillo. His head flopped forward with his chin on his chest, blood slowly dripping from a wound on his clean-shaven head.

Juh looked at Chokole, and saw for the first time what he took to be fear in her eyes. They both levered rounds into their Winchesters and kneed their ponies slowly forward along the trail, watching the bushes to either side closely for signs of an ambush or trick.

When they got to Cuchillo, they could see he was still alive, though unconscious. While Juh kept watch, Chokole slipped to the ground and walked to Cuchillo.

Slipping her knife from its scabbard, she cut the ropes holding him to the cross and caught him in her arms as he fell forward, gently laying him on the ground.

Finally convinced there was no one waiting to ambush

them, Juh jumped down and knelt next to Cuchillo as Chokole shook him awake.

As his eyes opened, he gasped and began to thrash around, trying to get to his feet, a terrified expression on his face.

Chokole grabbed his shoulder, pressing hard into the flesh with her fingers to get his attention.

"Cuchillo, what happened here?" she asked.

"They came out of the night! There was no warning."

"They attacked you while you were riding after them?" Juh asked.

"No," Cuchillo said, shaking his head but continuing to look over Chokole's shoulder, as if afraid the white men would return. "We were hidden on either side of the trail, waiting in ambush for them to ride into our trap, when suddenly they were there among us."

"You and the other warriors heard nothing of their approach?" Chokole asked.

Cuchillo shook his head. "I do not believe these men walk on the earth as we do. No one could get that close without making a sound."

"What are you saying?" Juh whispered, casting a worried glance at Chokole, as if he feared his friend might be delirious or out of his head.

Cuchillo reached out and grabbed Juh by the arm. "These men who are following us are demons from the underworld. That is the only explanation. They appear without warning and kill without mercy, and then disappear into the night as if they were never there. They do not fight like the other white-eyes and bluecoats."

Juh gently took Cuchillo's hand from his arm and stood up. I go to find the rest of the warriors with Cuchillo."

"See if you can find a pony for Cuchillo to ride back to camp," Chokole said. "I will get him up on his feet."

Twenty yards up the trail, Juh smelled blood and death nearby. He stepped into the brush next to the path and stopped, his eyes wide and his nostrils flaring. All of Cuchillo's warriors were lined up on the ground, their arms outstretched and their fingers touching, as if holding hands. The eyes and scalps had been removed, and their throats had been cut. Several sets of body parts from braves who had literally been blown to pieces in the battle were arranged nearby.

Juh wondered briefly why Cuchillo had been spared, and why the whites had taken the time and trouble to merely shave his head and not scalp him. White-eyes didn't think like Apaches, and Juh knew no one who could understand the strange ways of the intruders.

He glanced over his shoulder toward where Chokole was holding Cuchillo on his feet. He did know one thing. By the time Naiche was finished with Cuchillo, he would probably wish the four white-eyes had killed him like the others, for he was sure to be branded an incompetent warrior or worse, a coward.

Juh shook his head as he looked at what was left of his friends. He didn't believe for a minute what Cuchillo said about these white men being monsters from the underworld, but he knew one thing Cuchillo was right about . . . they certainly fought like demons.

Chapter 29

Falcon and his small band lay on their stomachs in heavy brush less than a hundred yards from the cross where the female Apache and the brave with her found Cuchillo.

Falcon propped his elbows on the ground and watched them through his binoculars as they cut him down. Though he couldn't hear what they were saying, he could read body language well enough to know they were worried, as he had hoped they would be, by what they'd found.

The woman warrior kept looking over her shoulder, her hard face glancing to and fro as if searching for imaginary enemies about to come out of the dark and pounce on them.

The young brave walked stiffly, carrying his rifle at port arms, and even from where Falcon lay he could see the man's knuckles were white where he gripped the long gun as if it were going to jump out of his hands.

Falcon smiled to himself. His plan seemed to be working. The usually imperturbable Apache, people who were generally thought to not know the meaning of fear or trepidation, were beginning to realize there were forces after them they could not escape, forces that could defeat them as easily as they were accustomed to defeating the white man's army. It was just what he wanted them to think.

After the brave managed to find and catch one of the ponies belonging to the war party, he and the woman helped the wounded Indian up on the back of the animal.

They slowly rode off back down the trail, both of the newcomers looking continuously back over their shoulders to make sure no one was there.

When they were out of sight around a bend in the trail, Jasper Meeks slapped Falcon on the shoulder. "I never would'a believed it was possible, Falcon," he said, sitting up and sticking a long, black cheroot in his mouth. He struck a lucifer on his pants leg and applied it to the cigar, puffing out clouds of evil-smelling smoke. "I never thought I'd see the day Apaches were spooked.

"It was a good idea you had, Falcon. Killin' them Injuns in the same manner they kill whites seems to have stuck in their craw. They don't seem to know what to make of it all."

"That's the plan, Hawk. Throw something different, something they're not used to, at them, and see how they react," Falcon answered.

"Well, it may be workin' like you said, an' it may be causin' the Injuns some troubles, but I still don't like it," Cal Franklin said in a low voice. "It just ain't Christian, doin' what we done to them bodies. They may be Injuns, but that don't mean we should cut 'em up like they was cattle being butchered."

Hawk glanced at Cal, his eyes hard. "Maybe you just don't have the stomach for this little war we got goin' on, Franklin."

Franklin turned his head to stare into Hawk's face, not giving an inch. "I got as much stake in this as you do, Hawkins. They killed my friends and partners, an' I came along to get vengeance. The Good Book don't say nothin' against vengeance."

"The Bible, if that's what you believe in, also says 'an eye for an eye and a tooth for a tooth,' my friend," Meeks said. "I personally don't believe in no God, but if'n there was one I can't hardly see how He'd object to doin' to the Injuns what they been doin' to white folks for years."

He took a deep puff of his cigar, lay back against the grass, and blew smoke at the stars overhead.

"Besides," he added, "what difference do it make what happens to your body after you're dead and gone? It's not like we was torturing those braves while they was still alive."

Hawk took out a plug of Bull Durham and sliced off a thick piece with his knife. He popped it in his mouth and began to chew as he talked. "Any time it gets too rough out here for you, feel free to hightail it on back to your mine, Franklin. We can get along just fine without you."

Before Cal could answer, Falcon interrupted. "Hold on, gentlemen. We need every gun we have, Hawk, and every man has a right to his own beliefs and feelings. If Cal doesn't feel right about the way we've been treating the dead Indians, he doesn't have to help with that part of it."

Hawk turned his head and spat, the brown liquid steaming in the chilly night air. "If'n you say so, Falcon," he said grudgingly, not looking at Franklin.

Falcon glanced at Franklin. "Cal, you have to realize why we're doing this. Cutting up those dead men has confused the Apache and made them stop and worry about what is going on. If they're confused and worried about us, they don't have time to go running around the country killing other people like they did your friends. Do you understand?"

Cal hung his head, looking at the ground as he made circles in the dirt with a stick. "Yeah, I guess so. I was just sayin' it bothered me, that's all."

"It bothers all of us, too, Cal. None of us likes doing that sort of thing. But we're in a war here, and sometimes in war you have to do things you wouldn't ordinarily do."

"I s'pect so."

"What's next, Falcon?" Meeks asked, still lying on his back and looking at the sky.

"I'm going to trail those three back to the Apache camp and keep a lookout on them. I want to make sure Naiche doesn't move his camp before we can get some help up here to clean them out."

"What about us?" Hawk asked.

"I'd like you to head on back to Tombstone and send a telegraph to Fort Thomas. We need to let the army know we've found Naiche's main base camp."

"Why can't Meeks and Franklin go to Tombstone an' me come with you?" Hawks asked.

Falcon looked at him. "Because it's going to be hard enough for one person to watch the camp without being seen. After what I did to their sentry last time, they're sure to have doubled the lookouts. Hawk, there is just no way two of us, no matter how careful, could escape being caught."

Hawk spat again, his face sour. "Well, all right, but that don't mean I got to like it."

"I figure it'll take the army two or three days to get a sizable force from the fort to here. Try to get them to agree to meet me here at this location early in the morning of the third day from now, and I'll let them know what the situation is at the camp."

"Them army commanders is stubborn," Meeks said. "What if they don't agree to wait for you to get there, an' want to head on in on they own?"

Falcon shrugged. "That's simple. Don't tell them where the camp is, just tell them you'll bring them here and I'll lead them the rest of the way."

"They won't like it," Hawk said.

Falcon gave a grin with no humor in it. "They don't have to like it. Just tell them it's either my way or they can stumble around in these mountains for the next year trying to find the camp on their own, while Naiche keeps on killing people."

As the others got their horses ready for the journey back down to Tombstone, Falcon worked on his rig. He took his spurs off and wrapped them in cloth so they wouldn't jingle or make any sounds. He tightened all parts of the saddle and reins so there would be no rattle or stray sound to give him away to the Indians he was tracking. Just before getting on Diablo, he took a small tin of bootblack from his saddlebag and rubbed it on his face. Though the moon was not full, there was still plenty of light to reflect off his white face and skin and give him away. After that, he removed his buckskins and replaced them with the black shirt and pants he generally wore on the trail.

When he was finished, he moved down the trail as silent as a ghost, and as black as night. By the time he was fifteen yards away from his friends, he was completely invisible.

"Damn," Franklin said, "That man is incredible. I can't even see him no more."

"Yeah," Meeks said, lighting another cigar. "I'm right glad he's not on my trail."

"Come on, boys," Hawk said as he swung into the saddle. "We got a long ride to Tombstone ahead of us."

After Meeks and Franklin got on their horses and the three men were on the trail, Hawk asked, "Jasper, you know anythin' 'bout the man in charge of Fort Thomas?"

Even though it was dark and he couldn't be seen, Meeks nodded his head. "Yep. His name's Colonel Grant."

"What's he like?"

"He's a big man, barrel chest, hair startin' to go gray. Been out here for some years now, but like most of the army brass, he still hasn't learned diddly 'bout how to deal with Injuns."

Hawk smiled grimly in the darkness. "Yeah, I know what you mean. The army, an' the politicians back east, keep thinkin' like they's dealin' with white folks. They just can't understand Apaches, or any Injuns, just plumb don't think like we do."

Meeks nodded again. "You're right, Hawk."

"You think this Grant will listen to what we got to say?"

"Who knows? Kind'a depends on his mood, an' what's been happenin' lately. If'n he's lost enough men to the redskins, then maybe, just maybe, he'll be ready to deal with us to get this war over.''

Franklin broke in. "Why wouldn't he listen to us? After all, we're trying to do him a favor and help him get rid of the Indians who've been riding around killing people."

Meeks gave a short laugh. "Cal, boy, you got a lot to learn 'bout the west. Army folks, lawyers, an' politicians are almost as strange in they thinkin' as Injuns. Only difference is, Injuns is more honest 'bout they intentions.''

Chapter 30

It didn't take Falcon long to catch up with the three Indians heading back to their base camp. He stayed well back of them, and even though they kept looking back over their shoulders; they remained oblivious to his presence.

Falcon, for his part, enjoyed this game of cat and mouse almost as much as he enjoyed the gut-wrenching excitement of life or death battle. A curious mixture of the cerebral and at the same time physical, Falcon had always been somewhat different from most of the men who lived in the West.

Perhaps that was why he enjoyed playing mental chess with Naiche. Move and counter-move, advance and retreat, it was a game the Indian leader had no chance of winning.

Falcon glanced at the sky, noting scudding, scurrying clouds and a moon that was getting closer to full every day. The clouds were sparse enough to show there would be no snow or freezing rain, for which Falcon was thankful. Sleeping outdoors in good weather was all right, but during winter storms it could try a man's soul.

As he rode the Dragoons hunting renegade Apaches with men who carried unusual nicknames like Hawk and

Jasper, he thought back to an earlier time, up in Wyoming Territory, where he'd assembled about the oddest collection of mountain men and gunfighters on earth. They'd given themselves downright different handles, and he had to admit that the name Falcon wasn't the least bit ordinary, either.

The whole thing had started when a power hungry cattleman hired gunmen to back his play. The Noonan boys intended to crush all the smaller outfits and put them out of business. They hadn't counted on Falcon MacCallister and some of his old mountain man friends showing up to take a side.

Noonan's foreman, Miles Gilman, also fancied himself a shootist and a bully . . . another mistake, made at the wrong time. The odds looked long against MacCallister's friends, but then it would to men who didn't know the MacCallister breed and their inclination to join a fight.

All across Colorado, Northern California, and New Mexico, Falcon had sent wires to old associates. Then he'd gone looking for one man in particular. . . .

Falcon knew he was being followed an hour after leaving the ranch. The man was pretty good, but Falcon was one hundred percent his father's son. *Nobody* was a better tracker than Jamie MacCallister.

Falcon had ridden through that country many times, but it had been a while, and his memory was busy trying to recall all the ins and outs.

After a few minutes, Falcon came to a spot he remembered. There was a tiny creek that flowed just behind a huge upthrusting of rock. If his memory served him correctly, he knew the place reasonably well.

He quickly swung in behind the rocks and ran back to deliberately cover his trail as clumsily as possible. Then, staying on rocky ground, Falcon got his rifle and ran to a smaller outcropping of rocks about forty feet away and directly across from the rocks that lay in front of the creek.

He made himself as comfortable as possible and waited.

The minutes ticked past and the sun grew hotter. The soft murmuring of the cold waters of the tiny spring-fed creek grew mighty appealing to Falcon. His mouth felt as though it were filled with cotton.

"Gettin' thirsty, boy?"

The voice and question came from behind him.

Falcon's hands tightened on his rifle and he waited for the shock of a bullet.

The bullet never came. Instead, a low chuckling reached Falcon's ears.

Falcon smiled as he recognized the voice.

"Big Bob Marsh," Falcon said, exhaling anxiety-filled air from his lungs.

"In the flesh, and as handsome to the ladies as ever," the man said, stepping closer.

Falcon stood up and the men shook hands.

"What in the world—"

Big Bob waved him silent. "I was about a hundred miles north of that pissant town in Utah when you put lead into Chet and Butch Noonan. If two ever deserved killin', them two did. But I knowed Nance would send men out lookin' for you. You took up with them smaller ranchers. I thought and thought 'bout where you might go to hole up. Felt you wouldn't go back to Colorado, so you wouldn't bring trouble to your kin. Then I 'membered that old cabin built into the mountain. Went there. But by the time I reached the cabin, you'd done hauled it outta there. Been trackin' you ever since."

"Now you've found me, an' a peck of trouble, too."

"You've knowed me a long time, Falcon. When did I ever back away from trouble?"

That was only the beginning of Falcon's gathering of old friends. Men with names like Puma, Mustang, Wildcat, Stumpy, and Big Bob Marsh, along with a gunman named Dan Carson, joined up with Falcon in the middle of a

wide street in a small Wyoming town where things between
the rich ranchers and smaller cowmen would come to a
head. Falcon remembered it well, almost like it was yesterday. . . .

The seven men spread out across the main street
through town, where the matter would be settled in blood.

"Must be fifty of 'em at least," Stumpy said. "An' another
twenty comin' behind that first bunch."

"That ain't all that many," Big Bob groused. "You can
bet Noonan and Stegman will be ridin' with them boys
back behind the bigger bunch."

"Get ready," Falcon called, just loud enough for his
men to hear. "They're going to be comin' up the street
straight at us in a few seconds."

"Just like I figured they would," Dan said.

"Yep," Mustang agreed. "You damn sure called this one
right, son."

"You boys know what to do," Falcon continued. "Soon
as the first lead flies, head for cover and then pick your
shots."

"You watch your butt, Falcon," Big Bob warned.

"Good luck, boys," was all Falcon said.

With a distant chorus of shouts, the mob led by Noonan
and Stegman put the spurs to their horses and lunged
forward, galloping down the street toward Falcon and his
line of men.

When they got within good pistol range, all seven jerked
two six-guns from leather and let them bang as fast as they
could cock and fire.

Twenty saddles were emptied in a matter of seconds.
Horses were rearing up and bucking and screaming in
fright. Wounded men were crawling around in the dirt of
the street, most of them getting trampled on by the hooves
of the horses that had been galloping directly behind them.

When the dust settled Falcon and the mountain men

were nowhere in sight, and the horsemen were trapped in the center of the street.

Falcon and three of his men opened up from one side of the street, while the three other mountain men opened up from the other. More saddles were emptied, and horses were going crazy from the smell of blood and the roar of gunfire and the screaming of the wounded gunhands.

Less than half of those who had arrogantly charged Falcon and his friends managed to get their horses turned around and gallop back out of town, many of them wounded. The street was filled with the dead, dying, and badly wounded.

Falcon and his men had not suffered even the tiniest of scratches.

Stegman was horrified at the carnage he was witnessing in the street, but Noonan was outraged.

"Dismount!" Noonan roared at his men. "Dismount and go after those bastards on foot! Kill them! Do it! I want all of you to go after 'em!"

A mob of hired guns spread out and began slowly working their way up both sides of the street, front and back of the businesses. There were Noonan and Stegman brothers and kids of the brothers and cousins and uncles, and so forth. For many of them, this would be the last fight. Their blood would stain the streets and alleys and boardwalks and businesses of the small western town in Wyoming.

"Just stay inside the church!" John Bailey told the people gathered for the church social. Preacher, get your choir together and give us some songs, will you?"

"My pleasure, sir," Reverend Watkins said. Come, sisters, let us raise our voices in song while the Philistines spill their blood in the streets."

Falcon came face-to-face with a bearded gunhand and shot him twice just as Big Bob lined up a paid gunny in his sights and blew him to hell.

Dan Carson stood in the doorway of a back door and

waited until a gunslick walked up . . . then he shot him in the head, and the man dropped dead.

Mustang stepped out of a building and blew one of the Noonan cousins out of one boot. The man was dead before he stretched out on the ground for the last time. Finally, one bare foot twitching, he lay still.

Puma called out to a gunslick. "Hey, you ugly bastard! I'm behind you!"

The man whirled around, and Puma gave him two .45 rounds in the chest.

Wildcat emptied one pistol into a knot of hired guns and sent two to the ground, mortally wounded. The other three jumped for cover and scrambled out of sight.

Stumpy leveled both pistols at several men who were trying to slip out the back of the building, and let his six-shooters bang. When the smoke cleared, two men were dead and the third was crawling away, out of the fight.

Suddenly there was a woman's scream, a terrible scream that cut the afternoon air.

After a few seconds, Falcon decided it wasn't a woman's scream; it was slightly off in timbre. He guessed what it was that made the sound.

A man staggered out from between two buildings, half his face gone and blood dripping from the terrible wound. The man tried to speak, but no words would come from his mouth, only muffled sounds.

"Jenny got him," Puma called. "I told you she was close by."

The man with half his face missing screamed in pain and then collapsed in the middle of the street and lay still, the victim of Puma's pet cougar.

"What the hell happened to Dick?" someone called. "I didn't hear no gunshot—"

"I don't know," another man replied, "but half his face is plumb gone."

A shot cut the afternoon, and a gunslick grunted and took a header off the hotel roof. He smashed through the awning, bounced on the boardwalk, and lay motionless.

"Falcon MacCallister, you son of a bitch!" Nance Noonan shouted.

Falcon did not reply. He stayed between two buildings, pressed up into a doorway.

"You've played hell, for a fact," Noonan cried. "But this ain't over."

For a fact, Falcon thought, *and if you had any sense you'd pull up stakes and ride on out to another part of the country— that is, if you had any sense.*

Then Nance Noonan signed his death warrant when he shouted, "I know you got kids, Falcon. And I know where they are down in Colorado. I'll kill them, MacCallister. I'll make certain none of your stinkin' offspring lives. They're dead, MacCallister. You hear me? Your kids is dead!"

Falcon felt an icy sensation wash over him, as if someone had thrown a bucket of ice water on him. He did not know it, but he was smiling. The smile was awful to behold. It was a curving of the lips that came straight from Hell.

"You're dead, Noonan," Falcon muttered softly, only the faint breeze hearing his words. "You're a walking-around dead man. No matter where you go, I'll find you and kill you."

A hired gun suddenly left cover and tried to make the side door to the general store. The guns of three mountain men barked, and the man stumbled and went down to his knees. He stayed in that position for a few seconds, then toppled over and lay still in the mouth of the alley.

"I'm done, MacCallister!" a man called. "I'm out of here. I'm holsterin' my guns and gettin' my horse and ridin' out, so don't shoot!"

Falcon maintained his silence.

"Me, too," another man shouted. "This is crazy. I ain't gonna die for no damn Noonan. I'm joinin' Pete and ridin' out now!"

"You yeller-bellied bastards!" Nance shouted. "I've been payin' you top wages for months, and now you turn yeller on me. You stand an' fight, you scum!"

"You go to hell, Noonan," another voice sprang out of

an alleyway. "It's time, past time, you understood that you ain't gonna win this fight. It's over, man. And I ain't havin' no part of killin' nobody's kids."

"That goes double for me," yet another voice added to the quitting declarations. "I'm done here, MacCallister. My guns is in leather. I'm through. I'm headin' out the back alley and ridin' clear of this town. You understand?"

"Git gone, then," Big Bob shouted. "All of you who want to live, ride out and don't never come back to this part of the country. If I see any of you again, I'll kill you on the spot. Ride out and don't come back. Hold your fire, boys. Let them ride clear."

Nance cussed all those who gathered up their horses, swung into saddles, and rode out. "You sorry bunch of yeller coyotes!" he shouted, his voice filled with rage. "You no-good, scummy bastards. Take a man's money and then turn yeller on him. Goddamn you all to hell!"

One of the men who had made up his mind to ride out told Nance how and where he could shove his words—sideways.

Then Nance again screamed out his anger at his departing gunmen.

"How about it, Nance?" Falcon finally broke his silence. "You and me in the street. You have the nerve to face me man-to-man, you sorry piece of crap?"

There was no reply.

Falcon again called for Nance to meet him in the street. Nance made no reply to the deadly invitation.

"We're out of here, MacCallister," yet another voice filled the late afternoon air. "We're done with this fight. They's five of us ridin' out. Hold your fire."

"Ten of us," another voice cried. "That about does it, MacCallister. Tell your boys it's over. We're through and done with it."

"Where's Nance?" Falcon shouted.

"He rode out just now. He quit. Him and all his brothers and kin went with him. We ain't stayin' here and takin' no lead for him."

"Ride out, then," Big Bob told them again. "But don't none of you come back. You're dead if you do."

"We understand. You've seen the last of us."

Falcon walked up to Mustang, leading his horse.

"Where are you off to?" Mustang asked.

"I got things to settle with Nance Noonan," Falcon told him.

He swung into the saddle. "Noonan made brags about what he was going to do. I aim to see he doesn't do them."

"I'll get my hoss and go with you."

"No, boys. You stay here until John Bailey gets him a few permanent hands hired."

Wildcat noticed then that Falcon had tied a bedroll behind his saddle, and his saddlebags were bulging with fresh supplies.

"Dean opened the general store for me," Falcon explained. "And I stocked up with what I'll need on the trail. I met with Willard, and he knows what to do with my money."

"No good-byes for John Bailey and his family?" Dan asked.

Falcon shook his head. "No. John will understand. I'll write him a letter once I get back to Colorado, and make certain my kids are all right."

The men shook hands all around.

"Good luck with your new lives, boys," Falcon told the mountain men. "I might drift back up this way one of these days."

That was probably a lie, and the mountain men knew it.

"See you, boy," Big Bob said, lifting a hand in hail and farewell.

Falcon sat his saddle for a moment, smiling at his friends. Then he turned his horse and rode out of town. He did not look back . . .

*   *   *

Falcon chuckled to himself as the memories made pictures in his mind. Looking back on it almost made him wish he had gone back to look up the old mountain men who'd helped him in that battle, but then he realized he'd been right not to. They were a strange breed, as fierce as mountain lions and as proud as peacocks. To a man they hated the idea of dying of old age in their cabins. That, and their intense loyalty to anyone they chose to call a friend, explained why they were always ready to join in a fight.

No, he thought, *it is better this way.* They would want to be remembered as they were, not as the old men they were fast becoming.

Chapter 31

From the semi-darkness ahead, Falcon heard the Indians he was following give a long, triple hoot like an owl. He knew they had come to the edge of the camp and were signaling a sentry. He quickly reined Diablo up and studied the surrounding terrain. Then he walked the stud up the side of the mountain slope into heavy brush until they were a couple of hundred yards off the path the sentry was watching. He tied the animal next to an exceptionally tall pinyon pine just below a distinctive outcropping of the ledge above them on the mountainside. He wanted to be sure to be able to find his mount if he had to leave the area in a hurry. He knew the odds of his getting to the camp, doing what he had to do, and escaping with his hair still attached to his skull were only about fifty-fifty.

After Diablo was seen to, with plenty of fresh grass nearby to graze on, Falcon started his long walk up the mountain. He'd left the horse a good ways away from the Indian camp so the animal wouldn't be tempted to nicker or call to the Indian ponies that were in the valley up above.

Luckily, the moon was at three-quarters and there were a few scurrying clouds in the winter sky. The moonlight was bright enough for Falcon to see where he was going and to avoid stepping on twigs or sticks and thus alerting the Indians to his presence, and the clouds provided occasional periods of almost total darkness so that he would be able to move freely without fear of being seen when he got near Naiche's camp.

As it turned out, even in the moonlight Falcon smelled the campsite long before he saw it. The pungent odor of roasting mule and perhaps other things he'd rather not think about tickled his nose and made his stomach growl, even though he knew he'd rather eat a live snake than anything cooked up by Apaches. He knew Indians would eat things that would make a billy goat puke, but evidently his stomach didn't care, for it continued to make sounds as he climbed toward the source of the smells. He patted his abdomen and then rubbed it vigorously to try and make it settle down.

It'll be a hell of a note, he thought to himself, *if you lose your scalp 'cause your stomach is howling for food.*

A low sound from up ahead, as if someone tried to stifle a cough, reminded Falcon he was not alone on the mountain. He stopped dead still and stood motionless next to the trunk of a pinyon tree, scarcely breathing.

After a moment, he picked out a shadow next to a juniper bush that was slightly darker than the surrounding leaves and branches. He stared past it, letting the image fall on the corner of his eye. Without really knowing quite why, he had found over the years that was the best way to see dim objects in limited light. A doctor in Denver had once told him it was because the cells of the retina that are most sensitive to light are arranged around the periphery of the retina, but Falcon didn't care why. He was just satisfied to know the trick worked when he needed it.

Moving slowly, an inch at a time, being very careful not to let his body be outlined against any moonlit areas, Falcon backed up until he could no longer see the sentry.

Once out of sight, he turned to the right and made a wide circle around the lookout, knowing that since he'd already killed one of the warriors who'd been standing guard, Naiche would likely have increased the number of men guarding the camp. He moved through the night like a wraith, silent and deadly, his Arkansas Toothpick in his hand, his other fist doubled and ready to strike if necessary. As before, he dared not use his pistol, for it would mean almost certain death.

After another hour of painstakingly slow progress, Falcon came to an overhang where he could crawl to the edge and have an unobstructed view of the Indian camp below.

He counted five fires scattered around the small area, arranged on both sides of the small stream running through the middle of the canyon. Squaws were roasting large chunks of meat on sticks arrayed over the flames, while some tin and pottery bowls were placed over the coals at the edge of the fires to heat beans and stews with God-only-knew what kind of meat in them.

He looked for the largest wickiup, hoping to find Naiche among the warriors walking around the camp. Sure enough, off to the right of the main body of tent-like structures, he saw the three he'd been tailing sitting talking to the man he thought was Naiche.

The one he and his friends had tied to the cross had tied a bandanna or some sort of cloth over his shaven head, evidently out of shame that he'd allowed himself to be captured alive. The woman, who seemed to have Naiche's ear, was talking in a voice so low that Falcon couldn't make out what she was saying.

He thought it strange for a female to be so trusted by the leader of the renegades, for he knew that women in the Apache tribes generally ranked little higher than dogs. Even so, here was one who carried a Winchester and sat and spoke with the leader as an equal. Occasionally, the other male warrior added something to what she was saying, and Naiche nodded and glanced toward the wounded man. Falcon thought to himself he wouldn't want to be in that particular Indian's moccasins—after failing twice in his master's eyes and getting all of his warriors killed both times. The chief of this band would most likely be very angry with the brave. There was no telling what punishment he would mete out.

Soon the powwow was over, and Naiche waved the three away and retired to his wickiup, presumably to go to sleep.

Falcon tried to make a count of the number of male warriors milling around the fires, but soon gave the effort up as impossible. The Indians moved around too much for him to make an accurate count, and at this distance, in the semi-darkness, he couldn't even be sure if some of the figures were male or female.

He squirmed a bit to get comfortable, and settled in to wait for the camp to get quiet as the rest of the Apaches began to head for their wickiups and sleep.

It was a couple of hours later when Falcon was startled out of a semi-doze by the sound of a stick breaking nearby. He slowly rolled onto his side, searching the ground in the darkness for his knife, which he had evidently dropped in his sleep.

He released the breath he'd been holding when his fingers closed around the handle of the Toothpick. Now, even if he were to be discovered, he had a fighting chance to defend himself.

Falcon held his breath and slitted his eyes to hide their whites as a young man strolled into view, holding hands with a pretty female of a similar age. Falcon knew he was practically invisible, lying on the dark humus of the forest floor with his face and hands blackened and his dark clothes, but the couple was walking directly toward him.

It seemed no matter how quickly he moved, one or the other would be able to sound an alarm before he could silence them both.

Luckily, the man stopped and took the girl by the shoulders, turning her to face him. He said a few quiet words in Apache that Falcon couldn't understand, then gently placed his lips against hers.

After a moment they broke apart, giggling, then the girl

turned and ran off back the way they'd come, laughing quietly over her shoulder.

The young warrior muttered some harsh words under his breath before turning and following her.

Falcon released his breath with a whoosh, grinning to himself. He'd heard of a few men being shot, and even one who was hanged, for the stealing of a kiss, but this was the first time he'd seen it save a man's life.

He slipped the knife back in its scabbard and rolled back over to take a look at the camp. The fires had almost burned themselves out, and except for a stray dog or two there was no movement at all among the wickiups.

Since it was obvious there was going to be no mass exodus from the area tonight, Falcon decided it was time for him to seek a more secure hiding place until the next morning. He crawled back from the edge of the precipice and then got to his feet and slipped off into the night.

After a while, he found a shallow cave musty with the odor of a long-gone critter of some sort who'd holed up here in the past. Falcon gathered some nearby brush and pulled it over the entrance, then crawled to the rear of the small enclosure and lay down. He needed to get some sleep. Tired men make mistakes, and tomorrow he was going to need to be at his best to do what he planned to do.

As he drifted off to sleep, he hoped he wouldn't snore too loudly.

Chapter 32

Falcon awoke just as dawn was breaking over the eastern peaks of the Dragoons. The cave was so cold he had to brush spicules of ice off his nose and eyebrows. He crawled to the entrance and peered out between the branches of the limb he had placed there to conceal the opening.

Once he was sure no one was about, he climbed carefully out into feeble sunlight, which gave little warmth, and got slowly to his feet. He stretched and did some slow exercises to get the kinks out of muscles grown stiff and sore from lying on the cold, damp earth of the hole in the ground.

His stomach growled once more, and his mouth watered as he smelled the aroma of breakfast cooking on open fires in the Indians' camp. He ran a dry tongue over gritty teeth, wishing he had thought to bring his canteen from Diablo's saddle. *I'd kill for a cup of hot coffee*, he thought as he used a fallen branch to brush away his footprints near the cave entrance. No need to let the Indians know anyone was there, since he might well have to make use of it again.

Just as he finished wiping away all traces of his presence, he heard the sound of hoofbeats and horses nickering from the camp just beyond the nearby ridge. As quietly as he could, he threaded his way through the dense undergrowth to the precipice and peeked over the edge.

Down below, he saw a couple of older men and Naiche climb on the back of three ponies being held by a younger warrior. Naiche called some orders to several men waiting nearby, but Falcon couldn't make out what they were.

Evidently they're going on a scouting party, he thought, *since they're aren't enough of them to be a war party.* Since Naiche obviously wasn't going to be moving the base camp any time soon, Falcon decided to head back down the trail toward Tombstone to see if Hawk and the others had made any progress in alerting the army to Naiche's current whereabouts.

Slowly, so as not to make any unnecessary noise, Falcon made his way back up the slope of the hillside toward where he'd left Diablo reined to a tree. He had no trouble picking out the tall pinyon or the distinctive outcropping of the mountain, and found his mount without any trouble.

After rinsing his mouth out and drinking his fill of water from his canteen, he stepped into the stirrups and spurred the horse down the mountain toward Tombstone, glancing back over his shoulder occasionally to make sure no warriors were on his trail.

Naiche saw the soldiers climbing a steep, winding trail into the Dragoons. Lying flat against a slab of stone, the fifty or sixty soldiers did not concern him as much as the scout who rode out in front of them, his face to the ground, a face all but obscured by twin braids of shoulder-length, orange-red curly hair.

Gray skies threatening snow or ice made it harder for him to see the man's features clearly.

"They have a scout now," Nana said. "He reads our tracks carefully . . . too carefully. Like an Apache, only his hair is the wrong color."

"I know him," Naiche answered. "I only know him by his description."

"Who is he?"

"His hair is red, and long, like an Apache, only he is not one of us."

Juh squinted into the distance. "Then who is this man who can find our tracks, no matter how carefully we hide them on the rocks?"

"He is called Mickey Free," Naiche said, remembering the stories. "He is half white. The white-eyes call him The Apache Hunter. Cochise told us about him, one of the last times our great leader talked to Geronimo. I was there. Mickey Free is from this land. He was a boy of ten or twelve when a band of Mimbres captured him and stole the livestock where he was working for a white man. For ten winters, Free lived as an Apache with the Mimbres and Mescaleros, kept as a slave to bring firewood to the lodges. He was kept in chains, and even some of the women beat him with sticks. While he was with our people he learned to track animals and men, to hunt deer and buffalo, and to steal horses from the Arapaho and Comanches. After ten winters, he escaped to live with the whites. He became a scout for the bluecoats. He lived at Fort Verde. He led the soldiers to the big battle at the place called Dry Gulch, where so many of our people were killed. He tracked down the Apache Kid, and led the soldiers to Victorio, following Victorio's tracks for three hundred of the white man's miles, a very long distance. It is said he has the eyes of an eagle, and he hates all Apaches for the way he was treated when he was our prisoner."

"He misses nothing," Nana observed, watching as the man Naiche called Mickey Free came to a fork in the trail leading into the Dragoons. The scout stopped for a moment. Without coming down from his horse, he led the soldiers onto the left fork, the direction Cuchillo and his warriors had taken when they started back to camp at Deer Springs canyon.

"You see?" Naiche asked. "He sees the prints of our ponies on solid rock."

"We must kill him," Juh whispered, lifting his rifle to his shoulder.

"The range is too far," Naiche warned. "We must be sure of the bullet that takes his life."

Naiche saw Mickey Free stop his pinto, then look directly up at their hiding place. "He knows we are watching him," Naiche said. "He is not afraid. . . ."

"Where did he learn the Apache secrets of covering the trail of a horse?" Juh asked.

"Some say he is more Apache than white man. While he was with the Mimbres, he learned many of our secrets."

"He will lead the bluecoats to our village," Nana said. "We must find a way to kill him before he does this. Our women and children will die."

Naiche recalled more of what Cochise told him, of how Free went after an Apache cousin of Victorio for the army's pay. Free found the Apache and killed him. His body was too heavy for Free to carry, since he only had one horse. To prove to the army that he'd found the right Indian, Free cut off the Apache's face, wrapped the skin and hair in the dead man's jacket, and dropped the rotting trophy at the feet of Al Sieber, the most notorious chief of scouts for the soldiers, in order to earn his reward at Fort Verde.

"Cochise said Free can track a shadow on a rainy night," Naiche said, again studying Free as he stopped to look up at their hiding place among the rocks.

"All men die when a bullet strikes the right place," Juh said. "Let me get in front of him and I will kill him. I can still see with these old eyes."

Naiche considered it. Nana and Juh were experienced in the ways of war, and both warriors were good shots. "We wait, until Free comes to the right place."

Nana frowned. "He knows we are here. See how he looks up at the mountain? The spirits are guiding his eyes to us. It is bad medicine."

"Is it possible he could have the power of the spirits with him?" Juh asked.

Before Naiche could answer, Free halted the soldiers

again and pointed up at the mountain where Naiche and the others were in hiding.

"He tells the bluecoats we are here," Naiche said. "He is warning them."

"What will we do?" Nana asked. "How can we lay a trap for the soldiers if Free is telling them where we are?"

Naiche found he was facing a new problem. Not only were four strange men with warrior-like instincts entering the Dragoons from another direction, killing and desecrating the bodies of his warriors, but now the dreaded Apache hunter, Mickey Free, was leading a large force of bluecoats toward their village from the north.

"We are surrounded by enemies," Juh observed. "The other white-eyes are approaching, and we can find no way to stop them or surprise them with an attack. Now this curious man with long red hair comes, bringing many soldiers, and he seems to know where we are, that we are watching him."

Juh had voiced Naiche's concerns only too well. The four men were only a nuisance because of their small number, but with Mickey Free leading so many soldiers into the Dragoon's higher elevations, it spelled trouble.

"We must move our camp again very soon," Nana said.

Naiche knew Nana had many winters of wisdom. It would be unwise to ignore his council. "Yes, but before we do we will kill the four whites who cut out the eyes of our warriors and take their scalps."

"We must find them first," Juh warned. "Some of our best trackers have been unable to pick up their sign. These four are very clever. They strike, then disappear into the forest like shadow-spirits."

Nana's and Juh's doubts would spread like a sickness through his younger warriors unless Naiche did something to stop it, and it had to be done soon. "We ride back to camp and pick the best fighters among us, those with battle experience. Then we look for the four white-eyes while the women and younger warriors take down our camp. We will move south, closer to the big river and Mexico."

"Why do we go south?" Juh asked. "There, the mountains have no trees, and water is scarce."

"Cochise told me the bluecoats cannot cross the big river into Mexico. Their strange laws make a river into a wall. If the soldiers come close we will escape to Mexico and look for the camp of Geronimo."

"His wise ways will help us," Nana agreed. "He may know of a way to kill this Apache hunter, Mickey Free. Geronimo is able to hide from anyone."

Naiche inched backward on the stone slab, signaling for the others to do the same. Down below, Mickey Free was talking to the leader of the bluecoats. For now, the soldiers were not climbing higher or moving at all.

Naiche hurried to his horse and, using a fistful of mane, he swung over the bay's back. "Be careful where you leave the print of a horse on our return to camp," he cautioned. "Free will come here to look for our tracks."

Silently, riding from rock slab to gravel beds in low dry washes, Naiche led his men away from the soldier columns and the Apache hunter. His spirit taunted him while they rode off, for it whispered that a brave war chief would not run and hide from someone like Mickey Free, or the four white-eyes who were coming into the Dragoons.

This called for an all-out attack on the four whites, to rid Naiche and his band of their trickery. Only then could they make plans to ambush the soldiers and kill the red-haired scout who led them.

Naiche wondered about Free. Could a white man, even one who had been a prisoner of the Apaches for ten winters, have learned all their battle secrets? Their hiding places?

It was not possible. Naiche intended to prove it.

As they rode back toward their camp, Naiche's mind was full of plans, things he would have to do. First he would get his women and children safe by moving the camp south. Then he would have to do something about the four white-eyes who were causing them so much trouble. Then there was the problem of what was to be done with

Cuchillo. His repeated failures had made Naiche's leadership seem bad.

The Indian leader shook his head to clear it of the ideas buzzing inside. Battle to the death was far easier than the responsibility of being chief to his people.

Chapter 33

Knowing there were no war parties in the vicinity allowed Falcon to keep Diablo on the trail, and he was making good time until the big stud raised his head and pointed his ears forward.

Falcon knew this meant Diablo had either heard or smelled something up ahead, so he quickly jerked the horse's head to the left and ran him up into heavy brush just off the trail.

He pulled his Winchester out of its saddle boot, levered a shell into the firing chamber, and waited. Before long, three riders came into view. Though they were being careful and were keeping the noise to a minimum, they didn't manage to spot Falcon in his hiding place.

Damn good thing I'm not one of Naiche's braves, Falcon thought, and considered for a moment bursting out of hiding and scaring the bejesus out of the three men. He decided against it, for they might go off half-cocked and fire a weapon, warning Naiche someone was on the mountain near his campsite.

Falcon walked Diablo out into the open just as Hawk and

the others came abreast of his position. "Howdy, boys," he called, shoving his Winchester back into its boot.

Other than a quick jerk of his head as Falcon called out his greeting, Hawk managed to hide his surprise at Falcon's sudden appearance in the bushes next to the trail.

Meeks wasn't quite so calm, and managed to get his pistol half out of its holster before he recognized who was hailing them.

Franklin's response worried Falcon the most. The miner didn't move, and barely looked up as Falcon approached. The man appeared to Falcon to be almost despondent, as if he had something heavy on his mind more important than his own survival.

Falcon rode out into the middle of the path, cutting his eyes at Franklin and raising a questioning eyebrow to Hawk. The big man shrugged while making a disdainful face. He'd made it clear from the start that he had very little respect for either Franklin or Meeks.

"You men have any trouble in Tombstone?" Falcon asked, looking at Meeks to see what his reaction was.

"None to speak of," Meeks replied. "We sent a wire to Fort Thomas requesting to speak with Colonel Grant or whoever was in charge of fighting the renegades."

"What was the reply?"

Hawk spat a brown stream toward Diablo's hooves. " 'Bout what you'd expect. The Colonel was busy at some social shindig, suckin' up to bigwigs from Washington, probably, an' the men out doin' the dirty work of chasin' Injuns wasn't in the fort right then."

"So, how'd you leave it?" Falcon asked, irritated at having to drag it out of them word by word.

"We left a message for any real soldiers who wanted a chance to kill some redskins to meet us at noon tomorrow or the next day just below Indian Head Peak. Said we'd be waitin' for 'em," Hawk answered, puckering up to spit again.

Falcon pulled Diablo's head around and glared at Hawk. "Hawk, you spit on my horse and I'll make you eat that plug, you hear?'' Falcon said in a low voice, letting the trapper know he wasn't going to take any more of his attitude.

Hawk grinned, and turned his head to spit to the side, as if he'd just be seeing how far Falcon could be pushed.

"Franklin, you look like a man with something stuck in his craw,'' Falcon said, his eyes on Cal. "Why don't you spit it out so we'll all feel better?''

Cal crossed his hands on his saddle horn and leaned forward, an earnest look on his face. "I don't think I can take any more of this, boys.''

"Any more of what?'' Hawk asked, an ugly sneer curling his lips.

"This butcherin' of Indians after they's dead.'' He shook his head, his lips tight and pale. "I've killed enough to last me a while. I'm done with ridin' the vengeance trail, boys, an' I'm gonna light on back toward Tombstone.''

"What'll you do then, Cal?'' Falcon asked, his voice soft and kind. He knew some of what Cal was going through, what any civilized man would go through doing what they'd done. He knew that if his Marie hadn't been butchered by renegade Apaches in the past, he would have had a hard time acting this way, too.

Franklin shrugged, looking back over his shoulder toward Tombstone. "First, I plan to sell some of my dust an' drink until I don't see those Injuns' faces in my sleep no more. Then I'll probably mosey on back to my claim and do a little more minin'.''

"Cal, you'd be wise to hole up in Tombstone until this Indian uprising is over,'' Falcon said. "Those renegades have hit your place once. Nothing says they won't hit it again if you go back there.''

Franklin nodded. "We'll see. I don't have no firm plans just yet. I only know I got to get away from all this killin'.''

Falcon nudged Diablo forward until he was next to Franklin. He held out his hand. "Good luck to you, then, partner.''

Franklin gave a half-smile, "Thanks, Falcon. You watch your scalp-lock, you hear?"

He nodded at Hawk and Meeks, then turned his mount and put him in a slow lope toward town.

"Damn coward," Hawk muttered.

"Hell, he ain't no coward," Meeks said, looking at Franklin's back as he rode off. "He's the smart one of the bunch."

"How about we make camp?" Falcon asked, his eyes searching for a suitable place. "I haven't eaten anything since yesterday, and I'm in dire need of some *cafecíto.*"

As they walked their horses up into the forest above the trail, he added, "Now, just where is this Indian Head Peak where we're supposed to meet the army tomorrow?"

Later that afternoon, Falcon left Hawk and Jasper Meeks at their camp and traveled back to where the Indians had their base camp. He wanted to see if Naiche had returned, and to see if any war parties were being formed.

He got to the precipice overlooking the camp just as the last wickiup was being dismantled, and found the women and children and warriors packed up and ready to move.

As the caravan of Indians pulled out of the valley and took a trail leading toward the southern edge of the Dragoons, where mountain slopes descended into flat desert, Falcon followed at a discreet distance.

He hoped Meeks and Hawk would have sense enough to wait for him at Indian Head Peak, along with the army. As soon as he found out where the Indians' new camp was going to be, he'd hightail it back to the meeting place.

The Indians, with Naiche in the lead, slowly wound their way south through the mountains, the trail descending toward the desert the farther south they traveled.

If they keep going like this, Falcon thought, *they're going to be on the desert floor before long.*

Just before the path turned and ran straight down to

the desert floor, Naiche turned his people off and led them into a small, box canyon that couldn't be seen from more than a hundred yards away. The Indians at the rear of the group covered the entrance to the canyon with deadfall branches and tree limbs after the rest of the people had entered.

Damn, Falcon thought, *if I hadn't seen them go in there, I'd never find the entrance to that canyon.* Even from the trail no more than thirty yards away, the entrance was camouflaged so well it was almost invisible.

No wonder they've managed to elude the army so easily, Falcon thought. *They can disappear in these mountains like a rabbit in a briar patch.*

He looked around and made a mental note marking the surrounding terrain so he could lead the army back to this spot, if they showed up tomorrow.

Before leaving, Falcon climbed to a ridge overlooking the valley below to take a last look. What he saw made him uneasy. The Indians were not erecting their wickiups, but were making what looked like a temporary camp. Wood was being gathered and cooking fires were being lighted, but there were no semi-permanent structures being put up. It looked to Falcon as if the Indians didn't plan to be here very long, possibly not even long enough for him to go and get the army and bring the soldiers back.

Now what to do? He had to decide whether to take a chance and go to Indian Head Peak and fetch the army, or to hang around here for a while longer to see just what Naiche's plans were. Falcon knew that if the Indians moved again without him following, they would once again disappear into the Dragoons, and it might be a long time before he would be lucky enough to find their camp again.

He pondered his choices as he sat and watched the Indian women cooking on their fires. It seemed to him he was always watching the Apaches eat while doing without food himself.

Chapter 34

Dawn came slowly to the Apaches' camp hidden in a pocket canyon where a tiny pool offered rare water in the southernmost part of the Dragoons, the driest section of this mountain range where wild game and grass were as scarce as water. The canyon where they camped now was aptly named Wild Pig Springs, since only the desert-dwelling javelina could find enough forage here to survive.

Retreating south from their Deer Springs hideout, Naiche and his followers would soon be forced to cross dangerous open desert flats to reach the Pedregosa Mountains that would take them to Mexico and the high Sierra Madres where Geronimo was said to be in hiding, raiding Mexican *rancheros* and villages for guns and horses and ammunition. *A retreat from the heart of the Dragoons had quickly become necessary as soon as Juh and Chokole returned with Cuchillo. The story of the bloody defeat and mutilation of Cuchillo and his warriors still rang in Naiche's ears after the wounded warrior and Chokole related what had happened at the north edge of the Dragoons.*

Cuchillo lay on a moth-eaten army blanket, groaning, his head still bleeding, as was a deep gash in his right side. Naiche sat crosslegged beside him, asking questions. Chokole and Juh listened in silence. The women and warriors who were not stationed in the surrounding mountains as lookouts prepared the camp gear and livestock to move again, on orders given by Naiche after word of the one-sided battle with the four white-eyes came. Smoked mule and deer meat and staples stolen from Bisbee and the wagon train were being loaded onto horses as rapidly as possible. Some of the women filled waterskins to tie to the backs of stolen cavalry horses for what Naiche promised would be a difficult journey across the desert to reach the mountains in Mexico.

"These white men . . . there are two who wear deerskins like the clothing worn by northern Indian tribes?" Naiche asked, more determined than ever to find out details about the men who were killing off his warriors a few at a time. He could never admit it to those around him, but only the dreaded Comanche to the east had proven to be worthy adversaries to Apache war parties, yet a new enemy with light skin was thinning the ranks of his fighting men.

"Yes," Cuchillo answered weakly. "One is very tall, big, and he moves like a mountain cat, making no sound with his feet. I saw and heard nothing when he moved among the rocks. It is as if his feet do not touch the ground. He leaves no tracks. He kills with a knife, the longest knife I have ever seen, and the blade makes no noise when it opens the flesh of his enemies. It does not seem possible, and yet I have witnessed it with my own eyes. He kills our best warriors and no one hears a sound, or sees a shadow."

A dark fear loomed larger in the back of Naiche's brain, a fear he dared not reveal to the others, for it would spread panic among his fighting men, and the women. *Is this man in buckskins not truly a man made of flesh and blood?* he wondered. *Could he be a Spirit warrior from one of the tribes in the cold country far to the north?* But the Apache were not at war with the Shoshones or the Utes or the Crow, so who *was* this white warrior? Who were the others with him, and why were they there, stalking Naiche's people? Why had they come to help the bluecoats make war on the Apache? And how could the tall warrior's skin be white if he was a spirit from another tribe? All the tribes known to the Apache were a dark, coppery color. These were questions without answers, troubling Naiche deeply as he questioned Cuchillo about the slayings.

One thing was clear . . . this tall warrior, and even the others with him, killed their enemies in the manner of an Indian. They knew secrets only known to the shamans about the Land of Shadows, how to cut out an enemy's eyes to make him blind in the afterlife so he could not hunt buffalo or deer, take a wife, or ride a horse in the next world. And these strange white men took scalps, proof they were not white-eyes in spirit or training. Soldiers and white buffalo hunters did not take Apache scalps.

So who were these men?

Naiche worried that they might not be men at all, men of any known race living upon the face of Earth Mother. The tall one made no sounds and left no tracks, as a spirit warrior might. Naiche had never seen a spirit warrior . . . he had only heard the stories—told by the old men of his tribe around council fires—of a day coming in the future when warriors from the Land of Shadows would return to Earth Mother in the form of flesh and bone to seek revenge against their enemies. But why were these light-skinned men entering the Dragoons enemies of the Apache? Were they spirits of the Comanches killed during the big plains wars so long ago, when Apaches battled the Comanche over hunting ground far to the east? All the Comanches Naiche had seen, including the most fearsome of all—the Kwahadie tribe known as the Antelope Eaters—were dark, like the Apache. The battles over the best hunting territory between the five Comanche tribes and the Apache bands had been fought more than thirty winters ago, and now there was an uneasy peace between the two lifelong enemies, since the white men came. These men were not Comanches . . . he was sure of it.

Naiche thought of a solution to the unrest among the

people here at Wild Pig Springs, for signs of fear were
everywhere on the faces of most of his followers. It would
be better to put the blame for Cuchillo's failure on Cuchillo
himself, calling him a coward, a man unfit to call himself
an Apache. While this was not true—for Cuchillo was a
born fighter with skills equal to any warrior in camp—if
he were made to look foolish for costing the lives of the
warriors he led to halt the four white-skinned invaders,
the people would have less fear of an approaching enemy.

Naiche stood up. "Come! All of you!" he cried. "Hear
what I have to tell you!"

Across the narrow canyon, warriors and women halted
their preparations to walk toward Naiche and the place
where Cuchillo lay on the blood-soaked army blanket.

Naiche waited for the others to arrive.

From the corner of his eye, he saw a question on Chokole's face. He would ignore it and carry out his plan,
hoping Chokole would understand that what he was doing
was necessary for the good of their people to keep them
from fear, from losing their hope of freedom in the war
with the bluecoats he had promised them. It seemed each
day he was being reminded of the often hard choices a
leader must make for the greater good of his followers.
Being a chief of his people, like being a warrior, was not
a job for the faint of heart.

Thirty warriors and women gathered around Naiche,
and by the looks on their faces they expected some addi-
tional bit of grave news . . . most had been shocked when
they learned what had happened to Cuchillo and his war
party when Chokole and Juh brought him back to Wild
Pig Springs, his head shaved and bleeding, telling a tale
about how all his warriors had been killed before a white
man tied him to a wooden cross. It was enough to stir the
worst fears of Naiche's Apaches, since they had never seen
this new blood-crazed enemy.

"Hear me," Naiche began. "My heart is heavy to say
these words, but I must tell you why we are leaving this
ancient place of refuge used by our forefathers. It is no

longer safe here, and one of our own . . . an Apache brother, is at fault. He has given the white enemy a chance to kill us.''

A whisper of concern went around the assembled men and women, as Naiche knew it would. The suggestion that a traitor, or a coward, was in their midst would turn fear into blame for what had happened to the others.

"Who?" asked an old woman named Cusi, the second wife of Nana.

Naiche looked down at Cuchillo. "A man we all believed was filled with courage. Cuchillo took his warriors into a trap set by the killer white-eyes. Their lives were his responsibility as leader of the war party."

"No!" Cuchillo protested, his voice thin with pain and loss of blood. "We covered . . . our tracks . . . and hid ourselves among the rocks very . . . carefully."

"All the others are dead," Naiche growled, reaching for a cavalryman's pistol taken during the attack at the ravine which was tucked into his belt, "except for you, Cuchillo. No Apache would allow this to happen to his brothers."

"No!" Cuchillo cried again, his dark eyes fixed on the gun Naiche aimed down at him. "We covered our tracks. We hid among the rocks and brush as we were taught during our training as warriors."

Juh backed away from the spot, but Chokole stood her ground with her gaze on Naiche.

"Do not kill him," Chokole said, her voice soft, without inflection. "We need every warrior who can fight these white demons."

"It is not enough," Naiche told her. "The lives of our best fighting men must be spared from a poor leader who forgets what he has learned about the ways of the Apache."

"Will you kill Cuchillo?" she asked.

"It is The Way. When a war leader costs the People the lives of his men, he must die."

Chokole wisely backed away to stand beside Juh. She realized the futility of trying to change Naiche's mind once it was made up. She was a warrior, but she was still a woman, and must mind her place when their chief spoke.

Naiche knew he had his audience convinced of Cuchillo's incompetence.

"I send our brother, Cuchillo, to join his ancestors," he said, cocking the hammer of the Colt. "May his spirit walk the dark places filled with sorrow for what he has done."

Naiche pulled the trigger. The gunshot rang out, echoing off the walls of the canyon around Wild Pig Springs.

Cuchillo's body jerked, his spine arching when a bullet went through his heart. He trembled, blood bubbling from his mouth. Then his muscles relaxed, and he fell back on the blanket with a quiet groan.

In his hiding place on a ledge overlooking Wild Pig Springs canyon, Falcon sucked in his breath at the sight of Cuchillo's cold-blooded execution. In all of his travels, he had never once heard of an Apache killing a brother warrior. He realized Naiche must be extremely worried to take such a drastic step. Perhaps his campaign of terror was working even better than he had hoped.

In single file, the Apaches left Wild Pig Springs leading horses and mules laden with supplies for the arduous journey across the desert. At the front of the procession, Naiche rode one of the fresh cavalry horses stolen from the soldiers.

Juh rode beside him on one flank. Chokole kept her horse in check on the other flank, watching the mountains and passes for sign of the enemy.

Juh glanced over his shoulder. "The People are afraid now, Naiche," he said.

Naiche understood their fear. For the first time in his life, he also feared an enemy. But as chief of the Chiricahua band, he could not allow his fear to show. "They are like the white man's sheep," he said.

"Chokole says it was wrong to kill Cuchillo," Juh went on in his constant monotone. "He fought the white-eyes with all his courage."

"He led his men toward death," Naiche answered, with anger he did not truly feel. "He was foolish. He was trained as an Apache warrior."

Juh looked up at the sky, a clear sky without a trace of clouds. "These men who come . . . I have a bad feeling about them," he said.

Naiche was irritated, even though he shared Juh's concern "You have become like an old woman. They are only men, mortal men."

Juh's eyes glassed over for a moment. "I had a dream, a vision. In my dream, these whites were from another place where men do not die in battle."

"These are the dreams of children," Naiche assured him, with his own private doubts clouding his judgement. "All men die when a bullet or an arrow finds its mark. Stop talking like a woman, Juh. You have seen many battles in your lifetime. When did you ever encounter an enemy who would not bleed when your arrow or your bullet was true?"

Juh said nothing more, guiding his horse down a steep trail toward the desert floor at the southern end of the Dragoons, where they would be forced to cross open land to reach Mexico.

He knew his dreams were not those of children, but warnings given from the Spirits that had always protected the People—when they were wise enough to obey the warnings.

After all, was that not why young men went to the sweat lodge—to make themselves ready for guidance from the spirit world?

Juh sighed but kept his mouth shut, hoping in his heart Naiche would not regret ignoring the Spirits' advice.

Chapter 35

Naiche halted his weary band for a brief rest stop in rugged foothills at the southern edge of the Dragoons. Beyond the hills lay a brutally dry desert, dotted with agave and barrel cactus, ocotillo plants and cholla, yucca and prickly pear, with scattered stands of mesquite trees offering the only possible hiding places—from the soldiers behind them led by Mickey Free . . . and the four strange white men, two of them dressed in animal skin Indian garb, Apache manhunters no one could identify who continued to stalk their every move toward Mexico, killing Naiche's warriors along the way.

Chokole shaded her eyes from the sun. "We will have no way to defend our people if they catch us out there, before we reach the shelter of the Pedregosas. Slowed by the animals and heavy packs they carry, it will take us two suns to enter the mountains, or perhaps three suns."

Their departure from Wild Pig Springs had been a sad affair, with the hasty burials of Cuchillo and his warriors. Naiche still felt a touch of regret for killing Cuchillo in order to put the blame for so many warriors' deaths on someone other than himself.

"We have no choice," he told the Apache fighting woman in a dry voice. "We must cross this desolate place as quickly as we can. The women will need to run, leading the pack animals. Anyone who falls behind will be left to die. Only the strongest of our people will make it to the land called Mexico, where the bluecoats cannot follow us. Tell this to all who have hope of living as free Apaches."

"We should wait for darkness," Juh counselled. "If the bluecoats see our dust sign on the horizon, or the four white-eyes, they will know where we are. We have no defenses in this open place."

Naiche was uneasy about any delay. "We are Apaches," he said. "We are trained to hide from our enemies when there is no place to hide. The Apache scalphunter, Mickey Free, is guiding the bluecoats along our tracks, and we have no tools to remove the iron shoes from our horses. The white-eyes in buckskins are also behind us. There is no time to rest. If we stay here to wait for darkness, they will be closer to us. Free will bring the soldiers, and all of us will die if we wait here for the sun to sleep. There are too many of the white-eyes for us to win a battle with them."

"We could lose a fight out in the open," Chokole warned as she gave their backtrail a careful examination. "Our people are frightened by the four whites who killed Cuchillo's warriors, and the soldiers coming from the north."

Naiche could never admit he had his own worries about Free and the buckskin-clad men. His role as chief of the Chiricahuas and leader of this renegade band forbade any demonstration of fear. "We have many-shoot rifles and bullets. Let them come to fight with us."

Nana, old enough to be wise in the ways of war, spoke. "We are too few, Naiche. The clever white-eyes have taken too many of our number to the spirit world. We know they understand our ways, our movements, and they can read our tracks too easily. Darkness will hide us when we cross this desert to the Pedregosas. It is two day's journey, perhaps more, as Chokole said, and we have no places to stop and fight where Earth Mother will give us rocks or big trees or cover to halt their bullets. We should cross this place at night, when they cannot see our dust sign in the sky. Out there on the empty desert, we will all be killed if they find our horses' sign and the direction we travel.''

Nana's experience fighting the whites gave Naiche a moment's pause. But he was certain the white-skinned killers were very close now, and Mickey Free would not be far behind them with the columns of bluecoats. "The iron on these soldier horses gives us away," he said finally. "This is the reason why they find us so easily. But we must have strong horses. Without them, we are helpless. The time has come for us to prove we are Apaches, in spite of the tracks we leave for them to follow. The white man's iron horseshoes are our enemy.''

"Yes," Chokole agreed. Darkness is not far away. I agree with Nana that we should wait for the sun to disappear, for with sundown the light is gone, and they will not see us or the hoofprints left by our animals.''

"Chokole offers you wise council," Nana said, giving the hills behind them his own careful scrutiny. "Even if they find us here, we have rocks and arroyos where we can fight them off with repeating rifles.''

Naiche recalled the wisdom of Geronimo, and how many times he had told the People it was better to hide and fight an enemy at the place and time where the advantage belonged to the Apache, and not the enemy. "Geronimo avoids direct contact with our white enemies. He leads them into traps where even a few good warriors can win battles against many times their number. If we wait here for the sun to sleep, we lose precious time. If we keep moving, we have the advantage of being far out in front of them.''

"Our people ... especially the women, are tired and

afraid of these white men," Nana said. "Under the cover of darkness they will have less fear."

Naiche turned to Nana, his eyes slitted with sudden anger. "I am chief of the Chiricahuas, a son of Cochise. The spirits guide me. We will cross this desert now, and put more distance between us and the whites while the sun warms the air. If we wait for darkness, the freezing cold will hamper our horses, and the women will not be able to travel as fast."

Nana lowered his head.

Chokole looked off at the horizon where the sun would fall below the desert in a few short hours, providing the darkness she and Nana wanted. "You are our leader, Naiche. I will do whatever you say we must do to reach safety. If you tell us to go now, we will go."

Across the desert floor, shimmering heat waves created the illusion of water in the distance. A hawk circled far to the south above the ocotillo spines, hunting, seeking prey before the darkness ended its chances of a successful feeding on the snakes and lizards it might find in a dry land. Riding currents of hot air, it rose on wings spread far from its body, a sure sign no danger lurked beneath it.

Naiche pointed to the bird. "The hawk gives us our sign. It hunts without fear. The way is clear across this desert to the mountains. Tell the women to run as fast as they can with the pack animals. It is time to go."

Chokole turned her horse and rode off at a trot back to the waiting women and horses. Naiche could hear her giving them his message. Farther back, a rear guard of armed warriors watched the foothills through which they had come since leaving Wild Pig Springs.

It was Juh who gave Naiche more cause for concern, when he pointed to a spot in front of them.

"Look beyond the cholla, Naiche," Juh said, his tone grave, filled with foreboding. "A coiled rattlesnake lies in our path. It is a sign from the spirit world to go in another direction, for the snake is a messenger of death."

Naiche heard the serpent's deadly warning rattle, and

he saw it coiled in the shade below a flat stone. His stomach twisted. The rattlesnake was, as Juh said, often a messenger from the next life sent by their ancestors to turn the People away from certain disaster.

More than anything else, even more than invoking the wrath of the spirits, Naiche feared being caught by the four unknown Apache hunters and the soldiers before more warriors joined them to use the many-shoot rifles lashed to the pack horses. What good were magic guns if he had no warriors to shoot them?

He slid off the back of his horse and drew his knife, for he meant to kill the rattlesnake silently as proof to Juh and the others that the serpent was not a bad omen foretelling some dark to come.

He strode quickly down to the rock where the huge rattler lay coiled. The snake watched him with cold, lidless eyes. He distracted the thick serpent with a sudden movement of his left foot, swinging it just close enough for a strike at the top of his knee-high deerskin boots decorated with porcupine quills and beadwork.

The rattler struck half the length of its body, deadly fangs bared. Naiche jerked his foot away just in the nick of time and sent his gleaming knife blade downward in a swift arc.

The tip of his knife caught the snake behind its broad head and tore through its layers of scales as Naiche pinned it to the ground. Coiling around his arm, rattling fiercely, it was helpless to inject its poisonous fangs into his flesh.

Naiche sliced the serpent's head off while its body still writhed with a life of its own. He stuck the rattler's head onto the tip of his knife and turned toward Juh and the line of Apaches waiting for him on the crest of a hill.

He shook the knife over his head. "See this, my brothers?" he cried. "We are Apaches! We will kill anyone who tries to stop us from joining Geronimo in Mexico!"

Nods of approval went down the row of warriors and women. By means of a simple demonstration, proving that the rattler was not a warning from the Spirits to turn away, Naiche had given his people new hope and courage.

"Follow me across the desert!" he shouted, mounting his bay with the snake's head displayed on his knifetip.

Single file, Naiche started downslope toward the welcome heat of the desert floor that would take them to the Pedregosas, then across the Mexican border to safety.

Chapter 36

Falcon watched through his binoculars as Naiche got on his horse, holding a knife with a snake's head on it, and led his people out onto the desert floor. He took particular note of the three warriors left behind as a rear guard.

Time to sow some more seeds of fear, he thought as he crawled backward from the edge of the ledge he was lying on. He pulled his Winchester from its saddle boot and eased over the hilltop, being careful to keep to heavy brush as he descended the side of the mountain toward the Indian guards. He took his time, making no noise, until he was a couple of hundred yards from the braves.

He stepped to a pinyon tree and braced his rifle barrel against a small branch stub sticking out. Slowly, he exhaled and increased pressure gradually on the trigger. The long gun exploded and kicked back against his shoulder. He worked the lever and switched aim before the echoes from the first shot had faded. Twice more, faster than it takes to tell it, he fired, knocking all three Indians off their ponies.

One was still alive by the time Falcon was able to scramble down the remaining hundred yards of hillside.

As Falcon stood over the Indian, a look of terror came over his face as the brave pulled his knife and slashed it across his own throat.

I guess I've got them thinking I'm some kind of monster, Falcon thought. That was good news, to see the Indians so afraid of him they'd rather cut their own throats than face him.

Falcon spent some time working on the dead bodies, then rounded up their ponies, tied the braves to the broncs' backs, and sent them out onto the desert in the direction Naiche and his band had taken. It would be nice if he could be there to see their faces when their rear guard showed up butchered like the others.

When he had washed the blood off his arms, Falcon gathered up as much dry timber and dead branches as he could and built a large pile in the center of the trail. He took a cigar out of his pocket, struck a lucifer on his pants leg, lit the cigar, then threw the match in the dry leaves.

Within minutes he had a roaring bonfire going, sending dark columns of cloudy smoke into the sky.

He looked back up the mountain toward the odd-shaped rock in the distance called Indian Head Peak by white folks. He hoped the army had shown up, and that Hawk and Meeks would recognize his smoke as a signal to come.

Once the fire was going well, he climbed back up the mountainside to Diablo. He decided he had time for a short nap, since he figured to be busy later that night. He took Diablo's saddle off, put his ground tarp on a bed of pine needles, and lay back for a *siesta.*

As he fell asleep he began to dream of another place where he'd tangled with Apache runaways from an Indian reservation. That time he'd found himself with some rather infamous company—none other than Billy Bonney, known in New Mexico Territory as Billy the Kid—a man virtually everyone thought was dead, shot down by Sheriff Pat Garrett. A bunch of Mescaleros hired by Thomas Catron up in Santa Fe rode to Lincoln County to raid the cattle ranch

of John Chisum. Falcon had quickly put an end to Chisum's
Apache problem. . . .

   Falcon walked over to the Kid where he was standing
above the man he'd shot.
   "Got him right through the heart," the Kid said, "only
he's still alive."
   "Won't be for long," Falcon observed, for even in the
dark of the pinyon forest an inky pool of blood was spreading around the body, easy to see.
   "He kinda whispered his name," the Kid went on in a
quiet voice. "Roy Cobb."
   "He called the other one Deke," Falcon remembered.
   "Cobb said they didn't work for Jimmy Dolan or Murphy
or any of the Lincoln County bunch. They came straight
down from Santa Fe, bein' paid by Thomas Catron, the
leader of the beef ring that started all this trouble. That's
what this feller told me just before he blacked out."
   "Somebody needs to pay a call on this Thomas Catron.
Tell him what happened to his boys and his Apaches here
tonight. It ain't over yet. There's still nine or ten Apaches
out there, and I intend to kill 'em all."
   "How come, Falcon?" the Kid wondered. "They don't
seem to want no more fight with us."
   "It's personal, Kid."
   "Personal? You've tangled with those same renegades
before?"
   "Not the same bunch, but they're renegades off a reservation, and that makes 'em fair game."
   "Fair game for a killin'? Mind tellin' me why you feel
so hard-line about it?"
   Falcon took a deep breath, gazing toward the open prairie where the renegades still sat their ponies watching the
trees where the shooting had occurred. He was remembering the worst moment of his life, when a band of redskins
had come down on his place while he was away, slaughtering his wife, Marie, butchering her like a fatted calf, cutting

her open, scalping her, leaving her alive to suffer miserably until she died slowly.

"You ain't gotta talk about it if you'd rather not," the Kid said.

"A band of renegades attacked my ranch while I was off on business. They took my wife with 'em. They had their way with her and then cut her open. Sliced off her scalp. My father told me when he found her she'd bled all over the place, so I know she suffered something awful."

"Was she . . . dead when he found her?"

Falcon merely nodded, turning away from the dying gunman from Santa Fe to walk to his horse.

"You're goin' after the others, ain't you?" the Kid said just as Roy Cobb let out his final breath.

"Sure as hell am," Falcon replied.

"I'll go with you," the Kid offered, hurrying to catch up to Falcon's longer strides.

"Nope," Falcon remarked. "This is my affair. Stay put until I'm done with 'em."

"You're gonna take all of 'em on by yourself?"

"Now you've got the idea," Falcon told him as he untied Diablo's reins and swung into the saddle.

He began thumbing cartridges into the loading tube of his Winchester rifle. Then he booted it and pulled one pistol at a time to check their loads.

"I'll damn sure ride out there an' help you," the Kid said again.

"I appreciate the offer," Falcon replied, reining Diablo away from the tree. "But this is my personal score to settle. It's been haunting me all these years. I can't sleep sometimes, picturing what my Marie must've looked like when Jamie found her."

"An' now you're out to kill every Indian renegade you run across. It don't matter what breed they are."

Falcon halted his horse just long enough to answer the Kid's question. "Those are renegades, son. The law says we don't fight each other any more like we did in the old days, before the big treaty at Medicine Lodge. These

Mescaleros broke their word to keep peace between us. They ran off looking for a fight with white men, and I aim to oblige 'em. Those renegades who killed my Marie ignored the treaty and went to war against me, against a defenseless woman. I'll make every redskin renegade I can find pay for what happened to my wife until I go to my grave. It's something I have to do.''

At that, Falcon had heeled Diablo through the pinyons toward the open valley, where nine Apaches were gathered in a low spot with rifles balanced across their ponies' withers.

Falcon rode to the edge of the forest. He jerked his rifle free, jacked a load into place, twisted Diablo's reins around his saddlehorn so he could guide the trusty stud with his knees. At the last Falcon pulled the Colt pistol from his left holster, fisting it, then bringing the Winchester to his right shoulder.

"Move out, Diablo," he said soft and low, urging the big stallion into a run straight toward the Apaches.

The Indians did not move, watching him gallop toward them out of a setting sun as if they couldn't believe their eyes—one man charging toward nine armed warriors. Falcon knew they must believe he was crazy.

Hell, he thought, *they may well be right.*

The smooth running gait of Diablo did nothing to bother his aim when Falcon drew a bead on one Indian and pulled the trigger on his rifle, a shot of almost three hundred yards, impossible for all but the best marksmen.

A shrieking Indian twisted off his pony, flinging his rifle high above his head as he fell head-first beneath the hooves of the other ponies.

Falcon gave the Winchester's loading lever a road agent's spin, twirling it around his outstretched hand, sending another brass-jacketed shell into the chamber. He was still too far out of range to use his Colt pistol, but he was sure the opportunity to use it would come.

Three Indians fired back at him, yet Falcon had anticipated their move by kneeing Diablo to the left and right so the big horse changed leads with every stride. A zigzagging target was virtually impossible to hit without a stroke of luck, and if Falcon had anything to say about it, the Indians were plumb out of luck today.

Falcon fired his rifle again as two slugs whistled past him into the night sky, while a third plowed up dirt and grass many yards to the right of Diablo's run.

The shot from Falcon's Winchester found another mark when a Mescalero in a fringed buckskin shirt yelped like a scalded dog and rolled, ball-like, off the croup of his prancing pinto pony to land hard on the ground behind it.

Again, Falcon gave the rifle a one-handed spin, a practiced move he accomplished so smoothly it seemed like a fluid motion, not the working of a steel mechanism in a man's hand.

Four more shots thundered from the swale in Falcon's direction, and all were wide misses. The Indians' ponies were hard to control with all the shooting going on, rearing on hind legs or plunging against the pull of jawreins.

Falcon aimed for an Apache and blasted him off his dappled gray. Blood flew from his ribs and back, and it seemed the big .44 slug had all but torn the Indian in half.

Diablo continued his charge toward the milling Indians as the powerful horse dodged back and forth under the signals from Falcon's knees.

The remaining Apaches suddenly panicked, as if they realized this crazy white-eyes meant business, and swung their ponies away from Falcon's headlong rush, drumming their heels into the ribs of their mounts.

Their retreat did nothing to discourage MacCallister's grin determination to blast the Mescalero renegades to their happy hunting ground. He asked Diablo for more speed and singled out one Indian to ride down and kill. Six Mescaleros remained, and if he had his way he meant to slaughter the entire bunch.

He fired at the escaping Apache and blew the back of the warrior's skull apart, with blood and hair and bone fragments flying high above the dappled pony until the dead Indian fell limply to the valley floor.

Turning Diablo after another target, Falcon aimed and fired twice with his Colt. Another warrior screamed in agony and went down hard.

Changing directions again, the scattering Apaches wanted no more of Falcon. Remembering Marie, he gave a mirthless grin. "Time for paybacks, you red bastards," he growled, asking Diablo for all he had.

Falcon rested aboard the big black stud on a hilltop to survey the scene below. Diablo was blowing hard, covered with a thick coating of sweat and foam. Falcon leaned forward to pat the big stud's neck, for he had run as if he were chasing the devil for Falcon—which, in a sense, he had been.

Spread across a starlit valley, lying in patches of dark blood, nine Mescalero Apache renegades decorated the north Chisum pasture. Men who had found all the excitement they could handle when they decided to leave the reservation and make some extra money by stealing.

He heard the Kid riding up the hill. As soon as the Kid got there he spoke.

"Never saw nothin' like it, Falcon." Kid removed his hat and sleeved off his face. Then he shook his head in awe. "You killed every one of 'em like it was all in a day's work."

He glanced sideways at Falcon. "You know, I used to think I was a pretty bad hombre, but you just showed me something. There's always somebody over the next hill who's just a little bit badder."

Falcon gave the Kid a lopsided grin. "Now you know why I keep telling you to get off the hoot owl trail and go straight. That trail only leads to one conclusion, and it's always the same, being stood up in a pine box for folks to take pictures of and stand around gawking at."

Kid nodded.

"You plannin' on goin' up to Santa Fe to have a talk with Catron?"

Falcon's thirst for revenge had lessened after the blood-bath, and he turned to the Kid. "Maybe later, but right now I'm heading on down to John Chisum's to tell him what happened."

He stared out across the field, almost completely covered in darkness now. "He's probably heard the shots and is wondering who's gone to war out on his spread." He stuck out his hand, "It's time you started that long ride to the Mexican border."

The Kid leaned out of his saddle, taking Falcon's hand. "It's been a pleasure to know you, Falcon MacCallister. Thanks for all you did to try to help me an' my friends. We lost the war in Lincoln County, that's for sure, but we damn sure made 'em pay in blood to get it done."

Falcon didn't want more conversation right at the moment. "Best you start riding, son. And good luck to you. If you're as smart as I think you are, you won't ever show your face in New Mexico Territory again. Let 'em all think you're buried up at Fort Sumner."

The Kid nodded and swung his horse off the hilltop, hitting a trot to the south. Crossing the dark valley, he glanced to his left and then his right when he rode past the bodies of some of the Apaches Falcon had killed.

Falcon watched the boy ride off, deciding the Kid's secret would always be safe with him.

He heeled Diablo off the grassy knob and headed for Chisum's South Springs ranch, with a tale to tell.

Just once, he turned to watch the Kid ride out of sight over a ridge.

"Good luck down in Mexico, Kid," he said to himself as Diablo carried him toward John Chisum's headquarters, *"Vaya con Díos, Chivato."*

Falcon tossed and turned as his dreams caused him to sweat, and his heart to beat faster. He relived in his mind his hatred for renegade Indians, and all that they had cost him. Not a bigoted man by nature, Falcon judged most people by their actions, not the color of their skin. Indians who were peaceable and obeyed the law had nothing to fear from him. It was the ones who flaunted the law, who declared war on the white man, that he hated with all his heart. The Indians had no honor about war. They killed women and children and civilians as well as soldiers who were on their trail, and they did it in the most brutal manner imaginable. For that reason, he would not rest until Naiche and his followers were captured, or were in their graves.

Chapter 37

"Dammit, Free," Captain Buford Jones shouted, "when are we going up in those mountains after Naiche? You've had us out here in the desert for two days doing nothing but riding around in circles."

The scout looked up from where he squatted on his haunches looking for tracks and signs only he could see in the hard-packed desert sand. He was a short man who appeared to be in his mid-forties, but with his white, glossy, gouch-eye and his long shaggy hair that he let fall down over his face to hide the eye from view, he could have been anywhere from twenty to fifty years old.

One thing was certain, Captain Jones thought, though he didn't dare say it out loud, the man sure enough had a lot of miles on him. He looked like he'd been rode hard and put up wet.

"Cap'n Jones," Mickey Free said in his Irish tenor voice, his brogue, normally thick as molasses in January, made even deeper by the evident sarcasm in his tone, "I would think after your last couple'a ventures up against Naiche, ye'd be a mite more careful 'bout rushin' into places ye ain't sure of."

Jones glanced around at the men in his command to see if they heard what Mickey said. He knew he wasn't the most popular commander since he'd lost almost all his men on his previous two outings, but he didn't appreciate a lowlife like Mickey Free impugning his abilities in front of his men.

Free had a terrible reputation among the officers of the army, and the only reason he got away with his insubordination was there wasn't a better tracker in the whole United States army. It was said that Mickey Free could smell Apaches from miles away even if there weren't any tracks to be found, and would follow his nose to where they were hiding. Unlike other scouts, who dropped back when fighting began, Free was always in the forefront, a maniacal grin on his ugly face as he drew down on and killed Indians. It was as if he had a driving need of some sort to kill every red man in the country.

"Just what do you mean by that remark, Free?"

Mickey shrugged. "Take it any way you like, Cap'n. But long as I'm scoutin' for this here *soiree*, we'll go about it my way. Do you understand, Cap'n?"

As Jones' face turned red and he sat straighter in his saddle, Mickey shrugged and spread his hands wide, an insolent smirk on his ugly face. "'Cause if it's not all right, I'll just shag my butt on back to the fort and let you carry on in your usual manner."

Jones clamped his teeth shut, trying his best to resist a sudden urge to pull his revolver and shoot this smart-talking sonofabitch right in the face. His resolve to do nothing was bolstered by Mickey's reputation as a cold-blooded killer, and Jones had a feeling that if he did go for his gun he'd be dead before he could clear leather.

He was saved from making a reply when a soldier rode up in a cloud of dust, his gelding covered with a thick coat of sweat and foam.

"Hey, Captain Jones, sir! I got a message for you from the telegraph at the fort," the young man called.

Jones reached out his hand without speaking, still fuming over the lack of respect for his rank shown by Mickey Free.

He took the telegram and unfolded it, squinting a little to make out the writing—he didn't intend to give Free any more ammunition to use against him by putting on his reading spectacles.

After a moment, he cleared his throat. "It says here, Mr. Free, that a group of cowboys up in the Dragoons have found out where Naiche is hiding his main force. They say if we'll meet them under Indian Head Peak at noon today, they'll lead us right to him."

"Uh huh," Mickey muttered, an expression on his face as if he'd tasted gall.

"What is the matter with you, Mr. Free?" asked Jones.

"It's just that I don't believe any cowboys could've just stumbled upon Naiche's camp and been allowed to ride away to summon us to them. Naiche ain't that careless, or that stupid. Does that telegram say who it is we're dealin' with?"

Jones glanced at the bottom of the paper. "It does mention a name here . . . Falcon MacCallister."

"The hell you say! MacCallister?"

"That's right. Why? Do you know him?"

Mickey rubbed his beard stubble for a moment, his eyes vacant as he thought back a few years. He'd been trailing an Indian for what seemed like months when he pulled up at a stage stop cantina to replenish his fading supply of Irish whiskey, or whiskey of any kind, for that matter. As he approached the cantina door, the Indian he'd been trailing stepped out with a pistol in his hand and a grin on his face. Mickey was sure he had only seconds to live, when suddenly a tall man appeared behind the Indian and grabbed him by the hair. The stranger yanked the brave's head back and slid a Bowie knife gently across his throat. He released the Indian and let him fall to the ground to die strangling on his own blood. When Mickey managed to make enough spit to talk, he asked the stranger's name. "MacCallister, Jamie MacCallister," he'd answered. When

Mickey offered to split the reward with MacCallister, he refused. Then the man bent, and quick as a rattler striking he'd sliced off the brave's face, rolled it up in the dead man's shirt, and handed it to Mickey. "Here's the proof you need to get your reward," MacCallister had said. Then, he'd winked and added, "An' bringing the man's face back wrapped up like a birthday present won't do your reputation any harm, either." He'd been right. That act of foolish bravado had made Mickey Free a legend in his own time, and gotten him any number of free drinks in bars all across the west.

Mickey looked up, snapping out of his reverie. "Know him? No, but I knew his paw. Hell of a man!"

Jones stared at Mickey with narrowed eyes. "So, you think we should trust this MacCallister to lead us to Naiche?"

"If he's anything like his father, I'd follow him through the gates of hell," Mickey said, a grin on his face.

He took two quick steps and jumped up on the back of a pinto pony he was riding. "Let's make dust, Cap'n. We're burnin' daylight."

Jones had no choice but to follow Mickey's lead, so he waved hand in a circle and shouted, "Follow ho!" as he spurred his horse into the dust cloud left by Mickey's pony.

Hawk and Meeks were sitting next to a small fire they'd built under the overhang of a rock to hide the smoke. Hawk paused with his coffee cup halfway to his mouth and cocked his head.

"Horses!" he said, jumping to his feet and walking rapidly to. He pulled out his Winchester and levered a shell into the chamber.

"Indians?" Meeks asked as he climbed onto the boulder and shaded his eyes as he looked down the mountain.

After a moment, Meeks smiled. "It's the cavalry, come to rescue us from the redskins."

"That'll be the day," Hawks said, a smirk on his face as he lowered the hammer of his rifle with his thumb.

It wasn't long before Captain Jones and his men rode into the clearing under the outcropping of rock that resembled an Indian Chief's head.

"Good afternoon, gentlemen," Jones said.

Hawk and Meeks looked at each other as if they didn't know which of them was being addressed as a "gentleman".

"Howdy, Colonel," Hawks said.

"It's captain, not colonel," Jones said.

"Which of you two is MacCallister?" Mickey asked, peering at them with his head cocked to one side as he looked out of his good eye.

Meeks stared at Mickey for a moment, then smiled. "Neither one of us is. He went on ahead to keep an eye on Naiche an' make sure he didn't move his camp. Would you be Mickey Free?"

Mickey nodded. "Yep." He was used to being recognized. After all, there weren't all that many men around who fit his description.

Hawk looked up at the mention of the name Free. "I didn't know you was in the area. Last I heared you was doggin' Cochise's tail."

Mickey yawned, as if what Hawk had heard was of no interest to him whatsoever. "Nope. That business's all finished now."

"Just who are you men?" Jones asked, irritated to be left out of the conversation.

"I'm John Henry Hawkins, but mostly I go by Hawk. This is Jasper Meeks."

Jones narrowed his eyes. "You the same Meeks who tried to take that wagon train through Indian country?"

Meeks face blushed a bright red. "Yeah, but it weren't my idea to go that way. The wagonmaster overruled my advice, an' they paid the price for ignorin' what I had to say."

Jones shook his head. "They certainly did. Now, what are you men doing up here during an Indian war?"

"We had business up here," Hawk answered.

"What business is that, Mr. Hawk?"

"Revenge. Them murderin' redskins kilt my kin ... butchered 'em like they was nothin'. I aim to kill a few Injuns for every one of my kin they slaughtered."

Jones cut his gaze to Meeks.

"What about you, Mr. Meeks?"

Meeks shrugged. "As you know, I suddenly found myself out of a job, an' I had nothin' better to do, so I decided to mosey around up here in the Dragoons for a spell."

"You after revenge, too?" Mickey asked.

Meeks gave a nasty smile. "Well, if any Injuns happen to cross my path, I don't intend to turn the other cheek after what they did to my wagon train."

Jones sat back against the cantle of his saddle. "Don't you men know it's the army's place to get the Indians back on the reservation?"

Hawk stared at Jones as he took a plug of tobacco and sliced off a piece. He popped it in his mouth and began to chew as he answered, "Yeah, Captain, an' we can all see you're doin' a damn good job of it, too."

"From what we heard in Tombstone the other day," Meeks added, "all you blue-bellies have managed to do so far is give the Indians a bunch of repeatin' rifles and some targets to shoot at with 'em."

"Word is," Hawk said, a malicious grin on his face, "casualties are running 'bout fifty to one, against you. At that rate, there'll only be one or two soldiers left when you finally kill all the redskins."

Mickey Free chuckled loudly, muttering under his breath, "You got that right."

"Enough of this talk," Jones barked. "Will you show us where Naiche's camp is?"

"You plannin' on just ridin' up the trail an' attackin' his people?" Hawk asked.

"Is there anything wrong with that plan, Mr. Hawk?"

Hawk snorted, glancing at Mickey Free. "Well, right off, I think it'd be a mite smarter to send your scout up there with me and Meeks an' let us take care of the sentries first. Otherwise, by the time you get to 'em, they'll be all dug in an' you'll have a hell of a time rootin' 'em out.

"He's right, Captain. I'll head on up to the camp with these two and scout out the lay of the land. After we've killed the guards, we'll come back and get you."

Jones nodded and spoke over his shoulder to his aide, "Tell the men to dismount. We'll prepare lunch here while Mr. Free scouts on ahead."

As they rode up the trail, Hawk looked at Free. "Mickey, tell me the truth. How do you stand workin' for idiots like that captain back there?"

Mickey laughed. "Well, I'll tell you, my friend, it ain't always easy." He hesitated a moment, then added, "But it's the surest way I know to kill me some Apaches."

"You hate 'em that bad?" Meeks asked.

Mickey's face clouded. "As long as there's even one of those bastards walkin' around free, I'll be volunteerin' to go get his scalp."

Hawk reined in his horse. "We'd better walk the rest of the way. It's only another mile or so."

The three men separated and spent an hour painstakingly creeping up on the ledge overlooking Deer Spring Canyon. Finally, after discovering there were no sentries stationed around the canyon, they met up on the precipice.

"Damn," Hawk said, "looks like they've flown the coop."

Down in the valley, cooking fires were still smoldering, lazy trails of smoke spiraling skyward.

Mickey stroked his beard-stubbled face. "Well, I guess if it comes to it, I can go down there and track the sons of bitches to wherever they've gone."

"Hold on a minute," Meeks said.

Hawk and Mickey turned and glanced at the trailsman.

He was facing away from them toward the southernmost part of the mountains.

"Look down there," he said, pointing.

Mickey shaded his eyes, then said, "I was wonderin' where MacCallister was. It'd be my guess that's a signal from him that the Injuns have taken out across the desert."

Hawk grinned. "Leave it to Falcon to send the army smoke signals tellin' 'em where to find Injuns."

Mickey started off back down the mountain toward their horses at a trot. "Come on, boys. Let's go get 'em."

Chapter 38

Falcon awoke with a start, covered with sweat that was fast becoming frigid as the late afternoon temperature dropped.

Stepping over to Diablo, he poured some water from his canteen onto his bandanna and wiped his face, trying to come fully awake. He glanced at the sun lying low on the horizon and realized he'd slept longer than he wanted to. Naiche and his band of renegades now had a good four hour start on him.

"Time to shag our tails, Diablo," he said, swinging into the saddle. As he put the spurs to the stud and leaned over his neck, he added, "I can't believe you let me sleep so long, fellah."

He could barely make out the tracks in the coarse desert sand in the failing sunlight, and occasionally had to get down off Diablo and cast around in a semicircle until he picked up the trail again.

Soon, he found himself thinking of Billy Bonney, and the adventures they'd had in New Mexico. He didn't recall his dream, so he couldn't figure out why Billy was on his mind, but with nothing else much to think about as he rode across the barren landscape, he let his mind roam back to those days.

Remembering his chance meeting with Billy the Kid, Falcon recalled some of the men he'd come to know during those troubles being heralded as the Lincoln County War ... he'd spilled a lot of blood on behalf of John Chisum during that affair. Chisum lost a great many good friends and neighbors to hired killers, both red men and white, from Santa Fe. Falcon found himself without options he could live with, for he wasn't made to sit idly and watch a one-sided fight with a good man like Chisum on the short end of things. . . .

When Falcon approached his cabin, after leaving John Chisum's South Spring Ranch, he saw three horses in his corral, eating hay and making themselves at home.

He eased off Diablo, and walked to the back of the cabin, stepping on his toes so as not to make any sounds. He doubted if his company was hostile—otherwise they wouldn't have left their horses in plain view—but he hadn't lived this long without being careful.

He filled his right hand with iron, pulled the back door open with his left hand, and stepped inside, immediately moving to the side with his back against a wall so he wouldn't be silhouetted against the open door.

One of the three men sitting at his table looked up, then turned to the others. "See, I told you he'd come loaded for bear."

Seeing the men sitting there, drinking coffee with their hands in plain sight on the table, Falcon relaxed and holstered his pistol.

The men's faces were vaguely familiar, but he couldn't place their names.

"Good evening, gentlemen. Mind if I join you in that coffee?"

"No, go right ahead," a tall, lanky man said. "We boiled plenty, an' it's good and strong."

Falcon poured himself a cup, tasted it, then added a little water with a dipper from the pail on his counter.

"Whew," he said, "this stuff's strong enough to float a horseshoe."

A second man, broad through the middle with a beard and moustache, said, "Sorry 'bout that. We been on the trail a good ways an' we needed something to keep us awake 'til you got here."

Falcon leaned back against the kitchen counter, his feet crossed at the ankles, sipped his coffee, and watched the men, waiting for them to explain who they were and why they were at his cabin in the middle of the night.

The tall, thin man built himself a cigarette, struck a lucifer on the heel of his boot and lighted it. Then he leaned back, coffee in one hand and butt in the other.

"Falcon, my name's Josiah G. Scurlock, but everybody just calls me Doc." He inclined his head toward his companions, "This here is Henry Brown and John Middleton."

Falcon nodded. Now he remembered. These men had been among the first group to join together and call themselves the Regulators.

"Howdy, boys. To what do I owe the pleasure of a visit from the last of the Regulators?"

Scurlock smiled. Evidently he was to be the spokesman for the group.

"We hear you were a good friend to the Kid, always there when he needed you, an' we also hear rumors it was you who took out Jesse Evans and a couple of his boys."

Falcon smiled and sipped his coffee, watching the men over the rim of his cup. He wondered where this was leading.

When Falcon didn't answer, Scurlock continued.

"When John Tunstall was killed, a group of friends and former employees of his joined together, to avenge his death."

He took a deep drag on his cigarette, then tipped smoke out of his nostrils as he talked. "When we all—Bob Widenmann, Dick Brewer, Charley Bowdre, Fred Waite, and the Kid—joined up, Falcon, we took a blood oath. We swore an oath to remain loyal to each other no matter what happened, and to make sure whoever killed John was punished."

Falcon began to see where this was heading, but he nodded and listened.

"Now, we ain't exactly proud of what we done back when things were getting hot and heavy. When the Kid got indicted for killin' Sheriff Billy Brady I was in Kansas, and both Middleton and Brown here were out of town, also."

Falcon stepped over to the stove and refilled his coffee mug, not adding water this time. He realized this was going to take a while, and he was bone-tired from a long day.

"Go on," he said, taking out a cigar and lighting it.

"Well, by the time I heard the news 'bout Kid's arrest he was already out of jail and on the run, so I didn't figure I needed to come back here and tell the truth." He looked down at his hands, folded on the table. "Falcon, it was me who put those slugs in Brady, not the Kid."

Falcon stared at Scurlock. *So the Kid was telling the truth when he told me he didn't kill Brady,* he thought.

"Now, don't get me wrong. All of us, the Kid included, did plenty of things we could'a gone to jail for, but we was acting as deputies, duly sworn and appointed."

"Cut to the chase," Brown said, looking as tired as Falcon felt. He looked over at Falcon, "What Doc is tryin' to say in his typical long-winded way, is that we're all feelin' mighty guilty that we took an oath to stick together, and then when the going got rough, we lit out and left the Kid to do our work, an' he got himself killed for it."

Falcon kept his mouth shut. No matter how good friends these were of the Kid's, too many people already knew he was alive. He wasn't about to tell anyone else the truth.

John Middleton nodded, his knuckles white where he was gripping his tin mug. "Yeah, so now we're back and we want to finish what we started, and make those that killed Tunstall, and the Kid, pay."

Falcon, his legs and butt aching from too many hours in the saddle, joined them at the table.

"And just how do you boys intend to do that?"

Scurlock crushed out his cigarette in an ashtray. "We're gonna kill Dolan an' the hired killers he's got with him."

Falcon shook his head. "I don't think that's such a good idea."

"Why not?" Brown said.

"First off, he's too well-connected, and too well-protected. If you did manage to kill him, his friends in Santa Fe and the army would never stop until all you men were hunted down and killed, or hanged."

"We're willin' to take our chances," Middleton said. "We owe it to the Kid, and the others who got killed tryin' to do what we all promised to do."

Falcon wagged his head again. "No. I think there's a better way."

"What's that?" Scurlock asked.

"Why not go after the men who did Dolan's dirty work for him? The Seven Rivers gang and the Dona Ana bunch, led by John Kinney."

Scurlock nodded, thinking on it.

"Those men are all known outlaws, and no one would mind overly much if you took them out. You could hit fast and hard, and get away clean, and you wouldn't have John Law on your trail for the rest of your lives."

"Would that hurt Dolan?"

"In the worst way. He'd no longer have them to do his bidding, and he'd lose all the cattle these men have been stealing to fulfill his government contract to supply beef to the Mescaleros. It would cripple his operations here in Lincoln County."

The three men looked at each other for a moment. Then Scurlock turned to Falcon. "Would you be willin' to ride with us?"

Falcon pursed his lips, then sighed. "I don't usually join causes, but in this case I might make an exception. These gangs have been riding roughshod over the entire county, and it's time someone took them down."

"How will we go about it?" Brown asked.

Falcon leaned forward, "I've got a plan. Here's what we'll do . . ."

The next evening, just before sunset, Falcon and the other three were on a ridge overlooking an area near Mesilla where the Seven Rivers gang were camped. There were close to two hundred head of stolen cattle the gang was preparing to drive to Santa Fe to sell to the government for Dolan. Falcon put his binoculars down and looked at the other men. "I count about twenty men. That makes it about four to one against us. You boys ready?"

Scurlock pulled his pistol out, opened the loading gate, and spun the cylinder, checking his loads. "Ready," he said.

The men climbed on their horses. "We'll ride in fast and hard, out of the west so's the sun'll be at our backs," Falcon said.

He wrapped Diablo's reins around his saddle horn, pulled his Winchester .44/.40 carbine out of his saddle boot and levered a round into the chamber, and loosened the hammer thong on his Colt sidearm.

Henry Brown put his reins in his teeth and pulled a Greener 10 gauge short-barreled shotgun from his saddle boot, filling his pockets with extra shells.

John Middleton filled both his hands with pistols, and stuck a third in the front of his pants, behind his belt for quick access.

They were ready to ride.

Scurlock looked at the others. "For the Kid," he said.

Falcon smiled and nodded. "And for all the other men these bastards have killed."

They leaned forward in their saddles and spurred their mounts, bounding over the ridge to ride out of the sun straight into the outlaws' camp.

As the four horses raced down the hill, several men in the camp, sitting around the fire drinking coffee and whiskey, looked up.

John Beckwith, the leader, said, "What the hell?"

Wallace Olinger, the brother of the man Kid shotgunned to death in his escape from jail, dropped his coffee cup and grabbed for his rifle, which was leaning against a nearby tree.

Falcon, pistol in his left hand and rifle in his right, raised the carbine to his shoulder and fired. His first shot took Billy Matthews in the left shoulder, spinning him around and knocking his pistol from his hand.

Brown veered his horse to the left and fired his Greener from the hip, the 00-buckshot loads tore into Matthews's chest, ripping it open and blowing his lungs to pieces, catapulting his body into the campfire, where it lay smoldering.

Scurlock rode toward Olinger, who began to fire his rifle as fast as he could lever the shells into the chamber. His second shot hit Scurlock in the side, cutting a shallow grove through his flank.

Scurlock didn't flinch at the burning in his side but took aim and thumbed back the hammer on his Colt Army .44. He fired once, missing, and then again, this time hitting Wally Olinger in the chest.

Olinger staggered back, but continued to fire until a bullet from Falcon tore through his lower jaw, shattering it and sending teeth and blood flying. Olinger fell to the dirt, mortally wounded. He lay moaning and trying to scream for help, but only managing a garbled gurgling through his ruined mouth.

Brown twisted in the saddle and fired his second barrel at a man running toward his horse. The molten lead buckshot hit John Beckwith just below his buttocks, tearing his left leg off at the thigh and shredding his right leg down to the bone. He sprawled, screaming in pain onto his face, to be trampled as Brown's horse ran right over his writhing body.

Two more men, trying to climb aboard bucking, dancing horses, were cut down by Falcon as he rode past, his .44.40 slugs hitting one mid-center in the back, and the other in the neck.

Scurlock saw John Long—the man who had set fire to McSween's house and fired into him as he was trying to surrender—jump on a horse and ride away, shooting back over his shoulder with a pistol.

Scurlock gave chase, firing his Colt Army until it was empty. Unable to reload with his mount galloping at full speed, Scurlock rode up next to Long and pulled a Bowie knife out of his belt. As he pulled his horse right up against Long's, he slashed out backhanded with the razor-sharp blade, cutting a long gash in the side of Long's neck.

Long grabbed his neck with both hands, blood spurting from between his fingers, and finally fell to the ground, his eyes wide, foamy blood running from his mouth and nose.

Middleton rode through the middle of the camp, straight at Buck Powell, who was crouched near the string of horses at the edge of the clearing.

Powell fired with both hands as fast as he could at the charging figure riding down on him. One of his bullets hit Middleton in the left shoulder, sending his pistol spinning out of his left hand. He drew another from his belt, thumbed back the hammer, and fired as he rode past Powell.

His shot hit Powell in the left temple, blowing a piece of his skull the size of his fist into the air, snapping Powell's head back and putting out his lights for good.

Middleton used his right hand to stuff his useless left arm into his belt so it wouldn't flop around as he rode, and whirled his horse to head back toward the camp.

He rode down one man who was running as fast as he could toward a distant grove of trees, trampling him under his horse's hooves, and shot another in the chest as he was putting a rifle to his shoulder to shoot at Falcon in the distance.

Falcon, his carbine empty, booted it and filled both hands with iron, firing with both as Diablo raced in circles around the camp.

Falcon blew three more men to hell, taking a bullet in his calf. He slowed Diablo long enough to wrap a bandanna around his leg to stop the bleeding, then continued his killing rampage.

Brown cracked open his Greener and was reloading when a black man rode right at him, firing a pistol over his mount's head. Brown looked up, staring death in the face, until the man was blown out of his saddle by Middleton, who grinned as he rode by.

Finally, it was quiet, except for the moaning and crying and shouting for help from the wounded.

Falcon, Middleton, Brown, and Scurlock gathered together at the edge of camp in the increasing darkness.

Falcon's nose wrinkled at the acrid stench of cordite and gunpowder, and the smell of blood and death was everywhere.

"You men had enough for now?" he asked.

Scurlock wheeled his horse around and surveyed the scene. There were at least fifteen dead, and four or five severely wounded. A couple of men had managed to make it to their horses and had escaped, riding leaned over their mounts as fast as they could.

"Yeah," he grunted. "I've got no stomach for shootin' wounded men."

Brown nodded. "Let 'em live or die on their own. I ain't plannin' on puttin' 'em out of their misery."

"Let's vamoose," Middleton said, his right hand over the hole in his left shoulder. "Our work here is done."

Falcon's attentions returned to the task at hand . . . that of tracking, harassing, and eventually killing the renegade Apache chieftain, Naiche, and his scalp-hungry warriors. This was no time for daydreaming. If the three dead men had been found by Naiche, he would know someone was close on his backtrail, and might well send a small war party back to remove the threat. Falcon needed all his wits about him to survive this trek across the desert.

He and Hawk and the others had been lucky so far going up against the Apache without suffering any casualties. Now that he was alone, he had to be doubly careful not to make any mistakes, because it only took one to cost a man his scalp.

Chapter 39

Cal Franklin was traveling fast as he left the Dragoons behind him, angling southwest toward Tombstone with his sacks of gold dust hidden in his saddlebags. He wanted no more of this three-man war between Falcon, Hawk, and Jasper pitted against bloodthirsty Apaches. He still recalled vividly what he'd seen from his hiding place in the cave, close to the cabin where he and Billy and Johnny and Frank headquartered while digging riches out of Arizona Territory rock. The slaughter he'd witnessed when his partners died still lingered in his memory, and he felt sure it would keep him awake at night for years to come. He didn't want to remember it any longer, yet it continued to creep into his slumber.

As he'd explained to Falcon and Hawk when they found him alive as the only survivor of the attack, he'd been asleep in a nearby cave, the beginnings of a new mine tunnel, when all the shooting and screaming and dying started. Cal had only his six-gun for a weapon, with six bullets and no more ammunition. What bullets they had were in the cabin, not really expecting any trouble. Thus he'd been forced to lie there at the mouth of the tunnel, to watch his friends and mining partners die the most horrible deaths anyone could imagine, and there'd been nothing he could do to save them. Shooting back at so many Apaches would only have gotten him killed, and his friends were already dead ... or dying painfully. Some might call him a coward for what he did, lying there in the darkness while his partners were being slaughtered, but Cal was alive. In his own mind he knew he'd done the right thing, the only thing he could do at the time.

He pushed the incident from his thoughts for now, intent on getting away from the Indians as rapidly as he could. He hadn't cared what Falcon or Hawk or Jasper thought about him for pulling out when he did. After so many years of failure and frustration seeking the mother lode, after finally finding enough gold to make him a rich man for the rest of his days, it was senseless for him to stay and remain involved in what MacCallister and the others were doing, tracking down and killing a few Apaches at a time.

I'm no Indian killer, he reminded himself. *I dig holes in the rocks, looking for gold.*

Crossing desert flats, pushing his mount to maintain a steady trot even though water for his horse would be scarce until he reached Tombstone, he rode into a shallow, winding arroyo to do as much as he could to keep from being seen. A huge column of cavalry from Fort Thomas was already entering the Dragoons from the north looking for the Apaches, and they were being assisted by one of the most notorious Indian scouts and Apache hunters in the southwest—a ruthless tracker and Indian killer named Mickey Free. Cal didn't know much about Free, only the stories folks told about him. In the opinion of most, Free was crazy, as mad as a mercury-sniffing hatter who happened to have a taste for Indian blood.

And Falcon MacCallister was no less an Indian killer when he went on a rampage, like the one he was consumed by now. Something from his past made him a driven man while going after the Indians, and he went about it with a methodical, almost casual intent. When it came to slaughtering and mutilating Indians, he seemed to derive some inner satisfaction from disemboweling them or scalping them the way Apaches did their victims. And his own personal touch—the gruesome blinding of Indians who were already dead—had all the earmarks of a man being on the verge of utter madness.

Following the arroyo, he felt safer being off the skyline in what was mostly flat country. Falcon had said the Apaches' tracks were headed this way, and he believed they were making a run for Mexico, but Tombstone, and safety for Cal Franklin, lay in almost the same direction the Indians were taking. He was certain it was worth the risk to get as far away from MacCallister, Hawk, and the soldiers led by Mickey Free as he could. There was sure to be more bloodletting if either bunch found the renegades, and Cal had seen enough blood over the past few weeks to last a lifetime, not all of the atrocities committed by the Indians. When it came to outright savagery, Falcon MacCallister wasn't all that different from the Apaches he was stalking across the Dragoons.

His footsore horse had begun to tire, coughing in the dry, dust-choked desert air. Cal slowed the gelding to a walk to give it a moment's rest. He quickly realized his mistake.

Two mounted Apache warriors swung their horses along the rim of the arroyo above him, both aiming Winchester rifles down at him with hatred slitting their coal black eyes.

"Stop. Drop guns!" one of them demanded in broken English, although there was nothing about the command Cal didn't understand.

"Sweet Jesus," Cal whispered, thinking about the sacks of gold dust, and what his life was worth.

He jerked his horse to a halt, then held both palms in the air to show they were empty.

"Drop guns!" the same Apache shouted, sighting along the barrel of his rifle with its muzzle aimed straight for Cal's heart.

Moving carefully, very slowly, he took out his pistol with a thumb and forefinger and dropped it in the sand beneath his horse. Then he pulled his rifle from its boot in the same slow fashion and tossed it down with a dull thud.

One Indian sent his horse down the sloping bank of the sandy ravine and stuck the barrel of his rifle against Cal's rib cage, jabbing him with plenty of force. "Ride. We show way," he said in a strange, guttural tone. However, once again Cal had no difficulty being sure of what the snarling Apache wanted him to do.

He picked up his reins and turned his horse to the south, the direction both Indians were pointing.

Then the Indian behind him jumped off his horse to retrieve Cal's weapons.

I'm sunk, Cal thought. *They're taking me to Mexico, or out in the middle of this desert someplace to rob me and cut me open, like they done Billy and my partners at the cabin. I'm gonna die howlin' for mercy just like they did, until a real slow an' miserable death takes me.*

Resigned to his fate, not knowing what he could do to stop the pair of Apaches from killing him and taking the winter's work from his saddlebags, he rode out of the arroyo heading due south toward a distant range of mountains.

The Pedregosa range was where a few old-time miners believed a fortune in gold and silver lay hidden somewhere in rocky peaks, a treasure that had eluded miners, including early Spanish treasure seekers, for over a hundred years. Cal had combed those same peaks for a couple of years, looking for likely spots that might contain quartz, where all gold was found. He'd found nothing and rode north, to the Dragoons a year later, a fateful choice, it now seemed.

His saddlebags filled with riches, Cal rode toward his destiny, sure in the knowledge he would not live long enough to spend a cent of it.

"Ride fast!" the taller of the two Apaches snapped, as

he slapped the barrel of his gun over the rump of Cal's exhausted gelding.

Cal's mount obliged the Indian with a long trot, limping slightly on its left forefoot. The Apaches appeared to be in something of a hurry, and Cal wondered if they knew the soldiers were close or if Falcon, Hawk, and Jasper might have been seen along the Indian's backtrail.

Cal, between grisly visions of what surely awaited him now, briefly pondered why only two Apaches had captured him. What had become of the main band? Falcon insisted it numbered somewhere between forty and fifty, in spite of the heavy toll he and Hawk had taken on some of them when they found Apache scouts away from the others.

These men are only scouts, he told himself. They were sent back by their chief to see who was following them, and how close they were. It was Cal's misfortune to be mistaken for a threat, when all he'd hoped to do was reach Tombstone with his scalp and his gold dust sacks intact. He had truly believed he could make it without dangerous incident.

It was small consolation. Cal Franklin, at his best, was never a match for trained fighting men. He was, by profession, a miner, not a manhunter, unprepared and without the skills needed to perform the bloody deeds he's seen Falcon, Hawk, and Jasper enact upon the Apaches they hunted in the Dragoons. Men like Falcon were a different breed.

I'm gonna die, he reasoned. *Never will get to spend a damn dime of all this gold we found. There ain't no such thing as justice in this life.*

As he'd expected, the two Indians guided him toward the far off outlines of the Pedregosas, yet something deep inside him whispered that he would not live long enough to see the mountains where he'd once prospected for gold.

They'll kill me before we get there, he thought, glancing around him at all manner of desert plants scattered across a sand and rock wasteland. *What an awful place to die when a man's got a fortune to spend.*

It was foolishness, he knew, to worry about the scenery where he would be tortured and killed by these Apaches. What did it matter if the last thing he saw was a cactus or a mesquite tree?

He'd been counting on seeing the insides of several saloons in Tombstone—like the Oriental, perhaps, and others—to spend some of his golden dust. But Cal Franklin wasn't going to make it. This was the end of the line. . . .

The warrior riding out in front made a sudden turn toward a distant thicket of ocotillo where a ravine made a sharp bend to the west.

That's where they're taking me, Cal thought. *That's where I'm gonna die.*

The Indian behind him with a rifle aimed at his spine rode closer to him now. Cal wasn't thinking about what would happen next, for he was resigned to it. He allowed himself to dream about what it would have been like to spend the gold in saddlebags.

They neared the ocotillo grove, and he saw shadows behind the stalks, the shadows of men and horses.

I wish I'd never left MacCallister an' Hawk an' Jasper, he thought. *It was a damned stupid thing to do.*

The call of an owl came from the brush. The warrior riding in front cupped his hands over his mouth and returned the bird's cry.

Cal's horse was now so lame it had difficulty in the deeper sandpits, struggling to free its sore leg. He gave little thought to the animal carrying him. More than anything in his life, he wanted to see the saloons of Tombstone again.

"Stop here!" the Indian behind him cried.

Cal pulled back on his reins.

"Get off horse!"

He obeyed the order, swinging down from the saddle on legs that trembled when they held his weight.

From the ocotillos, half a dozen Indians emerged from the brush cradling rifles. One of them pointed at him, and he was surprised to find that the Apache was a woman, even though she carried a rifle and pistol . . . and a knife.

"Come," one of his captors said, shoving the muzzle of a rifle against his ribs.

He trudged toward the brushy spot with his face toward the ground.

Chapter 40

Hidden in a sandy basin surrounded by spiny ocotillo stalks as a desert sunset emblazoned western skies, Chokole looked down at their white prisoner. They had stopped to rest their horses and the women who had run beside the pack animals while crossing the flats, after seven hours of nonstop pushing across dangerously open country. A favorable spirit sign had come since Naiche killed the snake, for a wind had risen toward midmorning which blew away the dust driven skyward by their horses' hooves moving at a fast pace.

"He is one of them," she spat in Apache, speaking to Naiche, pointing to a white man bound and gagged lying at the bottom of the sand pit. "I saw this one from far away, but he was with the two men in buckskins who killed our warriors. He wears different white man's clothing, but I am certain who he is. Let me kill him myself, Chief Naiche, for what they have done to our Apache brothers."

Naiche glared down at the sweating white man, his eyeballs bulging, about to burst from their sockets. He turned to Nana, one among his warriors who was old enough to have learned the most English.

"Ask him who the others are, Nana," Naiche said. "Tell him we will kill him unless he speaks true words."

Nana sauntered over on his badly bowed legs, strands of gray catching late sunlight in his shoulder-length hair bound to his head by a cloth band. Before he asked the prisoner any questions he took out his knife, showing the white man its gleaming, razor-sharp blade.

The white-eyes struggled to free himself of his rawhide bindings, making muffled sounds because of the bloody soldier's neckerchief tied over his mouth.

"You speak truth to me, white man, or I cut off your eyelids and tie you across a bed of red ants with your guts scattered like ropes around you."

The prisoner nodded quickly.

Nana bent down, and with the tip of his knife he cut the cloth away from the white man's mouth. "Who are these white men who follow us?"

"One . . . is named Falcon . . . Falcon MacCallister," the man stammered.

"Is he the silent one who wears deerskins and makes no sound with his feet?" Nana asked, putting the knife blade to their prisoner's throat.

"Yes . . . he's the . . . tall one who rides a black horse, an' has blond hair and blue eyes. He's an Indian fighter or somethin' like that. He's from up in Colorado Territory."

"Where is this place called Colorado Territory?"

"Up north . . . where it gits real cold in the wintertime. I ain't rightly sure why he left there. He never did give us no reason."

"Why does he follow us?"

"Some Indians killed his wife a long time ago . . . an' he ain't never forgot it. They cut her up real bad an' left her for dead, an' he swore a blood oath on all renegade Indians."

"Was it Apaches?"

"He never said, but . . . I don't think so."

As the white man hesitated, his eyes shifted and blinked rapidly several times. Nana, with the wisdom brought by many winters of life among the white-eyes, knew the man was lying.

"Look," the prisoner continued in a whiny, pleading voice, "I never was no part of all that killin'. It's them three others who done it to your braves."

"Who are the others?" Nana persisted, still drawing his knife gently across the bound white man's neck, just enough to draw a trickle of blood.

"One's called Hawk. He's an old army scout, I think. An' the other is a feller by the name of Jasper Meeks. He's a scout for wagon trains headed west. He's got real long, white hair."

"I saw this wagon scout with the silver hair," said a warrior standing in the circle around their prisoner in Apache. "His horse got away and he caught it. Then he took off and left the white people with the wagons to die. He is a coward."

Naiche understood some of what the white man said in his native tongue, although he turned to Nana for a translation of his next question. "Ask the white-eyes where the other three are now."

Nana grunted, returning to English when he spoke. "Where are the other three men?"

"Followin' your tracks, only MacCallister has some new idea about what he's gonna do when he gets real close to you. He said he was gonna kill all of you."

"A new idea?" Nana inquired.

"He's gonna leave the other two fellers some place an' come after you alone. That's what he said."

Now Nana chuckled, glancing over at Naiche. "The big one will leave the others soon to come for us by himself. He has said he will kill us all."

"He lies!" Chokole cried. "No warrior, not even a white warrior, would be so foolish. It is a trick, what this man tells us. Do not believe him."

Juh had been listening to all that was said. "I have seen this tall white-eyes with hair the color of wheat who rides the black horse. He kills without making a noise. He has been taught to hide on the face of Earth Mother like an Apache. My spirit voice spoke to me in a dream, saying this white man will be very hard to kill.''

Naiche turned to Juh, anger twisting his features. "Are you afraid of this white man?" he asked.

Juh wagged his head. "I am only telling you what my spirit voice whispered to me in my dream. I am not afraid of him, or of the others."

Chokole spat upon the face of the white prisoner. "We kill this one slowly, and leave him for the tall one to find. I will kill him in the old way."

Naiche knew it would be good for the others who followed him to see a white man tortured to death, proving to those who had doubts that Apache medicine was stronger than that of any white man.

He gave Chokole a nod of approval. "Kill him. Stake him out over the ants without his eyelids so his eyeballs will boil in tomorrow's sun. Cut his entrails from his body in the old ceremonial way. And scalp him. But leave him alive, so this tall one who calls himself a bird will hear his screams across the desert. It will be a message to him and his friends that we want war with him . . . that we are ready to fight him."

The warrior woman smiled grimly, satisfied with Naiche's decision. "I will enjoy cutting him," she said, loud enough to be heard by all the others. "Hear his cries, my People, and know that this is only the beginning of our war with the whites who have taken our land from us."

Naiche would not allow a fire, not even a small one to take the chill out of the late afternoon air, while Chokole fashioned wooden stakes from thick ocotillo stems and cut points in them, to be driven into the ground. Strips of rawhide soaked in a clay bowl of water not far away. Juh had found a red ant bed south of the ocotillo thicket, where he placed the unconscious white man, still bound hand and foot. The ants would come from their mound at sunrise, drawn to the smell of blood to feed.

"Tie him across the ant bed," Naiche ordered, somewhat concerned by their delay. "We have been here in one spot too long."

Chokole carried her stakes and the bowl of rawhide strips to the ant bed. Thirty-four warriors and women followed her to see the ritual. Five scouts had been sent out into the dark desert on foot to watch for the other white men, or the soldiers. All the Apaches knew what would happen the moment the white man began screaming. Anyone within hearing distance would be drawn to the sound, and they must be ready to hurry south, toward the relative safety of the Pedregosas.

Chokole walked up to the white-eyes, a strange gleam in her eyes. She put down her stakes and rawhide, then she drew her knife.

"You die, for the lives of the Chiricahua people you sent to the land of shadows!" she shouted, hatred for this white enemy thickening the sound of her voice until it was deep, like that of a warrior.

Kneeling beside his head, she seized the front of his hair in her left fist and made a quick, slashing motion across the skin covering his skull and forehead.

A shrill scream rushed from the prisoner's throat and his eyes flew open. "Oh dear God! No!"

She left him there, with blood pouring from a bare spot in his skull, his bloody scalp lock tucked into her belt. She took up the ocotillo stakes and hammered them into the ground with a heavy stone.

Juh began cutting the man's wrists free, only to tie them again with longer strips of rawhide to fasten to the stakes. They were wet strips of rawhide that would contract as they dried in tomorrow's sun, pulling their victim's shoulders and elbows and hips apart at the joints. But that pain would seem like nothing compared to having his abdomen cut open, and then loops of his intestines jerked roughly from his body cavity to have them tossed all around him. Removing the eyelids was a new touch for Apache, a form of torture learned from their lifelong enemies to the east, the Comanches.

"Please, no!" the white-eyes screamed, his thin voice ending an early morning desert silence.

Chokole actually smiled a genuine smile when she heard him call out for mercy.

She went about the rest of her preparations quickly, saving the trimming of his eyelids for last. All around her, the other Apaches, mostly the women, were preparing to move again, to run south as fast as they could travel until they reached the safe haven Naiche promised them in Mexico.

When the prisoner was staked across the sleeping ant bed, she drove the tip of her knife into the white man's belly and scooped out a fistful of sticky intestinal loops faintly resembling purple snakes when they slithered from her hand to land on the ground, where they were coated with a layer of caliche dust and sand.

"Ayiii!" she cried to the red and orange streaked heavens, painted by the sun as it inched toward the far horizon with the arrival of dusk.

"Ayiii!" the Apache women cried in a gruesome chorus of voices, a celebration of the white man's slow death lying across the ant bed.

"It is good," Juh said quietly to Naiche. "When these white enemies come to the sounds of his cries, they will know we will kill them all."

Naiche had his doubts, for he secretly feared the spirit dream described by Nana. Would this one white man be so difficult to kill? He looked back along the way they had come. Was this silent killer even now on their trail, following them so he could kill them one by one as he had been doing for the past several days?

"It is time to go now," Juh told him, handing him the thin rawhide jaw rein tied to the lower lip of his horse. "We have waited here too long."

Naiche swung aboard his bay and signaled the rest of

his band to move southward. Heavily laden pack horses led by the women, and twenty-two warriors, prepared to ride out onto the desert and travel all night to get to the far mountains and safety.

Chokole mounted her pinto and rode up beside him in the fading light. She pointed down at the dying white man staked out over the ant bed. "He will scream for many hours," she said.

"It will be a message to the other whites who follow our tracks," Naiche told her, giving the northern horizon a careful examination, looking for dust sign. "When they find him, they will know we are sending them a warning."

Juh overheard their conversation and gave the northern desert a passing glance. "The tall one will come," he told Naiche.

Naiche wondered how Juh could be so certain of it. Had his spirit voice foretold the future?

Suddenly, one of the five men who had been sent to watch their backtrail came running over a small hillock, shouting, "Horses come! Three riders are coming!"

Naiche whirled his bay around to face the young warrior. "From which direction?"

The man stopped, his chest heaving and sweat covering his body even though the morning temperature was still low. He pointed back the way they had come, toward the north.

"Only three riders?" Chokole asked.

When the scout nodded, too out of breath to speak, she looked at Naiche. "I told you the white man lied when he said the tall one was leaving the other two behind and coming by himself. It must be the three white-eyes who have been following us."

Naiche nodded, his eyes searching the horizon, watching three small dots appear and get slowly larger in the hazy late afternoon sunlight. His heart thudded in his chest, and his stomach roiled. At last, he was to come face-to-face with this man who had killed so many of his followers.

"Let me lead a small war party out to meet them,"

Chokole asked, her face fierce. "The tall one's tricks will be of no use on the desert flats. Even Apaches cannot disappear when there is no place to hide. Let us see if he is truly flesh and blood, or Spirit Walker."

Naiche looked at Juh and Nana to see what they would advise.

Juh shook his head. "It cannot be the tall one," Juh said with certainty.

"And why not, old one?" Chokole asked, scorn in her voice.

"It is not his way," the old man answered. "He would not be so easily seen. His way is to walk in shadows, to steal silently through the night on feet that make no sound, to kill without being seen. I know this from my visions."

Chokole snorted through her nose and turned her gaze to Naiche. She didn't dare say anything against the old one out loud, for the Apache revered the ancients, but she allowed Naiche to see her disagreement.

Finally, he told her, "Take ten warriors with you and ride out to meet the three who follow us." He stared into her dark eyes, his face like stone. "Chokole, do not return unless you have killed the white-eyes."

Her teeth flashed in a savage grin and she jerked her pony's head around. Holding her Winchester above her head, she gave an Apache war cry and quickly pointed out ten warriors to follow her.

As they rode off in a cloud of dust, Nana began to chant in a low voice, praying for the Spirits to guide Chokole's bullets to their marks.

After a while, when there was no sound of gunfire, Naiche rode to the top of a small hillock and peered into the distance. He could barely make out the war party returning in the semidarkness, leading the three horses and their riders back toward the tribe.

As they got closer his mouth became dry, and he felt a cold feeling in the pit of his stomach. He turned to Nana and said, "Keep the others here. Do not let them see what Chokole has found."

He kicked his horse into a gallop and rode out to meet the returning war party. As he got nearer, the images on the horses became clearer.

It was the three warriors he'd left to guard their backtrail at the juncture of the Dragoons and the desert. They were all dead, tied to their horses with sticks and rope, butchered as all the others had been by the tall one and his friends.

He held up his hand. "Stop here. I do not want the others to see this, for it will cause them to lose faith."

Chokole's face was twisted, as if she tasted something bitter. "What shall we do with them? They deserve a ceremonial burial, for they died honorably in battle with our enemies."

"Cut their ropes and leave the bodies here in this arroyo. Bring the ponies. We must be on our way before the blue-coats find our trail and follow us here. We cannot afford to be caught on the open desert."

"But—" Chokole started to say.

"Enough!" Naiche growled. "We will honor our fallen by singing songs of their bravery around our campfires once we are safe in the Pedregosas. Until then, we must keep on the move until we find cover."

Chokole nodded, her lips a thin, white line. She knew she must not say anything else. She glanced at the three dead warriors, whose mothers and sisters would be singing a death song tonight. She made a silent vow to kill the white-eyes who did this or lose her own life trying.

After the ponies were emptied of their burdens, Naiche led the war party back to the main body of his tribe. He reined his horse to a halt in front of his people, who were waiting for him to tell them what to do.

"Stay here and wait for the three white-eyes who follow us," Naiche said, pointing to the five men who had been watching their backtrail. "Hide yourselves well, and be brave in battle. You must kill them, and then you may rejoin our tribe."

He rode off, leading his people toward the Pedregosas that could barely been seen against the evening sky in the distance. Once there, they could make their way toward Mexico and join up with Geronimo and his warriors to form an unstoppable force that would drive the white man from their land forever.

Chapter 41

As Falcon rode through moonlight across the desert, he talked to Diablo in a low, soothing tone. It was something he'd done for years. He found expressing his thoughts out loud served several purposes. The tone of his voice reassured Diablo that all was well, and made the horse less skittish and less likely to buck or bolt if he came upon something unexpected in the semidarkness. In addition, speaking his innermost thoughts out loud allowed his more critical and logical conscious mind to pick them apart and find any obvious weaknesses or inconsistencies that might otherwise go unnoticed. The process had served him so well over the years that he now did it without thinking, automatically.

"Naiche must have found those three dead guards I sent on ahead by now," he murmured, sitting back against the cantle of his saddle in a relaxed manner as the big stud moved steadily through the night.

"So, he now knows even better that someone dangerous is on his trail. Hopefully, that will spur him to push his people hard, to make them travel around the clock without getting any rest. Tired warriors don't make good fighters, so the more he pushes them the better for me—and for the army if Hawk and Jasper ever manage to meet up with them. And if they recognize the fires I set as a signal,'' he added after a moment of thought.

As he remembered killing the three guards he found himself almost regretting his crusade against the renegades. After all, he reasoned, there was no way this particular bunch of Indians could have had anything to do with Marie's death. Perhaps he was becoming as bad as a lot of people who had settled the West, letting his thinking degenerate into the old adage, "The only good Indian is a dead Indian."

Searching his heart, trying to look deep inside himself, he came to the conclusion that he was being too hard on himself. He really had no particular animosity against Indians or any other minorities, in general. It was only the ones who took it upon themselves to break the law—to raid and kill and go to war against innocent people—that he hated and wanted to kill.

The murder of his wife Marie was only a symptom of the disease of disrespect for the rule of law. Understandable, maybe, in such a young, wild frontier, but a sickness he would do everything in his power to eradicate. It wasn't so much the letter of the law or the sometimes flawed men who tried to enforce it that Falcon believed in, but the general premise that if a collection of people were to live in close proximity there must be rules of behavior based on mutual respect and dignity which had to be followed. Those who took it upon themselves to ignore such common sense rules had to be punished or there was no safety for anyone in the land.

He further reasoned he would be acting no differently if a band of marauding white men were on a killing rampage. He would still feel the need to do all he could to wipe them out. The fact the killers were Indians was secondary to the need for their complete destruction.

After he came to this conclusion, he felt better about his mission, less afraid he was becoming hardened and callous to the killing he was being forced to do. His mind was cleared of all self-doubt, and he was able to concentrate on the job at hand, which was making life, and death, as miserable as possible for Naiche and his followers.

Without slowing Diablo, he reached back into his saddle-bag and pulled out the tin of bootblack and applied some more to his face. Earlier, he taken the precaution of wrapping burlap around Diablo's hooves, to muffle any sound the stud might make as they traversed the desert. He knew Naiche was sure to have posted more guards after finding his last three hadn't survived their assignment.

Falcon was both hampered and helped by the desert terrain. On the one hand there were precious few places any ambushers could hide, but on the other hand it was going to be almost impossible for him to arrive unnoticed across the miles of flat land. He was lucky the moon was only half full and there were plenty of scudding clouds to give at least intermittent cover of darkness.

The padding on Diablo's feet was so effective and his ride was so quiet that he could hear the occasional rattle of a snake disturbed in its slumber by his passage, or the swish and clatter as a lizard or kangaroo rat scurried out of his path.

From up ahead a faint cry came carried on the evening breeze. At first it was so low Falcon thought it merely the moaning of the wind, or the cry of a distant night bird. Soon it became louder, reminding him of the screech of a big female mountain lion in heat, screaming for her mate.

Suddenly, the cry changed and became screams for help, in a voice Falcon thought he could recognize through the agony.

"Damn, Diablo," he muttered as he pulled back on the reins and cocked his head, listening. "That sounds like Cal Franklin up ahead. If the Indians got to him and staked him out, that means they've got someone waiting to see if I take the bait."

He slipped out of the saddle, leaving Diablo ground-reined next to a mesquite bush. He took his shotgun rather than his Winchester with him, for he knew there would be no aiming in the darkness and he wanted something with a wide spread to it.

Crouching to keep from outlining himself against the horizon in case the moon came back out, he shuffled his feet to minimize sound and moved as silently as a wraith toward the terrible sounds ahead. As he walked, he loosened the rawhide hammer thong on his pistols and rearranged the scabbard of his Arkansas Toothpick so it was within easy reach.

The closer he got to the source of the sounds, the surer he was it was Cal Franklin making them. *The damn fool must have gotten careless and let some of Naiche's scouts take him prisoner*, Falcon thought. The one thing practically everyone in the area of marauding renegades agreed on was not to be taken alive, for the Indians left ample evidence it was a most horrible way to die. Knowing Cal, he had probably been riding along daydreaming about all his gold dust and what he was going to spend it on in Tombstone.

Every few feet, Falcon stopped dead still and held his breath, searching the darkness ahead for any sign of human presence. He realized that no man, not even an experienced Apache warrior, could sit for hours in dark waiting in ambush and the not make some noise, no matter how slight.

As he waited, Falcon heard the sound of a low, muffled cough from off to his right, then a sniff, as if the brave waiting there for him was coming down with a cold.

He shifted his direction slightly and crept forward, his Arkansas Toothpick in his right hand and his shotgun in his left.

Glancing upward, Falcon saw a large cloud moving slowly across the sky with all the majesty of a clipper ship sailing calm seas. The trailing edge of the cloud was almost to the moon, and in another few moments would pass it, leaving a brief period of moonlight shining down.

Falcon froze, staring ahead, waiting for light. When it

came, he could clearly see the outline of a man sitting fifteen feet ahead of him on the ground with his legs crossed in front of him and a rifle resting on his thighs. The man's head was nodding, leaning forward only to be jerked back upright as he caught himself dozing and tried to force himself to stay awake. *Naiche has been pushing his people too hard,* Falcon thought. Warriors falling asleep while waiting in ambush was a sure sign they hadn't had much rest lately.

When the next cloud covered the moon, bringing almost total darkness, Falcon laid his shotgun on the ground and eased forward, an inch at a time. As soon as he was in position, he clasped his left hand over the warrior's mouth and quickly slid the blade of his knife across his throat.

The man jerked once, then sighed heavily, almost as if he were relieved to give up his life and finally get some sleep. Falcon lowered him to the ground gently so as not to make any noise.

Figuring the other bushwhackers were arranged in a circle around the dying, moaning man, Falcon picked up his shotgun and began to move laterally around the area the sounds were coming from. He was in no hurry and moved slowly, knowing time was on his side. As tired as these warriors were, the closer to dawn it became, the harder it would be for them to keep their attention at peak levels.

The next two kills went without a hitch, the men dying silently as they had sat while waiting to kill Falcon. The fourth warrior must have been more alert than the others, or perhaps he heard the click of a pebble moving when Falcon attacked. He turned just as Falcon grabbed his throat, trying to bring his Winchester up to fire.

They wrestled in the dark for a few seconds until finally Falcon managed to slip the point of the Toothpick under his rib cage and angle it up to pierce his heart.

A dying spasm caused the brave's trigger finger to contract on the Winchester and it fired, exploding in the desert silence like a cannon shot, belching a foot-long flame out into the night, temporarily blinding Falcon.

The last of the sentries jumped to his feet, and in his excitement began to fire repeatedly at the place where he saw and heard the rifle shot. Bullets were pocking the desert sand all around Falcon as he rolled over toward his shotgun.

He grabbed the Greener and eared back the hammers, pointing the twin barrels toward the sound of rifle fire and firing blindly.

Just as the shotgun exploded, a whining bullet tore into Falcon's chest, hitting a rib bone and skipping along under the skin to exit out his back. Luckily the rib deflected the slug enough that it didn't pierce the chest but stayed just under the skin, causing intense pain but no lasting damage.

The buckshot from Falcon's shot spread out into a pattern ten feet wide at twenty yards, peppering the Indian and tearing him almost in two. He was blown backward in the air, arms flung wide, dead before he hit the ground.

When Falcon's vision came back took his shirt off and explored his wound with his hands. He figured he was all right when he took a deep breath and found only pain, no restriction of his breath and none of the dreaded bloody froth that meant a lung wound and certain death.

He rolled the shirt into a long cylinder and wrapped around his chest, tying it tight to minimize blood loss.

After making sure there were no more sentries, he made his way toward the sounds of crying and begging and moaning coming from the nearby depression in the ground.

No matter how many men a man has killed, or how many men he's seen left by Indians to die, when it's someone he knows personally and they're still alive and in agony, it rends the heart to see what cruelty one human being can impose on another.

There were tears in Falcon's eyes as he squatted next to Cal Franklin. He slipped the Toothpick under the rawhide thongs holding Franklin's wrists outstretched and cut them one by one, releasing the terrible tension on his arms.

Cal turned his head toward Falcon, exposing staring, sightless eyes covered with ants. "Who's there? Who is it?" he whined, his voice hoarse from his screaming and yelling.

"It's Falcon, Cal."

"Oh, thank God!" He reached with one of his newly arms and grabbed Falcon's shoulder. "Kill me, Falcon. If you've got any mercy in your soul at all, kill me quickly!"

Falcon glanced down and saw that Cal's intestines were spread all around him. The man had no chance at all of survival, but he might live for days in total agony.

Falcon drew his Colt and laid the barrel against Cal's temple. With his free hand, he stroked Cal's cheek. "Cal, you rest easy now, you hear?" Falcon said and pulled the trigger, putting an end to Cal Franklin's misery.

He sat back on his haunches, breathing slowly, waiting to regain enough energy to go out into the darkness and fetch Diablo.

He thought maybe he'd rest there the rest of the night and wait for the dawn to see if perhaps the army was on its way. He'd had no stomach to travel any further tonight. He'd had enough killing to last him a while, and he really needed rest. He didn't want to make the same mistake Naiche was making and push himself so hard he became ineffective.

After a while he got to his feet and went to find Diablo. On the way, reined to an ocotillo cactus, he found the five ponies belonging to the warriors left behind to kill him.

Once back at the area where the dead Indians lay, he took out his Arkansas Toothpick and walked to each body, slicing off the scalp locks one by one.

Taking the scalplocks to where the horses were tied, he affixed a scalp lock in each of the ponies' manes, leaving the bloody trophies hanging along their necks. After he was done with the grisly task, he cut their reins and fired his pistol behind them, sending them galloping off toward the distant mountains where Naiche was headed.

Falcon hoped they would send yet another message to Naiche that his days were numbered.

Chapter 42

The next morning Falcon woke up just before dawn. The air was frigid, and the sky was full of ominous looking clouds that bespoke of possible snow later in the day.

Falcon thought the desert must have been the last place God made, for it was filled with contradictions. Blazing hot and dry most of the year, it could turn freezing and have snow and ice at other times. He had seen the temperature in the day break one hundred and then fall to below freezing the same night.

He pulled on his fur-lined jacket and set about making breakfast. While the fire was starting and his coffee was heating, he used the time to bury Cal Franklin's body. With no wood available for a cross or other marker, he gathered a number of fist-sized stones and piled them over the grave to help keep scavengers from digging the remains up.

He didn't bother with the Indians' corpses, figuring coyotes and buzzards had to eat, same as worms.

Afterward, he sat next to the fire, enjoying for the first time in several days a period of relaxation where he could smoke a quiet cigar and a good cup of coffee. He had no supplies with him for a meal, so he chewed on some dried beef jerky and a few old biscuits that were as hard as rocks. *No wonder punchers call biscuits sinkers,* he thought, for they immediately sank to the pit of his stomach and sat there, waiting to cause mischief in his digestive tract later in the day.

As the morning sun rose he spied a dust cloud off to the north, coming from the direction he had traveled the night before. *I hope that's Hawk and Jasper with the army,* he thought. *If it's not, I can't afford to wait much longer. We've got to catch up with Naiche before he crosses the Rio Bravo into Mexico, or the army will be powerless to go after him.*

He emptied the rest from his coffeepot into his cup and brewed a fresh pot, figuring the men coming would be needing some after their journey across the desert.

Less than thirty minutes later the calvary arrived, led by Hawk, Jasper Meeks, and a gnome-like man with flaming red hair and a face only a mother could love.

The captain in charge reined his horse to a stop and tipped his head at Falcon. "I'm Captain Buford Jones, Mr. MacCallister. Your . . . associates here tell me you've been tracking Naiche and his band of renegades."

Falcon nodded, wondering why the red-headed gent kept staring at him so intently.

"That's right, Captain. They took off from here last night and headed straight south toward the Pedregosas and Mexico. I believe they're probably headed down there to try and join up with Geronimo, who I hear is on the warpath across the border.

As Jones opened his mouth to speak, the man who'd been staring at Falcon jumped off his horse and walked over to him.

"Ye be Falcon MacCallister, son of Jamie MacCallister?"

Falcon tensed. He never knew what such a greeting presaged. His father had many friends, but he'd also made his share of enemies also in his many years of traversing the west.

"That's right."

"I'm Mickey Free," the man said, breaking into a wide grin and sticking out his hand. "Your pappy saved my skin once, an' helped me out on some other matters a time or two. He was a real man, the kind you only run into once or twice in your life."

Falcon took Mickey's hand and shook it.

"Thank you," he said. "I was always pretty fond of him, too."

As they shook hands, Mickey's eyes glanced over Falcon's shoulders and he saw the five Indian corpses lined up a short distance away. He looked at Falcon and cocked an eyebrow. Then his grin got even wider, a feat Falcon would have thought impossible just a minute before.

"I see you been busy, Falcon," Mickey said, brushing by him to go take a closer look at the dead braves.

Jones and Hawk and Meeks dismounted as Jones told his sergeant to have the men dismissed for a meal break.

As they all walked to stand over the bodies, Jones's eyes widened and he stared at Falcon. "Mr. MacCallister, were these men killed by Indians? I notice they've all been scalped."

Falcon wagged his head. "No, captain. I did that myself, both the killing and the scalping. I tied the scalplocks onto their ponies and sent them on ahead to deliver a message for me to Naiche."

Jones drew himself up, a self-righteous expression on his face. "White men do not scalp their victims, Mr. Mac-Callister."

Mickey snorted a short laugh through his misshapen nose. "Kind'a depends on the man, Captain, don't it?"

His gaze flicked to the pile of stones nearby. "Who's the gent in the ground, Falcon?" Mickey asked.

"Friend of ours, name of Franklin," Falcon answered, drawing disbelieving looks from Hawk and Meeks.

"Ya mean ole Cal done got kilt by the Injuns?" Hawk asked.

"Yes, and he died hard," Falcon answered. "They worked on him a spell before I was able to end it for him."

Jones looked astonished. "You mean you killed your own friend in cold blood?" he asked.

Falcon's eyes got cold as ice. "I told you, Captain, he died hard. His eyelids were cut off, and his belly was opened with his guts spread out on the ground all around him. There wasn't any way he was going to survive, so I did what he asked and helped him to some peace."

"I cannot believe—" the captain started to say, when Mickey interrupted him.

"Believe it, Captain. If it ever happens to you, you'll be beggin' fer a blue pill just like Franklin did, an' you better hope there's somebody around to feed you one when you need it," Mickey said with feeling.

Jasper Meeks spoke up. "There might be worse ways to die, but offhand I can't think of one."

"Me, either," Hawk added.

"All right, gentlemen, point taken," Jones said.

"Would you men like some coffee?" Falcon asked.

"Only if it's strong enough to float a horseshoe," Mickey said.

"Oh, it'll float a horseshoe," Falcon answered, "but not the biscuits I ate this morning."

Within a few minutes, they were all standing around Falcon's fire, warming their hands and drinking coffee. Hawk stuck a wedge of Bull Durham in his cheek and the others built themselves cigarettes or fired up cigars.

Buford Jones took a long drink of coffee and asked, "Falcon, you and Hawk and Meeks have had several run-ins with Naiche and his men and you've managed to come out on top every time. Evidently you have some feel for how to deal with these Apaches. What do you suggest we do next?"

Falcon could hardly believe his ears. He'd never once before met an army officer who didn't think he knew it all, and had certainly never had one ask him for advice. Of course, he knew nothing of Jones's previous encounters with Naiche's men that ended in Jones's terrible defeats.

"Well, Captain, the one thing I do know is you'll never

defeat the Apache in a running battle or on horseback. Apaches, unlike most other Indians other than the Comanche, have no backup in them, and they won't stop fighting until the last man is dead. They don't have any word in their language for tomorrow, so all they live for is the here and now, unlike us whites who seem to think we're going to live forever. Thinking like that gives them an advantage in battle, 'cause they're not worried about surviving, as we are. They're only worried about dying with honor.''

Jones nodded. "So, what do you suggest, Falcon?"

"I think the best thing would be for me to try and flank Naiche and his group and come at them from the front. When they turn to try to avoid me, you and your men will be behind them, waiting."

Jones looked skeptical. "And just what makes you think Naiche, with his many warriors, will turn and run from just one man?"

Falcon grinned. " 'Cause I've gone to some trouble to make him fear me. So far, every war party he's sent out after my friends and me has come back to him dead. That'll be enough for him to take the easy way out and try to go around me if he can."

"I'll ride along with him, Captain, just to make sure thing' go the way he figures they will," Mickey said.

"I reckon Hawk and I'll do the same," Meeks added.

Falcon shook his head. "No, Jasper, I need you and Hawk to stay with the captain here, and show him how we arranged our ambushes of the war parties."

Jones frowned. "I don't need nobody to show me how to fight, Falcon."

"I know you don't, Captain, for the normal sort of fighting the army does. I'm quite sure you are excellent at leading your men in calvary charges. But this is Indian fighting. That's something else altogether, and you won't find any better teachers than Hawk or Jasper."

Somewhat mollified, Jones nodded. "All right, but just where do you think this is all going to happen?"

"If you've got a map showing the Pedregosas along the

border with Mexico, I'll show you. The mountains in that region are quite steep with lots of ravines and box canyons. There's only a few places where Naiche can cross easily, where the trail is such that the women and children traveling with him will be able to walk through the terrain.''

After Jones pulled out his map and Falcon showed him the area they were assuming Naiche would be in, Falcon took Hawk and Jasper aside.

"I'm counting on you men to keep Jones out of trouble."

Hawk frowned. "He's green as a two-foot high willow tree, Falcon. What the hell's the army thinkin', sendin' a man like that out to fight Injuns?"

Falcon grinned. "They don't have much choice, Hawk, 'cause men like you and Jasper are too smart to join the army and fight Indians for a living."

Jasper nodded. "I reckon that's true, Falcon. Men like us who've lived out here long enough to know which end of the porcupine to pet don't exactly take to takin' orders from some stuffed shirt from Washington. We'll try to keep Jones and his men alive until you flush Naiche our way." He shrugged, "After that, it's every man for hisself.''

"Fair enough," Falcon said. He stuck out his hand. "In case for some reason I don't see you gents again, it's been a pleasure riding with you."

The three men shook hands. Then Falcon climbed on Diablo and he and Mickey Free headed south-southeast to flank Naiche while Hawk and Jasper led the army troops south-southwest to come at him from behind.

Chapter 43

The Pedregosas lay in a long, uneven line, reaching southward to Agua Prieta across the border in Mexico. It was a mystery to Naiche and many Apaches how an imaginary line stopped the bluecoat soldiers from chasing them beyond a simple fence. It seemed senseless to a people who moved from place to place wherever they chose to go—fearing nothing but an enemy who might block their pathway to better hunting grounds by putting up a fight—but the white-eyes had many strange customs, like fences, which Naiche's people did not understand. It would not keep him from taking advantage of it—the most important one of all, the fence—now that they were on the run from soldiers and the three men who had an uncanny ability to track down and kill Apaches the way another Indian might.

After the skirmish with the three white men when they set their fire in the desert brush, Naiche found he had fewer than fifteen able-bodied fighting men. If Mickey Free led the soldiers to them now it would be a short fight unless Naiche could take his people to a fortified place higher in the mountains where rocks, scattered trees, and narrow trails would give them the advantage of cover.

He recalled the carnage done to his three rear scouts early today . . . their scalps missing, bellies cut open, and their eyes poked out as if someone had done it with a sharp pointed stick—a sure sign the men following them understood Apache customs and ways.

Nana, a veteran of many battles, was worried, too. Juh was preoccupied with watching their backtrail, while Chokole had said nothing since she cut the white prisoner's eyelids off and left him staked out across the ant bed. A curious silence gripped the women and younger warriors as they made their way higher into the Pedregosas. There were no more war chants, no celebrations of their freedom as there had been before. Everyone was waiting to see if the five warriors Naiche left behind to ambush the three whites were successful when the white Apache hunters were drawn to the shrill cries of pain from the prisoner Chokole gutted.

It was a gamble, that these cautious white men would ride up to the man staked across the bed of red ants, but Naiche felt it was a risk worth taking. His warriors were well hidden near the ocotillo grove, armed with repeating rifles, their horses tethered over a mile away in a second stand of ocotillo. If the white-eyes even came close to investigate the dying man's screams, they would make perfect targets for the Apaches' Winchesters in open desert surrounding the sandpit.

Off to the north, blanketing the desert flats they'd crossed to reach the mountains, a veil of smoke hung like a dark pall over the land. Naiche knew what the smoke meant. It was a way to draw the soldiers to their trail, a telltale sign of their passing and the direction they were taking. No doubt the fire was set by the three white men hounding their trail, seeking help from the bluecoats led by Mickey Free.

Nana rode over, after a long look at the smoke-filled desert behind them.

"It is a signal to the bluecoats," he said needlessly, for

every member of Naiche's band understood the smoke sign which was visible for miles, and why it was there.

"Mickey Free does not need smoke to tell them where we are and where we are going," Naiche said. "He reads our tracks and he knows we are headed for the mountains to make our escape to Mexico."

"He may try to convince the soldiers to cut us off, to get in front of us," Nana warned. "We will be caught between the bluecoats and the three white men . . . only I do not believe they are whites, not after what they did to Delgada and Boishta and his brother. These white-eyes kill like Apaches . . . marking their victims. Like the smoke covering the desert behind us, the way Delgada and Boishta and Sonsi were blinded is a message, telling us what they plan to do to us if they are able to find us."

"We are Apaches," Naiche said. "We fear no enemy on the face of Earth Mother. Only the Comanches are our equals in combat. These men are not Comanches. The prisoner Chokole left to die said one was from the north country where it snows."

"Perhaps they are Utes," Nana suggested, but it showed in his voice he did not truly believe it.

"They are white-eyes who have lived among some of the north tribes. Like Mickey Free, they have learned our ways, and we must expect them to think and act like Apaches," Naiche said, sure he was right about these white men. They were not members of any plains tribe he had ever seen or heard of, not Indians with white skin. There were times when he wondered if they were human, or if they could be spirit warriors from the Land of Shadows, for they seemed invincible at times, a thought he wouldn't share with the others, for it would instill fear in them.

Spirit warriors were the ghosts of dead Indians, according to Apache legend, and Naiche had never seen one. Most of his life, he had believed they did not truly exist except in the minds of the Old Ones.

Nana looked down at his wrinkled, battle-scarred hands for a moment. "It does not matter," he said. "They have killed half our number, and yet they keep coming. We must try to find a way to stop them if the ambush at the ocotillos fails."

Naiche had been considering it—another trap of some kind to stop or delay the three white-eyes if the ambush at the sandpit somehow went wrong—but very few among his warriors were clever enough to engage an experienced enemy like the men who followed them now.

"It might be best for us to send the others onward to join Geronimo while we pick a place, and a time, to halt them," he added, hoping it would not be necessary if they could be killed approaching the screaming man tied across the ant bed. He had given his five warriors careful instructions where to hide and wait in ambush. Isa led the ambush party, and Isa knew how to make himself seem to disappear.

"You and me and Juh are the most experienced when it comes to fighting a dangerous enemy," Nana said.

"Chokole is wise in the ways of war," Naiche told him, as the lines of Apache women passed him leading heavily laden pack animals. "The four of us could kill them easily, if we choose the time and the place."

"Chokole is brave," Nana agreed.

"Send for her. And bring Juh. The smoke gives us away to the bluecoats and Mickey Free. We must not allow them to catch us, or let this happen again."

"I will bring the others. Juh and Chokole will know what we must do if the trap at the sandpit fails."

Naiche gave the sign of agreement, still watching the smoky desert floor behind them for any sign that columns of soldiers were moving toward them.

Nana rode away to bring back Juh and Chokole, while Naiche considered a plan. The three whites were proving to be more troublesome than the bluecoats, or Mickey Free. If they could be stopped, Naiche was sure they could make it through the Pedregosas to Mexico. There was still a chance the ambush might work, but he'd been listening closely all day for the echo of rifle fire and heard nothing. Perhaps the distance was too great now.

Chokole came riding toward him, her face a mass of worry lines. She halted her pinto in front of him, yet she waited a moment to speak.

"Nana says we will go after the three whites," she said, her voice even, hard. She glanced over her shoulder. "This will not be easy, Chief Naiche. We should wait to see if Isa and Nednah and the others kill them. Or do you have another plan of attack that will be certain to take them off our trail?"

He did, although it would involve great danger for whoever was placed close to the white invaders. "Yes. The lessons I learned from Geronimo will work. Three or four of us will dig shallow pits in the desert sand. We will hide with our rifles under the flat leaves of the agave plant and lie in wait. They will follow our tracks, as they have since they came into the Dragoon Mountains. We hide in the small pits we dig, covered with brush and then we wait for them to ride close."

"This will be dangerous," Chokole said.

"Yes, but they know too many of the Apache ways of war, and they are killing us off a few at a time. We wait in the holes until they are very close, and then we kill them when our rifles will not miss, the way Geronimo killed the Mexican soldiers on the feast day of Saint Jerome. With an old Spencer rifle he was able to kill twenty Mexican *soldados.*"

"We only need to kill these three white-eyes, and the most important one is the big man who rides the black horse named MacCallister. He is the one who *must* die soon, or he will lead the bluecoats to us."

Chokole had spoken the truth. According to the white man they took prisoner, the man called Falcon MacCallister was the one responsible for so many Apache losses. "Yes," Naiche said bitterly. "This Falcon MacCallister must be the first white man to die."

Nana rode up with Juh, and they halted their horses in a half circle around Naiche.

"Tell us what you want us to do," Juh said. "Nana says we will go back to kill these three white-eyes. There have been no gunshots from Isa and his warriors. Either the white-eyes knew it was a trap and rode around it, or they may be waiting for the soldiers to join them."

Naiche watched his people moving up a steep mountain trail into the Pedregosas. "Come with me," he said to the others, after making sure the pack animals made it over the next rise. "I will show you how we will kill them. Send someone to the front to tell the women to keep moving. Tell them not to wait for us. The border into Mexico is only a few hours away, and there, they will be safe."

"Wait!" Chokole exclaimed, pointing north into the worst of the smoke. "Five horses come. It will be Isa . . . to tell us the white men are dead."

Naiche and Juh stared at the five darker shapes of horses moving through the curtain of smoke, for they were hard to see so far away through the smoke at such a distance.

But when Naiche got a closer look at the horses, anger began to well inside him. "The horses have no riders," he hissed, his teeth tightly clenched to fight back the rage building in him. "Isa and the others have been killed. The white men send back the horses as a message to us. Our warriors are dead."

Juh swallowed. "But we heard no guns," he said with his gaze still fixed on the riderless cavalry horses stolen from Fort Thomas.

"There are other ways to kill," Chokole told him darkly, a deep frown pinching her face.

Naiche's anger slowly changed to a touch of fear. Who were these white demons who killed Apaches without shooting a gun or making a sound? He had tried everything to halt them, and still they kept coming after him and his people. Were the three white men spirit warriors from another tribe?

"It is not possible," Juh said. "Isa picked four of our most trusted fighters."

"It is said spirit warriors can kill with a look . . . they do not need weapons," Nana murmured, his eyes downcast as if he were afraid to look at the horses coming toward them lest some magic take his soul, too.

"They were young and lacked battle experience," Chokole reminded him. "The years in prison at Fort Thomas made some of our young men careless. There was no chance to give them proper training as warriors."

Nana agreed hesitantly, though it was evident he still favored the spirit warrior idea. "Chokole speaks truth, Chief Naiche. There are only a few of us who were given a warrior's difficult training."

The five horses came toward them at a trot, drawn to the scent trail of the other horses climbing into the peaks carrying the Apaches' food supplies and guns. Naiche watched the geldings approach, wondering how the three whites could have known about the ambush awaiting them.

Juh voiced Naiche's concerns. "These white-eyes are far too clever for our younger warriors. The four of us remember what it was like to make war against the mighty Comanches . . . the Arapaho, and the Kiowas. We can kill these white men ourselves. Give us the word."

Naiche was torn by indecision . . . to keep on running toward Mexico, or stand and fight these white-skinned fiends . . . unless a bullet could not kill them. More and more, he was beginning to believe these men might be spirits without flesh or blood. He could find no other explanation for every attempt they made to escape them.

"Aiyee," Nana moaned as if to himself when the ponies finally came to them. Five bloody scalp locks could be seen hanging from the horses' manes.

He glanced at the others, his eyes wide with fear.

"There can be no doubt. These white devils are mighty warriors, be they man or spirit. We must be very careful when we confront them."

Chokole grasped her Winchester and held it high over

her head. "I swear to whatever spirits are listening, I will kill these men for what they have done to my brothers!"

Naiche nodded, but his eyes betrayed his doubts as he looked out over the smoke-covered desert and wondered just who—or what—was coming to meet them.

Chapter 44

Near the highest elevations, the Pedregosas offered shelter in many forms. Deep caves ran through the bowels of the earth. Steep-walled canyons crisscrossed the mountain range, providing a network of passageways where Naiche and his followers could stay out of sight while moving ever southward, although almost never in a straight line that would have made their journey that much shorter.

Here, Naiche felt relatively safe from the doggedly determined white men who had been glued to their trail since they broke away from the reservation and entered the Dragoons. His sense of safety, however, was not shared by Chokole or Nana, and Juh seemed unusually watchful now.

Naiche had abandoned his plan to lay in ambush for the white men at the base of the mountains. He would select the right spot when he came upon it and then prepare a deadly bushwhacking for the white-eyes from which he was certain they would not escape, if they were mere mortal men.

Chokole scouted the trail ahead. Nana, the most experienced warrior in Naiche's dwindling band, brought up the rear with two young warriors, staying back a mile or more, climbing to higher crests and ledges to watch patiently for any sign of the three pursuers.

As the day wore on until the sun was directly overhead, Naiche relaxed more and more. The maze of snake-like canyons they followed were ancient pathways to the land of Mexico, known only to Apaches who once roamed this rugged terrain. The white men had found it easy to track shod cavalry horses in sand and softer ground, but in the heart of the Pedregosas dark rock had been carved by wind and water since the beginning of time. Even a shod horse left little more than scratches on the surface of stone-bottomed ravines and gullies. Stunted juniper and pine grew on higher slopes, appearing to be clinging to walls of rock with nothing hut roots to hold them in place. The Pedregosas were one of the driest mountain ranges anywhere, in Naiche's experience, and only someone who knew where to look would be able to find scarce water for animals and men.

Naiche's calm was soon interrupted when Chokole came galloping her pinto mare in his direction . . . he could tell by the way she pushed her wiry little mount that she'd seen something amiss in the trail ahead.

He rode far out in front of the line of pack horses and mules to reach her, hoping she was not bearing bad news, yet all but certain this would explain her haste. She had spotted some form of danger ahead. He was sure of it.

She pulled her pony to a halt in front of his bay, and then pointed back down the canyon from which she had ridden. "I saw two of the white-eyes, Chief Naiche," he began. "They rode across the top of a ridge in plain sight. They did not try to hide from me."

It was puzzling news—two of the whites who had proven to be so clever allowed themselves to be seen against the skyline.

"Why did they show themselves?" Naiche asked, knowing that Chokole would understand why he asked this very simple question that did not fit the actions of cautious men.

"It is a trick," she replied. "They *wanted* us to see them, to follow them, thinking we would behave recklessly. I am sure they meant to lead me into an ambush."

He grunted his agreement. "You are very wise, Chokole, not to follow them. What else could it be besides a trick to lead you to a spot of their choosing, where the other whites would kill you with their rifles?"

"My heart told me this . . . not to follow them," she answered, still looking backward from time to time. "But this is also a sign that somehow, even without knowing these canyons, they have gotten ahead of us. They will be preparing an ambush where they believe we must travel."

Juh rode up to overhear the conversation, for he knew that Chokole's return to the main band meant trouble was waiting for them somewhere to the south, the direction they must take to get to Mexico.

"What is wrong?" Juh asked, searching Chokole's face as if he could read her thoughts before she spoke to him.

"Two of the white-eyes rode across a high ridge in plain sight," she told him. "They took no measures to stay off the horizon where no one would see them. It was a trick, of that I am certain."

"Yes," Juh muttered. "They hoped you would follow them to the killing place they picked out. It is grave news, to know they are ahead of us now. We will be forced to turn east or west to ride around them."

Naiche's anger, and his fear, returned. "They must be mounted on good horses," he said. "Only a strong animal with speed and endurance could get past us." He turned to Juh. "Go back and tell this to Nana. Leave the younger men to guard our rear. We will need our best fighters to confront them, and our best trackers to find out where they are waiting for us in the canyon."

"I will look for their tracks," Juh offered. "My eyes are still young enough to see the hoofprints left by a white man on a horse with iron shoes. After I bring Nana to you, Naiche, I will go alone to find their horse sign."

Chokole asked Naiche in a pleading voice, "Let me go

with Juh. Two pairs of eyes are better than one. I can show him the ridge where I saw the tall man on his black horse, and the white man with long red hair.''

"It was the red-haired one and MacCallister you saw?" Naiche asked, for the revelation caught him off guard. The prisoner they had left to die in the desert said that Falcon MacCallister was an Indian fighter from the northern regions. Perhaps MacCallister was not as smart or as cunning as they first thought, to ride out in the open. But how had Mickey Free gotten ahead of them to join MacCallister? Free and the soldiers were still far to the north, according to his scouts.

"Yes, the one called Falcon," Chokole replied. "He did not look down in the canyon even once when he crossed the ridge, and I knew then it was a trick to lure me to the place where they meant to kill me. The man with red hair rode behind him."

"You are wise," Juh said, staring south at towering walls of solid rock on both sides of the canyon they followed. "From up high on the rim, a good rifle shot could kill many of us. It is time to change direction when we come to the next fork in this ravine."

Naiche's worries had only worsened, now that Mickey Free and Falcon MacCallister were between them and the Mexican border. He wondered again if MacCallister and the other white-eyes were from the Land of Shadows, able to ride great distances as the spirits of dead warriors from another tribe. But why would a spirit warrior from some faraway place make war on the Apache? It made no sense.

Juh continued to study the canyon walls south of them, the direction they had intended to take. "It is impossible for them to overtake us," he said after a moment's thought. "These mountains are too rough for a horse to travel so quickly to take riders past us. We have covered many miles, and still we cannot outrun them."

Chokole rested her Winchester on her bare thigh. "I saw them clearly, Juh. The one called Falcon and Mickey

Free rode across the ridge. They rode slowly, giving me much time to make sure who they were."

Naiche remained silent. If Chokole, Juh, Nana, or any of his followers believed they were being chased by spirit warriors from the Land of Shadows, their will to fight would be broken. Free was a human man, known to be such by all Apaches. But what of MacCallister and the men with him? Could they be ghosts from a distant past who fought the Apaches long ago?

"Look for their tracks," Naiche said, privately believing that no ghost or spirit would leave tracks an Apache's eyes could see.

"I will bring Nana," Juh said, wheeling his pony around to ride north, where Nana and two warriors scouted their backtrail for soldiers.

"Yes," Naiche said, his mind elsewhere—on the possibility they were about to join a fight with spirit warriors, not mortal men. "Tell Nana to ride with you to look for the tracks made by Mickey Free and MacCallister, but do not follow them away from the ridge. I will lead our people to an offshoot canyon where we will ride in a different direction."

Juh heeled his horse into a lope, riding back along the dim game trail at the bottom of the canyon.

It was then Naiche noticed that Chokole was reading his face very closely.

"What is wrong?" he asked her.

She lowered her face, as an Apache woman must when she says something of importance to a chief. "I believed I saw fear in your eyes, Chief Naiche."

He would never admit being afraid. "You are wrong," he said gruffly. "It was only the angle of the sun. I am not afraid of these foolish whites, or Mickey Free. When we find them, we will kill them. Their blood will spill the same as any others. Find their tracks on the ridge. When our people are in a safe place I will follow their tracks and kill them myself . . ."

Chapter 45

Mickey Free reached up and rubbed the back of his neck. "I'll tell ye, Falcon, it do make my neck itch to have a bunch of heathen Apaches behind me an' me not doin' anythin' about it."

"I know what you mean, Mickey. It was real hard not to let that female and the others with her know we saw them down there in the canyon."

Falcon reined Diablo up at the edge of the precipice overlooking a deep canyon filled with juniper pine and other scraggly specimens of trees. Most of the vegetation in the Pedregosas was withered and yellowed, barely able to survive in such a dry, inhospitable climate.

Mickey walked his paint pony up to stand next to Falcon. He pulled a cloth sack of Bull Durham tobacco out of his shirt pocket and proceeded to build himself a cigarette.

When he had it going, he sighed deeply. "This has got to be the ugliest country I've ever had the misfortune to set eyes upon, Falcon. Even the snakes and scorpions look embarrassed to live here."

"I agree. I guess that's why the Apache's been the only people who ever even tried to settle in these mountains."

Mickey snorted through his nose. "Huh. The Apache are dumb enough to live anywhere. They're like animals, Falcon. Huntin' an' eatin' an' breedin', that's 'bout all they think about."

Falcon cut his eyes to Mickey. The hatred the man felt for all things Apache was evident. It almost oozed out of his skin like sweat when he talked of them.

"Why do you hate the Apache so much, Mickey? I know they took you when you were a child, but there's got to be more to it than that."

Mickey sat puffing his cigarette for a moment without speaking, his eyes far away, thinking of another place and another time.

"You ever talked to somebody who's been in prison, Falcon? Someplace really bad, like Yuma Territorial Prison? All they do is complain that the food was bad, the guards were mean and brutal, and they were worked too hard."

He shook his head. "That's nothin' compared to what those bastards did to me, every day for ten years. I've got scars on top of scars 'til I don't hardly have no feelin' in my back anymore. Beaten, starved, worked until I dropped every day, treated worse than the mangiest cur in the village . . . it was a hell that I prayed every day to be delivered from."

Falcon pursed his lips. "I know all that, but . . . there seems to be more . . ."

"You're right. There was this squaw, a little bit of a thing called Onasha. She wasn't real bright, kind'a like her brain never grew to catch up with her body. Well, she got to bein' nice to me, would bring me water when it was hot, things like that. One thing led to another, an' me being a normal boy of 'bout sixteen with all the cravin's of the flesh that go with that age, one day I just kind' a grabbed her and tried to kiss her. One of the young warriors saw what happened an' ran off to tell the chief of the tribe."

Falcon thought he knew what was coming next. "What did they do?"

"That night, they gathered the entire camp an' made

me strip naked and stand in front of them while the squaws all laughed and pointed at me. Then, they brought Onasha out of her tent, stripped her naked, an' did the same thing. After a while, with her cryin' and bellerin', not really understandin' nothin' of what she'd done to deserve this, the young warriors all took her out in the darkness an' had their way with her. Afterwards they slit her nose to show she was dishonored, a whore."

A single tear formed in Mickey's eye. "She ran off in shame, an' I never saw her again." He shook his head. "Don't know if'n she killed herself or what. An' all because she was kind to a white-eyes."

"They are a hard people," Falcon said, looking away as Mickey reached up to wipe his eyes. "They have to be to survive in places like this."

A few minutes passed without either man speaking. Finally, Mickey said, "Now, tell me again why you think the sight of the two of us is going to make Naiche turn his entire band of renegades around and head back into the trap the army's settin' for him."

"They'll do it because we're the unknown. Naiche knows what to expect from the army. Every time he's gone up against them, when he's had proper weapons he's beaten them, so the army holds no fear for him."

"But we do?"

"Yeah. Naiche must know you're here by now, and you're about the most famous Apache hunter and killer there is. And every time he's sent warriors up against me, they've come back dead. That's got to worry him some, maybe enough to make him change his direction away from Mexico and back toward where Major Jones has the army waiting for them."

"What if it don't?"

Falcon smiled. "Then you and I are in for some heavy fighting. Matter of fact, I do expect a small war party to come up here looking for us. My bet would be that Naiche will send four of five of his most trusted and experienced warriors to sneak up on us and see if they can kill us."

"No wonder my neck's been itchin'. What do you figure on doin' 'bout that, Falcon?"

"Why, we're going to disappear into thin air."

As Mickey looked at him like he was crazy, Falcon stepped out of his saddle and handed Diablo's reins to Mickey. "Here, lead my horse over there toward that trail that leads back into those arroyos."

As the Indian fighter walked the horses off, Falcon picked up a dead juniper tree branch and followed along behind, walking backward while erasing the animals' hoof-prints in the fine sand and caliche dust. Once they were onto harder packed shale and rock, he climbed back onto his horse. When they looked back, their tracks walked up to the edge of the canyon and then disappeared, just as Falcon wanted them to.

"What now?" Mickey asked.

"Now we find some cover, someplace we can defend if Naiche's war party manages to find us."

He pulled Diablo's head around and headed deeper into the maze of arroyos and small canyons that made up the Pedregosas, making sure to keep the horses on ground that would show no prints and leave no trail.

Several hours later, Chokole followed Juh and Nana with three other warriors as they trailed the white men.

Nana often had to get off his pony and get down on hands and knees to find the tracks in the areas where the ground was hard, or where the sand cover had been blown away by the everpresent winds.

Chokole watched the two old warriors' every move. It was always possible to learn something of tracking from men as experienced as these. Between them they had over one hundred years of living and fighting the white man.

It was almost like magic to the younger warriors how the old men could track horses over this terrain when they could see nothing. A broken twig, a dislodged pebble, the smell of horse urine where animals had relieved themselves, sprinkles of tobacco spilled while making a cigarette, all these things were noticed by Juh and Nana as they followed the white-eyes deeper into the Pedregosas.

Finally, they came to the ledge overlooking the canyon where Chokole had been when last she'd seen the pair. Juh and Nana got off their ponies and bent low over the ground, spreading out in ever widening circles, shaking their heads and talking softly to one another.

After a while, they walked back to the edge of the cliff and looked down into the canyon, as if looking for bodies that might have fallen off the ledge.

"What is wrong?" Chokole asked. "Where did they go?"

Juh looked up, his eyes worried. "There are no further signs. The tracks of MacCallister and Mickey Free end right here."

Nana nodded his head in agreement. "We have searched for fifty paces in every direction. There is no sign they left here."

"But that is not possible. Men and horses cannot fly," Chokole said scornfully.

"You are correct, Chokole," Juh said, staring out over the canyon. Then he pointed to high in the sky where a pair of hawks soared overhead, riding air currents while looking downward toward earth. "Men and horses cannot fly, but spirit warriors from the Land of Shadows can."

"Bah!" she spat. "You talk like old women around the campfires at night. Mickey Free is no spirit warrior. He is merely a white man who takes pleasure in killing our people."

"But what of MacCallister?" Juh asked, his eyebrows raised. "He walks without making a sound, he kills warriors who lie in wait to kill him without being seen, and he walks his horse over the edge of a cliff and disappears into the air. Is this not the behavior of a spirit warrior?"

Chokole felt gooseflesh prickle the back of her arms and Juh was spooking her, as well as the three young warriors with them. She saw them looking over their shoulders and gripping their many-shoot rifles so hard their knuckles were white. This would not do. She could not allow this old man to bring fear into the band led by Naiche.

"Enough," she said. "Even if, as you say, MacCallister is a spirit warrior, what of Mickey Free? His tracks also disappear."

Juh shrugged, looking at Nana. "Perhaps MacCallister killed Mickey Free and made him a spirit warrior, also, or perhaps he wrapped his arms around Free and his horse and carried them aloft with him. Who knows the ways of spirit warriors?"

Chokole jerked her horse around by its nose rein. "Let us search this way," she said, pointing toward a faint trail leading down into some arroyos and canyons. "Perhaps your eyes are merely too old to see the signs that are there."

She heeled her pony down the trail, looking back once to make sure the others followed her as she made her way down the side of the mountain toward the maze of canyons running in all directions.

Nana looked toward the heavens, mumbling under his breath as if he were praying to whatever gods he believed in to keep him safe from spirits that killed silently and then took wings to escape their pursuers.

Juh merely kept his eyes on the ground in front of them. perhaps hoping he might find some sign showing he was dealing with mortal men after all, and not some demons from the afterlife.

They progressed this way deeper and deeper into the rabbit warren of canyons and arroyos, with Chokole and Juh and Nana leading the way and the three young warriors bringing up the rear.

In the third canyon that they searched, they came to a sharp bend in the dry streambed they were following. After Chokole and Juh and Nana turned the corner, the first of the three braves in the rear pulled his pony to a halt, levering a shell into the firing chamber of his Winchester.

"What is it, Kotah?" asked one of his companions.

"I heard a twig break in that bush over there," he said,

aiming his rifle at a thick bramble bush intertwined with a halffallen down mesquite tree.

As he drew a bead on the bush, he heard a double thump behind him and turned quickly, his bowels turning to water as he saw the other two warriors lying bleeding on the ground, their throats cut and two men sitting astride their ponies.

Kotah opened his mouth to scream just as the long, razorsharp knife hurled by the man in black struck him in the chest.

His scream came out a strangled gurgle, and he stared at the hilt of the knife handle protruding from his chest, then back at the men who had killed him. His eyes slowly crossed and he fell from his horse to join his friends in the dusty caliche and sand of the streambed as he died choking on his own blood.

Falcon jumped off the Indian's pony and bent to retrieve his Arkansas Toothpick from the dead man's chest.

Mickey slipped off his pony and looked up at the ledge overhanging the canyon where he and Falcon had waited until the warriors were in the right position for them to leap down upon their ponies and kill them with quick slashes of knives across their throats.

Mickey shook his head. "I swear, Falcon, jumpin' down on those hosses was like somethin' outta a dime novel."

Falcon grinned and used a branch to brush away their footprints as he and Mickey clambered back up the wall of the canyon.

"So now you feel like Black Bart the famous stagecoach robber, huh, Mickey?"

Mickey grunted with effort as he climbed the steep wall of the ledge. "Black Bart wasn't never crazy enough to try somethin' like that," he growled.

They had barely scrambled out of sight above when Chokole and Juh and Nana came galloping back around the bend in the trail, their rifles held out in front of them as if they expected trouble.

"Aiyee!" Nana cried as he saw the three warriors lying

in the dirt. The kills were so fresh one of the men was still bleeding, his lifeblood pumping out of his throat in a crimson stream, to be soaked up immediately by the thirsty soil.

As luck would have it, Falcon and Mickey startled a small covey of quail from a bush as they ran by, sending the birds flying out over the canyon with a loud thumping of wings.

"Look, Chokole," Juh called, pointing at the pair of quail as they flew overhead. "The two spirit warriors take wing."

Nana raised his rifle and began to chant in a deep guttural voice, nodding his head to some inner rhythm only he could hear.

"Hush, old one," Chokole said, her head cocked to the side as she listened, hoping to hear hoofbeats, or any other sound that would convince her they were not dealing with spirit warriors.

She had never believed much of the drivel spouted by the old one's who sat around the campfires, amusing the younger children with their tales of spirits and gods and other supernatural things. She was always more sensible, believing only in the strength of her mind and the fierceness of her hatred for all things brought by the white man.

When she got down off her pony and could find no signs or tracks in the dirt, the hair on the back of her neck stirred, and she felt the first glimmerings of fear. Perhaps they were dealing with spirit warriors, after all for who else could kill three of their bravest young warriors without them making a sound?"

Chapter 46

After stripping the bodies of their rifles and knives, Chokole and Juh and Nana rode as rapidly as they could back toward where they thought Naiche would be.

At first he was so furious that Chokole thought he might shoot them all, but then, when he heard Juh's story of the hawks and later the quail, his face blanched white.

Even Geronimo, as great a leader as he is, cannot fight the spirit warriors, Naiche thought.

"Tell the people we turn back," he told Nana.

"But Naiche," Nana protested, "the army is back there. That way lies sure death."

Naiche looked toward the sky, searching to see if any hawks were soaring above to overhear his orders. "Better to die facing an enemy that can be killed than to be taken to the Land of Shadows by spirit warriors, and have no chance of an honorable death," he answered, his face stern.

Chokole stepped forward. "Do not listen to the old ones' tales, my chief. I am sure if we push forward we will prevail and be able to join up with Geronimo. Then the two greatest chiefs of the People will lead us to victory against the white-eyes."

Naiche turned to face her, and both his eyes and his visage softened as he looked at her. "It is too late for that, Chokole. For some reason, we have angered the spirit world, and it sends warriors to defeat us. Warriors against whom we have no chance, for they can neither be seen nor heard when they come to kill our young men. Our only chance is to defeat the bluecoats and then proceed to meet Geronimo along some other path. Perhaps if we show enough bravery in our fight with the white-eye soldiers, the Spirits will forgive us and leave us to our destiny."

Chokole, with tears in her eyes, took out her knife and slashed it across her left forearm. She sleeved her arm across her face, smearing it with blood, then held her bleeding arm high above her head. She gave a war cry and turned to face the other warriors in the camp. "We go to meet the white soldiers, to live or die as the gods decide," she yelled. "Who will follow Chief Naiche with me?"

The warriors all took out knives and slashed their arms, holding them up and chanting war whoops and yells as they ran their ponies.

"Dammit, Mr. Meeks, we're the cavalry!" Captain Buford Jones said with feeling. "We're supposed to do our fighting on horseback, not hunkered down in the bushes and behind rocks. I don't much hold with bushwhacking . . . that's the way the Indians do their fighting."

Jasper glanced at Hawk, whose face was screwed up with an expression as if he'd tasted some week-old milk that'd turned to vinegar.

The men were having trouble convincing Jones to get his men situated and hidden and ready for when the band of renegade Apaches came boiling out of the Pedregosas like bees from a disturbed nest.

Hawk leaned to the side and spat a brown stream right next to Jones's highly polished boots.

"Excuse me, Cap'n," he drawled. "I know you horse soldiers are real proud of yourselves, but tell me, just how much luck you had fightin' the Injuns your way?"

Jones blushed a deep crimson. "Well, uh—"

"Way I hear tell," Hawk continued, glancing out of the corner of his eye at Jasper with a smirk on his face, "you plumb got your butts kicked but good last few times you went up against the 'Paches on hossback."

"Why you sonofa—" Jones began, rage in his voice.

Jasper held out his hands. "Easy there, Captain. It's no shame to have lost a battle to the Apaches. Hell, the only people on earth meaner or better fighters than the Apache are the Comanche."

He paused to put the cigarette he'd built in his mouth and light it. "Now, the point Hawk an' I are tryin' to make to you is, the only way to beat the Injuns is by playin' by their rules."

Mollified a bit, Jones asked, "Which are?"

"Strike when they don't expect it, an' strike from hidin' when you got 'em boxed in twixt your riflemen, where they don't have no place to run to."

Hawk nodded, evidently feeling he'd needled Jones enough for one day. "That's the way we been doin' it with Falcon, an' we've had some good luck with it."

"But how do you know where the renegades will come from?"

Jasper spread out a map of the Pedregosas on the ground and pointed at it with his finger. "Look here, Captain. This trail we're guardin' is the only one that's relatively level for ten miles in either direction. The way I hear it, Naiche is travelin' with women and children in his group. My guess is he'll try this trail rather than have all them people try to climb up and down canyons and arroyos on their journey."

"That brings up another point, Cap'n," Hawk said. "Better tell your men not to hesitate to shoot at the women and even the bigger kids. It don't make much difference whether the bullet in your brain is fired by a brave or a squaw, yore just as dead, an' I sure as hell don't want to end up with a tomahawk in my back 'cause one of your boys is bein' a gentleman.''

"Suggestion noted, Mr. Hawkins," Jones replied with ill-concealed contempt. He looked around at his men, "Sergeant, assemble the troops. Mr. Hawkins and Mr. Meeks will show you where to position them for maximum effect against the hostiles."

"Yes sir," Sergeant Brautman answered, throwing a smart salute at the captain.

Hawk spat again, saying to Jasper in a stage-whisper, "I hope these boys can fight as well as they salute."

Chapter 47

Naiche led his people down the trail northward. His plan was to exit the Pedregosas and turn southwest, staying on the desert floor until they had traveled a safe distance away from the spirit warriors, then turn back south and cross into Mexico there. He hoped they would be able to do it before the army caught up with them, but in any case he figured fighting the army was less dangerous than going up against the spirit warriors who had been killing his men a few at a time for weeks.

The column of his people was spread out in a thick line for several hundred yards, with Naiche, Chokole, Juh, and Nana leading the front and the rest of the young warriors bringing up the rear, as a guard against a rearward attack from the spirit warriors.

Chokole glanced around her as she rode, looking at the tall cliffs of the canyon walls on both sides.

"I do not like this trail, Naiche," she said after heeling her pony up next to his.

He looked up and to the side, but his mind was clearly elsewhere. "It will be all right, Chokole. The enemies we have to fear are either behind us or out in front of us."

"But what of these confined canyons? They would be perfect places for an ambush."

Nana, overhearing her words, snorted. "Huh! The white soldiers are too dumb to do as we do in battle. That is why, with the aid of the many-shoot rifles, we are so easily able to defeat them."

Juh chuckled. "If the white-eyes could fight like the People, then we would have much to fear, but as it is their leaders are men with little courage and no honor. In our last battle, their chief ran from the field to save his own life, leaving his men to die."

Nana nodded. "That is something an Apache would never do."

Jones, from his vantage point high on the canyon wall, let the entire procession get within the jaws of their trap before he took out his sabre, held it high over his head, and brought it down in a slashing arc.

Immediately from both sides of the canyon, withering fire from the soldiers hidden there rained down on the Apaches.

Nana's throat was pierced by a slug, killing him even before he realized they were under attack.

Juh's shoulder was grazed, the force of the bullet turning him half around before he raised his rifle and began to return fire. His second shot hit a young calvaryman from Ohio in the forehead, ending forever his adventure out west.

Naiche's horse reared on its hind legs at the first gun-shots, thus saving the chief's life. He levered shells into his Winchester and fired as fast as he could pull the trigger, which seemed even faster than the two shots a second advertised by Governor Winchester.

Chokole, seeing the way ahead blocked by two men in buckskins, standing in the middle of the trail firing into the crowd, hollered at Naiche, "Chief, come this way!"

They both pulled their ponies' heads around by jerking

on the nose reins and galloped toward the rear of the column as fast as they could. They were not abandoning their people, merely trying to find a way to lead them to safety.

As they neared the bend in the trail behind them, two men rode into the open. One had hair the color of a blazing sunset, braided in two braids in the Apache style. The other sat tall in his saddle astride the biggest, blackest stud Chokole had ever seen.

Naiche jerked back on his reins, a look of terror on his face. "It is the spirit warriors!" he yelled.

Chokole looked over her shoulder. "I will take the one with flaming hair. The other is yours."

She leaned over her pony's neck and heeled its flanks hard, pointing the Winchester ahead with one hand.

Mickey Free, seeing her charge, gave a bloodcurdling scream and charged at her, an Army .44 caliber pistol in his right hand.

Chokole's rifle clicked on an empty chamber. She was out of ammunition. She threw the rifle aside and pulled her knife out, holding it high overhead as she returned Mickey's yell and continued to charge him.

When he saw her throw down her rifle, he holstered his pistol and pulled his Bowie knife out, spurring his horse until blood flowed from its flanks.

As they passed by each other, they both swiped with their blades. Chokole's cut a shallow slash in Mickey's right arm, while his slipped through her neck muscles all the way down to bone, severing her right carotid artery. She continued riding for twenty yards as if nothing had happened, then tumbled off her pony, dead before she hit the ground.

Seeing this, Naiche took a deep breath, gave a yell and a whoop, and charged at Falcon, firing as he rode.

Falcon leaned low over Diablo's head and kneed the big stud into action, straight at Naiche.

Halfway there, Diablo stumbled in a depression in the ground, covered over and made invisible by a patch of scrub grass and weeds. Falcon, caught by surprise by Diablo's faltering, was catapulted over the horse's head onto a patch of sand.

Unable to believe his good luck, Naiche reined his pony to a halt and took careful aim with his rifle at the spirit warrior.

Just as he pulled the trigger, the red-headed spirit warrior rode between them, taking Naiche's bullet in the side of his chest. Mickey was spun around and thrown to the ground by the force of the blow.

As Naiche levered another shell into the chamber, Falcon rolled over onto his stomach and drew his Colt. Firing by instinct, without aiming, he put two slugs in Naiche's chest and one between his eyes, blowing out the back of his head and sending hair and brains flying.

As soon as he saw there was no further danger, Falcon scrambled to his feet and ran over to where Mickey lay, breathing heavily and holding his chest.

"Damn, that hurts," the little man groaned, a blood-stained grin on his face.

"You crazy fool!" Falcon said as he sat and cradled Mickey's head in his arms. "Why did you do that?"

"Just repayin' an old debt," Mickey answered. "I owed your pappy one for savin' my bacon a few years back."

Falcon looked up and whistled, bringing Diablo on the run. He got to his feet and reached into his saddlebag and brought out a slab of fatback bacon wrapped in a cloth. He took the meat and placed it over the hole in Mickey's chest, holding it tight.

Mickey laughed, then coughed and groaned. "I thought for a minute there you was gonna fix me my last meal, partner."

Falcon grinned. "No, but a doctor once told me if you covered a chest wound with meat or lard, sometimes it would seal the hole and let it heal. I figured it was worth a chance."

Mickey took a deep breath. "Damned if I ain't breathin' better. Hell, now I'm gonna owe you for savin' my life again. You damned MacCallisters just keep on gettin' me in your debt."

"It could be worse," Falcon said. "It could'a been Buford Jones who saved you."

Mickey scowled. "You're right, Falcon. That would truly be unbearable."

Chapter 48

After saying good-bye to Hawk and Jasper, Falcon headed back toward Colorado. He took the trail that wound through Tombstone, wanting to pay his respects to the Earps and his new friend, Doc Holliday.

He found Doc at his usual place, playing poker at the Oriental Saloon. All in all, Doc looked better than he usually did.

"Howdy, Doc," Falcon said, standing before the table.

Doc looked up and grinned, then took a deep draught from the whiskey bottle that was always by his side.

"Howdy do, Falcon," Doc replied. "Care to sit in for a spell?"

"No, I don't like to gamble with friends, Doc. It hurts me too much to take their money."

Doc leaned back his head and laughed. "Me neither Falcon. 'Course that still leaves me a whole passel of people to take money from."

Falcon tipped his hat and started to leave. "Well, be seeing you, Doc."

"Hey, Falcon," Doc called, "did you hear the news?"

"What's that, Doc?"

"I hear they found Johnny Ringo stuffed in the fork of an oak tree, a couple of .44 slugs in his chest."

Falcon arched an eyebrow. "Any word on who killed him?"

"Why, I swear I don't know, Falcon. The way that boy talked, there wasn't anyone in the territory who was fast enough to get the drop on him." Doc paused and pretended to be thinking, then smiled a sly, cat-smile, "Why, perhaps that boy shot himself out of shame for the way he's acted all these years."

Falcon cocked his head. "Doc . . . ?"

Author's Note

Some have written that Falcon MacCallister was a cold-blooded killer who terrorized the West, killing hundreds of men for sport after his wife's death in 1876. Actually, the number of men who fell under Falcon's guns was much lower than that and there was no sport involved.

It is true that Falcon was a gunfighter, and it is also true that he was a skilled gambler, but it is not true that he was an outlaw and highwayman. That is nonsense, for Falcon was a rich man at the time of his wife's death.

He began riding what some called the 'owlhoot trail' through no fault of his own.

Falcon MacCallister was the spitting image of his father, Jamie. He stood six feet and three and was heavy with muscle. Just like his father, Falcon literally did not know his own strength.

And just like his father, Falcon was quick on the shoot. Jamie and Falcon were both known as bad men. In the West, being a bad man did not necessarily mean being a brigand. It just meant that he was a bad man to crowd.

And Falcon was a bad man to crowd.

* * *

Historical figures depicted in *Cry Of Eagles* are shown as faithfully as possible, as was the fight at the OK Corral. Doc Holliday and the Earps, Johnny Ringo, the Clantons, and events around Tombstone during that era are described as most historians have recorded them, with only slight changes for dramatic effect.

Naiche and Chokole were real characters. Naiche was a son of Cochise, who was the most widely known Chiricahua Apache chieftain in their history. Naiche's actual fate, and Chokole's, are unknown or unproven, although some spotty records do exist, claiming they lived to a ripe old age, others describing their bloody demises. Naiche became Chief of the Chiricahua Apaches after Cochise's death and the death of his older brother Taza.

Fort Thomas was a military post and Apache Indian agency in southwestern Arizona Territory during the period, regarded as one of the worst of all Indian reservations when it came to conditions and cruel treatment at the hands of military leaders and Indian agents. Apaches wore metal tags around their necks, even the babies, in order to be counted. Rations at Fort Thomas were meager and usually spoiled: a handful of weevil-ridden meal or moldy flour, a slice of half-rotted beef, and water. Starvation and sickness often drove many Apaches to escape this brutal treatment by their white captors, and almost certain death as a result of malnutrition or disease.

Delshay, Chief of the Tonto Apaches, was beheaded by a commanding officer at Fort Thomas, and his head was placed on top of a pole in the middle of the fort's parade grounds, remaining there for years as a grinning, fleshless skull, a reminder to Fort Thomas' Apache prisoners of what could happen to troublemakers.

The most infamous and deadly of all Apache warriors was most certainly Geronimo. During one of his many captures, President Grover Cleveland ordered Geronimo hanged. The order was later rescinded. Geronimo served as a role model for many resentful younger Apache boys for his unparalleled skill as a guerilla fighter, whether in irons or roaming free in the Dragoons, or in Mexico.

Geronimo escaped many times, and led the last vengeful bands of Apache renegades in battles against white men in the southwest until his final surrender, when making war against superior numbers of white soldiers with better weapons made his struggle all but hopeless.

Many older Apaches remained stubbornly unreconstructed during imprisonment, even after they were moved to Fort Sill in what is now Oklahoma. Geronimo was one of the worst, often taunting soldiers, "You could never catch me shooting when I was free!"

Naiche was no different while in captivity, and Chokole was certainly one of the bravest Apache women in history, a skilled guerilla fighter until the last, a rare example of women as warriors when record numbers of defeats against army patrols thinned Apache ranks.

Tom Horn knew Naiche and Geronimo, and most likely, Chokole. Horn warned President Theodore Roosevelt that Geronimo was known among his people as The Human Tiger, and that he would never give up his old ways. The same was said of Naiche, albeit not as often, since Naiche made more efforts to live in peace with whites until the final wars broke out over inhumane treatment at the San Carlos and Fort Thomas reservations.

An Apache named Nana died at Fort Sill in 1905, to the end accepting nothing the white man had to offer. His last words were "I can see the mountains of our homeland!" But there is some doubt this was the same Nana who fought with Naiche and Geronimo. Nana was a fairly common Apache name, and at the time few white citizens cared about the actual identities of Apache prisoners. They were regarded as little more than captive animals, heathen savages who had to be incarcerated, or killed outright to allow for expanding white settlement of the West.

Some records indicate Naiche lived to be an old man, living in Mescalero, New Mexico, while others claim an imposter posed as Naiche to give the freedom-loving

Apaches continued hope that he was with Geronimo in Mexico—until Geronimo's final surrender, at which time no record of an Apache named Naiche exists among the prisoners taken.

A number of the older warriors, who had known life as free men on the open prairies, killed their wives and then themselves when reservation life became too bleak. They had seen their people die by the hundreds, of the white man's diseases for which they had no natural immunity, of starvation, and in some cases, by execution for minor offenses.

But the annals of the American southwest will reveal that the Apaches killed more white settlers, travelers, and soldiers than almost any other plains tribe, with the possible exception of the far more numerous Comanche bands. Apaches were savage, brutal people toward their enemies. White men, paid to hunt down and kill the raiding Apaches, were rare, and their careers were most often very short.

Mickey Free is an actual historical figure, and his skill at tracking and killing Apaches is well documented. Men like Free, and the fictional Falcon MacCallister, were appreciated by folks living in frontier outposts. Getting rid of the bloodthirsty Apaches became a celebrated event in small settlements. Free was in fact a twelve-year-old boy tending stock on a ranch in Arizona when Apache warriors swooped down on them, stole twenty head of stock, and took him with them. For the next ten years he lived as an Apache, learning to track, hunt, fish, shoot, and kill in Apache fashion. His real name was Felix Martinez. Al Sieber, the famed chief of U.S. Cavalry scouts, described Free as half-Irish, half-Mexican, half-Apache, and whole son of a bitch . . . he meant it as a compliment. It was said he could track a shadow on a rainy night. He had fiery red hair, a small red moustache, and a mug that "looked like a map of Ireland." Most often described as ugly, his left eye was cocked at an odd angle, probably the result of a cataract. He let his stringy red hair fall over his face to hide it, and usually wore it in twin braids in the style of plains Indians.

MacCallister, and the real-life Indian fighters from which he is drawn, saw nothing wrong with fighting fire with fire. An uncounted number of Apache scalps were taken in Arizona and New Mexico Territories during the late 1800's by white, or half-white, bounty hunters. Monies were paid by territorial governments and the government of Mexico for Apache scalps, and few if any questions were asked as to how they were taken.

Geronimo died at Fort Sill in 1909. With him was Asa Daklugie, son of Ishton. His death is well-documented, and no doubts exist as to his fate.

Were the last of the free Apaches captured or killed by the soldier patrols in Arizona before 1896? No one can be certain.

In 1913, Pancho Villa told General Hugh Scott he knew of bands of "wild" Apaches still living in the high mountain valleys of the Sierra Madre. The Mexican government reported a raid on a Mexican village west of the Sierra Madre by "wild" Apaches in 1934—the last recorded, although poorly documented, attack by renegade Apache warriors anywhere. Yaqui Indians living there, lifelong enemies of the Apache, were positive in their identification of the raiders as North American Apaches.

Men with bitter scores to settle for Indian depredations against their families and friends roamed the West until the end of the century. Such was the man named Falcon MacCallister, a man haunted by bloody memories. . . .

THE EAGLES SERIES BY
WILLIAM W. JOHNSTONE

THE FIRST MOUNTAIN MAN SERIES BY
WILLIAM W. JOHNSTONE

THE MOUNTAIN MAN SERIES BY
WILLIAM W. JOHNSTONE